The Law of the Land

*She Died Unshriven
Without Fear of Favour
The Queen's Constables*

DAVID FIELD

CONTENTS

She Died Unshriven
Without Fear of Favour
The Queen's Constables

She Died Unshriven

Chapter One

Thomas Lincraft clomped grumpily into the main room of the house in Barker Lane that he shared with his wife Lizzie and their two children, clearly in one of his stern moods. He sat down at the breakfast table and ran his hand casually through his black mop with its first few streaks of grey, clearly indifferent to his appearance, even though he would be on full public display in an hour's time. His wife Lizzie, ever sensitive to his moods, leaned down and kissed the top of his head, at the same time tactfully sweeping several large dandruff flakes from the shoulders of his jacket.

'There's cheese this morning,' she advised him breezily. 'I kept it hidden from the kids, but the milk's gone sour, so it'll have to be small beer. Only one, mind – we want you at your best for the inquest.'

His only reply was a non-committal grunt before he enquired after their two children.

'They're in the grassy ground, playing with that barrel hoop that Robert found; he said that Lucy could play with it as well,' Lizzie advised him as she poured his beer, then took the jug away in case he was tempted.

'See that you bring them inside if it comes on to rain,' Tom instructed her as he cut himself a thick slice from the two-day old black loaf. 'It looks pretty gloomy out there, but not half as gloomy as it'll be *indoors* in the Shire Hall.'

'Please don't pick another fight with the Coroner,' Lizzie pleaded. 'You seem to be determined to annoy the man, and if you want to be appointed as County Coroner's Clerk when Matthew Barton takes his pension…'

'Who says I do?' Tom argued. 'You're the one that wants me to become Greville's lackey. For myself, I'm happy to stay a Constable.'

'Not even the *only* Constable for the County,' Lizzie reminded him. 'There's five of you, and you're not even the most senior of them. But provided you doesn't get up Greville's nose, like you seem determined to do, then we're bound to go up in life, given the number of bad folks you've brought to justice these past years.' Tom's immediate reaction was a snort.

'If it means toadying up to that lazy old fool Greville, then I don't want the job, so stop going on about it. It gives me a headache, some days.'

It was the only real tension in the otherwise happy ten-year marriage that had produced two children. Lizzie was ambitious for her brawny, rough cut former carpenter husband to rise above what many regarded as a lowly status in the market town of Nottingham, but Tom had his own deeply ingrained reasons for wishing to dedicate his life to preventing injustice, since he'd seen it in action many years ago, in respect of two of his closest family members. This brought him into frequent conflict with County Coroner Sir Henry Greville, one of two appointees for the County of Nottinghamshire to this prestigious office under the Crown by virtue of the vastness of his estates and the closeness of his friends at the Court of Queen Elizabeth with Keeper of the Great Seal Sir Nicholas Bacon.

Sir Henry regarded this office as no more than his natural entitlement, and clearly resented the many hours that it kept him from his preferred hunting pursuits; in consequence, he was a great cutter of official corners, and took great offence when Tom – who Sir Henry regarded as a nit-picking old woman – insisted on peering into the dark corners of every accusation that was brought to his attention, never concluding guilt until the last vestige of doubt had been expunged.

What made matters worse was that it was not the proper function of a constable to investigate allegations of criminal conduct; a constable was merely required to bring in those accused of crime by others, in addition to apprehending those they saw blatantly committing offences under their noses. Tom had a reputation for pursuing doubts that he should be ignoring if he was to stick to the duties for which he was remunerated.

His frugal breakfast complete, Tom fastened his short cloak by its throat clasp, picked up the staff of office that had rattled many a skull during alehouse brawls, kissed Lizzie goodbye, assured her that he would acquit himself respectfully, and set off down Barker Lane towards High Pavement, from which the sonorous bells of St Mary's parish church boomed out their proud message that yet another nine o'clock communion had been celebrated. He turned into Stoney Street, acknowledging the occasional greeting with a silent nod, and within five minutes he was standing outside the Shire Hall, watching the eager spectators making their way through the open front doors.

The inquest to which they were all attracted was a 'county' matter, so it would be heard in the Shire Hall, rather than the Guildhall, further down at Weekday Cross, which dealt with 'town' matters. He muttered with resignation as he made his way through the front door, then mounted the staircase that led up to the jettied first floor courtroom that was one of the few chambers in the modest market town that could host something as public, and as important, as an inquest.

These were just as much a form of entertainment for those with nothing better to do as the regular Assize courts held in the same courtroom, to which the matter before them today would no doubt be referred by Coroner Greville, once he had achieved the result he appeared to have set his mind on. He would also no doubt, as usual, wish to see it concluded by dinner time, even though Tom retained lurking doubts regarding the formal evidence that they would be hearing.

The dead girl was allegedly one Amy Brindley, formerly a maidservant in the manor house of Anthony Featherstone, the middle-aged hereditary Squire of Lenton Gregory, on the road west out of Nottingham as it headed towards Derby. She had been missing for some weeks, and what was believed to be her body had been discovered, in a woeful state of decay, buried in a paddock on the Featherstone estate, and Coroner Greville had wasted no time in ordering the arrest of Featherstone himself, on suspicion of the girl's murder. This no doubt owed much to Greville's unabashed Catholic leanings, whereas Featherstone was a regular, and highly regarded, 'prophesier' in the 'Dissenter Chapel' in Halifax Lane that Tom also attended, making no attempt to hide his angry contempt for the murderous intolerance of the Church of Rome that had taken the lives of his father and brother during the reign of the former Queen Mary.

The courtroom was already near full, and buzzing with excited conversation, as Tom walked to the side table in order to confirm his attendance in response to the formal summons that had been sent by the Coroner's Clerk, the ageing Matthew Barton, and he was then instructed to take a seat on the bench reserved for witnesses. Across the room were two other long benches, for the jury that the Coroner had summoned to the inquest into the death of Amy Brindley. The fact that only twelve had been called – the minimum number permitted by law – was a further indication that Coroner Greville regarded the matter as cut and dried, and Tom sighed as he took his seat, noting that Greville had cut another corner by summoning townsmen to a county inquest, because it was quicker, although of dubious legality.

A few minutes after nine, the Clerk disappeared through a door behind the 'bench' at the far end of the courtroom, re-emerging only a minute or so later with Coroner Sir Henry Greville in all his finery, his florid face emphasised by the whiteness of the ruff at his neck, and his impressive height increased considerably by the feathered green bonnet. Everyone rose as he entered, and remained standing until the Clerk had announced the formal opening of business, to which he added the traditional – and no doubt compulsory – 'God Save Her

Majesty', before inviting those in attendance to be seated. Sir Henry cleared his throat noisily and announced to the nervous looking men on the jury bench that

'This inquest has been convened for today, the Nineteenth day of July in the year of our Lord 1571, in order to enquire into the circumstances of the death of a girl believed on credible evidence to have been one Lucy Brindley, a maid of some twenty four years, whose body was discovered buried on the land of one Anthony Featherstone. Witnesses shall be called, and evidence shall be heard, and it shall be your solemn duty at the end thereof to determine the cause and manner of her death. If it be your concluded opinion that said death may be attributed to the hand of another, then you must not shrink from so announcing, naming that other should it be within your ability to do so. I charge you all, in my capacity as Coroner for the County of Nottinghamshire, and in the name of Her Majesty Queen Elizabeth, to perform your solemn duty without fear or favour, and to render a true account thereof in due course, as you shall answer to God on the Great Day of Judgment. The first witness, Master Clerk, if you will.'

The first witness was George Wolstenholme, Steward to the estate of Anthony Featherstone, a pinch-faced, somewhat haughty, individual who clearly regarded himself as a man of some importance as he stood solemnly in the place designated for witnesses, waiting politely for the questions to commence. Having given his name, age and occupation, he nodded enthusiastically when asked by Sir Henry 'You knew the girl called Amy Brindley?'

'Indeed, sir. She was employed as a general maid in the same household in which I have the honour to serve as Steward.'

'And what were her duties, pray?'

'General in nature, sir, as befits someone of that rank within a properly run house. She would light fires, see to the dusting of the main rooms, and make beds, as part of her regular duties. She would also serve wine and other refreshments on those occasions when the master had visitors.'

'And were those occasions frequent?'

'Not latterly, no, sir, since my master is somewhat advanced in his years, and not given to extensive socialising.'

'Did this Amy Brindley give good service?'

'So far as I am aware, sir. There were never any complaints about her work, if I might express myself in those terms.'

'So had she applied for a letter of good name, you would have supplied her with one without any qualm?' was the Coroner's next question. Wolstenholme seemed somewhat ill at ease when asked this, so Sir Henry pushed a little harder.

'Why do you hesitate, Master Wolstenholme?'

'Well,' the witness replied with a slightly flushed countenance and a pained expression, 'It was only talk among the other servants, you understand, but she was said to be – well, one might say "free with her favours", if I could put it like that.'

'Promiscuous, say you?'

'A rather strong word, if I might be permitted to say so without any disrespect to your good self, sir. But I had occasion to dismiss a coachman who struck my Assistant Steward, and when I enquired as to the cause of their dispute I was advised that Amy had been – well, "carrying on" would perhaps be the appropriate word - with the coachman when the Assistant Steward was under the impression that Amy and he had a – a – an "arrangement", shall we say? Regrettably, it also transpired that said arrangement was of a "financial" nature, if I might express it in those terms.'

The colour rose slightly in the Coroner's face as he stared back intently at Wolstenholme.

'We are both men of the world, witness. Are you saying that the lass charged *money* for her favours?'

'So I was led to believe, sir. I had no personal knowledge of the truth of that, you understand, but . . . '

'Yes, quite,' Greville cut him off. 'But your previously expressed reluctance to supply this dead girl with a letter of good name was as a result of what you had learned of her acts of prostitution?' Wolstenholme went even paler in the face as he nodded. 'Again, a somewhat harsh description, if I might make so bold . . . .'

'This is a coronial inquest, witness, not the swearing in of a bishop!' Greville thundered. 'I need the truth here, as do the good members of the jury who are sitting with me. Did the girl charge money for her sexual favours, or did she not?'

'Regrettably yes, sir. Or so it would seem.'

'Thank you. Now, on another matter, you testified earlier that the dead girl's duties included making beds, is that not so?'

'Indeed, sir,' Wolstenholme smiled, glad to be on more palatable ground.

'Including the bed of the master and mistress of the house?'

'There's been no Mistress of the house these four years and more, sir, since the Mistress Arabella passed out of this life with the sweating sickness that took so many in this part of the country.'

'So your master, Anthony Featherstone, is a single man?'

'A widower only, but yes, sir.'

'A widower is a man without a woman, witness – let us not play with words. I appreciate your loyalty to your master, and it is to be commended, but the fact remains that your master was without a female in his bed. Correct?'

'Correct, sir.'

'But someone who had duties that took her into that bedroom was the believed dead girl, Amy Brindley, also correct?'

'Yes, sir.'

'So the same Amy Brindley who is known to have sold her body to at least one member of the household had official duties in the bedroom of your master?'

'Only domestic duties, sir. I would hesitate to suggest that they were anything other than that.'

'Whether or not they were is a matter for the jury to determine, Master Wolstenholme,' Greville smirked. 'You are permitted to stand down, unless there is anything else you wish to advise the jury?'

'No, sir – I've said all I know about the matter.'

'Indeed, while at the same time advising the jury of additional matters upon which they might wish to speculate,' the Coroner replied with a long stare across at the jury bench. 'Very well, stand down.'

Tom ground his teeth in silent displeasure as he heard the good name of a dead girl dragged through the mud for no apparent reason other than seeking to point the jury towards a finding that would best suit Sir Henry's political and religious bigotry. It was bad enough that the poor girl's future had been snuffed out like a candle, but to blacken her reputation like that with nothing to substantiate it but backstairs tittle-tattle was an unjustifiable additional indignity.

Tom knew only too well how people could be condemned without any opportunity to defend themselves by the merest whisper and innuendo, even from those who had pretended friendship, and sometimes even kinship, with their victims. He pressed his lips tightly together, as if to ensure that his mouth would remain resolutely closed, when he heard the next witness being called. She was the overweight and slightly malodorous lady who had been sitting next to him, taking up more than her fair share of the bench space, and no doubt she was about to kick the tragic girl even harder in her remembrance.

In response to the opening question, the lady boomed out her qualification for being the object of everyone's attention.

'Harriet Marsh, aged forty-three years, widow, and Housekeeper of the Featherstone manor house.'

'And in that capacity you knew the dead girl?' Greville enquired with an encouraging smile.

'Yes indeed, sir – *very* well.'

'We heard from the previous witness his belief that the girl was a whore. Would that accord with your assessment of her character?'

'Most definitely, sir, to the point at which I had complained to the Master regarding her carry-on with the other servants, not to mention others she might be meeting with on her days off.'

'So the Master – Anthony Featherstone – was aware that the dead girl was not above selling her favours for the right price?'

'He most certainly was, sir.'

'And what was his reaction?'

'He did nothing of which I was aware, sir.'

'You mean he did nothing to dismiss her from his service, or to chastise her regarding her immorality?'

'Not so far as I am aware, sir.'

'Do you have any ground for believing that he might have taken the opportunity to avail himself of the same services – the "immoral" ones, I mean?'

'None whatsoever, sir. And if I might make so bold as to say so, I would not have thought that he was given to that sort of thing, sir.'

'But one never knows, does one?' Greville argued with another meaningful stare towards the jury benches. 'A gentleman such as Mr Featherstone would have much to lose, would he not, were it to become known that he was in the habit of dallying with female servants? So he would be anxious to keep that knowledge from you, would he not, along with everyone else in his service?'

'I suppose so, if you put it like that.'

'And if the girl in question – the object of his depraved lust for young flesh – were to threaten to make the matter public, he would have every reason to wish her out of the way, would he not?'

'Again, if you say so.'

'I do not say that this is what happened – that must remain a matter for the jury – but please advise us how long the girl had been missing from her duties.'

Mrs Marsh thought long and hard before replying. 'It must have been a couple of months, anyway.'

'So, since we know that a body believed to be hers was discovered on the third day of this month – July – you would say that she had been absent from her duties since sometime in May?'

'Yes, sir, that would be about right.'

'Was there any speculation, at the time, about why she might have left so precipitously? I take it that she did not give notice?'

'No, sir – she just up and left. There were some who thought that maybe she'd found a better position somewhere else, and some who thought that perhaps . . . well, perhaps, given her Godless life, that she might be in the family way, if you'll forgive me for mentioning it, sir.'

'You must mention everything that you think may be relevant to how she came to meet her violent end, witness,' Greville smiled encouragingly. 'Did she give any ground for believing that her sinful ways might have been her downfall? That they might, as matters fell out, have led to her death?'

'No, sir. It was just the speculation among the household, sir.'

'But if she *was* with child, the person who had got her into that state would also have benefitted considerably from her demise, would they not?'

'I suppose they would, yes, sir.'

'Anything else you can tell us, witness?'

'Not really – except that she was otherwise a most likeable lass, sir. Very open and friendly, like.'

'And possibly very open and friendly with the wrong person. Yes, thank you for your attendance, witness. You're free to leave, should you so wish, as indeed are you, Mr Wolstenholme. I'm sorry, I should have advised you of that earlier. Now, where are we? Yes, I think we have time, before we adjourn for dinner, to hear from the man who discovered the body. Mr Hoskins, would you step into the witness space please?'

So far as Tom was concerned, matters were about to go from bad to worse. It was one thing to hear the good name of a tragically murdered girl dragged through the midden of public opinion, but now he had to sit and listen to a most blasphemous set of untruths from a man who should be ashamed of himself for perpetuating Popish fairy tales among a gullible and largely naive group of his fellow citizens in order to cover up what he had *really* been up to that afternoon. Tom gritted his teeth once again, and kept his eyes on the floorboards as Ben Hoskins gave his full name, announced his age as being thirty-four, and described his profession as that of tanner.

'I believe,' Greville began with an open and inviting smile, 'that you were the one who discovered the body believed to be that of the unfortunate Amy Brindley?'

'I didn't know what her full name were then,' Hoskins began, 'but yes, I found her body right enough, along with others of my acquaintance.'

'Would you tell the jury, if you would, how this came about?'

'Yes, glad to be of assistance, Your Worship. It were like this, you see. I were coming back from a trip in my wagon to Derby, on business, when my horse kind of reared up in its shafts and gave a whinny of fear. I looks up, and there were like this here ghost in the middle of the road I were driving along. "Lenton Lane", we calls it.'

'Did I hear you correctly, witness? Did you just mention a "ghost"?'

'That's right, your Highness. A girl, it were. A young lass maybe in her twenties, no more than that, wearing a blue gown of some sort, looking pale in the face, and with a bright light all around her.'

'So what did you do?'

'I nearly shit myself, to be honest. Sorry, but it's the truth. I were just wondering how to get out of her way when she said something.'

'And what did she say?'

'She said as how her name were "Amy", and she'd been working for the squire of the manor whose land I were passing at the time, and as how he'd done her in because she were expecting his bubby, then buried her in the bottom paddock, next to the road I'd been travelling down.'

'And what did you do next?'

'I got down off the wagon, and followed her into the paddock, like she insisted. I were scared to do anything else, to tell you the truth. It's not often a ghost tells you what to do.'

'Then what, witness?'

'She led me to a piece of ground under a big oak tree, and said as how I'd find her body under it if I dug down a few feet. It looked as if she might be right, because there were a patch of grass what looked different from the rest, so I promised her I'd come back when I had something to dig with, and she kind of smiled, then disappeared out of sight.'

'And did you keep your promise?'

'Yes, but not straight away, mind. I went back into town and called in at the Guildhall and told Constable Lincraft what had happened. I don't think he were inclined to believe me at first, but I reminded him that it were his public duty to deal with complaints and suchlike, and he agreed to come back with me. But first we had to borrow some tools from local folk, and most of them offered to come with us. Then we went back and found the body. Horrible, it were – all shrivelled and stinking.'

'Yes, thank you, witness. I believe that another witness will be describing the body in more detail later. Is there anything else you can tell us?'

'No, that were about it, so far as I can remember.'

'This "ghost" that confronted you – what reason do you have for believing that it really *was* the spirit of the dead girl?'

'Well, for one thing, she were dressed just like the body when we dug it up – the same sort of blue smock, anyway. And of course she'd been able to tell me exactly where she were buried.'

'Yes, quite. And I believe you said that she named her murderer to you?'

'Aye – she said it were the man she worked for – him what owns the big house up at Lenton Gregory.'

'And she told you why he'd murdered her?'

'Yeah – she were in the shit with a bubby what were his. Sorry – my language can get a bit rough and ready sometimes, you know?'

'No need to apologise, witness, since it must be quite an ordeal even recalling those dreadful events. You're free to go now, if that's all.'

Hoskins scuttled back to the witness bench while Coroner Greville was announcing a one hour adjournment for dinner, and everyone made their way out into the noonday gloom. Including Tom Lincraft, who was cursing quietly under his breath.

Chapter Two

Thirty minutes later Tom was still muttering as he sat perched on the lowest of the steps before they met the rutted road in front of the Shire Hall, oblivious to the heavy rain drops that were landing spasmodically on the shoulders of his cloak, and which gave early warning of something worse to come from the leaden skies that had been lowering over the town since daybreak.

A few feet behind him, and set into one of the upper steps, was the gibbet on which were regularly displayed the bodies of those hanged as highwaymen or traitors, allegedly in the name of justice. Fortunately there was nothing on display today, or else Tom would have sat elsewhere, but the mere sight of this gruesome reminder of the cruelty of which 'the established order' was capable brought the nightmare memories back.

Somewhere down south, in a part of London known as 'Smithfield', was a plaque on which were inscribed the names of those Protestants who had been burned to death there sixteen years ago, in the course of the evil and tyrannical persecution ordered by the former Queen Mary, and enthusiastically pursued by her senior clerics. In the case of the true believers of the old city this had been the Bishop of London, and two of the names on the inscription were that of 'Lincraft'. His father Edward and his older brother Richard, mercilessly betrayed by Tom's cousin Francis in return for absolution of his sin of lying with his own sister.

Tom had never spoken another civil word to cousin Francis since Tom, his mother and his younger brother, had fled north and finished up in Nottingham, taken in as an act of charity by his mother's carpenter brother. In fact Tom and Francis had never met since, but were the two ever to come face to face while Tom was armed, he would be likely to end his life on the gallows, after spending its last few months in his own lock-up. He had never forgiven Francis, and never would, but night after night his prayers contained a tearful plea to be relieved of the memory of that day.

He'd been kept securely indoors in what had then been the family home in Newgate Street, but this had lain only just round the corner from the execution site, and even locked inside the rear room of the humble house he'd been able to hear the agonised screams and shrieked curses of those condemned. For days afterwards the air in the cramped, narrow streets reeked of seared human flesh, and it must have been then that Tom resolved, as a mere youth of thirteen, that he would never again give credence to anything that emanated from the Church of Rome, or any of its posturing prelates. Even less would he subscribe to Catholic rites, or any of the blind superstitions promoted by clergymen in order to hold their flocks in fearful thrall with tales of Hellfire, Purgatory and the machinations of the Devil.

This included a belief in ghosts, those allegedly earthbound spirits that rose from dank graveyards and river marshes to terrify the living, and urge them back onto the paths of righteousness. They no more existed than did Purgatory, in Tom's opinion, and even though the so-called 'Dissenter' group of which Tom was an ardent member were condemned even by those who followed whichever flavour of the English Church was approved of from year to year, he was proud to be counted among those who regulated their conscience in accordance with the word of God as they understood it from their study of the Bible, and without the intervention of priests who told them what to believe, and what was signified by the mumbled Latin phrases of their blasphemous observances.

He could not, and would not, believe in ghosts, and he was damned if he was going to sit by silently while a Coroner's jury of honest, decent folk were hoodwinked into concluding that Ben Hoskins must have known where Amy Brindley's body was buried because her ghost had confided that knowledge to him. Ben Hoskins, of all people – an incorrigible drunkard and brawler who had tasted Tom's staff across his head more than once over the years. There was one other obvious reason why Ben had known where Amy was buried, and Tom much preferred that explanation to the one that Coroner Greville was clearly urging his jury towards, namely that the girl had been done to death by Anthony Featherstone, whose religious fervour was even greater than Tom's, and who preached the word of God with all the power and simplicity of a latter-day Disciple.

'I thought you'd be coming home for your dinner,' Lizzie chided him from where she stood a few feet away, hands on hips, and cutting into his surly thoughts. 'I saw Peter Baker passing our window, and I was told by his wife that he were on that jury. I was expecting you back at the same time. That were ages ago - have you still got time to come home for some lamb stew?'

'I'm not hungry,' Tom growled, and Lizzie was all set to leave it at that since she recognised the stubbornness in his tone. Then to her surprise Tom opted to explain further, as if unburdening himself of a great weight.

'That stupid bloody Coroner seems determined to see Anthony Featherstone hang for the murder of that girl what were found in his paddock. Bad enough that Greville's a bastard Catholic, while Anthony's aye preaching the truth of God's word to them what's prepared to accept the Lord's good grace, but the only evidence against Anthony is some daft bloody ghost story told by an even bigger bastard what couldn't even lie straight in bed! I'll not see Anthony swing on Gallows Hill on the word of Ben bloody Hoskins and some pretended ghost!'

'But if that's what the jury reckons is the truth of the matter, what can you do?' Lizzie pointed out, in the hope of making Tom face reality and avoid yet another confrontation with the Coroner that would do his future prospects no good.

'What I can do,' Tom retorted as the colour began to rise from the base of his neck, 'is to make sure that the jury learns the truth, and not just Ben Hoskins's version of it! There's a crying need for me to smell out some more facts to put to the jury.'

'But the inquest'll be over by supper time, won't it?' Lizzie objected, but Tom shook his head vigorously. 'Not if I gets *my* way!' he insisted, and Lizzie wished him good luck as she slipped sadly away for home.

There was a lengthy delay once everyone had reassembled upstairs, and as Greville lurched slightly heavily into his seat on the bench an hour later, it was obvious that Her Majesty's Coroner for the County of Nottinghamshire had dined well at the expense of a swift conclusion of the business in hand. Or perhaps, Tom mused darkly, Greville regarded the matter as so foregone that there was no need for an efficient use of time.

Fully expecting to be the next – and final – witness at the inquest, Tom was somewhat taken aback to hear one 'Amos Bridges' being called into the witness space. He was a grizzled middle-aged man with the sort of dark leathery skin that can only be acquired after a lifetime out of doors, and it came as no surprise to anyone to learn that he was employed as a gardener on the Featherstone estate. He was taken through the formalities, during which he revealed his age to be a surprising sixty-three. He was then asked when he had last seen Amy Brindley. He screwed up his lined face in thought, and replied 'That would have been when I were planting out the late carnations under the front winders of the big house. The Master likes them seeded in the hothouse, then bedded out in full bloom in May.'

'And did you speak with the girl when you last saw her?'

'Yeah, like I always did. She always liked to chat about the plants when she came outside, and that day were her day off, and she were going out somewhere or other. Anyway, she stopped and complimented me on this year's carnations. A fine young lass, she were, and what happened to her were a shame and a sin, so it were.'

'Did she say where she was going?'

'Not really, but it must have been somewhere a way away, because she were wearing her big boots. Real proud of them she were, but they was expensive, so she only wore them on days when she was going into the town, or somewhere like that.'

Something in Tom's brain registered faintly, and he made a mental note of 'boots' for when he had more time to puzzle out what had triggered a thought process in his head.

'And this was a day in May, you say?' Greville persisted, and Bridges nodded. 'I couldn't tell you properly what day it were, but it were the last time I ever saw her.'

'Do you recall what she was wearing?'

'Kind of,' Bridges conceded. 'Them boots, like I said, and a blue smock what come down to the heels of the boots. But no bonnet as I can recall.'

'Did she say where she was going?'

'No, but like I said, it must have been a good way away – maybe the town?'

'Did you see anything of your master at this time?' Bridges thought for a moment, then shook his head. 'No, but then I didn't often see him on warm days like that was. That's why he probably waited a day or two more to borrow the spade, since it came on all cloudy a few days after I'd last seen that Amy lass.'

Greville's eyes lit up with enthusiasm as he picked up the point.

'Did I understand you to say just then that your master borrowed a spade from you a few days after you last saw the dead girl?'

'Yeah, that's right. Come as a bit of a surprise, as you can imagine, the lord of the manor doing his own gardening. And at his age, too. He's not like me – we're about the same age, you see, but whereas I been active all my life, the Master's led a more privileged life, and he tends to puff and blow a bit, even if he's just walking out to the coach.'

The impatience was visible on Greville's face as he waited for the old man to finish reflecting on the advantages to be had from an active life, then raised his hand and subjected the witness to a penetrating stare.

'I want you to think very carefully about this, witness. When your master borrowed the spade, did he give any indication of what he wanted it for?'

'No, not then. He were a bit secretive in his manner, and he just said that he had some digging of his own to do, and that he'd return the spade the next day, which he did.'

'So you have no idea what purpose he put that spade to?'

'Oh yeah, I have. Sorry, only you asked me if he said anything about what he wanted the spade for, and he didn't, like I said. But I saw him using it later that day, when I were on my way home.'

'And what was he doing?' Greville enquired eagerly. Everyone waited in frustration as Bridges screwed up his eyes in concentration, and allowed a good thirty seconds to elapse before replying.

'Well, let me see now. He were digging down in the bottom paddock – the one what we keeps for winter bedding for the horses. I called out a cheery "Good Night", but I don't reckon he could have heard me, because he never looked up. He's a bit deaf at the best of times, and it were beginning to get dark anyway. It'd come over a bit cloudy that day, like I said earlier.'

'This "bottom paddock" to which you refer, witness,' Greville prompted him eagerly, 'is it the one closest to the road that they call "Lenton Lane"?'

'Yeah, that's right.'

'The paddock in which the body of Amy Brindley was discovered?'

'Aye, the same one.'

'Now please think carefully, witness. Whereabouts, in that paddock, did you see your master digging?'

'Just under that old oak tree that should have been taken down years ago. I remember that, because it's got dangerous ever since the worm got into the old trunk, and sooner or later it's going to come down. I were a bit concerned in case it come down while the Master were digging under it.'

'And this was a few days after you last saw the dead girl?'

'Yeah.'

A smile of satisfaction appeared on Greville's face, then he summarised what they had just heard for the benefit of the jury as he fixed them with a meaningful stare.

'So, it seems that a few days after the dead girl disappeared your master – Anthony Featherstone – borrowed a spade from you, and was then to be seen digging around the base of the old oak tree in the paddock nearest to Lenton Lane. The same oak tree under which the body of Amy Brindley was later discovered?'

'Yes,' Bridges replied reluctantly, as the full implications of the evidence he had just given became clear in his own mind. 'But that don't mean . . . .' he began, before Greville pierced him with a glare of challenge.

'Doesn't mean *what*, precisely, witness? Bear in mind that it's for the jury to draw the obvious conclusions from your evidence. Are you admitting that you might have misled that jury, albeit innocently?'

'No,' Bridges conceded weakly, and appeared to be greatly relieved when he was told that he was free to go. As he walked slowly towards the door with a sad, and slightly guilty, look on his face the first dull roll of thunder could be heard from the west. Greville smiled as he addressed the jury.

'Just one more witness, then perhaps we can all get home before that storm hits us. Constable Lincraft, please.'

Tom stood stiffly upright as he acknowledged his name, age and occupation, and was asked to describe the events that had brought him into the case.

'I were down at the Town Gaol, just completing duties for the day, when Ben Hoskins burst in with a most unlikely tale about him having seen a ghost.'

'It's for the jury to determine what's likely and what's not,' Greville reminded him sharply. 'Just give us the *facts* as you recall them, and leave the opinions to those authorised to draw them.'

'The *facts*,' Tom continued without any obvious indication that he felt chastised, 'were that Ben Hoskins were of the belief that if we dug down beneath an oak tree on the estate of Andrew Featherstone, we'd find the body of a dead girl.'

'And what was your reaction?'

'Like I said, I don't believe in ghosts.'

'I meant what did you *do* in response to this allegation?' Greville replied testily. 'I assume that you knew your duty, as one of the County Constables?'

'Of course,' Tom replied grumpily. 'You can ask anyone you like in this town, and not one of them could accuse me of neglecting my duties.'

'So what did your duties require you to do on this occasion?' Greville enquired frostily, and Tom cleared his throat.

'There was a report of a body buried in a field, so naturally I were obliged to follow up on it. But since I didn't fancy digging with my bare hands, I went in search of picks and spades and suchlike. When the men I were borrowing them off learned what they was wanted for, they offered to come and help with the digging, and we set off in Hoskins's wagon and went to where he reckoned we'd find a body.'

'And did you?'

'Obviously, else we wouldn't all be here today,' Tom replied sarcastically, to appreciative titters from some of the jury members that seemed to annoy Greville. 'It were a lass in her twenties, to judge by what were left to be found,' Tom added.

'It's important that the jury get all the information you have available, Constable, even if it may be unpleasant to hear, so please don't spare us the detail.'

'Very well,' Tom persevered. 'We could smell it before we even got down to it, and one of the picks sent up a shower of something cold, sticky and stinking before we realised that we'd dug down far enough. About six feet or so, so someone had gone to considerable trouble to bury the evidence of their wicked act. We scraped back the soil at that level and there were this lass in a blue smock and a pair of boots, with a ribbon of some sort round her neck. It were tied tightly inter the bones what was showing through the rotted flesh, so I reckon she'd been strangled.'

'And what were your next actions?'

'We managed to get what were left of the poor lass into the back of the cart, and brought it into town. It were too smelly to take into the Guildhall, so we left it in the wagon in the side lane, and I arranged for one of the women from town that we use for that sort of thing to come and strip the body. Normally it'd be washed as well, but there didn't seem to be any point this time, so as you know I reported the finding to you, and you authorised for the poor lass's remains to be buried in St Mary's graveyard. On the north side, the Reverend insisted, since she hadn't received her last rites before she died. Seems like you got to make an appointment to be murdered these days, if you wants a decent Christian burial.'

This provoked further titters, to Greville's obvious annoyance, but they were too close to the completion of the inquest, so far as he was concerned, so he persevered.

'What further actions did you take, on my authority?'

'Well, you seemed to be of the opinion that suspicion had fallen onto Anthony Featherstone, on account of what the ghost was supposed to have told Ben Hoskins, so I went to his manor house and told him that he were under arrest on suspicion of the murder of a girl called "Amy". I did so with great reluctance, I may add.'

'No you may *not!*' Greville shouted. 'Your eagerness or otherwise doesn't come into this, unless you wish the jury to believe that you carry out only those duties that accord with your finely developed legal knowledge.'

This time the titters were directed against Tom, who bridled as he fired back the riposte 'No, Coroner, I go by the evidence. The proven *facts*, that is – not the tittle-tattle and prejudice that's led a fine Christian gentleman to be locked away in the Gaol for the past week or two.'

'That's quite *enough*, witness!' Greville bellowed. 'Are you presuming to tell me my job? The duties entrusted to me by no less than Her Majesty?'

'Of course not, Coroner,' Tom replied coldly. 'I just follow the proven facts, that's all.'

'And you consider that the jury do not have sufficient facts upon which to reach their verdict today?' Greville challenged him, to be met with the cool response from Tom that 'There's one very important fact that has yet to be proved.' Greville went red in the face as he fired back sarcastically with 'Perhaps you might wish to advise us, from the depth of your legal knowledge, of what precisely that is, Constable?'

'The identity of the victim,' Tom replied with an arrogant smirk.

'But everyone who's given evidence today has advised us that the missing girl was Amy Brindley.'

'No - and with respect to your office, Coroner – the witnesses who've given evidence today have all *assumed* that the body in the paddock were that of Amy Brindley. For certain, Amy Brindley is missing. For certain the body found in the paddock were dressed in the same manner as that described of the missing girl when she were last seen. But no-one's said for certain that the body's Amy Brindley's. Only some make-believe ghost, if you're daft enough to believe Ben Hoskins.'

'Once again, let me remind you,' Greville shouted, even redder in the face, 'that it's for the fine gentlemen of the jury here to decide who to believe, and who not to believe. It's your job as Constable simply to respond to what you're told by others, not to embark on your own investigations. Surely the testimony given by Master Hoskins is the only evidence we can rely on regarding the true identity of the body?'

'We still need something better than the say-so of a ghost!' Tom objected. 'Something more positive to tell us if the body were Amy Brindley's or not.'

'But the body was too far gone for that, surely? And she's been decently buried for some time now,' Greville argued, suddenly less sure of his ground, and Tom nodded. 'That's the case, but there may be other ways of proving who the girl were.'

'You have further witnesses that you've so far failed to disclose?'

'No – I need to make further enquiries,' Tom smirked back. Greville's face was now a delicate shade of turkey cock as he underlined what that would require.

'If you are to make further enquiries, which is not what you are strictly speaking employed for, then this inquest must stand adjourned, must it not?'

'It must, if we're to do things proper by the law, and find out for certain who the dead girl were' Tom reminded him. 'An inquest is supposed to determine who the dead person were, how they died, and why. We know *how* she died, and you've assisted the jury greatly in coming to a conclusion about who done her in. But we can't do nothing more 'til we knows for certain who she were. And "who she were" will assist greatly in concluding who murdered her.'

The inquest was adjourned to groans of resignation from the jury, and with furious looks from Greville towards Tom, but he had made his point and achieved his objective. Now he had to put his skills to the test, and act way beyond his official duty, in order save a probably innocent man from a terrible fate on Gallows Hill, the designated place of public execution on the northern outskirts of the town.

Chapter Three

'If Peter Baker puts sand into the next load of flour we buys from him, don't be surprised,' Lizzie grumbled as she came in carrying a large bag of vegetables that she began cutting into small portions to supplement the potage that had now been on the simmer for three days, into which she'd made a point of throwing the leftover lamb from the previous day.

'And why might that be?' Tom enquired from his chair in the corner, staring into space.

'Because it were you what insisted on that damned inquest being put off for a week. Peter's on the jury, as you must have noticed, and his wife Martha could barely give me the time of day when I met up with her at the vegetable stall in Weekday Cross. And instead of getting under my feet while I cleans the house, why don't you take yourself out for a walk or something?'

'It's still raining outside,' Tom reminded her, then wished he hadn't as Lizzie threw the knife down angrily on the battered old worktop and stood glaring at him, hands on hips.

'I *know* it's bloody raining, since I were the one what had to go out in it to get the best of the turnips for the pot.'

'Don't swear in front of the kids.'

'The kids are outside.'

'In that rain? Do you want them to shrink?'

'At least if they shrink, there'd be less risk of them tripping all over your big feet. Ain't you got no work to do?'

'Plenty, but I'm just taking a minute to decide what order to do it in.'

'You'd better have something to show for causing that there inquest to be put off to another day,' Lizzie grumbled as she picked up the knife and continued cutting. 'What was you thinking of?'

'I were thinking of poor old Anthony, in that there Gaol every day, accused of something I don't think he did.'

'It's not your job to decide who's guilty and who isn't,' Lizzie reminded him. That's the job of the jury, not you.' Tom sighed.

'Of course. But they can only decide on the facts what they're given, and Greville's decided for himself that it were Anthony what done it, which suits his purpose, since it'd be one less Dissenter for the world. And a damned fine one, at that.'

'Now who's swearing?' Lizzie grinned back at him. 'And trust you to bring religion into things where it don't belong.'

'It belongs in everything we do in life, as I thought you knew,' Tom replied as he fixed her with a disappointed look. 'If you didn't have to look after the kids on them evenings when I'm at the Meeting House, then you'd know what a fine preacher Anthony is.'

'Does that make him less of a murderer?' Lizzie challenged him. 'You're the first to keep reminding me of all the wicked things they did in them monasteries, before the old King changed the way we worshiped God. You can be a fine preacher and still meddle with innocent boys and girls, or so they tell us when we ask why all them so called holy places was closed.'

'That's just the point,' Tom argued. 'They was houses of sin, right enough, but they was *Catholic* houses. The new religion what me and Anthony follow is nothing like that.'

'Says you,' Lizzie retorted as she took a handful of diced turnip and threw it into the gruel pot over the fire. 'For all you know, your precious Anthony Featherstone took advantage of the poor lass what were working for him, then done her in when it were all about to become general knowledge.'

'You're as bad as the bloody Coroner,' Tom muttered, then apologised for his language before he could be chastised for it. 'He as good as told the jury what they should be deciding, namely that Anthony did the poor lass in because she were carrying his child. And all because some make-believe ghost told Ben Hoskins that were the way it happened. Would *you* believe anything Ben Hoskins told you? I'd rather believe in ghosts than the truth coming out of Ben Hoskins's mouth!'

'Mary Draycott reckons that her mother's ghost visits her house every Sunday,' Lizzie commented, to a derisive snort from Tom.

'It's a pity she don't do the washing while she's at it! Her kids smell of piss all the time, according to Robert. Ghosts are for Catholics anyway, which suits Greville of course.'

'Is this all about your religious differences?' Lizzie demanded. 'Because if so, you're ruining your chances of ever stepping up in life. But leaving all that aside for the moment, what makes you so sure that your precious friend's innocent of what he's accused of?'

'Just a feeling in the guts,' Tom advised her. 'It's all too neatly cut and dried, to my mind. There were a witness called to the inquest – Anthony's gardener – who I never got to speak to, and his evidence were the final sinker, if you start with the prejudiced belief that

Anthony's guilty, or with the intention of *proving* that he is. You've got to ask yourself who went out to the estate and spoke to that witness in the first place, because it weren't me. And according to what the man said, you could believe that Anthony were seen burying the body.'

'What does Anthony say to that?' Lizzie enquired, and Tom rose from his seat, walked to the table, embraced Lizzie once she'd held the knife out of harm's way, and kissed her on the forehead.

'Thanks for that,' he said gratefully. 'You've just helped me decide where I'm going first this morning.'

As he walked, head down in order to avoid the puddles that had formed in the ruts of Stoney Street after yesterday's storm, he began to rehearse the questions that he must ask of one of the most inspirational Christians he'd ever known. It would be both painful and embarrassing, but certain questions had to be asked. To divert his mind momentarily he reflected on the matter of the boots that had been on the feet of the dead girl, the issue that had rung a faint bell in his head – always something to which he paid attention when conducting his customary enquiries into any complaint that was brought to him. Enquiries that he was not authorised to make, and which would one day land him in serious trouble. Then it finally clicked into place like the good carpenter's joints that he had been taught to make all those years ago.

Sir Henry Greville seemed determined to bully, or at least persuade, the inquest jury into concluding that Anthony Featherstone had murdered Amy Brindley because she was carrying his child. But why would Anthony do so somewhere outside, when he clearly had the run of his own spacious house to himself – a house in which the girl was confined by her own domestic duties? And yet the girl whose body had been dug up was wearing boots, and despite what Tom had argued in order to have the inquest delayed, and prevent Anthony from being committed for trial, there seemed little doubt that this body was that of Amy Brindley.

She had clearly set out somewhere, possibly to meet someone, and that someone might well have been the one who had done her in; either that or she had been the victim of a madman she'd encountered as she walked through the estate on her way down towards Lenton Lane. In either case, why should it be thought that her murderer had been Anthony Featherstone? It didn't make any sense that he would have lain in wait for her in open view on his own estate, when he could more easily – and certainly more privately – have done the deed in some dark corner of his own manor house.

Down in the basement of the Shire Hall, the turnkey looked through the flap in the heavily studded oak door, then acknowledged Tom's right to access the dismal, cold and dank cell corridor. He drew back the creaking door on its groaning hinges, and gestured with his head for Tom to enter the cell containing Anthony Featherstone. Tom winced slightly against the smell of unwashed body as he did so, and shook Anthony's hand warmly as he rose in greeting from his iron pallet with its straw bolster.

'I'm sorry you're still here,' Tom mumbled, but Anthony smiled reassuringly. 'You have your duty to perform, Tom, and there can be no exceptions – not even for a good friend, as I can hopefully regard myself in your case. That miserable excuse for a human being that serves my food, when he can remember, tells me that I'm likely to be here for a good while yet. Is that true?'

'Yes, afraid so,' Tom admitted as he lowered his gaze, unable to look Anthony in the eye. 'And that were my fault, I'm sorry. I got the inquest delayed, because there's lots more questions to be asked. By me, that is, even though it isn't strictly speaking part of my job. And I have to start with you, I'm afraid. The way things were going, Coroner Greville was set on getting the jury to send you for trial to the Assizes, charged with the lass's murder.'

'That doesn't surprise me,' Anthony sighed. 'He and I have been at loggerheads for some time now, regarding our religious differences, which of course you share with me. For some reason he seems to have taken it upon himself to investigate Dissenters such as ourselves with a view to reporting them to Queen Elizabeth as likely sources of organised rebellion against her rule. Quite why is anybody's guess, but my own suspicion is that it's in order to divert attention from his own Catholic friends, who may be plotting precisely what he's accusing us of.'

'That's a scandal, and unworthy of even a disgrace to public office like Greville,' Tom protested. 'At first I thought he were just being slack and lazy as usual, but from what you said just now, maybe he's got darker reasons.'

'Almost certainly,' Anthony confirmed, 'so what other information do you require from me?'

'First of all,' Tom replied, slightly red with embarrassment, 'there's the matter of the personal morals of the lass Amy Brindley, always assuming that it's her body we found buried in your paddock, though that's looking more and more likely by the day.'

'What do you mean by "personal morals"?' Anthony enquired. 'You refer to her looseness in matters of the flesh?'

'You knew?' Tom enquired, glad to be relieved of that part of the enquiries he felt driven to make.

'Of course I knew,' Anthony smiled. 'My Housekeeper Mrs Marsh would never shut up about it, and was demanding that the poor girl be dismissed.'

'But you didn't?' Tom persisted, and Anthony shook his head. 'Our Lord, when faced with the harlot who was being stoned in the marketplace, urged the crowd "Judge not, lest ye be judged", remember? He also instructed the girl "Go though, and sin no more". I obviously chastised the girl, and warned her of the road to Hell that she was in danger of walking, but why should I dismiss her? Had I done so, I would have been as guilty as the mob seeking to stone the harlot, would I not?'

Not for the first time Tom was humbled by the man's simple humanity, and the grace of God that was evident in his every thought and deed. Even to *think* this man capable of murder was blasphemy, and to actually accuse him of it a mortal sin. Tom's resolve strengthened to do all in his power to free this wonderful man of even the whisper of sin, but there was still something very difficult that he had to broach with him.

'Your gardener Amos Bridges told the inquest that you borrowed a spade from him, but you wouldn't tell him what you wanted it for,' Tom advised Anthony. 'You can see how that made things look black against you.' Anthony smiled.

'I didn't tell him what I wanted it for because he never asked. But even if he *had* asked, I would have probably been obliged to commit the sin of telling a lie, for the best of reasons.'

'Can you tell *me*?' Tom enquired hopefully, and Anthony nodded. 'Of course, but I must swear you to secrecy, for all our sakes.'

'And what's it got to do with me?' Tom enquired fearfully.

'All of us in the Dissenters' Chapel,' Anthony replied as his face took on a more serious look. 'Mind, I mentioned the attempt by Sir Henry to prove that we are all plotting against Queen Elizabeth?' When Tom nodded, Anthony continued.

'I had heard a rumour that Sir Henry was about to visit houses in the county on some excuse or other of searching for evidence of plots against the throne. Some sort of self-appointed mission on his part to divert attention from Catholic intrigue, as I conjectured earlier. Anyway, as it happened there were things in my possession that it would not have been good for Sir Henry and his ferrets to discover.'

'Are you *sure* you can tell me?' Tom enquired, heart in mouth, and Anthony smiled. 'Of course I can, since you share my religious fervour for the truth, and what I am about to reveal doesn't bear directly on your investigations into the dead girl.'

'Go on,' Tom invited him.

'You have presumably heard of Henry Barrow, since he is frequently mentioned during our meetings?'

'The philosopher what were imprisoned down in London, simply for visiting another Dissenter what'd been imprisoned by the Bishop of Winchester?'

'That's the man. He also wrote several treatises that are regarded as treasonous, if not heretical, even by those Protestants who pose as true Christians at Elizabeth's Court. The best known of these treatises are alleged to attack the Church establishment, when in fact they simply assert, as you and I believe, that every man must make his obeisance to God in his own way, without resort to an established clerical order of archbishops and bishops. This could be interpreted, not simply as heresy – which it clearly is not – but as treason, since Her Majesty is "Supreme Governor of the Church of England", which puts her at the head of all those clergymen who cannot accept – even in Protestant terms – that every man may make his own direct communion with God.'

'So what's this got to do with why you wanted a spade?' Tom enquired, totally at a loss.

'I had several copies of this man's writings in my house,' Anthony explained. 'They had been printed in the Netherlands and smuggled into the country, and I was reluctant to burn them, since I found them to be such a source of inspiration. I therefore determined to bury them, in an old metal casket that I had. I must admit to a certain cowardice on my part, not wishing to be caught in possession of these writings, and perhaps being imprisoned – or even worse.'

'You was seen burying them, by your gardener,' Tom replied with a smile. 'And to make matters worse, it were not long after the girl Amy disappeared, and in the same place where her body were found in due course.'

'Under that old oak?' Anthony confirmed. 'Yes, that was indeed unfortunate.'

'It were more than that, with respect,' Tom explained. 'That were why I did what I did to get the inquest put off to another day. The jury had just heard that you'd been seen digging under that there oak, and if they'd been allowed to come to a decision that afternoon, you'd now be awaiting trial at the next Assize.'

'I shall always be grateful to you for that, Tom, but how can you use the truth to secure my release?'

'Did you have some valuables in your house, what you could have been burying?' Tom enquired, 'and if so, could they have been buried in that there casket you mentioned?' Anthony frowned.

'I can't ask you to tell a wicked lie like that, Tom – even to secure my freedom.'

'I don't necessarily have to tell a lie,' Tom smiled. 'There's ways of saying things that gives the wrong impression, without actually telling an outright lie. But do you want folk to know that you had treasonous writings in your possession?'

'Obviously not, so I'll leave that matter to your conscience, Tom. I only ask that you don't perjure your own soul simply to save my neck.'

'That may not be necessary, if I can prove that you was digging somewhere other than where that lass's body were buried.'

'And how can you do that?'

Tom knelt down in the dust of the earthen cell floor and drew a cross with his finger.

'This is the oak tree, right?' He then drew a straight line below it in the dust, adding 'And this is Lenton Lane, see? Now, show me whereabouts near that old oak you buried them there papers in the casket.'

Anthony knelt next to Tom and made a mark slightly to the north of the cross. 'There – on the side of the oak closest to the house. I was fortunate to find a soft patch between the roots, so I dug there.'

'And you didn't go back and take the casket out of there later?' Tom enquired eagerly, and Anthony smiled.

'I didn't have time, dear friend, since it was only a few days later when you arrested me, on the order of Sir Henry. I hope you can tell me that this poor unfortunate girl was buried somewhere else?'

'Indeed she were,' Tom enthused, his heart much lighter. He made another mark in the dust, to the right of the oak tree. 'There. If where she were buried could be called the "east" side, you buried your casket on the "north" side. All I have to do now is dig where you told me, and that clears your name. D'yer want me to save them papers what's in the casket?'

'Obviously, but you'll be taking a huge risk for your own safety, if you're caught with them.'

'I won't be,' Tom grinned, 'because they'll be locked safe inside a cupboard we constables has in the Guildhall, where we keeps important bits of evidence. If I get caught with them, I'll have to admit that they got dug up on your land, mind you, and claim that I know nothing about what's written in them.'

'Excellent!' Anthony smiled. 'I'm very blessed indeed, to have a friend like you.'

'I'm the one what's blessed,' Tom assured him, 'to be able to claim the friendship of such a powerful man of God as yourself. I've got to go now, but keep your spirits up, because bit by bit I'm pulling apart the web of lies what led to you being locked away in this terrible place.'

The smile of satisfaction was still on his face as he walked through his own front door in anticipation of his dinner. He was a little puzzled that Lizzie hadn't laid out the wooden boards from which they ate their frugal meals, but the reason for that was revealed when Lizzie poked her head through the doorway from their adjoining bedroom.

'You're needed down at Ben Hoskins's place before you sits down to your dinner,' she advised him. 'Seems that he wants his lad taken up for stealing from him.'

'What, Oswyn Pike, the lad what helped us dig for Amy's body?'

'I don't know his name.' Lizzie protested. 'Just that Ben wants you down there as soon as you can. You'll have to put off your dinner.'

'I'm not putting off my dinner on the say-so of Ben Hoskins, so just serve it up,' Tom instructed her.

'You'll leave it until after your dinner?'

'*Well* after – and maybe not until tomorrow. This afternoon I need to see a man about a spade.'

Chapter Four

Tom was whistling quietly to himself as he crested Zion Hill and looked westwards down the long slope towards the meadows, orchards and streams of Lenton, his destination that afternoon. He could do with a stiff walk after that heavy dinner, and Ben Hoskins and his petty complaint could wait until Tom was well and truly ready. It was over two miles to Anthony's manor house at Lenton Gregory, and the walk back would be a lot more demanding, since it would be mainly uphill, but the rain had finally cleared, and it promised to still be fine and sunny when he walked back for his supper in the early evening, since the light would remain until around nine o-clock, given the time of year.

He cast his mind back to when he'd come down this slope on the front of Ben Hoskins's wagon, with five others clinging to its outer edges as they sat inside it, swaying and bumping through and over the many ruts in the well-worn country track to Derby while the implements they'd brought with them clattered and rolled around their feet. There was something about that trip that was worrying away in the back of Tom's brain, but it would have to wait until he had a spare moment among his jumbled thoughts, since the next step in his investigations promised to be crucial.

Who had taken the trouble to speak to humble estate gardener Amos Bridges, and learn from him facts that almost resulted in Anthony being committed for trial charged with murder? Was Tom merely embarrassed since it hadn't occurred to him to speak to someone so lowly who worked outside the manor house itself, or was he correct to be suspicious of the fact that someone had sought Amos out, and perhaps put words into his mouth through bribery or fear? The only manor employees Tom had spoken to had been the Steward and the Housekeeper, and their evidence at the inquest had not varied from the version of Amy Brindley's duties that they'd reported to him, although he'd been taken by surprise by the references to her character that had been forced out of them by Coroner Greville.

It was high time that Tom spoke to anyone else who might be employed on the estate from who he hadn't yet sought information. Once again he reminded himself of the thin, almost invisible, line between seeking out witnesses for a future inquest and making enquiries of his own. But it was a line that he had occasionally crossed in the past, and this time he felt more than justified.

Amos Bridges was easy enough to find, weeding in a vegetable plot to the side of the manor house. Tom called out to him, and the old man straightened his back, smiled and walked towards him.

'Mr Bridges, I'm Constable Lincraft, one of the County Constables.'

'Aye, I remember you from when you come to speak to the Steward and the Housekeeper. You was at the inquest as well, I seem to remember.'

'That's right, I was. I was wondering how *you* came to be there, though,' Tom replied with the warmest smile he could manage in the circumstances, 'since I never spoke to you when I first come up here.'

'It were someone from the Coroner's office,' Amos advised him. 'An old feller, a bit official like, and he spoke to everyone what works on the estate.'

'Matthew Barton?' Tom enquired as his face darkened in annoyance.

'That sounds about right,' Amos confirmed. 'Like I said, he spoke to all of us except Jane Netherfield, what comes in every week to do the laundry and sewing. She weren't in that day, so that Barton feller missed her. Then me, the Steward and the Housekeeper was told to come into town for the inquest.'

Tom thought quickly, and came to the angry conclusion that Barton had been very selective regarding the witnesses he'd summoned. Those who had testified could all give accounts that tended to suggest that the dead girl had been in an immoral relationship with Anthony Featherstone, whereas there must be others in and around the estate who could give different accounts, and perhaps point the finger away from 'the Master'.

'I'm sorry that I might have given the impression that the Master had been burying the poor lass,' Amos cut into Tom's ruminations. 'It were just that the feller from the Coroner asked me if I'd noticed him doing anything unusual about the time that Amy went missing, and I remembered the spade he borrowed.'

'About that,' Tom enquired, since Amos had raised the point, 'you told the inquest that you'd seen the Master digging under the old oak in what you calls the "bottom paddock" – the one alongside Lenton Lane.'

'Aye, that's right.'

'Now, think carefully,' Tom urged him. 'Whereabouts exactly under the oak was he digging?'

'How do you mean?'

'Well, you said you was on your way home when you saw him digging – that right?'

'Yeah – so?'

'So you was coming down that track what I walked up from Lenton Lane a few minutes ago, right? So you'd be able to see the oak, and the Master, and Lenton Lane, right? Now then, were the Master digging on the side of the oak nearest to you, or on the side nearest to Lenton Lane, or to either side?'

'Definitely the side nearest to me,' Amos replied with certainty. 'The Master had his back to me, and the oak were in front of him. That's why he didn't see me coming down from the house, and like I said, he's a bit deaf, so he probably didn't hear me when I called out a "Good Night" to him.' Tom smiled.

'Thank you, Mr Bridges. You can console yourself that you said nothing at the inquest to make things worse for your master, because the body were buried to the *side* of the oak, not at the front.'

'Thank God for that,' Amos breathed with relief. 'It's been on my conscience ever since.'

'And you'd like to do your bit to clear his name?' Tom enquired hopefully, and Amos nodded. 'Of course I would.'

'Well, first off,' Tom replied, 'give me the names of *everybody* what works in the house.'

'Well,' Amos replied as he screwed up his heavily lined brow in thought, 'there's the Steward George Wolstenholme, as you know already, and Mrs Marsh the Housekeeper. Then there's Tom Belton, the Under-Steward, Jim Batley the coachman, Nell Sampson the Cook, and Bessie Helms, what works in the kitchen and scullery. And of course Jane Netherfield, what comes in to do the washing and sewing once a week.'

'And what day of the week's that?' Tom enquired. 'Wednesday,' was the reply.

'You mean tomorrow?' Tom enquired by way of confirmation, and Amos nodded. 'Yeah, today's Tuesday, ain't it, so tomorrow will be Wednesday. She normally gets here about eight in the morning, and she's here all day.'

'Looks like I'll be back tomorrow, then,' Tom smiled. 'And when I does, can I borrow that spade?'

'Don't go getting your clothes all mucky,' Lizzie instructed Tom the following morning as he sat eating his bread and lard. 'Why do you need to dig on Featherstone's land anyway – you looking for another body or something?'

'No thanks,' Tom grimaced at the memory. 'One was bad enough.'

He called in at the Guildhall for long enough to take one of the horses that were kept in the stables at the back for the use of Town officials, then he saddled it up and rode sedately through Weekday Cross, up into Bridlesmith Gate, through the town square and back out under Chapel Bar on his return to Lenton Gregory. When he came back in the other direction he hoped to be carrying a casket in front of him on the horse's neck, which would be far preferable to lugging it back on foot, and there was no way on God's earth that he could leave it at the manor house to be discovered, since for all he knew there was someone in the household who was working with the Coroner to see Anthony Featherstone end his days on the gallows.

An hour later he was seated in the well appointed main room in the manor house, the bright sunlight casting cheery beams across the wood panelling as he was tactfully making enquiries of Under-Steward Tom Belton regarding his relationship with Amy Brindley.

'It's obviously all a bit of an embarrassment,' Tom was telling him, slightly red in the face. 'I'm very fortunate to have kept my position in the circumstances, and George Wolstenholme was most generous and understanding about the whole business.'

'You had no reason to believe that Amy were being disloyal to you with the coachman?'

'Of course not!' Belton protested. 'I thought it was just some special arrangement that Amy and I had. If I'd known she was such a whore, I obviously wouldn't have laid a hand on the girl.'

'But you paid her money nevertheless?'

'Yes, but not for – for *that*. Our relationship was much more natural than that, but not long after we started – well, shall we say "meeting"? – she told me all about her widowed mother in Mansfield who was being threatened with eviction from her cottage after her husband – Amy's father - died, so I was happy to give her a shilling or two from time to time. Not every time we – we – we "did it", you understand, so I never associated the payments in my mind with what we were doing. I got the shock of my life when I discovered that she'd given the coachman the same story, and had been going to it with him as well.'

'Did you do it here in the house?' Tom enquired bluntly, far from being inclined towards sympathy for the man, who shook his head.

'Obviously not, for fear of being caught out. We had our own little spot, in the ruins of the old priory across the Derby Road out there.

The place was only closed down for good a few years ago, and the old dormitory that housed the monks still retains its roof. We'd arrange to meet down there after sunset on maybe two evenings a week.'

'And you had no reason to believe that she were taking others there?' Tom enquired cruelly, and Belton shook his head, on the verge of tears.

'Obviously not, and I'm *so* ashamed.'

'The coachman what you had the fight with,' Tom prompted him. 'Did he have the same arrangement with the lass? To meet her in the old priory, I mean?'

'No idea,' Belton replied. 'I'd imagine so, but we didn't get down to that level of detail before the fight broke out between us. He was dismissed, and as I mentioned already I regard myself as fortunate to have retained my position here.'

'As it says in the Good Book, "Go though and sin no more",' Tom replied with an unkind smirk. 'Now, can you tell me where I'll find Nell Sampson and Bessie Helms?'

'In the kitchen, where do you think?' Belton replied, glad to have retrieved something of his dignity from the conversation.

The only person in the steam-wreathed kitchen was a portly middle-aged lady who was stirring a pot full of something or other as if determined to reduce it to broth. Rivulets of sweat were running down her rosy cheeks from the lower hem of her bonnet down to the several folds of her chin, and she frowned as she saw Tom standing hesitantly in the doorway.

'Come in, if you're coming in,' she instructed him, and Tom walked into the wall of appetising steam with a smile.

'Coney stew,' the woman advised him. 'It needs a firm hand if you wants it softened up, and these here coneys ain't all that young. Still, with the Master away I only have to feed the household staff, and they'll eat anything you puts in front of them. You the Constable come to ask about that whore what worked as a maid until she got what were coming to her?'

'That's right,' Tom replied with his second encouraging smile of the day, as he rapidly came to appreciate why the Coroner would not have appreciated what the Cook could have told him about the life led by Amy Brindley. 'Knew her well, did you?'

'Not half as well as a lot of menfolk around these parts,' Nell replied with a sneer. 'She were a right baggage, and no mistake. Off every night to wherever she plied her trade, and no shame. It were obvious that sooner or later she'd pick the wrong 'un to raise her skirts to.'

'So, you don't believe she were killed by anyone here at the manor house?' Tom enquired hopefully.

'I doubt it,' Nell replied. 'The coachman what got himself dismissed for belting Tom Belton had slung his hook long before Amy disappeared, and as for Tom himself, well he's a right wet 'un as he couldn't knock the skin off a milk pudding. He won't even chase the rats out of this kitchen, so I don't fancy his chances of killing a big strong lass like Amy were.'

'What about the Master? Tom enquired tentatively, and Nell turned on him with an angry glare.

'I'll not hear a word said against him, do you hear me? The Master's a fine Christian gentleman what treats his staff with respect. You hear about that sort of thing going on in other households, of course, but not *this* one. That's what I told the Coroner's feller, so if you come in here to get something bad said about the Master, you picked the wrong person, and you can leave my kitchen right now!'

'Do you have any idea how many customers Amy had, and if any of them liked knocking lassies around a bit?' Tom enquired hopefully, and in an attempt to deflate the Cook's wrath, but Nell shook her head.

'She never did anything openly round the house, so we never got to see any of her other gentlemen friends, if you could call them gentlemen,' Nell snorted derisively. 'Bessie reckoned as how she took them down to the priory, what's all closed down now.'

'Bessie Helms, the kitchen girl?' Tom enquired as he looked round the kitchen pointedly. 'I don't see her in here, and I'll need to speak to her as well.'

'Depends whether or not you're prepared to breathe in a dose of the shits,' Nell advised him bluntly. 'It were nothing I cooked, mind, but she's been in her bed for two days now, with a right case of the runs. You'll find her room out the back, above the stable.'

'I might wait until another day,' Tom replied with a grimace. 'In the meantime, what can you tell me about the last time you saw Amy?'

'That were the day she went out and never come back. She come in here for her dinner, and she seemed mighty pleased with herself. Her and Bessie was talking about where Amy were off to on her day off, and there was talk of Amy paying Bessie back some money she owed her. That'd be the first time she'd ever done that, so wherever she were off to, her customer must have been rich.'

'And how were she dressed, can you remember?' Tom prompted her, earning another snort in response. 'All fancied up as usual, with that blue smock she always wore when she were going to it with her fancy men. Maybe it were easier to lift up or something. And as usual she were wearing her fancy boots, which makes me think her man that day were something special. She were even wearing that silver brooch thing what she claims to have been given be some feller in town what were her admirer. The poor bugger probably had no idea what a whore she really were. Pass me that ladle, would you?'

Reluctant to become a voluntary kitchen hand, and even more reluctant to be invited to sample what was being beaten into submission in the pot, Tom made his excuses and left via the scullery door that led onto the back green, where a woman in her mid twenties was hanging items of bed linen on the rope in the sunshine. She smiled invitingly, and he walked over.

'You by any chance Jane Netherfield?' he enquired, and the woman nodded.

'That's me. Are you looking for some sewing to be done? Only you've got a nasty rip in your shirt.'

'Goes with the job,' Tom smiled back. 'The fool what done that got my staff round his head, and right now he's in the Town Gaol for assaulting a constable of the law. That's me – Constable Thomas Lincraft.'

'Well, Constable Thomas Lincraft, come and take a seat on that bench over there while I go and get a needle and thread, and sew up your shirt in exchange for you telling me what you propose to do to catch the swine who killed Amy. That's why you're here, isn't it?'

Ten minutes later Tom was leaning in towards Jane as she deftly sewed up the tear in his shirt, and preparing to ask her what she knew of Amy Brindley. She sighed as she bit off the end of the thread with a 'there you go – all mended, and no charge if you find my friend's killer.'

'She were your friend?' Tom enquired, surprised by both that revelation and the cultured way in which the woman spoke.

'She certainly was,' Jane confirmed. 'My best friend – in fact, just about the *only* friend I ever had, until I met my lovely husband. The people in the house told you she was a whore, presumably?'

'Yeah – that's how everyone seems to remember her.'

'Everyone except me. Did they tell you how generous she could be to people she loved?'

'No – definitely not,' Tom confirmed, somewhat confused by the conflicting report he was receiving. Jane smiled.

'She was definitely a whore, but she had her good side too. She was an orphan, and she'd learned to survive, so when someone like me came along with no idea how to make it alone in this world as a woman, she took pity on me. I'd been brought up in a convent orphanage, where I'd learned to do needlework, wash clothes, and speak correctly, in the belief that I'd one day make a good wife to a freeholder, or maybe even a country squire. Then the convent was closed down, and I found work in a country house just outside Derby, where the Master's son proposed marriage to me after he seduced me and got me pregnant. Then he began beating me, and I lost the baby after one of his more brutal attacks. I ran away, and met Amy while walking towards Nottingham on the road from Derby. We got talking, and Amy persuaded me that men weren't worth it, except for what could be wheedled out of them one way or another.'

'I hope she didn't teach you to go whoring, like her?' Tom enquired, horror stricken by the thought, but Jane smiled and shook her head. 'She certainly offered, but it didn't appeal to me, so she let me share her room in the stables here, doing the washing and sewing for the household until I met this wonderful man who'd just lost his wife to a fever, and needed someone to look after his three children. He works one of the farms on the estate, and to cut a predictable story a little short, we were married last year, and I add to the money from the farm by doing sewing and washing, both here on the estate and elsewhere. But without Amy's natural kindness, I dread to think where I'd have finished up.'

'That's a completely different Amy to the one I heard about from them in the house back there,' Tom admitted, confused by these new revelations.

'They no doubt spoke as they found her,' Jane smiled, 'and I'd be the first to admit that she was no saint. She seemed dedicated to using men, exploiting their obvious weakness in carnal matters, and she could be as hard as the winter frost when it suited her. Some men she actually felt sorry for, like the Assistant Steward of the estate here, but most of them she despised, and if she believed that they were cruel towards other women beneath them, like their wives or servants, then she made sure that they paid her the most. As for other women, if they made it clear that they looked down on Amy because of the life she led, then she'd go out of her way to be unpleasant towards them, and flaunt all the money she made from whoring. After all, that's just a physical – almost animal – thing, and it's what's in your heart that matters. Amy and I understood each other, and we were good friends.'

'I'm trying to find out who killed her, so anything you can tell me about who her regular "customers" were will obviously help,' Tom explained, uncomfortably aware of his rough manner of speech compared with Jane's educated tones. She appeared to think for a moment, then added what she could.

'There was one particular man recently, who Amy seemed to despise more than the others, to judge by the way she spoke about him. Someone from the town, I believe, although as usual I think she would have taken him to her favourite spot in the priory ruins. This man was apparently quite wealthy, but mean-spirited, and he and Amy would often argue about the money he'd give her for her favours. I spoke to her for the last time on the day she disappeared, and she seemed very happy about some scheme or other that involved getting more money from this man. She was very keen to tell me how she was going to be wearing the neckband that I'd made for her, which she was always so proud to wear. If she was still wearing it when you found her body, I'd appreciate getting it back some time, because it'll remind me of our friendship.'

Tom felt a lump rising in his throat as he remembered how a blue neckband appeared to have been used to strangle the girl found under the oak tree, and he shrank from telling this lovely lady the complete truth.

'There *were* a blue neckband round her neck, right enough,' he confirmed, 'but how can we tell if it were the one what you give her? A blue neckband is a blue neckband.'

'Not this one,' Jane assured him. 'I made it specially for her on her birthday last year, and I embroidered her initials on it. "A.B" in gold thread. If that's on the garment, then I'd be very grateful to get it back, as a keepsake.'

'Consider it payment for the sewing,' Tom smiled as he bid her farewell and collected his horse from the stable, chuckling quietly as he nudged it down the drive, then into the paddock on the left that sloped gently down to Lenton Lane, with the large, and elderly, oak at the bottom. He pulled the spade from where he'd fixed it under the bridle leathers and walked towards the familiar oak that brought back some horrible memories. His spirits lifted again as he noticed the paler patch of grass roughly three feet square in front of the oak, and he stood on the rim of the blade, which sank effortlessly into the loose soil as he deployed all his body weight. At the two feet depth he heard a dull thud, and within minutes he had Anthony's casket in his grasp.

He took a while to remount the horse with the casket under his armpit, but eventually he managed the delicate manoeuvre, and after returning the spade with grateful thanks he set the horse's head down the drive, and then out into Lenton Lane, with a huge grin on his broad face.

It had been a worthwhile day. Not only could he now explain why Anthony Featherstone had been digging beneath the old oak, but he believed he had a means of identifying the body buried nearby as that of Amy Brindley.

Chapter Five

Tom looked up from the breakfast table to where Lizzie stood in the bedroom doorway with an accusing look on her face, holding up the shirt he'd taken off the night before.

'It's maybe as well you decided to change your shirt, since you been wearing this one since Easter. I were waiting to sew up that hole in the shoulder, but it seems like you done it yourself. Would you care to mend the hole in Robert's while you're at it?'

'I didn't mend it,' Tom smiled back. 'It were the woman on Anthony's estate what does all their washing an' mending.'

'Well, the next time you go up there, you can take her all *our* washing as well,' Lizzie advised him sarcastically. 'How did you get on up there, anyway?'

'I think I can now prove that the dead girl was Amy Brindley,' Tom smiled back at her, but she shook her head disapprovingly. 'I thought that were already decided at the inquest. Weren't you trying to find out who killed her?'

It was Tom's turn to shake his head. 'You know nowt about how these things are done, so leave the finding out to me.'

'You're not supposed to do things like that, anyway,' Lizzie reminded him, and Tom nodded. 'I'm not supposed to do washing and mending neither, so I'll leave that to you.'

'Leave some of that bread for the kids as well. Anyway, you'll need to call in on Ben Hoskins, because he were round here again while you was out yesterday. He's threatening to report you if you don't arrest that there apprentice of his for stealing from his house.'

'I've got better things to do than answer to Ben Hoskins's beck and call.'

'Then you'd better set about them, while there's still some bread left. And take that tin box with you, instead of leaving it by the side of the bed. I stubbed my toe on it twice already.'

An hour later, inside the Guildhall, he took the key for the constables' cupboard from the Senior Turnkey to whom it was entrusted, and took a deep breath before he opened it and placed Anthony's casket safely inside. Already stored inside were various items that would be offered as 'evidence' at future trials for theft, robbery, rape and coin clipping, but the items he was seeking still smelt as bad as they did when they were stripped from the corpse of a long-dead girl.

He braced himself to investigate in the matted folds of the blue smock, and his hand came to rest on the item he was seeking. He unfolded the blue neckband, then gagged as a minute piece of decomposed flesh fell from it onto the floorboards. His determination was rewarded as the neatly embroidered initials 'A B' could clearly be seen on one end of the neckband, the gold thread slightly soiled, but still visible to the eye. The dead girl was undoubtedly Amy Brindley, but, as Lizzie had reminded him earlier, he still needed to prove who'd killed her. Someone other than Anthony Featherstone, that is. With a sigh he replaced the rest of the clothing from the dead girl, locked the door, returned the key to the man entrusted with it, and sat staring at the neckband.

'That smells disgusting!' fellow Constable Giles Bradbury complained from where he sat in the corner of the communal office, sharpening a quill ahead of making a list of stolen items he'd recently removed from the house of a man now two floors below in the cells. 'Can't you take it outside or something? Better still, take it and stick it under Ben Hoskins's nose, and tell him to take a deep breath. I'm sick of the bastard coming in here, demanding that you look into that stealing what he's accusing his lad of. I offered to look into it myself, but he's insisting that it's got to be you.'

Giles was very much Tom's junior, a fresh-faced, broad shouldered, ginger haired former farm hand who was very popular with the ladies. He was the perfect person to have at one's back in an alehouse brawl, and he all but hero-worshipped Tom, with his quiet intelligence and incorruptible soul. The two men worked well together, and Tom would perhaps include Giles in his enquiries into the death of Amy Brindley should the need arise, but for the time being he was obliged to work alone, since he didn't want to risk Giles being dismissed for adopting Tom's habit of investigating a crime rather than just reporting it and jailing the alleged offender.

'The next time Ben Hoskins comes in here complaining, tell him to go and piss in his bonnet,' Tom growled. 'And if he wants to know why I'm not available, tell him that I'm too busy investigating a false allegation against Anthony Featherstone what he started with all that nonsense about a ghost.'

'You've really got your teeth inter that business.' Giles observed. 'Can't you just leave it be?'

'No I bloody can't,' Tom insisted. 'I'm not going to be party to the wrong feller being hung. And it's time I carried on trying to find the *right* feller!'

He was already over a mile west of the town, riding slowly past the boundary of the Featherstone estate, when he realised that he'd formed no plan of action, and had no reason to be where he was that he could recall, other than a strong desire to get out of the town and back to where it had all started. Ahead on his right was the fateful oak tree under which had been discovered both a rotting corpse and a casket full of politically dangerous writings, and he reined in the horse and sat staring at it as other horse riders, wagons, and the occasional person on foot passed him by on either side. And that set off another train of thought.

It was highly unlikely that Amy had been murdered here, whatever the time of day, since there was a constant flow of people back and forth to Wollaton, Beeston, Bramcote, and beyond, all the way to Derby. It might be easy enough to bury her here at dead of night, but not to strangle the life out of her even under the cover of darkness, when her screams might attract attention. So where had it been done? From what he'd learned on the estate yesterday, it might well have been in the grounds of the old priory, but even then the removal of the body would have to have been done at night. And whoever it was would have required at least a horse to sling the corpse over, or perhaps a wagon of some sort. And of course a spade.

Suddenly his mind clicked back to something that had niggled at him the previous day, and a light began to grow brighter around an idea that had been subconsciously taking shape ever since the inquest. He found himself reliving in his mind the arrival of Ben Hoskins at the Guildhall, claiming to have seen a ghost, and demanding that Tom organise a search under the old oak. The wagon had been empty, but when Tom had raised the obvious objection that they had nothing to dig with, Ben had urged him on with the insistence that he had a spade available. That had not been enough, as Tom had pointed out, and in the final wagonload that had hastened out of town before the light faded had been three spades and two picks, along with their owners. The fact remained, however, that Ben Hoskins already owned a spade when he had come calling with the unlikely tale of a ghost in Lenton Lane!

Or was it just wishful thinking on Tom's part? He had no love for Ben Hoskins, and he wouldn't entertain for one moment the suggestion that the location of the girl's corpse had been revealed by her ghost. He'd already decided, well before the inquest, that Ben's knowledge of the existence of the corpse was more likely to have been as the result of the evil company he kept, and that Ben might be doing one of them a favour – or had perhaps been earning a disgraceful shilling or two – by inventing the ghost story, but would it not also fit what was known of the matter for Ben to have been the one who did Amy in?

Ben was well known as a violent man when in drink, but who was to say that he wasn't like that when sober? He also had a reputation as a womaniser, and had narrowly escaped more than one charge of rape when he'd managed to persuade, or bribe, some of his equally wicked friends to testify that the victim had been either a prostitute, or so drunk as not to remember what she'd consented to up a dark alleyway. So, all the pieces would fit.

Except the pieces that pointed directly to Ben's guilt, while Coroner Greville was determined to see Anthony Featherstone swing for it. Perhaps Greville knew the truth, and was being bribed or threatened by Ben himself, Tom mused, then shook his head to rid himself of the thought. The two men moved in totally different circles, and Ben was unlikely to possess sufficient wealth with which to bribe Sir Henry. Or had Sir Henry been the fancy new friend that Amy had been boasting of, who'd done her in when she threatened to reveal his association with her? Tom found himself smiling openly at the thought of being the one to reveal that delightful piece of information, then checked himself. He was here to find Amy's murderer, whoever that might have been, and not to settle old scores.

So where to next? His eyes wandered instinctively to the south – to his left, where the crumbling tower of the former Lenton Priory was just visible over the tops of the trees. He might as well make the trip now, before returning to the estate and asking for directions to the house where Jane Netherfield lived with her husband and family, so that she could positively confirm that the neckband that Tom had wrapped around the horse's bridle, in the hope of killing the smell from it with God's good air, was the one that she had made for Amy.

One could almost believe in ghosts, he told himself as he guided the horse slowly through the grass and weed clumps between the old priory buildings that the moss and ivy were rapidly claiming for themselves. Several crows were croaking their protest as he approached each building in turn, wondering which of them might have been the former dormitory that had housed the monks, and he had almost persuaded himself that the faint echo of chanting was drifting from the largest of the buildings, which had presumably been the chapel in the days when men had idled away their days in gluttony and sexual debauchery contrary to the laws of nature. Then ahead of him, in the grass, he saw something glinting in the sunlight, and he commanded the horse to stop, then slid down from the saddle.

He bent down and picked it up, a silver coloured brooch of some sort, somewhat tarnished after spending some time lying at the mercy of the elements, but with the image of an eagle above a castle still quite visible. Tom turned it over, but there was nothing on the reverse to indicate who might have owned it. Then with a start he remembered something the Cook had said as he'd sat talking to her through the coney-flavoured fog. Hadn't she recalled how Amy Brindley had been proudly showing off a silver brooch she'd received as a "present" from her latest, wealthy, admirer – the one she was heading out to meet on the day that she never returned?

On a whim, Tom looked to the side of where he was standing, at a long, low building that seemed to be connected to the chapel at its far end. He knew nothing about the monastic life, but it would make sense for the dormitory that housed the monks to be connected under cover to the place to which they had to walk, at all times of day and in all kinds of weather, in order to conduct their services of worship. Emboldened, he walked through the brick opening that had presumably once possessed a door before some local farmer had removed it for service in a cow barn or something, and he was in a narrow passageway down which a family of rats scattered before his advancing boots.

There were openings every few feet down this passageway, each of which gave access to what appeared to have once been a room big enough for just a bed. These must have been the individual monks' cells, put to a far from holy purpose by a local whore a few years after the departure of the last monk who had presumably put it to a similar purpose, but now a scene was beginning to play itself out inside his head.

He turned and walked the few feet back to the point at which he'd gained access to the corridor, the place where his horse was grazing happily in the long weedy grass. He confirmed that the spot in which he'd found the brooch lay directly in the path a person would have taken carrying a body over his shoulder, and creating enough movement, when heaving the body either onto a horse or into a wagon, for the brooch to have slipped from the inert corpse, silently and unnoticed, particularly if the deed had been done in darkness. There was every chance that this tiny piece of silverware was the final confirmation that Amy had accompanied her special gentleman friend to their usual place of assignation, not realising that she was about to whore herself into a lonely grave under an oak tree. But he needed to return to Lenton Gregory to have this confirmed.

Back in the estate kitchen he was treated to a frosty stare by the Cook, who was accompanied by a lumpy girl with straggly red hair as they stood together peeling parsnips.

'If you've come for more scandal about the Master, just turn round and go back the way you come,' the Cook instructed him, but Tom stood his ground and smiled at the girl.

'Are you Bessie Helms, by any chance? And if so, are you feeling better?'

'I ain't done nothing wrong, if you're the Constable.'

'I am, and I don't believe you have,' Tom smiled back reassuringly. 'But somebody done something wrong to your friend Amy, and I'm trying to find out who that were.'

Bessie looked enquiringly at the Cook, who nodded over the parsnip she was peeling.

'No harm done, I suppose. But take it outside, and if he tries to get you to say something untrue about the Master, come back and tell me, and I'll give him what for.'

Once outside, Tom gestured to the bench at the side of the drying green where he'd sat talking to Jane Netherfield the previous day, and invited Bessie to sit by his side on it. She still appeared reluctant to talk at all, so Tom began by taking the silver brooch from his pocket and holding it out in the palm of his hand, where the girl could see it.

'Do you recognise this?'

'It were Amy's!' Bessie shouted excitedly. 'She were always showing it off, and boasting that she'd been given it by some fancy feller in town what she were going to make a lot of money out of!'

'By whoring?' Tom enquired, but Bessie shook her head, then went slightly red in the face. 'I won't get in any trouble, right? Only I knew what she were up to, and I didn't warn nobody about it.'

'You'll only get in trouble if you *refuse* to tell me what you know,' Tom advised her in a stern voice, and that seemed to do the trick, as the girl launched into a breathless litany that left Tom even more convinced that he was on the right track.

'Well, it were like this. Some time ago Amy told me about this special feller she'd met, what had lots of money, and were prepared to spend it on her if she let him do things a bit on the rough side, if you gets my meaning. You knew she were a whore, so I'm not telling any tales out of order? Well, she seemed to take delight in telling me all about it when she come back from her trips down to the priory. You knew that's where she took them, right? Well, I haven't had a man yet – not the proper way, anyway - and Amy seemed to find it funny to tell me all about how it's done, what her various men friends liked to do, and how she could always charge them more if it were something special. She were always after money, and before she got her regular men friends she used to borrow off me for her fancy clothes and stuff, except I never got any of it back – she could be proper mean like that.'

'The special gentleman she'd just met?' Tom prompted her, before she could get even further off the point.

'Yeah, sorry. Anyway, a few months back she told me that she'd been inter town for something or other – probably whoring – and she'd met this man in "The Bell" – that's an alehouse, right?'

'Know it well,' Tom replied with a grin, and Bessie continued, seemingly encouraged.

'Well anyway, this feller were well off in some trade or other – leather, I think she said it were – but whatever, he promised her twice as much as she normally got if she'd agree to him doing it a bit rough. She must have said yes, because once or twice she come back with bruises on her face and arms, but boasting as usual about how much she'd got from this new found feller. It were always her day off when she met him – Wednesdays – but after a week or two she didn't seem quite so cocky in her manner, and I asked her if something were wrong.'

'And?' Tom enquired eagerly, and Bessie frowned.

'I were coming to that, weren't I? Seems they'd started falling out about how much money he were supposed to be giving her, and she were thinking of giving him over. But not until she'd made him pay through the nose one last time.'

'And that were the day she went missing – the day she went out to meet him one last time, and the day he probably done her in?' Tom enquired eagerly, and Bessie's face fell.

'Don't you want to know what she were planning on telling him?'

'Not really.'

'Well, I'm going to tell you anyway, because I thought it were right clever.'

'She told him she were expecting his baby?' Tom enquired, earning himself a look of scorn from the girl.

'You're not that bright, are you?

'I'm the bloody Constable, so mind your manners!' Tom fired back, and Bessie lowered her head.

'Sorry, but since she were such a whore, what man's going to believe her when she claims that the baby's his?'

'So what was she going to tell him?'

'That she had the pox, and she reckoned it were him what she'd got it off.'

'And were that true?'

'No idea, but she were going to threaten to go round every alehouse in the town and warn all the girls that he had the pox, unless he handed over lots of money.'

Tom thought for a moment, before conceding that this would indeed be a very strong motive for someone to murder the stupid girl, making a threat like that in an isolated place to a man who liked to play 'a bit rough' at the best of times. But there was something important he needed to find out.

'Did Amy ever tell you this man's name?'

'Only his first name – "Benjamin" it were.'

'Are you sure?'

'Course I'm bloody sure – she were forever going on about "My rich Benjamin feller", an how he owned his own business somewhere in the town.'

'What sort of business?'

'Dunno exactly, but I think it were something to do with leather.'

'Did you tell the Coroner's Clerk all this when he were talking to all the staff on the estate?'

'Yeah, and he said I'd be called to tell what I knew at that there inquest thing. But only the Steward and the Housekeeper were called for, in the end.'

'So you could have told the inquest all about this "Benjamin" feller, and how Amy were meeting with him on the day she probably got herself murdered, but you was never allowed to, is that right?'

'Aye – I thought it were a bit strange.'

'It were more than that,' Tom grumbled. 'But the inquest were put off for a week, and it'll be on again next Monday. Could you and Jane Netherfield come into town, to the Shire Hall, that day?'

'I can only speak for myself, but if it'll help hang the bastard what killed Amy, then of course I will. And I reckon Jane will, too, because she were Amy's special friend. But will they want to hear what I can tell them?'

'Trust me,' Tom assured her as he rose from the bench, 'they'll get to hear what you've got to say whether they like it or not.'

DAVID FIELD

Chapter Six

The smile disappeared from Tom's face only when he was guiding the horse down Bridlesmithgate on his way back into the cluster of houses around St Mary's that was 'home'. But before he could put his feet up ahead of supper being served, there was a call of duty he really ought to attend to if he was to avoid Ben Hoskins causing trouble for him, just at the time when Tom was planning even worse trouble for Ben Hoskins.

It was too much to believe that a ghost had conveniently told Ben where to find Amy's body; that had been obvious from the beginning. Add to that the fact that Ben owned a spade, that he was known to be violent when drunk, and prone to violence towards women, throw in the fact that Amy had, shortly before her death, been immorally associating with a 'Benjamin' who claimed to be a wealthy dealer in leather, and a very clear picture was forming in Tom's mind.

But a picture in his mind would not be good enough. He needed facts, and although he had a good deal more than had been revealed to the inquest jury during the first day, he only had until next Monday to gather together the necessary strands of proof that would at least ensure that Anthony Featherstone was cleared of suspicion. What would be even more satisfying would be proof that the poor girl had been murdered by Ben Hoskins. She may have been a whore, but who was Tom to judge? And hadn't he been set a fine example by Anthony himself, with his Christian obedience to the example set by Our Lord when confronted with a woman being stoned for adultery? Poor young Amy had no-one to ensure that her brutal and pitiful death was avenged unless Tom did what he perceived to be his duty.

His reflections on his duty wrestled with his eagerness to get home and have his supper, but conscience won the day, and halfway down Bridlesmithgate he nudged his horse left towards Pilcher Gate, where Ben Hoskins conducted his tannery business from a squalid yard at the side of his imposing jettied three-storied residence.

'About bloody time,' Hoskins growled as Tom tied his horse to the post and held his breath against the foul smells that came with the man's trade. 'But you're too late, of course, as always. The little bastard ran off when I caught him at it, and fuck knows where he's got to by now – halfway to Leicester, I shouldn't wonder!'

'Does he come from Leicester?' Tom enquired, but Hoskins shook his head.

'Not now – he come from there originally, or so he used to tell me, but he were lodging with an aunt of his in Beeston somewhere before he come to live with us. You might find him there, but I doubt it. Anyway, stay right where you are, while I get the stuff I caught him with.'

Hoskins bustled inside, and Tom took the opportunity, after a couple of deep breaths, to look inside the sagging workshop that Hoskins presumably called his business premises. Tom, as a carpenter before he became a constable, knew next to nothing about the tanning trade, but even he knew that it consisted of converting cow hides into leather by soaking them in disgusting mixtures of dung and urine. But although he looked around carefully, there were no cow hides in sight, and nothing by way of finished leather goods.

'Yeah, trade's been a bit slack these past few weeks,' Hoskins admitted, seeming to read Tom's thoughts as he reappeared in the workshop entrance carrying a small leather bag. 'Anyway, here's the stuff I found in the thieving little bastard's room in the stable back there.'

'He lived with you, right?' Tom enquired, and Hoskins nodded. 'Like all apprentices, it were part of his duties to live on the premises, and mix all the potions for the tanning. But lately he didn't have all that much call on his services, and he were mooning around the house a lot. That's when he must have took all this stuff in this here bag – it were found in his room above the stable, and as you can see it's items of my wife's jewellery. "Ellie", her name is – the wife, I mean. Will you need to speak to her?'

'Later, perhaps,' Tom suggested. 'Right now, it seems I have to go in search of Master. . . .what's his name again?'

'Pike – Oswyn bloody Pike. What sort of name's *that* to give a lad – Oswyn? Mind you, if he were stealing the wife's jewels, maybe he's a bit – you know – an arse fiddler?'

'You want him arrested for *that* as well?' Tom enquired sarcastically, and Hoskins shrugged. 'Please yourself – but you got to find the little bugger first. It's your bloody slackness that led to him slipping away, so find the thieving shit and lock him up!'

'You're late for your supper,' Lizzie complained as she stood in the front doorway watching him tying the horse to the hitching rail that he rarely used. 'And does I have to feed the bloody horse as well?'

'I fed him up at the Guildhall,' Tom explained, 'and since I'm going to need him tomorrow, I thought I'd let him bed down in the back garden.'

'It'll be the first use you've made of that in years,' Lizzie remarked sourly as she walked back into the house, where Tom could hear utensils being slammed down on the table. He sighed and went in, wondering whether or not he'd be punished further for his lateness by way of dry bread and even drier leftover meats.

'Where you been all this time, anyway?' Lizzie demanded as she slopped potage into his wooden bowl, and Tom took his opportunity.

'I been out at Lenton, doing my job, and I reckon I've got enough new facts to save Anthony's neck. Then I did what you been on at me to do for days now, and called in at Ben Hoskins's place, to investigate that thieving what he reckons his apprentice lad's bin up to.'

'And has he?'

'Dunno yet, since the lad up and ran away when he were first accused. That's why I need the horse tomorrow. He's maybe skulking out Beeston way.'

'So, what was you saying about saving Anthony's neck?'

'Well,' Tom smiled triumphantly as he put down his spoon in order to allow the contents of his supper bowl to cool down, and pulled the end portion off some freshly baked bread, 'the Coroner were trying to make out that Anthony done the lass in on the estate, right? At least, that's what he wanted the jury to decide. Well, as it so happens, the lass were meeting a gentleman friend called "Benjamin" on the day she were last seen, and her favourite spot for doing that were the old priory buildings down the road in Lenton.'

'They reckon them's haunted,' Lizzie observed with a shudder. 'Are you saying that the girl were done in down there, so that her ghost will haunt the place as well, along with all them monks?'

'The only ghost of Amy Brindley that exists is in the mind of Ben Hoskins,' Tom insisted. 'I told you before, I don't believe in ghosts, but I do believe in evil people that are still alive.'

'So what did you learn down at the old priory?' Lizzie enquired, and Tom smiled. 'I found something that belonged to the dead girl, and were probably lost when she were being carried out of there, dead.'

'So you can prove that the girl were at the priory when she were murdered?' Lizzie smiled, 'that's something at least.'

'I can also prove that it were probably her latest fancy man what killed her, then took her body out to the Featherstone estate and buried it under that oak tree, probably late one night,' Tom added triumphantly.

'So all you have to do now is prove who that fancy man were,'

Lizzie reminded him with a mocking smirk, 'and are you going to eat that potage or just play with it?'

'I'm going to eat it when it lets me, and stops burning my mouth,' Tom replied, 'and as for proving who the fancy man were, I reckon I'm pretty close to doing that. I'm told by reliable witnesses that his name were "Benjamin", and he were in the leather trade. How many of them can there be?'

'You can't mean Ben Hoskins, surely? I know you can't abide his wickedness, and I know he's been pushing you to arrest that lad of his, but where's your proof? Are you sure you're not pointing the finger at him just to get your own back?'

'D'you really think I'm that mean?' Tom enquired, and was not entirely consoled by the fact that he received no immediate denial. 'Well, mean or not, I've got my duty to do, including my duty to eat this potage.'

'It's not my fault I never know what time you're coming home at night,' Lizzie complained, 'and it's all you're getting, so be a good boy like Robert and eat it all up.'

The next morning, when he reported for duty and announced that he was intending to travel to Beeston, Giles Bradbury was looking glum.

'I don't know where you been these past few days,' he grumbled accusingly, 'but there were a snotty-nosed feller from the County Sheriff's Office here yesterday, asking why you've been neglecting your duties lately. Apparently, there's been complaints from the Coroner, and from Ben Hoskins. And while we're on the subject, there's a stack of complaints about stuff going missing from land down by the Leen River – mainly fruit and stuff. I ain't had time to deal with any of it, and anyway it's your turn down there. I got bitten by a rat last time I were down that way.'

Tom thought quickly. The complaint from Ben Hoskins he could understand, mean-minded bastard that he was, and in any case Tom was on his way to investigate that particular complaint. But the one raised by Coroner Greville was of a different order altogether, and could be an attempt by the man to get Tom removed from office before he stirred up any more complications regarding what Greville clearly regarded as the simple matter of sending Anthony Featherstone to the gallows. Along with the loss of any further authority to investigate the truth behind Amy Brindley's murder, which strictly speaking was not part of his duties anyway, would come the loss of use of the horse he was riding to and from Lenton, and today even further out west, to Beeston. And if all went to plan, he'd need some way of transporting witnesses from Lenton into the town.

He hurried down to the basement of the Shire Hall and demanded admission to Anthony's cell. The man rose with a hopeful expression on his face, and Tom nodded in confirmation.

'I'm now able to prove, as near as don't matter, that the lass were done in at the old priory,' he advised Anthony, 'then buried at dead of night under your oak tree. And I'm pretty close to being able to prove who's guilty of the crime, so chin up. But I need something from you.'

'Anything – just ask,' Anthony smiled back.

'May I assume that you still keep a coach on your estate, since you've still got a coachman?'

'Yes – do you wish to borrow it?'

'Yeah – also another horse, if that would be possible as well. And I maybe might need to hide a young boy on your estate. Not sure about that yet, but maybe he could help that gardener of yours in exchange for his keep?'

'Yes, of course – anything you need. If you let me have a quill and a piece of vellum, I can give you a note to the Steward, advising him that you have total authority over the estate in my absence.'

'I don't have time,' Tom replied, 'but thanks anyway. I got to be going now, but with a bit of luck you'll be out of here within the next week.'

Three hours later, having made discreet enquiries in the two main streets of the village of Beeston, four miles to the west of the town, Tom slipped from his horse at the front fence of the cottage in Manor Lane, hitched him to the rail, drew his staff and pushed open the front garden gate. A young man was hoeing between two lines of vegetables, and he looked up in apprehension as he saw Tom walking towards him with a raised weapon. Tom smiled reassuringly.

'Oswyn Pike? I'm told that this is your aunt's house, so you must be him. You've got nothing to fear from me unless you try to make a run for it, in which case you'll get this lump of wood round your head. I don't believe you stole from Ben Hoskins, but there's some information I needs from you.'

'You're the Constable, ain't you?' Oswyn frowned back suspiciously. 'I remember you from when we dug up that body.'

'And that's what I want to talk to you about.'

'*I* never done it!' Oswyn all but shrieked, and Tom gave him a reassuring grin. 'If I thought you had, believe me I wouldn't have just walked through your gate – I'd have kicked it down, then smacked you over the head and tied your hands together. I'd also have brought a couple more fellers with me.'

'So, what d'you want to know?'

'Simple. The day we found that body, when did Ben Hoskins set off from his tannery, and where were he off to?' Oswyn thought for a moment before replying.

'After breakfast it were, but not for some time after. I thought it were odd, because he said he were off to Derby to get some cow hides for the tannery.'

'And what were odd about that, exactly?' Tom enquired hopefully.

'Well, for one thing we hadn't done any business for a week or two, and I don't reckon the Master could have had any money to buy new hides. He always paid for new hides from money he'd made from the last lot of finished leather, and there hadn't been any sales for a week or two. I had no work to do, and was just sitting around the place making myself useful – tidying up the tanning shed and suchlike.'

'And the second thing that were odd?' Tom persisted.

'Well, when he were going to Derby he normally set off at daybreak. I know it takes four hours to get there, because I been with him a couple of times. Then he wouldn't get back 'til supper time, but that day he were back not long after dinner, as you know yourself. So I don't reckon he'd been anywhere near Derby, to tell you the honest truth.'

'So how long were he gone, altogether?'

'Maybe four or five hours – no more than that, anyway, then when he *did* come back, it were with you.'

'So he didn't come back with any cow hides before coming back with me?'

'No.'

'Well there were nothing in the wagon when he called me out to dig for the body, so where do you reckon he might have been?'

'No idea,' Oswyn shrugged. 'But that were nothing unusual for him in them days. He'd taken to disappearing without telling me where he were going. It always seemed to be on a Wednesday, and I reckoned as how he'd taken to gambling, because he never seemed to have any money. He hadn't paid me for weeks, and the meals were getting smaller and smaller. I reckon he accused me of stealing as an excuse to get rid of me.'

'About that,' Tom smiled, 'Like I said, I don't think you stole anything at all, but tell me how it come about that you was accused of it.'

'It were a fix,' Oswyn replied with a grimace. 'I were cleaning out the shed for the sake of something to do when he comes racing in with a bag of some sort that he claimed had some of his wife's jewels in, and reckoned he'd found it under my bedding in the loft where I used to sleep. It were a ridiculous lie, but he insisted that he were going to call in the constables, and I got scared, because it were just his word against mine, so I ran off, and now you've found me. I ain't done nowt against him, so why would he accuse me of something I ain't done?'

'That's easy explained,' Tom smiled. 'He wanted you safely locked up, out of the way, because of something you know that he don't want anybody else to know.'

'Like what?'

'That's what I'm here to find out,' Tom advised him. 'And I reckon it might have something to do with that spade of his, and one time when he went missing, taking the spade with him.'

'That makes sense!' Oswyn enthused, 'and it explains why he blamed me for losing it!'

'Go on,' Tom urged him, and Oswyn's face took on a reflective expression as he recalled the events in question.

'It were some time ago now, but there were one night when he come home real late. My room were in the loft above the stable, and I were still dozing off when I heard him stabling the horse and cursing really loud. I reckoned he'd lost a lot of money at the cards or whatever, so the next day I kept my head down, because he could get a bit rough when he were in a bad mood – just ask his missus. Anyway, I spent the day cleaning out some of the last of the cow shit what we hadn't used, and putting it into the pile at the back of the yard, using the spade what we kept for that. Then the next night he were gone again, and the following morning I went looking for the spade, because I still had some shit left to shovel out of the shed. I couldn't find it, and then the Master lifted it out the wagon and give me a right telling off for leaving it in there, except I hadn't, see? I just put it down to the fact that he'd lost all his money gambling, and were expecting him to beat either his missus or me, which he normally did when things weren't going right for him. But not this time, because he seemed to have his mind on something else.'

'And when were this, as rightly as you can remember?' Tom enquired eagerly, but Oswyn looked blank until prompted further. 'Were it before the day we found the body?' Tom demanded impatiently.

'Oh yeah, a long time before that,' Oswyn confirmed. 'Maybe a couple of months before then?'

'So sometime in May, you reckon?'

'Yeah, about then. Does that help you?'

'It certainly does,' Tom smiled, 'but it don't help you much, because you're going to be looking for a new trade.'

'Can't I just stay here with my Auntie?'

'You could, once you've told the Coroner what you just told me. But before that, you've got to go into hiding somewhere. I found you too easily out here in Beeston, and Hoskins might come looking for you as well, so how do you fancy doing a bit of gardening work out on a big estate in Lenton?'

'If you says so, but can I finish this weeding before I goes? And do you want to stay for your dinner?'

It was mid afternoon before the two of them left Beeston, with Oswyn perched uncomfortably on the neck of Tom's horse as he walked him carefully along the track that joined the Derby Road at Wollaton, then up the final mile to Lenton Gregory, where Tom dropped Oswyn off with instructions to Amos Bridges that he had a new lad to help him with the estate gardening, on the orders of the Master. Then Tom persuaded the coachman that the spare horse had been loaned to him by Featherstone, and set off for home, after declining the offer of an early supper. He was leading the spare horse by the bridle as he entered Low Pavement at the foot of Bridlesmithgate, and turned towards the Guildhall in Weekday Cross, where a group of armed men were waiting for him.

Chapter Seven

'Am I being arrested?' Tom enquired as he opted to remain in the saddle in response to the apparent leader of the group stepping towards him.

'Thomas Lincraft?' the man enquired, and Tom nodded. 'You must know that, since your face's familiar, and we've met before. I just can't remember when, or why.'

'I'm Ralph Ireton, from the office of the County Sheriff, and I'm here to advise you that you've been suspended from office.'

'That doesn't particularly surprise me,' Tom grunted. 'Who was it what complained, and have you got any intention of listening to my side of things?'

'The complaint is two-fold,' Ireton explained. 'First of all a complaint of dereliction of duty from a Master Hoskins, who asserts that for two days you declined to investigate a charge of theft by his apprentice.'

'Hoskins is a trouble-making, loud-mouthed, bullying old pisspot,' Tom growled.

'Yes, he spoke highly of you too,' Ireton replied, to appreciative titters from the men around him.

'And more to the point,' Tom added hotly, 'I've just come from talking to the lad what's supposed to have stolen from him.'

'But you don't have him in custody,' Ireton pointed out, and Tom smiled. 'Because the lad's innocent. Hoskins was lying.'

'That's for a court to decide, or did you regard yourself as a judge and jury as well as a Constable?' Ireton grinned. 'That probably explains the second source of complaint – taking it upon yourself to investigate crimes, and interfering with the natural process of these things.'

'Coroner Greville?' Tom enquired, and Ireton nodded. 'Since you were clearly expecting that complaint, presumably I need not acquaint you with its content?'

'He no doubt complained that I caused a delay in an inquest he were pretending to conduct, when the wrong man were about to be sent for trial, just so he could get his supper on time. It just so happens that I'm preparing for the truth to come out, in my capacity as a resident of the county.'

'Not any more you're not,' Tom was assured. 'Not while misusing your powers as a Constable, anyway. Step down from that horse, put it back in the stable, and hand over your staff of office.'

Tom did as requested, after assuring Ireton that the second horse was his, and made his way back into the constables' room in the Guildhall on the pretence that he had some personal items to collect. Giles Bradbury looked up from his desk, his face a picture of embarrassment. 'It weren't me, honest!' he assured Tom, who smiled encouragingly.

'I know who it were, right enough, and now I'm even more determined to prove one of them wrong, and the other one guilty of murder. But first I need you to turn your back for a minute, while I gets something out the cupboard.'

'You're suspended from duty,' Bradbury objected, 'and it's more than my job's worth to let you into that cupboard.'

'And how do you know I'm suspended, when I didn't know myself until a few minutes ago, outside there? And I didn't tell you anything about that, did I?'

'No, but the Sheriff's men come in here, and said they was looking for you, to suspend you from duty.'

'But you didn't know for certain that they had, did you? Now shut your noise, and get your head back into them papers, while I gets what I needs from that cupboard.'

Giles did as instructed, and Tom swiftly removed the ribbon that had been around Amy's neck when she was murdered, the brooch that Tom had found in the grass at the old priory, and the bag of jewels given to him by Hoskins. He tucked them all into his jacket and sauntered out with a cheery farewell to Giles, and an instruction to keep his seat warm until his undoubted return.

He would need to act quickly, before word of his suspension reached the ears of their neighbours in the town, and in particular the Hoskins family. But he also needed to secrete away the vital pieces of evidence that he'd removed from the cupboard, and where better than the overgrown garden about which Lizzie was always complaining, and which even their own children refused to play in any more, preferring the rough open ground a few doors down from the house?

'You decided to plant turnips, or what?' Lizzie demanded as she surveyed him from the rear door of their house. Tom looked up at her and nodded down at the hole in the ground he'd just made with a large stone with a rough edge, into which he'd placed the all-important items before covering the hole over with the aid of his boot heel.

'If you see anyone exploring down here, stop them,' he instructed her sharply, and she burst out laughing. 'You're joking, ain't you? Who'd want to go exploring in that overgrown mess? And apart from leaving your horse to graze in it, you've shown no interest in it yourself in all the years we've lived here, so why now?'

'There's important evidence planted in there,' he advised her. 'Well it's the first thing I've ever known you plant,' she goaded him, 'so it must be important. Now, do you want this here supper or not?'

The next morning he was awoken by Lizzie shaking him roughly by the shoulder, and he opened his eyes to the sight of one of her 'Tell me what's going on, and don't lie to me' faces.

'I just met Martha Collinton in the street. You've been suspended. Why didn't you tell me?'

'I were too busy answering your questions about the garden. Looks like I better get a move on, before it gets to be common knowledge.'

'And where you going at this time of day? Looking for a new job?'

'No, doing my old one. I'm off to see Ellie Hoskins.'

'But you've been suspended!'

'She doesn't know that yet, with a bit of luck. Now, out of my way, because I just got a clever idea.'

He dressed hurriedly and rushed into the garden, where he retrieved the bag of jewels, into which he placed the silver brooch after cleaning it as carefully as he could. Then he saddled the horse and led him into the street, before trotting him the short distance into Pilcher Gate and slipping down from the saddle at the front door of the house next to the tannery. He was about to knock when he heard a woman's voice from the roadway alongside him.

'Constable Lincraft, I believe? Are you seeking Benjamin as usual? And what has the stupid oaf done this time?'

Somewhat taken aback by the woman's polite, educated manner of speech, he turned and smiled. 'Are you by any chance Ellie Hoskins?'

'I'm *Eleanor* Hoskins, certainly,' the woman replied haughtily. 'Only Benjamin insists on lowering me in everyone's eyes by calling me "Ellie". So I repeat – what has he done this time? Or have you perhaps come to return my jewellery, and have you arrested Oswyn Pike?'

Tom smiled, reached into his jacket, and produced the small bag of jewels like a travelling conjurer earning a few pence by entertaining the crowds on market day.

'These are yours, that right?' he enquired innocently, omitting to advise her that all but one of them had been handed to him by her own husband only recently. She examined the contents eagerly, nodding as she identified each item in turn.

'That's my amethyst ring, certainly. And my pearl necklace – not real pearls, obviously, since Benjamin saves the real ones for his lady friends. And you've found my silver brooch! That was the first thing to go missing, and it was given to me by my father for my sixteenth birthday. It has the family crest on it, and is very precious to me – I'm *so* glad it's been found, since it's all I have left to remind me of better days.'

When Tom looked puzzled, she continued.

'My father was Richard Linacre, the brewer. We were quite wealthy, with our own family crest, then he died, and the business failed very quickly. I was reduced to working for a living, maintaining the saddlery owned by my aunt on my mother's side, to which Benjamin used to deliver leather. He was nothing like the man you know – the man you've taken into custody several times. He was handsome, charming, kind, attentive, in fact the exact opposite of what he is now, with his drunken ways and his association with women of quite the wrong sort. And he's not above beating me when in one of his foul moods. But anyway, you don't want my life story, do you? You're only here to return my jewels.'

'So, you have no hesitation in saying that this silver brooch were once yours?' Tom enquired, barely able to contain his excitement, 'and you're sure it went missing before the rest of them jewels?'

'Quite certain – why?'

'Because it's mighty important in a matter that I'm involved with at the moment, and I'll need to keep it, just for a day or two,' Tom advised her as he reached out his hand, and breathed more easily once it was back in his possession.

'When can I claim it back for good?' Eleanor enquired, and Tom gave her a reassuring smile.

'If you come to the Shire Hall on Monday next, the chances are you'll get it back then. Right now, I need to go about my business.'

'No you fucking don't!' came a bellow from the entrance to the tanning yard, and there stood Ben Hoskins, armed with one of the long poles used to stir raw cow hides around in his tanning vat. 'You been suspended, so you've no business asking questions here, or anywhere else! It's the talk of the town that you're not a constable any more, so what you up to, eh? As for you, you useless lump of maggot food,' he yelled across at Eleanor, 'what you been telling him?'

'Nothing!' Eleanor replied with a fearful look. 'He was just returning my jewellery, honestly! I didn't know he wasn't a constable any longer!'

Hoskins glared at Tom. 'If I were you, I'd leave town without further delay, shithead! I'm going to report you to the Sheriff for impersonating a constable, and you'll likely finish up in your own cell, so piss off now, while you can. A long way away, if you knows what's good for you!'

Fortunately Tom was in the process of climbing into the saddle before Eleanor spoke again in her eagerness to appease Ben's wrath.

'There's no harm done, and at least I got all my jewellery back. Even that lovely silver brooch that my father gave me all those years ago. Although Tom Lincraft's taken it back again – claims he needs it for evidence or something.'

The look on Hoskins's face was that of a pole-axed calf in a slaughterhouse as Tom allowed himself the luxury of a rude gesture in his direction before cantering off down Pilcher Gate on his way out of town.

'I've got all the evidence I'm going to need,' Tom told those gathered around him in the estate kitchen, while the Cook served them all bread and cheese. Jane Netherfield had just arrived on her husband's horse, having been summoned by Bessie Helms when Tom first arrived. Bessie had run excitedly all the way to the Netherfield farm, and had travelled back perched on the mount's neck, but she seemed not to be lacking reserves of energy as she snuggled as close to Oswyn Pike as she could get while they all sat around the big table.

'So why do you need us?' Oswyn enquired suspiciously, and Tom's reply was 'Because each of you can supply a little bit of the whole story. Jane can tell the Coroner that the neckband on the body what we found in the paddock were made by her as a present for Amy. That proves that the body were likely Amy's, as far as anything can. Then Bessie tells the jury all about Amy's new rich feller what she were bragging about, and how she probably set out to meet him that day when she never come back. Wednesday – her day off, and her day for meeting her rich feller. She can tell us his name, as well – "Benjamin". And the fact that he had a leather business, and that Amy were going to try and get money out of him on the day when she set out to meet him.'

'I hope I can remember all that,' Bessie whispered apprehensively, and Tom smiled back at her reassuringly. 'Remember that she were your friend – all of you – and that this will be the only chance you have of sending the feller what who killed her to the gallows.'

'She weren't *my* friend,' Oswyn objected, and it was his turn to get a confident smile from Tom. 'Neither were Ben Hoskins,' Tom reminded him, 'But it's you that can tell the jury how he were often out late on Wednesday evenings. And how he come back all flustered one Wednesday night, then disappeared in his wagon the next night, probably carrying a spade.'

'It sounds as if you're leaving it all to us,' Jane objected, 'and how do we know that the Coroner will listen to what we have to tell him?'

'As far as that goes, he won't have any choice,' Tom replied with yet another smile, 'because he's obliged to listen to any evidence that can be made forthcoming in the matter. That's the law.'

'But how does any of this prove who it was that killed poor Amy?' was Jane's next objection, and Tom tapped his nose conspiratorially as he reached into his jacket and extracted the silver brooch. 'That's my job. Now, which of you wants to tell the Coroner that Amy always wore this brooch when she were going out for the day all dressed up?'

'I can do that,' Bessie confirmed gleefully, 'but how does it prove anything about who killed her?'

'Because I can prove who gave it to her in the first place,' Tom beamed back at them all. 'Ben Hoskins were a bit too clever for his own good when he tried to accuse Oswyn of stealing his wife's jewels, just so he had an excuse to get rid of him. Ben knew that Oswyn could tell all about the two late nights and the spade, which is why he had to get him out of the way, before I went asking questions.'

'I'm glad you brought him here,' Bessie gushed as she leaned over and kissed Oswyn on the cheek. 'But how does we get to the town in time for next Monday?'

'In the Master's coach,' Tom advised them. 'Before coming out here, I called into the County Gaol to see him, and he wrote a note what orders the Steward that you're to be allowed to use the coach to come into town on Sunday. And that I'm to be given the money for you all to stay in a decent inn on Sunday night. I'll come and get you from there on Monday morning, and take you all to the inquest.'

'So who *did* give the brooch to Amy?' Bessie persisted, 'and how can you prove who it were?'

'That's going to be the tricky bit,' Tom admitted. 'But be ready when I come up on Sunday to follow your coach into town.'

He had one final matter to attend to before he could go home for supper. He presented himself at the Senior Turnkey's desk in the front entrance to the Guildhall and asked to speak urgently to Constable Bradbury. Giles appeared, somewhat reluctantly, and gave Tom an awkward grin.

'I'll take a guess that you're going to ask me to do something I shouldn't,' he muttered, and Tom gave him a reassuring smile.

'Depends how seriously you takes your job, don't it? I want Ben Hoskins arrested for murder sometime on Sunday. And at the same time I want you to lock up his wife on suspicion of being his accomplice, and to bring her to the inquest on Monday in the Shire Hall.'

Chapter Eight

The courtroom was even more crowded than it had been on the first day, as Tom led his witnesses towards the side bench. Coroner's Clerk Matthew Barton gave a startled squawk and bustled across to challenge them with a testy 'We haven't summoned any more witnesses for today!'

'Maybe *you* haven't,' Tom replied with a smirk, 'but I spent the week doing your job for you. And the purpose of an inquest is to get to the truth. So, you just sit quiet in your corner over there, and let's get to the truth. Not *your* version of it, of course, nor the version what the Coroner thought he were getting, but the *real* truth.'

Barton scuttled away through the back door to warn Sir Henry Greville that the adjourned inquest looked like taking up more than the hour or so that they'd anticipated, and Tom smiled down reassuringly at the nervous looking group on the witness bench.

'You'll be fine, so don't worry. Leave the fancy lawyer arguments to me, and just remember what it is that the jury over there needs to hear.'

He'd spent the whole of the previous day – Sunday – taking his witnesses through what each of them had to advise the Coroner's jury, first of all in the kitchen at Lenton Gregory before they'd taken the coach down into town, then again in an upstairs room of The Bell, where they were all accommodated overnight. Tom had picked them up there in the morning, and guided coachman Jim Batley through the market place, then down Bridlesmithgate and along High Pavement until they reached the Shire Hall.

There was a slight commotion as Giles Bradbury led Eleanor Hoskins into the courtroom with her hands tied together, and with a resentful look on her face. As they came up to the witness bench she gave Tom a frosty look. 'Was this really necessary?' she enquired, and Tom nodded. 'We wanted to make sure you turned up to say your little piece. All we need is for you to tell the Coroner that this here silver brooch were once yours.'

'And that will prove that my pig of a husband murdered his latest fancy woman, as I understand it?'

'How did you know that?' Tom enquired with a puzzled frown, to which she replied 'You'll hear soon enough. Then you'll hear something you probably *didn't* want to hear, regarding whether or not

Benjamin Hoskins goes to the gallows.'

Tom looked enquiringly at Giles Bradbury, who shrugged his shoulders dismissively.

'There were no sign of Ben Hoskins at his house, so he must have run off. No doubt this lady played a part in that, so make sure that she don't take them ropes off her wrists. I'll be in the back of the courtroom, just in case.'

Any further conversation was cut short by the entry of the Coroner, who threw himself angrily onto his seat on the bench, then called out loudly for 'Thomas Lincraft'.

Tom stepped forward to stand in front of Greville, who pierced him with a glare that was no doubt intended to be intimidating. 'What's the meaning of this outrage?' Greville demanded, 'and why are there more witnesses to be heard?' Tom treated him to an oily smirk.

'As you yourself ordered, Coroner, this inquest was adjourned for a week in order for me to get more facts about the dead girl. You'll no doubt be pleased to learn that I've done that, and a good deal more besides. I can now give the jury more idea of who murdered her.'

'And how many witnesses will this involve?'

'There's five in all, Coroner, including me.'

'But you've already given evidence,' Greville objected, 'and the law says that you can't do so twice during the same inquest.'

'Begging your pardon and all that,' Tom smiled mockingly, 'I gave evidence the first time as a Constable. Since you took it upon yourself to have me suspended from duty, I'm not a Constable this morning, and I claim the right to give evidence in my own right, as plain simple "Thomas Lincraft", who's got something to tell the jury that'll help them to get to the truth of the matter.'

'I'm not sure that I can allow that,' Greville insisted as he looked towards the jury bench, where a whispered conversation was going on. After an awkward pause, one of them raised a tentative hand, and Greville nodded. 'What do you wish to say?'

The man cleared his throat and then announced that 'I'm Peter Baker, sir, and I speaks for the rest of the jury when I asks if we could hear what Tom Lincraft has to say. Even if he's *not* a constable any more, we all trust him.'

'Oh, very well,' Greville conceded grumpily. 'Tell us what you've got to waste our time with, Lincraft, and let's get this over before dinner.'

'I were going to be the last to give evidence, Coroner,' Tom advised him, 'since what I has to say will tie together what you'll be hearing from the others.'

'And I suppose you've also organised the order in which we're to hear this additional evidence?' Greville demanded, and Tom nodded. 'With your leave, Coroner, the first one's Jane Netherfield.'

Jane stepped into the spot designated for witnesses, and smiled nervously as the Coroner demanded her personal details.

'Jane Netherfield, sir, wife of George Netherfield, of Sands Farm on the Lenton Gregory estate. I'm aged twenty-seven.'

'And what have you to tell us?' Greville enquired in a tone of voice that suggested that he couldn't care less, but Jane had rehearsed her part well, and she held out her left hand, in which was the blue necktie.

'I was advised by Constable Lincraft, as he then was, that this necktie was found around the throat of the dead girl whose body was dug up on the estate. I can identify it by the embroidery, since I made it, and gave it as a present to a friend of mine who worked on the same estate of Anthony Featherstone. Her name was Amy Brindley, and she worked as a maid in the manor house there.'

Greville glared, first at Tom, then at the jury. 'I suppose that resolves any remaining question regarding the identity of the dead girl. Do you have anything to add, witness?'

'Only that she didn't deserve to die that way,' Jane murmured sadly.

'Very well, you're free to go if you wish, or you can rejoin the others on the witness bench,' Greville conceded, before treating Tom to a sarcastically exaggerated smile and the question 'Who's next?'

Bessie Helms rose shakily to her feet and stood on the spot vacated by Jane. She was visibly trembling as she responded to the first question.

'I'm Bessie 'elms, sir – spelled with a "H" – and I works in the kitchen of the manor house where Squire Featherstone's the Master. I knew Amy Brindley, what were a friend of mine, in a manner of speaking, and I know as how she'd lately got herself a new gentleman friend.'

'By all accounts she had plenty of those,' Greville muttered loudly in an audible aside to the jury. 'Was there one in particular that you were aware of?'

'Yes, sir – one by the name of "Benjamin", what were wealthy, and owned a leather business here in the town.' She broke off briefly when a derisive snort could be heard from Eleanor Hoskins, which was silenced by a glare from the Coroner. When Bessie appeared to have fallen silent, Greville urged her on with 'What about this wealthy gentleman friend, witness?'

'Well, sir,' Bessie continued, 'she were in the habit of meeting him in the ruins of the old priory, and . . . . '

'For the purposes of whoring?' Greville demanded, and Bessie shook her head. 'I'm not sure why she were meeting with this "Benjamin", sir, but . . . . '

'It's been well established that the girl was a whore, witness, so don't try to deny it. She may have once been your friend, but she's dead now, so no harm can come to her reputation any longer. Let's just agree that she was in the habit of meeting this mysterious "Benjamin" fellow for the purpose of whoring, although more's the pity that she chose to do so in what was once a fine house of God that now lies in ruins due to poor counsel given to our former King. So, we now know that her latest customer was called "Benjamin", and that he worked in the leather trade. Is there anything else, witness?'

'Quite a bit, sir, if you'll pardon my continuing,' Bessie persevered as she held out her hand and unclenched her fingers to display the silver brooch. 'Not long before she died, Amy took to wearing this silver brooch what she said had been given her by this man called Benjamin. She were wearing it the last time I saw her, pinned to the blue dress what she always liked to wear for best. She were off to meet this here Benjamin feller, except this time things wasn't so rosy between them, and she were fixing on giving him the "goodbyes". Only she were also going to ask him for more money, see, else she were going to spread bad stories about him in the town here.'

'Disgraceful!' Greville spluttered. 'Little wonder the cunning whore got herself killed! Although that hardly excuses the man himself – this "Benjamin" person – from associating with her. However, it begins to look as if the blame for the death may lie outside the Featherstone estate. And take that smirk off your face, Lincraft! Anything else, witness?'

'No, sir – except the dead girl were my friend.'

'Well, hopefully you've learned to be more discerning over your choice of friends. You may resume your seat, witness. Now then, Master Lincraft, who's next, and why is that lady sitting with her wrists tied?'

'For reasons that will emerge in a short while, Coroner,' Tom replied brusquely. 'The next witness is Oswyn Pike, if you please.'

Oswyn looked down at the floor as he was glared at by Greville, who barked at him as he demanded his name, age and occupation.

'I'm Oswyn Pike, sir, I'm nineteen years old, and I'm a gardener.'

'And why are you here?'

'I used to be apprenticed to Ben Hoskins, sir. In the tanning trade, it were.'

'And?'

'And well, he went and dismissed me for stealing, except I didn't.'

'Stealing what, exactly?'

'Jewels, sir. His wife's. Except I didn't.'

'And what has this to do with the dead girl, unless one of those jewels was the silver brooch that was being worn by the dead girl when she was last seen?'

'It weren't, sir, because I never stole owt – honest!'

Greville allowed himself a loud theatrical sigh for the benefit of the jury, then glared down at Oswyn.

'I may be missing something important here, witness, which means that the jury probably are as well, but what can you possibly tell us that has to do with the death of a girl we now believe to have been Amy Brindley?'

'I were dismissed for nowt, sir.'

'So you said already, and this is getting very tiresome.'

'Tell him *why* you were dismissed,'' Tom whispered hoarsely from his seat on the witness bench, earning himself a ferocious look from Greville. 'Let the witness speak for himself, Lincraft – you'll get your turn in a minute, if we ever get past this dithering boy.'

'I were dismissed for what I knew about Master Hoskins, sir,' Oswyn yelled desperately, and Greville nodded. 'We're finally getting somewhere, if God is on our side. What was it you knew about this Master Hoskins?'

'That he were staying out late every Wednesday night, and he blamed me for misplacing a spade, except I didn't.'

'Let's start with the bit about Wednesday nights,' Greville sighed, and Oswyn now had the bit between his teeth.

'Well, sir, every Wednesday he'd set off on his wagon on the pretence of going to Derby or somewhere to get cow hides for tanning. But he never once come back with any, and the business were fading fast, because he weren't selling any leather goods neither, see?'

'So your employer's business was in a bad way, and he was pretending to travel to an adjoining town to purchase more hides. Was he not simply seeking to preserve his pride, and pretending that his trade was still thriving?'

'But why did he need a spade, sir?'

'Ah yes, the spade,' Greville repeated as he rolled his eyes in a theatrical gesture towards the jury, some of whom smiled, and all of whom were wondering where this was all leading. 'Do *please* tell us about the spade, since we're all agog to learn about it.'

'Well, it were like this. There were one Wednesday night when he come back real late while I were lying awake in my bed above the stables, and it were after that when I heard him stabling the horse and cursing about something or other. He did a lot of cursing, did the Master.'

'What was he cursing about?'

'No idea, but the next night he were off out again.'

'And this would have been a Thursday – not your master's normal night for going out?'

'No – that were the point. Then the next morning I found the spade we used for shifting cow shit lying in the bottom of his wagon. He blamed me for it being there, but the day before I'd left it against the side of the tanning shed, like I normally did. And that's it, really.'

'That's *what* precisely, witness? What on earth has this got to do with the dead girl?'

'Well, just that Ben Hoskins took a spade with him when he went out on the Thursday night, and he knew that I knew, and that's why he dismissed me on a false charge of stealing his wife's jewels.'

Greville shook his head as he ordered Oswyn back to his seat, then glared at Tom.

'I hope your next witness makes more sense, Lincraft.'

'So do I, Coroner,' Tom replied with an exaggerated smile, 'since it's me.'

'What about the lady with her hands tied in front of her?'

'She'll be giving her evidence after me, sir. But since you expressed your confusion and displeasure, a moment ago, regarding how all these bits of evidence fits together, I thought I might oblige the court with an account of the enquiries I spent the past week following up.'

'Enquiries you were not authorised to make in your capacity as a County Constable,' Greville reminded him, and Tom smirked as he replied 'Which makes it perhaps as well that you made sure I were dismissed from that office, so that I could continue to ask questions like any ordinary person. And I got some answers for the jury to listen to.'

'Oh, very well. But get on with it, because the morning's slipping away from us.'

'Well, sir,' Tom began, 'as you'll have gathered, the first thing I did was try to find out who the dead girl were, since we'd had to put off this inquest to find out. We'd all been assuming that it were Amy

Brindley, but there were no proof of that. Anyway, I went to the Featherstone estate, and I spoke to the witness Jane Netherfield, who told me about the blue necktie she'd made for the lass Amy. I remembered that there'd been a blue necktie round the neck of the dead girl – in fact, it looked as if it had been used to strangle her.'

He was obliged to pause at this point when Jane Netherfield gave a light squeal and burst into floods of tears. Bessie Helms put her arm around her in a consoling gesture, while Eleanor Hoskins managed to extract a kerchief from her bodice, which she held out awkwardly in her roped hands. Bessie gave her a whispered thanks, and passed it on to Jane, who blew her nose loudly, then gave a bubbling apology to Greville for the interruption. Greville nodded his acknowledgement, then called for Tom to continue.

'Well, once Jane Netherfield had identified the necktie, and it seemed to be proved that the dead girl were indeed Amy Brindley, I asked around the estate regarding the girl's habits. It were Bessie Helms what told me that the lass had a lot of gentlemen friends . . . '

'She was a whore, you mean!' Greville corrected him loudly, and Tom inclined his head in silent agreement. 'She were certainly intending to seek a large sum of money from her latest admirer, and it may be that's what led to whoever it were doing her in. I were also told by staff on the estate that her favourite place of assignation with her latest gentleman – who she told Bessie Helms were called "Benjamin" – were the old priory down the road a bit, on the other side of Lenton Lane. So, I went looking down there, and found that silver brooch lying in the grass just outside where the monks used to have their bedrooms. The way it were lying gave me the idea that maybe it got lost when Amy were struggling with whoever killed her, or maybe when her dead body were being taken away to be buried in the field on the Featherstone estate. And that's something else, by the way.'

'Please don't change the subject at this point,' Greville instructed him. 'Come back to the point about the burying of the body later, if you must. But what about the brooch?'

'Well, I'd already been told by Bessie Helms that the lass Amy had been given it by this feller called "Benjamin", who were in the leather trade somewhere here in the town. So, I took the brooch back to the estate, and Bessie said that right enough, it were the brooch in question. So now I knew I were looking for a feller called "Benjamin" what had a leather business here in the town, who'd given Amy that brooch during one of their meetings.'

'And did you find him?' Greville enquired, now apparently absorbed by what Tom was advising the inquest.

'I reckon so,' Tom smiled. 'It just so happened that Benjamin Hoskins, what owned a tanning business a few streets away from where I live, were demanding that I arrest his apprentice for stealing jewels from Ben's wife. This were Oswyn Pike, as you knows, and when I found him at the place he'd run away to, he told me all about Ben Hoskins's night-time movements, and the business with the spade.'

'Are we talking about the same Benjamin Hoskins who gave evidence, on the first day of this inquest, about having seen the ghost of the girl Amy, who'd told him where to dig for her body?'

'The very same, sir, and you'll recall as how I weren't prepared to believe in all that nonsense about ghosts. But Ben Hoskins were right about where the body were buried, so how did he know? There were one other possible reason for that, and then the lad Pike told me about the business with the missing spade. He also told me something he didn't get round to telling us this morning – do you want him back as a witness?'

'No, God forbid!' Greville replied hastily. 'Just tell us what he told you.'

'Well, sir, he said that on the day Hoskins claims to have seen the ghost, he set off late for what he claimed were another trip to Derby. And you'll recall that Hoskins told this inquest that he were on his way *back* from there when he saw the ghost. Well, the lad Pike told me that it used to take him fours there and four hours back, so the times didn't fit. It were only the middle of the afternoon when Hoskins come back inter town with the story about the ghost, so where had he *really* been? And it were then that I learned that Hoskins had a spade.'

'Perhaps you can now tell us what you learned about the site of the girl's grave, since we've got to that part,' Greville suggested. 'The "something else", as you called it earlier.'

'Ah yes, that,' Tom smiled. 'You remember as how, on the first day of this inquest, the Featherstone estate gardener – Amos Bridges – said he'd seen his master Anthony Featherstone digging under the same oak tree where the body were found? Well, naturally, I enquired of Featherstone himself about that, and he told me that he'd been digging on another side of the old oak from where the body were, and that he'd been burying something precious in a tin box. I borrowed a spade and dug where he told me, and sure enough there were a tin box, right where he said I'd find it, so that put him in the clear so far as concerns the digging.'

'And what was in the box?' Greville enquired eagerly, but Tom shook his head. 'I never opened it, sir.'

'But where is it now?'

'In the Guildhall, locked away safe in a cupboard where we keep items of evidence.'

Greville seemed disappointed with the answer, but was equally anxious to move matters on.

'Coming back to your earlier evidence, witness – this brooch that you believe may have been worn by the dead girl at the time when her body was being moved. Did you ever find out who its owner was?'

'I did indeed, sir, and it's this final lady who'll be giving evidence. She's Hoskins's wife Ellie, sir.'

'*Eleanor*!' the lady in question shouted indignantly by way of correction. Greville nodded. 'She's your final witness, you say? And all she'll be doing is identifying this silver brooch in front of me here on the bench? If so, we'll take her evidence now, even though it means that dinner will be a little late. Perhaps it would be easier, and a little more dignified, were you to remove her wrist restraints. This is all assuming that you've finished your own evidence, of course.'

A minute later Eleanor Hoskins was standing in the witness space, rubbing at her wrists where they'd been chafed by the ropes. She announced her name, and the fact that she was married to Benjamin Hoskins, then gave her age as thirty-seven.

'Mrs Hoskins,' Greville said in a tone of respect that had not been bestowed on any of the previous witnesses, 'I'm advised that you can identify this brooch as yours – is that correct?'

'It is,' Eleanor replied calmly, and Greville continued in the same tone.

'Do I take it from what we heard earlier that you believed this brooch to have been stolen from you by the witness Oswyn Pike?'

'That was what my husband told me, and I had no reason to believe otherwise. But I now know that he gave it as a gift to his latest whore, and that it somehow got lost in the long grass while he was carrying her body to his wagon after he killed her.'

Greville raised his hand in a silencing gesture.

'That's only conjecture on your part, surely? Certainly, the evidence we've heard this morning might give rise to that inference, but you can't know for certain, can you?'

'Oh yes I can,' Eleanor replied defiantly. 'Because he confessed it all to me. Just before I killed him.'

THE LAW OF THE LAND

Chapter Nine

In the stunned silence that followed Eleanor's revelation, a few sharp intakes of breath could be heard from the jury benches, and Greville's mouth opened and closed several times before he found the words.

'You're prepared to admit to having killed your husband, say you?'

'I'm actually quite proud of it,' Eleanor replied calmly, 'and the world's a better place without him.'

Greville gestured with his hand for Tom to step forward again, and nodded towards Eleanor, as she stood silently before the bench. 'Perhaps this woman should be restrained with ropes again, Constable.'

'I'm not a constable no more, remember?' Tom smirked back, 'but Constable Bradbury's somewhere in court, so he can take care of that.'

Once the ropes were back around Eleanor's wrists, Greville demanded that she explain her extraordinary confession in more detail, and she smiled as she duly obliged.

'When Constable Lincraft left our house that morning, after telling me that he'd found my silver brooch, my husband Benjamin seemed like a man in the grip of some sort of seizure. He was trembling, and white in the face. I asked him what was wrong, and he responded by ordering me into the house. I was concerned that this might foretell another beating, so I hid a knife in the folds of my gown. A few minutes later he came into the house, and demanded – Benjamin never "asked" for anything, he always demanded – that I lie about the brooch.'

'He wanted you to deny that it was yours?' Greville enquired, but Eleanor shook her head. 'No, he wanted me to say that I'd actually seen Oswyn Pike slipping it into his jacket, but I refused. I said that it wouldn't be fair to accuse the boy in that way, and perhaps have him falsely imprisoned, and then Benjamin told me that he'd given the brooch to his latest whore – although he didn't quite put it in those terms – and that the girl had died accidentally when they'd been struggling. I asked what they'd been struggling about, and where, and Benjamin told me that they'd been down at the old priory, and that the girl had threatened to accuse him of raping her.'

'So, the girl was killed by accident?' Greville enquired, but Eleanor shook her head.

'So Benjamin tried to insist, to begin with. But then I asked him why he'd been with the girl in such an isolated place in the first place, and accused him of whoring with her. He became quite angry, and shouted that she'd been worse than a whore, and she deserved to die for trying to extract money from him. I told him that I didn't believe that she'd died by accident, and that I had no intention of risking being sent to prison for lying to the authorities about his involvement in the girl's death. Then he began raving and shouting that he'd "choked the daylights out of the little harlot" – his words, not mine – and that he'd do the same to me if I didn't help him to cast the blame on Oswyn Pike. I unwisely replied that Oswyn Pike was a better person that he was, and that I wouldn't tell a lie that would see him hang, and that's when Benjamin flew at me and tried to strangle me to death. God must have been by my side when he urged me to arm myself with that knife, and you'll find Benjamin's body in the shit pile at the back of the house, where it belongs. "Ashes to ashes, dust to dust, and shit to shit", as far as I'm concerned. You can take me away now, if that's the appropriate procedure.'

In what seemed like a dream, Tom stepped forward instinctively, then stepped back, red-faced, when he remembered that he was no longer authorised to take criminals into custody, and watched as Giles Bradbury led Eleanor out of the courtroom, after allowing himself a sly wink in Tom's direction. As Eleanor disappeared from sight behind the double doors that led into the corridor, Greville seemed to start from a reverie of his own, and turned to address the jury.

'Would I be right in thinking that you have heard enough to enable you to bring in a true verdict in the matter with which you were originally charged, before this amazing turn of events?'

There was an excited murmuring between the twelve men, before the one they had elected as their spokesman on the first day replied 'We have, Coroner, and we have a verdict.'

'Proceed, and my clerk will record it,' Greville instructed them, and the spokesman - elected since he was the only literate one amongst them - rose to his feet, held up the piece of paper that contained the outline of what he had to say, and announced that 'We, the members of the jury called to enquire into the circumstances leading to the discovery of the body of a female in Lenton Gregory on the third day of July in this year of 1571 find that the body was that of one Amy Brindley, maidservant of one Anthony Featherstone, and that she was killed feloniously by the hand of one Benjamin Hoskins of Nottingham on some date prior to the said third day of July.'

Greville frowned at the spattering of applause that rippled through the courtroom following this pronouncement, then fixed Tom with another of his steely glares.

'That no doubt brought you a great deal of somewhat unnecessary satisfaction, Master Lincraft, but I shall ensure that the thorough investigation that you conducted into this case is reported to the Sheriff of Nottinghamshire, and no doubt the miscarriage of justice that led to your suspension from your duties as Constable will be overturned in due course.'

'Talking of miscarriages of justice,' Tom replied with a broad smile, 'will you now order the release, of Anthony Featherstone, without any more delay? He's spent too long down below here already.'

'Yes, of course. And now let's all adjourn for dinner.'

As Greville rose from the bench and lumbered back through the door to his private chamber, Tom turned to look back smilingly at his witnesses, and was almost knocked flat as they ran to embrace him, thank him and congratulate him on his triumph. They insisted on all but dragging him down Stoney Street to the 'Old Angel', where they celebrated with ale, bread and cheese, using up the remainder of the money entrusted to them by the estate Steward for their accommodation. Much later that afternoon Tom looked over the top of his fourth mug of ale to see Lizzie standing in the doorway in her customary battle pose, hands on hips.

'They told me I'd find you in here' she frowned. 'I don't think you'll need any supper after this lot, so if you can find your own way home when the ale runs out, you'll find me with my feet up, enjoying a snooze.'

'I obviously can't thank you enough,' Anthony Featherstone beamed as he raised his brandy goblet in a salute to Tom, 'and you, Mrs Lincraft, must be exceedingly proud to have such a God-fearing and honest man for a husband.'

'He has his moments,' Lizzie acknowledged gruffly.

'And this was undoubtedly one of them, for which I shall remain eternally grateful,' Anthony smiled.

They were spending the weekend as Anthony's honoured guests on his estate, and had just finished an excellent dinner. Robert and Lucy had been sent to explore the grounds under the supervision of Amos Bridges, and the adults were relaxing in front of the log fire that had just been lit against the encroaching dampness of the early Autumn afternoon. They would be returning home the following day, after a hearty breakfast, in the same estate coach that had brought them from Barker Lane earlier that day, and Tom would be returning to duty on Monday morning, reinstated to his former duties, but with the rank of 'Senior Constable' that the County Sheriff had insisted upon, much to Greville's chagrin, when news reached his office of the exemplary investigation conducted by Tom that had narrowly avoided a horrible miscarriage of justice.

'What will happen to poor Mrs Hoskins?' Anthony enquired sadly, but Tom smiled back reassuringly. 'She likely won't hang, anyway. For one thing she did us all a kindness by ridding the town of one of its worst, and for another she did what she did to defend her own life. I reckon she'll be released to live what's left of her life as a widow woman.'

'Talking of happy endings,' Anthony smiled, 'it looks as if I've acquired a successor to old Amos when he retires. He speaks highly of his new assistant, young Oswyn, and to judge by the attention he's receiving from the girl Bessie in the kitchen we're likely to have a married couple living above the stables before too much longer. But what I can't understand,' Anthony continued as he swirled his brandy around in its goblet, 'is why the man Hoskins was so stupid as to draw attention to the existence of the body. It could have lain there forever, and none of us any the wiser.'

'Probably not,' Tom replied. 'I seem to remember that you use that bottom paddock for winter bedding for the horses in the stable, right?'

'Yes, but so what?'

'When does you harvest it?'

'Early Autumn, while it's still turning brown, and is long enough to make decent stall bedding. In fact, we'll be making a start on it in a few weeks' time.' Then the realisation hit him, and he smiled. 'Of course, it might have been noticed then that there was something different about the patch where the girl was buried.'

'Also the patch where you buried them papers,' Tom reminded him. 'I can keep them for you for a while if you like.'

'Yes, that might be best,' Anthony agreed. 'But I hope you didn't have to tell a lie about them to the Coroner.'

'No,' Tom grinned, 'When he asked me what were in the box, I just told him I hadn't opened it, which were true.'

'All the same,' Anthony smiled in a mocking expression of disapproval, 'you must say an additional prayer for forgiveness at our next meeting. But surely the man Hoskins had nothing to gain by having the body discovered earlier than it might otherwise have been?

He was simply drawing attention to himself in the most unbelievable of ways, with all that nonsense about a ghost.'

'It's nonsense to you and me, because we follow the true faith, but there was plenty of others what was prepared to believe it. Even Lizzie here, though she won't admit it now.'

'Leave me out of this,' Lizzie insisted as she smiled lovingly at Tom anyway.

'And,' Tom added, 'we got lucky that Hoskins just panicked when he did, and thought that maybe by making himself the one what drew attention to the body, he'd be the last person to be suspected. We constables rely a good deal on folks like Hoskins being stupid. That's how we catch most of them, even though we're not supposed to go investigating the way I did.'

'Well,' Anthony smiled as he raised his glass, 'Here's to Senior Constable Lincraft catching many more stupid criminals, even if he breaks the odd rule in the process.'

'So long as he don't finish up as stupid as them,' Lizzie added with a smile.

On the Monday morning a small crowd of Guildhall staff had gathered to cheer Tom back to duty, and he was handed a mug of ale by a grinning Giles Bradbury. The two men made their way into the inner office once the others had begun to drift back to their various duties, and Giles shook his head in quiet disbelief.

'Just to think that a week ago you were suspended from duty, and now you're back in here, promoted to "Senior Constable". But you deserve it, and I has to admit that you put up quite a show at that inquest – better than some lawyers I've seen.'

'I had to break a few rules, remember,' Tom reminded him. 'Don't go picking up my bad habits.'

'But how can they be said to be bad, if you gets the right result in the end?' Giles argued. 'If it hadn't been for you poking and prying where you shouldn't, poor old Anthony Featherstone would be on his way to the gallows. That's why I took this job – to see justice being done to the right folks for the right reason.'

'Me too,' Tom admitted with a rueful grin. 'But as you can see from what happened to me, you're in danger of treading on the wrong toes sometimes.'

'I'd like to work with you on your next matter, if that'd be acceptable to you,' Giles said with a sheepish grin. 'I wants to learn how to do things the way you do.'

An hour later he got his wish. There was a sharp thump on the door, and the Chief Turnkey poked his head round after opening it with obvious urgency.

'Tom, there's a feller out here what reckons he's just found his father hanging from a roof beam in the mill he owns down by Leenside. Could you look into it?'

'Tell the man we'll be right out,' Tom assured him, then caught the smile on Giles's face.

'Well, you said you wanted to learn from me, didn't you? Off your arse, and let's go and risk being bitten by rats.'

Endnote

It's a truism that novelists should write about things with which they are familiar, and after half a lifetime working as a public prosecutor my familiarity with the lives and work of senior police officers brought Detective Chief Inspector Mike Saxby to life with ease. I also recall that, like the rest of us, they have private lives and families. But, unlike the rest of us, the two often conflict, as I hope I have underlined in this first novel in the series. Likewise, in the next, 'Justice Delayed', we get to learn what drives the somewhat crumpled and dishevelled DI Dave Petrie, as well as delving further into the researches conducted by investigative journalist Jeremy Giles, whose murder becomes the focus of Mike Saxby's next enquiry.

My creation of the fictional 'Brampton' will fool nobody resident in Nottingham, given the occasional references to its location, but again I was writing about a place I know well, while availing myself of the freedom to describe settings such as the police headquarters and the layout of a North Midlands English city. I hope I will be forgiven this little subterfuge, and that you were sufficiently drawn into the professional and personal lives of the characters to want to read more. I would particularly value your feedback on this new project of mine, either by way of reviews on Amazon or Goodreads, or more directly on my website page, davidfieldauthor.com. I look forward to hearing from you, and thank you for taking the time to read this book.

David

Without Fear or Favour

David Field

Chapter One

Tom Lincraft, Senior Constable for Nottinghamshire, and his eager colleague Constable Giles Bradbury, were racing hard to keep up with Robert Franklin in his enthusiasm to show them his father's corpse. Down Turncalf Alley, and through the marshy ground that lay between it and the Leen River, the two men puffed and panted to keep up with their informant. Tom was the older of the two, at thirty years of age, but he was hardened by many a chase through the narrow back lanes of the town, and he was only a few yards behind the younger and naturally fitter Giles as they squelched to a halt in the boggy grass in front of the mill.

It was now almost August, and the wild flowers that decorated the flood plain in promiscuous abundance were daring to expose their stamens for the bees to spread their pollen, only to have them trampled down by heavy constabulary boots as the two men doubled over at the end of their enforced run, anxious to refill their depleted lungs.

'Not bad for an old codger!' Giles grinned as he straightened up.

'Mind your manners, you cheeky young beggar!' Tom growled between hoarse intakes of laboured breath. 'You come down here to learn how I does things, not to see how fast I can run. And keep your big boots out of that muddy mess to the side there.'

'D'you want to see this or not?' Robert Franklin demanded from the platform itself, his face betraying his annoyance at the delay.

'Just getting our breath back,' Tom assured him as he led the way, then launched himself forward onto the wooden boards of the mill platform, prior to raising himself back to his feet. He leaned down and helped Giles up behind him, and the two officers of the law turned in order to contemplate the reason for their being summoned down to Leen Mill.

The body of Edward Franklin was swinging slightly in the morning breeze from the main beam of his own flour mill on the north bank of the river. The big wheel was motionless, indicating that the sluice had not been opened before the man who had run the family mill had seemingly opted to end it all. The morning sun had been playing on his corpse for at least two hours, judging by the number of flies buzzing enquiringly around his face, and Tom frowned as he walked around the circular platform that led to the grinding stones, and took a long hard look at the back of the man's head.

'I can't believe he done it!' Robert Franklin wailed. 'There were no reason for it, because trade were good, and we had a good flow of water these past few weeks. *And* we had a full order book. What can I tell Mam?'

'Tell her he *didn't* do it,' Tom replied quietly and distractedly, and Giles moved round to stand next to Tom as he whispered 'What have you found?' Tom continued staring at the fly-ridden overweight carcass suspended from the creaking rope as he spoke quietly from the corner of his mouth.

'Ever seen a person what had hung himself?'

'Of course I have,' Giles replied, slightly aggrieved. 'I've been a Constable for two years and more, and I've had my fair share of them. Why?'

'What colour were their faces?' was Tom's next question.

'Purple and black, most of the time.'

'Most of the time, or *all* of the time?' Tom persisted, and Giles conceded 'Well, *every* time, since you ask.'

'And what colour's *his* face?' Tom continued with a nod towards the body swinging in front of them.

'Well, it's not purple nor black, anyway,' Giles conceded, and Tom nodded.

'So what does that tell you?' Giles thought for a moment, then gave up the struggle. 'It's different from the others?' he offered weakly, and Tom nodded.

'It's different because he didn't hang himself.'

'So why's he dead, and why's he hanging there?' Giles challenged him, and Tom sighed. 'Use your bloody eyes, man.'

Giles peered carefully at what was dangling in front of them, then finally noticed what Tom had spotted immediately. 'That looks like a big lump on the back of his head,' he observed.

'Big as a bowling ball,' Tom agreed. 'And how do you reckon he came by that?'

'Maybe when he took the dive off the platform?' Giles suggested, and Tom shook his head. 'It's wet out there, remember? Wet and muddy. To launch himself off this here platform, he'd need to climb onto it with the rope round his neck. Do you see any boot marks on the platform apart from them what we just made?'

'No,' Giles conceded. 'I get you. So he didn't hang himself, you reckon?'

'I'd bet my life on it,' Tom replied. 'So tell me, as your first lesson in separating the truth from what we was supposed to think, how did this feller come to be dead?'

'Somebody crowned him to the back of the head, then strung him up to make it look like he'd done himself in.'

'Correct,' Tom smiled. 'You're learning, boy. Now, you're a big strapping feller – could *you* have done it, all on your own?'

'I doubt it,' Giles conceded. 'So there was more than one of them, you reckon?'

'Definitely two, and maybe three or more,' Tom confirmed. 'He were a big feller, as you can see, and once he were dead, he would have been pretty heavy to lift.'

'A dead weight, you mean?' Giles joked, then apologised as Tom shot him a foul look.

'Part of what you'll learn from me is to show respect for the dead,' Tom growled as he jerked his head to where Robert Franklin was sitting on the edge of the platform entrance, facing outwards with his head in his hands, sobbing quietly. 'And now we got to ask questions of the poor bugger what found him – his own son, remember. But before that we got to look at the ground out there.'

'Why?'

'Because it's got a lot to tell us, that's bloody why!' Tom advised him in an irritated tone. 'Now get back down there with me, and don't put your boots anywhere unless I says you can.'

Back on the ground, with Robert Franklin still making sobbing noises five feet above their heads, Tom led the way slowly to a patch of churned up mud and grass to the side of the mill, and pointed downwards.

'What can you make out down there?' he enquired of Giles, who frowned.

'Looks like somebody did a lot of dancing around,' he agreed. 'Take a closer look,' Tom insisted, and when Giles remained silent Tom became fractious again.

'Have your never seen a horse?' he demanded, and Giles looked more closely. 'Yeah, I see what you mean. There's hoof marks in that there mud.'

'More than one,' Tom added. 'See, there's one with a full set of nail marks, and another what's missing a couple? So two horses at least, and maybe more.'

'But that could have been done by horses what was calling at the mill,' Giles objected, and Tom nodded. 'Now, what questions should we be asking of this poor sod what just lost his father?' Giles shrugged, and Tom sighed. 'Listen and learn, young feller. But first of all, pick up that spur what you obviously missed.'

Giles did as instructed, and listened attentively as Tom walked back to where Robert Franklin was sitting and adopted a sympathetic tone.

'It must have been quite a shock, finding your Dad like that, but I needs to ask you a few questions. That alright?'

Robert nodded, head down, and wiped his nose roughly on the sleeve of his shirt as Tom began.

'First of all, how does folk deliver their grain, and collect the finished stuff, from this here mill?'

'By horse and cart, obviously,' Robert replied, and Tom continued. 'Does any of your customers come from the nobility, or maybe just the rich folk up in the town?'

'No,' Robert replied with a shake of the head. 'There's Peter Baker, up in Stoney Street. He's probably the richest of them, but in the main our customers is all more humble folk – folk with long gardens what grows their own grain, then brings it to us to have it ground.'

'And they uses horses and carts, yeah?'

'Yeah. Some of them just uses barrows and suchlike. Peter Baker has a cart, and we've got one of our own, what we sometimes uses to deliver to folks what don't have their own. That's it, over there where the horse is grazing.'

Tom nodded sagely. 'It's just that we just found a spur in the mud to the side there. Can you think of any visitors to the mill lately what had spurs on their boots?'

'Definitely not,' Robert assured him. 'Spurs is only for the rich folk, and most of them uses the mill further down on the Trent, alongside Hethbeth Bridge.'

'Very well,' Tom replied as Giles moved alongside him. 'My fellow constable and me is of the opinion that your Dad didn't hang himself. We think that someone whacked him on the back of the head, then hung him up to look as if he'd done the deed himself. So there's some comfort in knowing that. But the problem with that, see, is that we got to take the body back to the Guildhall and let the Coroner know as how there's been a murder.'

'I understand,' Robert nodded sadly, 'but what do I tell Mam?'

'Tell her that we're going to be asking questions around the town, even though it's not officially part of our duties. We're supposed to just lock them up when somebody else gives us the facts that entitles us to do that. I don't suppose your Dad had any enemies? Anybody who'd want to kill him?'

'No,' Robert replied sadly with a shake of the head. 'He were a popular kind of feller, you know? You need to keep well in with folks if you're running a business like ours, and Dad were always smiling and laughing, joking with the customers and so on. He liked his pot of ale, too, and he were always standing his turn when he had the money.'

'Where did he drink?' Tom enquired. '"The Bell", on Beastmarket Hill,' Robert replied. 'Do you know it?' Tom and Giles both grinned as Giles replied 'There's not a constable in the county who don't know The Bell.'

'Yeah,' Robert conceded ruefully, 'it can get a bit rough some nights, but Dad were well respected. He always liked to play skittles out the back of there. In fact, me and him were there last night 'til quite late on.'

'Playing skittles?' Tom enquired, and Robert nodded. 'Dad were, anyway. With some new feller we'd never seen in the town before.'

'Was your father gambling?' was Tom's next question, and Robert shrugged. 'I wouldn't know. I were too busy chatting to Polly, the lass what serves the pots in there. She can be right friendly, if you know what I mean.'

'Know her well,' Giles murmured with a glint in his eye, and Tom stared his disapproval as he continued with his questions. 'Did your Dad seem to be getting on well with this new feller he'd just met? Could they have had a falling out over something? You get the idea – could this have been the person what come down here this morning and did him in?'

'I thought you said there had to be more than one,' Giles reminded him, then fell awkwardly silent in response to the glare that he earned himself.

'My colleague's right to remind me of the fact that there was likely more than one of them what did the deed,' Tom conceded, 'but for all we know, this feller weren't travelling alone, and your Dad might have done or said something to make him angry.'

'That don't sound like Edward Franklin,' Robert replied with a shake of the head. 'But you may be right, because I couldn't think of anybody here in the town as would want to do my Dad any harm, so it must have been a stranger. And the feller looked a bit – well, like as if he were anxious about something.'

'Any idea what?' Tom prompted him, but Robert shook his head. 'No, not really. But he were always looking behind him, like he expected somebody to sneak up with a knife or something. And he disappeared once or twice, claiming that he needed to check something in his room. It got Dad a bit annoyed, because then the skittle alley would get claimed by other players, and Dad had to wait 'til this feller come back down again.'

'Your Dad told you all this afterwards, did he?' Tom enquired, and again Robert nodded. 'Yeah, when we was walking home down through Greyfriars. We always made sure we was together if we come back from The Bell late at night, in case of footpads, you know?'

'Very sensible,' Giles acknowledged. 'So that were the last time you seen him?'

'Yeah, although he shouted a good morning as he left to open the mill this morning,' Robert recalled. 'That were our normal way of doing things. Dad would get up first, fix himself some breakfast, then come down to the mill in the cart to open up the sluice and get the wheel turning. Then I'd come down an hour or so later to help lift the first load up onto the platform and then onto the stones.'

'So you still lives in the same house as your parents?' Tom queried. 'That's right,' Robert confirmed. 'I never married, so it were easier for all of us if I lived at home and worked the mill with Dad, as well as doing things for Mam, like fetching water and chopping wood.'

'And this morning were no different?' Tom pressed him. 'Your Dad left the house an hour before you, that right?'

'Yeah, near enough. It's only a five minute walk to the mill from where we lives, in the mill cottage under the Castle rock.'

'And when you got here this morning, you found your Dad hanging the way he was when you called us in?'

'That's right, yeah.' Tom thought for a moment before explaining what was on his mind.

'To my way of thinking, your Dad were killed during that hour. But whoever done it either got lucky, or they knew your normal arrangements, and was waiting for him to turn up for work as normal.'

'Or somebody followed him,' Giles added helpfully, and Tom nodded. 'Good point, Giles.' He turned back to Robert. 'You didn't hear no noise of horses or nothing before you set out for the mill?'

'No,' Robert replied, 'and the track from the house to the mill's pretty quiet at that time of day. The sun had been up a good couple of hours, but it were still early in the working day.'

'And you saw nothing as you was coming down to the mill itself?' Tom enquired. 'A couple of town doxies lying in the grass, fair gone with the drink by the look of them,' Robert recalled with a faint smirk. 'I don't reckon they could have done it, not the state they was in. But nobody else, no.'

'Is owt missing from the mill?' Giles enquired. 'You know, bags of stuff, or tools, or even maybe money? Somebody could have been robbing the place when your Dad caught them at it.'

'Nah,' Robert replied with a shake of his head. 'There were nothing of any value left here when we wasn't here to guard it.'

'Which brings us back round again to the likelihood that whoever did it were interested in killing your Dad for personal reasons,' Tom concluded. 'We'll need to get his body up to the Guildhall, so can we borrow that wagon of yours?'

'Yeah, of course,' Robert agreed. 'Do you need a hand to get the body into . . . I mean, down to . . . .'

The pain was written all over his face once again, and Tom took pity on him.

'No thanks, that's why only big strong fellers is appointed as constables. We can look after that, but you can help us no end if you can think of somebody what wanted the old man dead.'

'I really can't,' Robert confirmed in a voice that was almost a plea to be excused further questions, 'but maybe you should find out a bit more about that feller that Dad were playing skittles with last night. He looked a bit on the rough side, and I can't be sure that there wasn't a couple of other blokes watching them playing, but like they wasn't interested in skittles, if you get my meaning.'

'We'll certainly pay a call on the proprietor of The Bell,' Tom assured him as he and Giles climbed back onto the mill platform. Tom took the large knife from the belt at his waist, swung the staff of office that hung from the same belt to one side so that it didn't impede his movements, and instructed Giles to lean out over the well beneath the platform, take the weight of the corpse, and be prepared to drape it across his shoulder when it slid down following the hasty slashing of the rope. Together they lowered it from the outside of the platform into the waiting cart, hitched up the grazing horse and set off back up the roughly defined track through the wet undergrowth, on their return to Turncalf Alley and back into the town proper.

'Did you take a good look at his face?' Giles enquired as soon as they were out of Robert Franklin's hearing. Tom looked sideways at him with raised eyebrows, and Giles duly obliged. 'He were making noises like he were crying, but there was no tears. I always pay attention to folks's faces when I'm asking questions, and you can learn a lot from the looks on their faces. Not a tear in sight, that one.'

'So you reckon he weren't too unhappy about his old man being dead?'

'Why would he? He gets to inherit the mill, from what he were saying.'

'So you're prepared to conclude that it were the son what did for the father?'

'Not yet, no. I'm just saying that he weren't all that upset, that's all.'

Just before they reached the entrance to the narrow Turncalf Alley, Giles appeared to be looking intently to his left, towards the foot of the Castle rock as it descended into Leenside. He caught the flicker of something light coloured and muttered to Tom that he'd be back shortly, then set off at a quick trot in the direction of the movement he'd spotted. A few moments later Tom clucked with impatience as he watched Giles talking in an easy manner with two women whose facial expressions even from that distance left little doubt that they were enjoying the exchange.

'What were that all about?' Tom chided Giles as he reappeared with a wide grin on his face. 'We needs to get this body back to the Guildhall, and alert that useless Coroner Greville that he'll need to give up a day's hunting in order to conduct an inquest. It were no time for you to be making yourself agreeable to the ladies.'

'They was no ladies, believe me,' Giles leered back at him. 'Two of the biggest whores in town, but very keen not to be run in for it, so I keeps them sweet by *not* running them in, and in return they gives me lots of information about who's doing what around the town, and who to.'

'So?' Tom enquired, far from mollified by the explanation.

'So they been lying out there all night, and believe me they smelt as if they had as well. They must have been the two what Robert Franklin saw when he were on his way to the mill, and he weren't the only one they saw while they was coming round from the night before.'

'And?'

'Two, or maybe three, blokes on horses, coming over this here bridge out of town, a little while after they heard the miller's cart heading for the mill, and maybe an hour before they saw "the younger feller", as they called him, heading the same way. They heard shouting from the direction of the mill as well, but thought nothing of it at the time. Looks like you was right after all.'

'I hope you got their names,' Tom muttered, and Giles grinned.

'I've known their names ever since I ran them in one time for strutting their arses in the Market Place on market day. That were two years ago now, and they smelt a lot better in them days. But I knows where to find them, and they're always more than happy to oblige the authorities, if you get my meaning.'

'Only too bloody well,' Tom grumbled. 'Come on, we've got a body to deliver. And tonight we might try a game of skittles.'

Chapter Two

'Trust you to find an excuse to go drinking ale,' Tom's wife Lizzie chided him as she cleared the supper things from the table, and ordered their son Robert to stop pulling his younger sister Lucy's hair as they wrestled and tumbled in the darkening corner of the all-purpose room in which they would soon be required to climb into their bedding. 'And you should be ashamed, taking that innocent young Giles with you and teaching him your sneaky ways.'

'Being sneaky's the only way to get to the truth in this town,' Tom insisted. 'That's how I got to be "Senior Constable", remember? I wouldn't accept all that shit from Ben Hoskins about finding that girl's body because her ghost told him where to find it, when all the while it were Ben himself what had put her there.'

'Shit', Robert repeated almost under his breath, and Lucy giggled. Lizzie's face reddened with embarrassment and anger as she smacked Tom across the back of his head and glared at their two offspring. 'Ignore what your father says, because I always do,' she advised them, then glared back down at Tom.

'Since your language's only fit for the alehouse, maybe you shouldn't waste any more time getting down there. Take your key with you, because I'll be locking the door after you've left, since you took the trouble to fit that lock in the first place. There were a girl misused down the lower end of Fisher Gate the other night, as you must know. A pity you can't use your desire for the truth in order catch whoever done that.'

'The lass were in the the White Boar 'til it closed that night, or so I heard in the same town gossip that you must have heard, and no doubt she could hardly walk by then,' Tom replied huffily. 'Little wonder she weren't able to defend herself, or even call for help. Assuming she *wanted* any help, that is.'

'Typical!' Lizzie fumed. 'Just because she were a lass on her own don't give anyone the right to do what some animal did to her, and when she has the courage to complain to the constables, all she gets is "You've only got yourself to blame." I only hope that nice Constable Bradbury isn't picking up the same bad attitude towards women. He's a right handsome spunk, is that one, and I bet the lassies is throwing themselves at him. I just hopes that he treats them right, that's all.'

'He certainly seems to be well in with the town harlots, anyway,'

Tom muttered as he pulled his cloak from its hook behind the door and kissed Lizzie on the cheek that she offered him. 'Let's see if he's any good at catching murderers,' he added as he ducked under the lintel on his way out into the street.

'Fancy a game yourself when this lot have finished?' Giles enquired as they sat on the bench to the side of where two local men were arguing over the rules that governed the game of skittles. Tom shook his head with a knowing smile. 'You're only asking because you reckon you're better at it than me. That's not why we're here, anyway. Keep your eyes peeled for strangers.'

'How am I supposed to know who's a stranger and who isn't?' Giles complained. 'You know the town folk far better than I do, on account of the fact that you've been a constable for more years than me. We'd be far better off enquiring of the landlord, wouldn't we?' Tom allowed himself a hollow laugh.

'You're not wrong when you claim not to be so familiar with town folk. Have you ever attempted to get information out of Ted Hollins?'

'Is he the landlord?' Giles enquired, and Tom smirked triumphantly. 'See, you don't even know the bugger's name! Have you never had occasion to break up fights in this place? There's plenty of them on Saturday nights.'

'More than once,' Giles replied, 'but I never dealt with the landlord. Just Polly, that lovely lass what serves most of the pots in here. She's always very grateful when I steps in.'

'I dread to think how she shows her gratitude,' Tom muttered, 'but talking of pots, it's your turn.'

Ten minutes later Giles returned with a rueful smile, but empty handed. 'I think I just met the landlord. Is he a big feller with a baldy head and a wart on his chin?'

'That sounds like Ted Hollins, right enough,' Tom confirmed. 'And where's our ale?'

'Polly said she'd bring them down to us. Don't worry, they're paid for. Only that there Ted Hollins didn't seem all that keen to serve me when I asked him if he had any strangers staying here.'

'What did he say, exactly?' Tom enquired, and Giles frowned.

'He said that the *only* people what stay here is strangers to the town, and that if they lived locally, they wouldn't need a bed for the night in The Bell. He had a point, I suppose, but when I asked about a feller what were playing skittles with Edward Franklin last night, he told me to fuck off, and it were then that Polly offered to bring us the drinks.'

Tom snorted derisively. 'No wonder he told you to fuck off. It's all over the town that Edward Franklin were found dead early this morning, after he were in here playing skittles last night, and landlords like Ted Hollins can't afford to get their names associated with stuff like that. I just hopes we doesn't have to wait too long for them drinks.'

'While we does,' Giles said encouragingly, 'tell me why you turned out so different from other constables. I mean, why is that you won't just settle for what people tells you when they makes an official complaint? How come you always has to make your own enquiries?'

'It's personal,' Tom growled defensively as he let his eyes drop to the floor. 'Obviously it's personal,' Giles persisted, 'but if I'm to follow in your footsteps, you might at least tell me what's led to you getting up the noses of the likes of Coroner Greville when you takes it upon yourself to investigate matters what's best left alone.'

Tom sighed deeply, and looked Giles in the eye. 'Does you really want to know?' he enquired reluctantly, and Giles nodded. 'Of course I does, else I wouldn't be asking you, would I?'

It fell silent for a moment during which Tom was clearly battling with some inner emotion before he began to explain.

'I grew up in London, in a place called Newgate. It were pretty rough in them streets, but my father and older brother was a bit different from the normal run of folks down there. They was only common labourers, working in the wharfs along Thames Street, but they somehow found God. Not the fancy kind, with bishops and suchlike swinging them incense bottles and prattling away in Latin. The true religion – the way of Tyndale and his likes, who took the word of God straight from the Bible, and not from priests what wasn't fit to call themselves men of God, the way they carried on.'

'You one of them Protestants, then?' Giles enquired, and Tom smiled. 'Indeed I am, and proud to admit it. But there were a time when it weren't safe to say that you was.'

'It still isn't, in some quarters,' Giles reminded him, and Tom nodded again. 'But I'm going back to a time before now, to the reign of Queen Mary. "Bloody Mary" they called her, and she were well named. She ordered her bishops and suchlike to hunt out all them what was Protestant, and have them burned for what were classed as heresy.'

Giles shuddered. 'They reckon it were a terrible way to die, although I were just a babe in arms when all that were happening.' He caught the look of pain on Tom's face, and hastened to apologise. 'Look, forget what I asked, if it's bringing back bad memories.'

'It is,' Tom admitted, 'but you're entitled to know. My Da and my older brother Richard was Protestants, and the church they went to down in Blackfriars were always a pain up the arse to the Bishop of London, a Catholic murderer called "Bonner". On the orders of Queen Mary he sent soldiers into the Blackfriars church on a night when my Da and brother was in there, worshipping God like good Christian men. All the names of them in there was taken, and they was given a week in which to admit that they'd been misled, and to "recant" their beliefs, as it was called. But they was told that they could only recant the once, and that if they ever once went back to their old ways there'd be no saving them.'

'I think I'm beginning to understand,' Giles began, but was silenced by the look on Tom's face. 'You understand bloody *nothing*, so don't try and pretend you do!'

'Sorry,' Giles replied in a small voice. 'Go on.'

'Well,' Tom continued as he took deep breaths to overcome the emotion that the memories were provoking, 'My Da and brother weren't the sort that heroes is made out of, so they recanted. But we had these cousins, see? Dad's sister Martha had two kids – a boy called Francis and a girl called Catherine. They was all Catholics, but for most of the time we all got on well enough. Then Francis – the evil *bastard* that he were – took a fancy to Catherine in a way that he shouldn't have done, and his mother – my aunt – caught them at it, and reported it to their priest, who threatened Francis with the fires of Hell if he didn't earn himself absolution from his wicked sin.'

Tom was breathing heavily, and Giles was becoming concerned for his health, and raised a hand in the air. 'Look,' he urged Tom, 'if this is all getting a bit much for you . . . .'

'Hear me out!' Tom all but yelled, causing a few people round them to look up enquiringly, and Giles nodded. 'If you say so,' he conceded placatingly.

'I says so!' Tom replied heatedly, then lowered his voice to complete the horrible story he had to impart.

'Like I said, Cousin Francis were seeking absolution. Then he learned that Bishop Sodding Bonner were seeking information about any people what had renounced their recantation, and was still attending Protestant services. So in exchange for absolution, Francis agreed to hand over names, and to make himself look even better in the eyes of the priest what were offering him the way out of Hell, he added the names of Dad and my brother Richard.'

'And that were a lie?' Giles prompted him, and Tom nodded as tears of bitter anger welled up in the corner of each eye. 'Yeah – a wicked, evil fucking *lie*, an' if I ever catch up with Cousin Francis I'll swing for the cunny! Sorry about the language there, but it still rankles something fierce, and you *did* insist that I tell you.'

'So they was executed?' Giles enquired, and Tom nodded as he shuddered. 'Burned at the stake in Smithfield, along with loads of others, all on the same day. They locked me in the house so as I couldn't watch, but it were only just round the corner in the next street from our house in Newgate, and so help me God I can still hear them screams!'

Giles, embarrassed and horrified by what he'd just heard, waited patiently until Tom appeared to have calmed down and looked back at Giles with an embarrassed smile of his own. 'So now, young feller, you knows why I never accepts anyone's word about the guilt of somebody else without I check for myself. It's all too easy for someone to be condemned on the word of someone what means them no good.'

'Here's your pots,' a melodious voice announced as a most attractive young lady smiled seductively into Giles's eyes and handed each man a jug of ale. 'Ted told me to leave them sitting on the counter until the beer went flat, but I thought it would be better for me to sit on your counter before the froth went out of everything. You haven't lost *your* froth I hope, Giles?'

She plumped herself down on Giles's knee and gave him a lingering kiss, while Tom looked on disapprovingly. She certainly fulfilled every man's dream of a pot girl, with long black hair, the most enchanting glittering blue eyes, full breasts and curving hips under her simple brown smock. Once Giles had disentangled his face he leered across at Tom with a look of salacious pride and advised him that 'This is Polly.'

'I didn't imagine she were the minister's wife,' was all that Tom could manage by way of reply, and Polly giggled. 'I don't fancy being anyone's wife just yet. Maybe when I've begun to lose my looks, and Ted decides to look for another girl to attract the men in here. By then my arse will be black and blue anyway, with all the attention it gets from pinching fingers.' She giggled again at the look of shock on Tom's face, then began nibbling Giles's ear before advising him that 'We should be closing before much longer – d'you fancy coming upstairs with me then?'

'I don't know when we'll be finished in here,' Giles replied as he squeezed her breast, 'but here's something to be going on with.' Tom gave a loud cough and reminded them both that 'We're here on official constabulary business.'

'Oh yeah,' Polly remembered, 'that were another reason why I brought the pots myself, rather than leave them for Ted to get around to it. You was asking about a stranger what were playing skittles with Ed Franklin last night?'

'That's right,' Tom confirmed. 'Can you describe him for us?'

'I can do better than that,' Polly replied with a smile. 'I can tell you where you can find him – upstairs, in the large back room on the first floor. He's been here for two nights already, and there's three other fellers what seems to hang around him, except they isn't staying here. They just wanders in here every day about dinner time, and moons around the front door back there, watching who's coming in and out.'

'Are they out there now?' Tom enquired, and Polly nodded. 'One of them's the size of a bloody cathedral, with a big bald head and a scar down his cheek, while the second one looks like he might be his brother, except he's got plenty of hair, although it's in need of a good wash. The third one seems to be in charge, and he looks like a ferret with the pox, on account of all the horrible pussy boils on his face. The way he looks at me, I wouldn't want to be caught down in the cellar on my own with him.'

'I'll go and take a look,' Tom volunteered, and smiled down at Giles as he stood up to leave. 'I'm sure you can find something to amuse yourself with while I'm gone.'

When Tom returned with a worried frown, Polly was busy flirting with the line of men waiting to play skittles, and Giles was finishing his pot of ale. He caught the look on Tom's face, and enquired as to its cause. Tom sat down and unfastened the strap that attached his staff of office to his belt.

'I hope you can trust that little baggage what was sitting on your knee when I left just now, because I think our landlord may be tipping off them three fellers what may be guarding the bloke you was asking about when you ordered the ales. He was talking to the ferrety looking one, and pointing out the back here. Best have your staff handy, just in case.'

Polly breezed past them on her way back into the main room, blowing a kiss to Giles as she did so. Tom kept his eyes trained past her as three men answering the description she had given only moments earlier appeared in the narrow alleyway between the main room and the skittle alley. One of them grabbed her arm and hauled her back down towards Tom and Giles, and Giles whipped round urgently as he heard her cry of pain. Then he leapt to his feet and raised his staff in the air, just as landlord Ted Hollins appeared in the doorway and yelled 'That's him! That's the feller what were asking about your friend!'

'Let go of the lassie!' Giles demanded, then stepped back slightly as the man with the poxy face drew a sword. 'Says who?' the man demanded, and Giles announced that he was a local Constable. The man spit into the rushes and grinned. 'Suits me – I always wanted to kill me one of them.'

'Come and give it a try, then!' Giles challenged him, but the man's grin didn't fade as he turned to his two companions. 'Seems like they only hires blind fellers as constables in this shithole of a town.' Then he turned back to Giles, adding 'As you can see, there's three of us.'

'And there's two of *us*,' Tom announced as he rose to his feet wielding his own staff at shoulder height. The man spat again into the rushes and cackled with laughter as he continued to leer at Giles.

'Brought your Dad with you, did you? Very well, let's start the dancing.'

The man holding onto Polly by the arm gave her a mighty shove, sending her crashing into the side wall with a shriek. She bounced off the wall, then ran past Ted Hollins in the doorway, calling him a 'rotten bastard' on her way through to the safety of the main room. Ted tactfully withdrew behind her, leaving the three recent arrivals squaring up to Giles and Tom in the narrow passageway. The current skittles game had been hastily abandoned as those in the skittle alley pressed themselves against the back wall, and looked on fearfully as the five men stepped slowly and cautiously towards each other.

The man with the sword advanced menacingly towards Giles, who stood his ground with his staff at waist height, while Tom remained a few feet behind Giles, awaiting his opportunity whichever way matters went. Giles smiled as he saw the first muscle movement from his opponent that betrayed his intention, and was ready when he lunged towards him, raising his weapon with a view to slicing Giles's head from his shoulders. This was by no means the first time that Giles had faced an armed idiot, and as the sword arm swung in a wild 'haymaker' arc towards him he jumped deftly sideways and brought his staff down hard on the man's forearm. There was a sickening crack of bone, followed by an agonised scream, and the sword fell to the rushes as the swordsman collapsed in a screaming heap and Tom stepped forward, picked up the sword and advanced on the other two assailants, who fled as if pursued by all the demons of Hell.

'Get up!' Giles ordered the man with the injured arm, and when he continued to kneel, whimpering loudly and nursing his arm Giles grabbed him by the hair and hauled him to his feet. 'Not so brave now, are we?' Giles gloated, then made a serious mistake by remaining too close to his prisoner, who lashed out with his booted foot and kicked Giles in the groin, then staggered back through the main room and out into the street, followed by Tom, who halted in the doorway, uncertain which way to go.

'They went up towards Chapel Bar!' Polly yelled from where she was standing with a shocked expression in the centre of the room. Tom cursed under his breath, then announced his intention of going back to see how Giles was faring.

'Is he hurt?' Polly wailed, and Tom grinned. 'Yeah, but I'll leave you to find out where exactly.'

He moved back towards the narrow passageway that led to the skittle alley, and as he did so there was a sudden furtive movement from the foot of the stairs that led to the upstairs rooms, and Tom turned quickly as a middle aged man ran behind him, heading for the door. Just as he reached it Polly stuck out a foot, and the man fell over it and landed in a sprawling heap in the doorway. Tom turned quickly and hastened to pinion the man to the floor, while Polly advised him that 'This is the feller you was looking for – the one what were playing skittles with Ed Franklin the night he got killed. I'll go and see to Giles.'

Just then Giles appeared from the passageway, white in the face and hobbling awkwardly. 'You alright, Giles?' Polly enquired hoarsely, and he grimaced. 'I'm still alive, sweetheart, but I don't think I'll be back when you close.'

'Too right you won't,' Tom advised him as he hauled the man to his feet. 'You and me is going upstairs to see what this feller's been hiding in his room that were so important that he needed three ruffians to guard him.'

Chapter Three

Tom held the man firmly by his tunic collar, even though he displayed no sign of attempting further escape, and Giles followed behind as they mounted the rickety staircase to the first floor. Down in the public room, Polly and Ted Hollins were clearing away empty pots after they'd decided to close for the night, since most customers had scuttled out once the fighting had finished.

'The big room at the back – that's what Polly said,' Tom reminded Giles with a backward glance as he reached for the door handle and pushed hard. The door rattled in its frame, but didn't open, so Tom commanded Giles to search through the man's pockets.

'I'm surprised a place as rough as this has keys to their rooms,' Giles observed with a smile as he extracted a massive key from the concealed pocket in the man's tunic and unlocked the door. Tom shoved the man inside roughly, and instructed Giles to block the doorway exit. Then he looked around with an experienced sweep of his eyes.

There were several large bags in various locations around the room, and Tom opened each one in turn while Giles studied the face of their captive carefully as he did so. The bags all yielded nothing but bales of cloth, which Tom tipped out onto the bare boards with mounting frustration.

'Satisfied?' the man enquired sarcastically, and Tom glared back at him.

'I might have been, if you hadn't tried to make a run for it, my friend. What are you hiding?'

'Nowt', the man replied stubbornly as his eyes flickered involuntarily towards the pallet in the corner piled high with bedding. Giles smiled to himself as he advised Tom that 'Our friend here seems quite interested in all that bed linen and stuff on the floor over there – maybe you should take a look inside it.'

Tom walked to the side of the room where the pallet lay under the mullioned single window, took the sword that he'd acquired during the earlier fight, and which he'd attached to his belt, then began turning over the tangled bedding with the point of its blade. His search soon revealed another bag, a heavy one that jingled merrily when he prodded it with his sword.

'Finally we're getting somewhere,' he growled as he bent forward and pulled at the drawstring. When it failed to open he looked more carefully and gave a sigh of satisfaction. 'This must be mighty precious to you,' he observed with a backward smile at the man who'd been hiding it in his bed linen. Then he transferred the smile to Giles. 'Any good at picking locks?' he enquired, and Giles nodded. 'I learned a lot from fellers I used to collar in my days down in the lower town. There's not a lock you can't get round if you've got the right tool. You take over guard duties on the door, and leave it to me.'

'Try not to bust it completely,' Tom chuckled, 'since once you've opened it you can show me how it's done.'

After a couple of experienced twists inside the crude heavy lock with a piece of thin metal that had been concealed within his tunic, Giles gave a triumphant chuckle, and the lock fell into the bedding. He pocketed it, then turned his attention back to the bag, whose drawstring he pulled open with one single action borne of practice with girls' bodices. He peered into the bag, then gave a cry of surprise.

'Give Ted Hollins the good news that this feller won't have any bother paying his reckoning,' he advised Tom, then reached inside and withdrew his overloaded hand, from which fell several silver coins. 'There's hundreds of them just like that inside this here bag,' he gloated, and Tom gave their prisoner a sick smile.

'Let me guess,' he said with heavy sarcasm, 'you was on your way home after selling a cow at the Saturday market.'

'It's not mine, honest!' the man insisted, and Tom noted an unfamiliar accent. 'I'd already come to that conclusion,' Giles advised him, 'since there's enough coins in there for half the cows in England. So where did you get it from?'

'Some feller in London,' the man advised them, and Tom laughed. 'Does he know it's missing yet?' he enquired with further sarcasm, and the man looked even more bewildered. 'I didn't steal it, honest! I were given it to bring to Nottingham.'

'Then your mission is accomplished, is it not?' Tom enquired, thoroughly enjoying the exchange. 'But was it really necessary to have Edward Franklin murdered?'

'I haven't done no murder!' the man protested, on the verge of tears, and Giles nodded. 'I'm inclined to believe you, friend, but what about your three travelling companions? The ones what was all set to murder *us* downstairs?'

'I don't know nowt about what they've been up to!' the man wailed. 'I don't even know their names. Not their full names, anyway.'

'Well, let's have their first names, shall we?' Tom requested, and the man nodded nervously. 'The feller with the scar calls himself Thomas, his brother's called George, and the one with all the pimples is Gerald. But that's all I knows about them, honest!'

There was a heavy knock on the room door, and the surly face of Ted Hollins appeared from round it. 'If you're taking this feller down to the Guildhall charged with the murder of Ed Franklin, I wants my money. He's due me twelve shillings in all.'

'Pay the man,' Tom instructed Giles with a smile, and Giles reached into the bag and withdrew a single coin, which he threw onto the floor at Hollins's feet. 'There you go, a fine silver sovereign – keep the change, and put it to my credit over the counter the next time I'm in here. Either that, or pay someone to get rid of these bed bugs.'

'Where d'you get that?' Hollins enquired in amazement as he picked up the coin, bit it, spat on it, then rubbed it back to a shine with the sleeve of his shirt.

'Ask your customer here,' Tom muttered as he stepped forward and took a firm hold of the man's tunic collar. 'Except you can't, because he's coming with us.'

'There were another girl attacked while you was swilling ale in The Bell,' Lizzie complained as she cut the top crust off the fresh loaf. 'Mary Draycott told me when we was at the baker's stall up the road there. Maybe you should make your enquiries in The White Boar, because that's where the lassie were dragged out from, they reckons. That's two this week – the place is obviously getting dangerous for lassies.'

'It's already dangerous for anyone what drinks their ale,' Tom muttered as he smeared a generous helping of lard across the crust that Lizzie had just handed to him. 'But I can't be in two places at once.'

'Well, if you hadn't dragged Giles Bradbury down there with you, maybe he could have done something,' Lizzie suggested, and Tom sighed.

'You're getting like the rest of the people in this town. When will you all accept that we can't stand at every street corner, or up at the counter in every alehouse, just in case something happens while we're there? And if we're there, then of course it *won't* happen. Even if Giles hadn't been with me last night, there's nothing he could have done to prevent another lassie being set upon. We can only follow up on what's reported to us, and no doubt when I go down the Guildhall this morning the matter will be awaiting our attention.'

'Well we can only hope that it gets it,' Lizzie conceded grumpily.

'And you should probably leave it to Giles anyway, since the poor lass what has to tell all the horrible things what was done to her will feel a lot more comfortable telling them to a handsome feller like Giles. Why did you need him last night, anyway?'

'Because we're both looking into the murder of Edward Franklin, that's why.'

'I heard as how he'd hung himself,' Lizzie objected, and Tom smiled. 'Good. If you heard that, given all the old gossips you hang around with when you go out to the markets, then our plan must be working. We've put it about officially that he hung himself, and that's what we wants folks to believe, but for my money he were done in by two, maybe three, fellers what wanted it to look like suicide.'

'Why would anyone want to do that?' Lizzie demanded, and Tom put down the bread and cleared his mouth before replying in a tone that suggested that his patience was wearing thin.

'Clearly to cover up the fact that somebody wanted him dead. What I've got to work out is "why" – and then, of course, *who*. But you've just got me thinking. If it's still general tittle-tattle round the streets that Franklin hung himself, how come the landlord of The Bell knew that someone had done him in?'

'That's something else you'll have to work out, if you ever gets off your arse,' Lizzie chided him as she removed the remainder of the loaf. 'That's all the breakfast you're getting, if you wants any dinner later on, so go and earn your keep down at the Guildhall. And prove to me that a live girl what's still having to come to terms with what were done to her is more important that a dead miller.'

Giles was already sitting behind his desk as Tom walked into their shared room in the Guildhall and enquired how Giles was feeling.

'Still a bit sore in the gentleman's chambers, thank you for asking. There were another girl ravished while we was arresting that wet pudding last night. At the *back* o' The White Boar this time, but she'd been in there the whole evening, or so I been told. That makes two this week.' Tom raised an arm to silence him.

'Give over, I'm sick of hearing it from Lizzie, who thinks we should be investigating that first, rather than Ed Franklin's murder.'

'And should we?'

'What's your opinion?'

'Does it matter?'

'Of *course* it matters. I'm quickly coming to learn that you seem to be close with every lass in town what likes to flaunt herself in public.

Should we let these attacks continue, as a warning against that way of living, or will these girls complain if we start putting in a presence where they'd rather be free to ply their trade?'

Giles looked genuinely shocked. 'You're not seriously classing all these girls the same, are you? Are you saying that every girl what wants to go out of an evening and enjoy a drink, and some convivial company, is a whore?'

'No, course not. But some of them is, and I'm not prepared to waste valuable time chasing after fellers what's naturally attracted to doxies but doesn't want to pay their outrageous prices.'

'How do *you* know how much a doxy charges?' Giles demanded with a grin, and Tom shook his head. 'I doesn't, obviously, but you gets my point.'

'I'm not sure I does,' Giles countered, 'but we can't just ignore two brutal rapes connected with the same alehouse in the same week.'

'Then the sooner we get this Franklin murder out of the way, the better,' Tom nodded by way of ending that particular line of conversation. 'Has the Coroner been advised?'

'Yeah,' Giles confirmed, 'and the body's down in the cellar, awaiting his permission for a burial.'

'That'll be St Mary's again,' Tom muttered, 'and no doubt another burial on the north side, unless we can produce a bishop what can testify that poor old Ed got the last rites while he was being done to death. That there minister's far too High Church for my tastes.'

'Let's fight them battles we can win,' Giles suggested. 'Starting with that grovelling feller down in the cells.'

'What did you do with all that money?' Tom enquired, to which Giles replied with a cheery 'Spent it all on doxies. They charge too much these days, didn't you know?' Then he saw the look on Tom's face, and added 'Sorry – it's locked away in the Town Clerk's vaults.'

'Right, let's go and talk to the man whose name we don't even know yet. At least, I assume not, unless he were that obliging when he were being booked in?'

'He calls himself "Thomas Browne", with an "e" on the end,' Giles advised Tom as he looked down at the note on his desk. 'He was most particular about that.'

'Is your name really Thomas Browne?' Tom enquired sharply as the two of them confronted the crumpled individual cowering in the corner of the tiny cell.

'Yeah, honest!' Browne insisted. 'So what does Thomas Browne do for a living – apart, that is, from murdering Nottingham millers?' Tom demanded sternly

'I didn't murder no-one, honest I didn't!' Browne wailed, close to tears, and Tom considered that his man had been weakened enough to get some more useful information out of him.

'Tell us about the money,' he demanded. Browne nodded eagerly, and began his tale.

'I'm a draper by trade, with a nice line of business based in Shrewsbury, from which I travels all over the Midland counties, like Warwickshire and Leicestershire. I don't come to Nottingham all that often, but if you wants the truth I'm telling you about being a draper, you can ask Ralph Meadows up in Goose Gate, because once or twice I've been able to put him in the way of some fine damask bolts imported from Spain. A lot of my stock is imported from foreign countries, and that's why I were in London – a week or so ago it must be now.'

'Where you were given all those silver coins?' Giles enquired in a cynical tone, and Browne nodded. 'It sounds hard to believe, I know, but I were down in the wharves at Rotherhithe, buying up some silk what I already had an order for, when this rich gentlemen called me over to one side and asked if I were interested in doing business with royalty. Naturally I said yes, and he told me that he were connected to the likes of the Earl of Leicester – her what the Queen's said to be mighty fond of – as well as the Duke of Norfolk, the Earl of Essex and lots more beside. But first I had to prove that I could be trusted with money. Lots of money.'

'Do you believe all this shit?' Giles enquired as he turned to Tom with a mocking smile. Tom shook his head. 'Not yet, anyway. Keep talking, friend.'

'Well anyway,' Browne continued as if his life depended upon it, which in his mind it probably did, 'the next thing I know we're in this alehouse across the river – on the north side, near the Tower, and I'm being introduced to them fellers what was with me in The Bell last night. In fact, they've been with me every step of the way since I left London, and to be perfectly honest with you good gentlemen, I'm mighty relieved to be rid of them.'

'And why's that? Tom prompted him, and Browne grimaced.

'Well, I was told that they was there to guard me and that money what I were travelling with. If anyone was to ask, I were to pretend to be plying my normal trade around the country, while carrying this here bag of coins what I was meant to deliver to someone here in Nottingham.'

'Who?' Giles demanded sharply, but Browne shook his head. 'I weren't told – just that the man would contact me, and that I were to stay at The Bell, and speak to nobody on my travels about the money what I were carrying.'

'When did you leave London?' Tom enquired, and Browne thought for a moment before enquiring 'What day's today?'

'Tuesday,' he was told, and he nodded. 'That must be right, because there were a big church parade two days ago when we went through Leicester, so that day must have been Sunday. So that must mean that I were given the money last Thursday, give or take a day, because I think we was on the road for four nights in all.'

'You and them three bodyguards, you mean?' Tom asked by way of clarification. 'All four of you?'

'Yeah,' Browne replied ruefully, 'but as it turned out they was more like gaolers than bodyguards. Everywhere I went they was following me – they never stayed at the same inn, but wherever I were staying the buggers would be there all the time, hanging around by the door or insisting that I stay in my room. It weren't too bad when we was on the road, but once we got here to Nottingham I had the days to myself, just waiting for someone to turn up and claim the money. Just sitting around in that gloomy bloody room for hour after hour – and the food they serve in that there Bell is just shit.'

'How come you was allowed to play skittles with Edward Franklin, then?' Tom enquired suspiciously, and Browne grimaced. 'That were a big mistake, for me *and* him, as it turned out. I were allowed to sit and watch the games when I made a big noise about being cooped up in that room all day. I were sitting there, just watching the other players, when this feller come up to me and asked if I wanted to play. I'd played a few times back at home, so I said yes, and while we was playing he started to ask me where I was from, because I talked different from him. Then it occurred to me that he might be the feller what was meant to collect the money, so I asked him. He didn't seem to know what I were talking about, but I think that Gerald feller – one of the so-called bodyguards, like I said – had overheard us talking. The three of them was sitting alongside the game, you see, like they didn't even trust me to play skittles. Two of them forced me back into the room, then held me up against the wall and demanded to know what I'd meant by asking this feller if he'd come for the money, and what I knew about him. All I knew about him was that he ran the mill down by the river, and that's what I told them. Then they locked me in the room, and come back yesterday morning and told me that they'd "fixed the problem". That's what they said, but you've probably worked it out for yourselves that they done for the poor feller, just because I were stupid enough to ask one silly question of the poor sod.'

'From what you're telling us,' Giles thought out loud, 'the identity of the person you was meant to hand the money over to is a closely guarded secret, along with the very fact that you was here to hand over money in the first place.'

'You're not wrong there,' Browne confirmed with a sad nod. 'From the minute I took that there money, my life hasn't been my own. And now I suppose you're going to charge me with murder.'

'Not necessarily,' Tom replied, 'but from your point of view that's the only good news. You'll be kept in this cell, if only for your own safety, until we catch the other three. What can you tell us about them three, or the feller you was supposed to hand the money over to?'

'Nowt, I'm afraid,' Brown replied sadly. 'I appreciate you hiding me down here, because now I've been talking to you I don't think I'd stay alive for very long once I were back out in the street. As for the other three, I think they're Londoners – they talk like Londoners, anyway, and they was sent by that rich feller what I met in Rotherhithe, so I reckon they could be working for somebody important – maybe even royalty, or at least nobility of some sort.'

'We're going to be conducting a very thorough search for them three,' Tom advised him, 'and you've given us their names – "Thomas", "George" and "Gerald", as I recall – but anything else you remember – *anything*, mind – will make our work a lot easier.'

'Their horses, for example?' Giles added. 'You obviously travelled up here by horse, so did the three of them have their own horses, and if so where are they stabled now? And come to that, where's yours?'

'Mine's in the stable at the back of The Bell,' Browne advised them. 'As for the others, I've no idea. Not in the same stables, probably. But somewhere pretty close by, I'd reckon, if that helps.'

'It's a start,' Tom admitted grudgingly, 'although there's lot of stables in the lower town. But thank you anyway. Enjoy your stay.'

Chapter Four

'Well,' Tom remarked as they returned to their room upstairs, 'it's looking pretty likely that we know who done Ed Franklin in.'

'Yeah,' Giles agreed with heavy sarcasm, 'and it looks as if I were wrong to suspect the son. All the same, I'd like to know why he weren't as upset as he tried to pretend he were about his old man being dead.'

'He stands to inherit the mill, as you pointed out to me earlier,' Tom reminded him. 'And who knows how things was between them? Not all fathers and sons gets on well together. No, my money's on them three what tried to do us in, just because we was making enquiries about them. Guilty consciences or what?'

'Even if you're right,' Giles pointed out, 'we still has to find the three of them.'

'Any ideas?' Tom enquired, but Giles shook his head. 'Tell you what, though,' he observed, 'if Browne were telling the truth about not knowing who were to be collecting all that money, then at least one of the three what were keeping a close watch on him must know. Otherwise, how would they know if the money were being handed over to the right person?'

'You're right, of course,' Tom agreed, 'but that doesn't go any further towards telling us who they are, and where we can find them, does it? And right now, I don't give a shit *who* the money were intended for – the most important matter for us is to find them what murdered Ed Franklin.'

'But don't you think the two matters might be connected?' Giles suggested. 'The feller in London what trusted them three to keep an eye on Browne must have instructed them to kill anyone who got in the way of the money being handed over, or finding out who was to be collecting it, and that were the big mistake what Ed Franklin made when he got too friendly with Thomas Browne.'

'Obviously,' Tom sighed with irritation. 'So when we find the three of them we can ask them that question as well,' Tom frowned. 'But we still got to find them, hasn't we? So how do you propose that we does that?'

'How about releasing Browne and following him until them three comes after him?' Giles suggested, and Tom smirked as he looked pointedly at Giles's groin. 'You keen to get your nuts kicked again?

And you were lucky you didn't finish up with anything worse than that.'

'You wouldn't say that if you was living inside my hose this morning,' Giles joked with a grimace, 'and as for anything worse, you may have noticed how I dealt easy with that sword what you're still wearing.'

'You're not the only constable what's disarmed a feller with a sword,' Tom grunted, 'and there's a limit to the number of times you can get away with it. There's only the two of us, and three of them, so let's not set out to be heroes.'

'Do you know any better way of finding them three?' Giles challenged him, and Tom shook his head. 'No, but I knows a safer way – we start searching the local stables for three horses what was delivered there some time on Sunday. And we can make a start on that before either of us even thinks of having dinner.'

By the end of the morning they'd examined every stable on the south side of the town, but had found no trace of the three mounts that the ruffians accompanying Browne must have stabled. As they stood outside the last of them, they argued over whether they should keep going on the north side after dinner, but Tom was of the strong opinion that they should go back to The Bell and tackle Ted Hollins over his apparent knowledge that Ed Franklin hadn't committed suicide.

'We'd be just chasing our own tales round in circles,' Giles objected. 'We should stick to the one line of enquiry until we get answers, so I reckon that we should continue looking at stables.'

'And how well does you know the north side?' Tom challenged him. 'At least here in the lower town we knew where to look; for all we know there's stables on the north side what we don't even know about.'

'All the more reason why we should be looking,' Giles countered. 'And how long before the Sheriff starts asking why we're not doing something about them girls what's been attacked?'

'Like what?' Tom demanded. 'We're not supposed to make up our own complaints, remember? We just has to arrest them what's accused by others, and has any of them girls what reckons they was attacked come forward and made official complaints? They're just rumours at the moment, and my wife Lizzie's got more information about them than us.'

'There's one girl complained, according to the paper what were on my desk this morning,' Giles advised him. 'If I hadn't spent the morning smelling horse muck with you, I'd have been dealing with it.

Anyway, it's time for dinner, so let's meet back at the Guildhall after then, and see if you can come up with something better than staring at horses' arses.'

'Have you done owt about them girls what was attacked?' Lizzie demanded as she served the pickled pork and cabbage. Tom shook his head.

'Don't *you* start – Giles has been rattling my ear about that half the morning,' Tom complained. 'And so he should,' Lizzie fired back. 'That's what you gets paid for, isn't it? What *have* you been doing, anyway?'

'Searching all the stables south of the market for three horses, but we hasn't found them yet,' Tom grumbled, and Lizzie stared at him in disbelief.

'Two sworn Constables of the Peace, and even working together you couldn't find just three horses in what must be eight or ten stables?'

'Not just any old horses,' Tom explained patiently. 'Three horses what belong to the three fellers what attacked us in The Bell last night.'

'So they can go for you again?' Lizzie demanded with raised eyebrows. 'And for all it's worth, let me remind you that it's not your job to go looking for offenders. You're just supposed to lock them up when somebody else makes a complaint. Why is it you always has to try and go one better, and stick your nose in where it's likely to get cut off?'

Tom sighed. 'We've had this conversation more than once, and the answer's the same one as I've given you time after time. A lot more crimes gets properly solved if I asks a few important questions of people what can supply the answers, and I never takes somebody's word for it without checking. Otherwise I'm no better than the Chief Turnkey.'

'You never *have* got over how your Dad and brother died, have you?' Lizzie enquired sympathetically as she placed a consoling hand on Tom's head. 'Don't you think it's time you gave that a rest?'

'*Never*!' Tom growled as he pushed his dinner plate away from him. 'There's nowt wrong with this dinner – I'm just not all that hungry, I'm afraid.'

Down in the lower town, only yards from the Guildhall, Giles had a very healthy appetite as he sat on the bottom step of the plinth of the

Weekday Cross that marked the boundary between Low and High Pavements. His lodging was only just across the road, above a baker's shop from which he was in the habit of purchasing a freshly baked loaf from the second firing of the day, then selecting some fruit from the stall that was always positioned a few doors down, in front of the apothecary's chambers. He'd then sit and watch the world go by, mentally noting who was going where, who was talking to who, who seemed furtive and who looked unusually wealthy, while he chewed enthusiastically on his dinner.

He'd been doing this for the best part of two years, and it was by watching the comings and goings that he'd developed his enquiring nature, and his talent for reading peoples' minds from their actions and facial expressions. He was happy to be working more closely with Tom, since he also seemed to have a taste for poking around in corners, and forming his own conclusions about crimes reported by others, rather than taking their word for it.

But Giles was obviously not meant to enjoy a quiet dinner today, and he groaned as he heard the complaining yell from behind him, and turned to smile at Susan Coleridge as she bore down on him with a disgruntled look on her wind-browned face.

'*There* you are, you useless piece of empty cheesecloth! Sitting on your lazy arse, instead of making sure that the streets is safe for decent honest girls like me! I just come from the Guildhall back there, wanting to know what's being done about the feller what done me behind The White Boar, and I'm told that you and that other useless pisspot Tom Lincraft's spent the whole morning admiring horses!'

'Morning Susan,' Giles smiled warmly once he'd cleared his mouth of the plum whose stone he hurled after a strutting pigeon in the road in front of him. 'I read that note we was left about you being set upon last night, but we've been too busy investigating the death of Ed Franklin.'

'He done himself in – everybody knows that,' Susan objected as she plumped down beside him and placed a hand on the sleeve of his jacket. 'But now that I've found you, don't you want to know what happened?'

'The note said you was ravished,' Giles replied with a slight smirk, 'and I think I knows how *that* were done. If you tell me who done it, I'll have him taken in, then put him on the list for the next Assize.'

'He didn't give me his name, nor – so far as I recall from our brief acquaintance - did he tell me where he lives,' Susan replied caustically. 'He were a stranger, I think – at least, I'd never seen him before, and I hardly got a good look at him, since he had me from behind, if you get my meaning.'

'And where were this, exactly?' Giles enquired, genuinely sympathetic, since Susan was not one of the town doxies who probably deserved every perverted act inflicted on them.

'Out the back of The White Boar,' Susan advised him indignantly. 'I'd gone there with brother Jack and his wife Sarah, after we'd spent the day working in them fields out Sneinton way what's owned by Earl Manvers. We'd all been paid for the day, and when we come back up through Fisher Gate we decided to have a small refreshment. Except it turned into a big one, then Sarah dragged Jack back home when he fell over through the ales he'd drunk, and that left me on my own.'

'You should have left with them,' Giles commented as he bit into another over-ripe plum. 'A lass on her own isn't safe in the likes of The White Boar,' he added, and Susan smacked him across the bonnet.

'D'you think I didn't know that, you ninny? I weren't that far gone, except I needed to do a tinkle before I set off home, so I nipped out the back into that there field where all the men goes to piss. They does it, so why shouldn't lassies, when they're caught short? Anyway, I'd just finished when this big bloke jumped on me from behind and did what I just told you.'

'And you didn't get a good look at him, you reckon?' Giles enquired somewhat unnecessarily, and Susan tutted.

'You wasn't listening proper, was you? Or does I have to draw you a picture? He had me from behind, and not in the normal place for that sort of thing. And when I struggled he give me these here bruises. All I can tell you is that he had a bald head – I felt that when I reached behind me to try and push him away. But he were too strong. And it were black as a pig's arse out there, so I didn't see owt else. But I think he might be the same feller what were inside the White Boar earlier, shouting the place down about the quality of the ale. He were right about that, but if it's the same feller, he had a big scar down his face, like someone had tried ploughing it with a knife or something.'

Giles was immediately all ears. 'A big bloke with a bald head and a scar, you said?'

'Yeah – d'you know him?'

'Not as well as I'd like,' Giles smiled back. 'In fact I'd like to make his better acquaintance, although not quite in the same way that you did.'

'This is nowt to laugh about!' Susan complained. 'And I'm not the first, neither. It's being put about that Alice Winters were given a few bruises by the same feller the night before – after he'd done her, of course. But that were down the road a bit from The White Boar – an alleyway down Malin Hill where she'd taken him by way of business, if you follow me.'

Giles had no difficulty following her. Alice Winters might be getting well past her prime, but she still earned a precarious living as a town doxie, and that might explain why she'd made no official complaint to the authorities. No-one was likely to believe the complaint of a whore that she'd been beaten black and blue by a 'mark', even though a physical beating was not one of the normal services impliedly offered by women of her sort. But at least Giles knew where she lived, and his lively enquiring brain was already buzzing, particularly when he remembered where he'd last seen her.

'How d'you know it were the same feller?' he demanded eagerly, and Susan smiled sardonically. 'Taking more of an interest now, is you? How come you're more interested once it's a whore what got done, when you couldn't be bothered when it were an honest girl like me?' Giles gave her the benefit of a long leer.

'I remember learning all about your honesty down in the Trent Meadows a couple of years back, so don't give me that, Susan Coleridge.' She giggled and smacked him playfully across the nose. 'You're obviously still a naughty boy, Giles Bradbury, and any time you wants to go back down into the Meadows, just let me know. But not 'til you finds that beast what likes it the other way. To judge by what he done to me and Alice, it's only a matter of time 'til he kills someone.'

'He may have done already,' Giles replied darkly, 'and it just so happens that I'm already looking for him in connection with another matter, so I'll let you know when we find him, and then you can tell your story at the Assizes.'

'Will I have to?' Susan frowned. 'It's kind of embarrassing.'

'I can teach you how to tell your story without being too shy about it,' Giles assured her. 'We might even practice down in the Meadows.'

'You'll never change, you randy cockerel you,' Susan smiled as she leaned forward and kissed him. 'Make it soon, though.'

When Giles got back to the constables' room in the Guildhall, Tom had been there for almost an hour, and was getting fractious from the inactivity. He looked up with an annoyed expression and demanded to know why Giles was late. 'Or was you having dinner with the Duke of Newcastle?' he enquired sarcastically.

'Better than that,' Giles beamed. 'I got a line on that brute what's been attacking girls in The White Boar.'

'I thought we agreed that would have to wait while we find Ed Franklin's killers,' Tom complained, but the smile remained on Giles's face as he revealed his latest information.

'One and the same, it seems. The bloke what attacked and ravished Susan Coleridge were almost certainly one of them three what attacked us last night, and what may have done for Ed Franklin. The one with the bald head and the scar down his mug.'

'So now we got another reason for finding him,' Tom conceded, 'but that don't tell us where to look exactly, does it?'

'I've got another girl – well, a woman, really – to talk to. One what didn't complain because she's an old town doxie, and nobody would've believed her if she'd complained. Nor would they have been likely to give a shit, more's the pity. But she might be able to tell us more about one of them three fellers at least.'

'Not before we've gone back and spoken to Ted Hollins,' Tom reminded him. 'I were going to go down there on my own if you wasn't back in the next ten minutes or so.'

'Well here I am,' Giles smiled, 'and if I'm forgiven for being late back from dinner on account of what I found out, we can go together.'

The look on Ted Hollins's face said it all as they strode into the main room of The Bell and made for the counter, where Polly was washing pots in the sink. She smiled lovingly in Giles's direction and enquired if he was feeling better 'where you was kicked.'

'Haven't had time to try it out yet, Polly,' Giles smiled back. 'Well, I don't mind assisting you when you decides to,' she smiled back, and Ted had heard enough.

'Get on with your work, you shameless baggage. And as for you two,' he glared at Giles and Tom, 'have you come in search of a pot of ale, or do you plan on causing another fight in here?'

'We didn't start that last fight,' Tom reminded him, 'and as the landlord what was playing host to them what did, you'd be best advised to keep quiet on that subject. We've come to inspect your stables, as it happens.' Ted shrugged his shoulders. 'Please yourselves. Mind and take a spade each and shift some shit while you're in there.'

'Talking of shit,' Tom persevered, 'how come you mentioned to us last night that Ed Franklin were murdered?' 'Because he were,' Ted persisted, and it was Giles's turn to ask a penetrating question. 'And what made you think that, when the story around town were that he'd hung himself?'

'I don't know what were being said around town,' Ted replied, 'but it were being said in here that somebody had done for him.'

'Said by who?' Giles persisted, and it was Polly who answered 'By one of them blokes what attacked you two. The one what kicked Giles in the you know whats.'

'I thought I told you to get on with your work,' Ted growled. 'There's still a few pots what needs to be cleaned.'

'And still a question to be answered,' Tom joined back in. 'How did the man with the poxy face know that Ed had been murdered?'

'So it's true then?' Ted enquired, at which Tom slammed his fist down on the counter, making Polly jump and causing Ted to step backwards in an involuntary movement.

'Stop pissing us about, if you wants to carry on running this place! We're damned near certain that Ed Franklin had his head smacked hard before he were strung up to make it look like suicide. And what's more, we're equally damned certain that it were done by them three what was frequenting this place, guarding that guest of yours what had a big bag of silver coins to deliver to someone here in the town. So you can see why we think you might know a bit more than you're telling us about them three. Like their full names, where they comes from, and where they been staying since they come to Nottingham.'

'No idea, and what's it got to do with my stables?' Ted bluffed. Giles was almost as angry as Tom at the man's uncooperative attitude, and his response was delivered in a cold voice.

'How many horses in there at the moment?'

'Just the one,' Ted replied evasively. 'And yesterday?' Tom persisted, at which Ted's eyes dropped to the counter. 'There might have been more yesterday – you'd need to ask the stable boy.'

'Who's no doubt been told by you to keep his mouth shut,' Tom sneered. 'But we'll ask him anyway. Stable out the back, is it?'

'He was lying about them horses,' Giles assured Tom as they walked through the back of the empty skittle alley towards the stables. 'His eyes gave him away.'

'I saw that for myself,' Tom insisted, 'but I don't think we're going to fare any better out here than we did in there.'

'Let me try something sneaky,' Giles grinned as they entered the stable, at the far end of which was a ragged youth rubbing down a fine mare in the end stall who Giles recognised even from that distance. He stormed down the passageway alongside the five stalls, grabbed the youth by the collar, and hauled him, protesting loudly, two feet in the air, using only one hand.

'Ben Tanner, isn't it? Ben Tanner what got done for stealing from washing lines up in Cow Lane? The beak told you that if you ever come up before him again you'd be dangling on the end of a rope, mind? Well, that day's come, you little rat!'

'I hasn't stole nothing!' the terrified youth protested, and Giles did his best to look unimpressed. 'That right? Then what did you do with the horse what that big bloke with the baldy head and the scarred face left here on Sunday?'

'I didn't steal no horse, honest!' the boy squealed. 'Then where is it, cunny?' Giles demanded, and the youth was only too anxious to explain 'He took it out of here on Monday morning!'

'That's not what he says!' Giles persisted in a menacing tone, 'so unless you can prove that he's been telling us lies, by telling us where we can find his horse, you're coming with us!'

'Honest, I don't know!' Ben croaked, on the verge of tears. 'All I know is that he asked me where there was a stables further out of town somewhere. Him and his two friends – they had a horse each stabled here on the Sunday, but they took them out before it even got light on Monday morning. Them and another bloke – a cripple - what was with them, and when they come back they asked where there was a good stables well away from here. Honest, that's the truth!'

'And what did you tell them?' Tom demanded as his first contribution to the conversation. The boy looked appealingly towards him as he answered 'Dan Bradwell's place, up on the Derby Road, just out of town, above the Castle there.'

Giles let go of the youth's collar, and he collapsed into the straw. 'You'd better be telling us the truth, else we'll be back with a rope!' Giles threatened him as he and Tom walked away, each with a carefully concealed smirk on his face.

'That were a bit rough on the poor lad,' Tom said in a tone of voice that nevertheless betrayed his admiration.

'And if we'd gone in there all polite and asked the same questions, we'd have got the answers Ted Hollins had told him to give us. Doing things my way, we've now got a likely stables to go to and wait 'til the fellers turns up for their horses. And we knows that there was somebody else with them when they collected their horses. For my money, Robert Franklin's back in the picture.'

'And how did he get up here?' Tom challenged him. 'We still needs to find them three fellers, anyway, because they're obviously mixed up in all this. They're probably out somewhere today, so we'll leave it for the moment. In the meantime, I owes you a favour, and the least I can do is help you collar this feller what's been attacking girls in The White Boar. That should keep Lizzie quiet as well, until I tells her that I'm going to be spending another night swilling down beer in an alehouse.'

'Ever tasted the ale in The White Boar?' Giles enquired with a quizzical smile, and Tom grinned back.

'Bloody good point, but we at least has to pretend to, while we waits for a bloke with a bald head and a scar on his face to try the same trick once too often.'

Chapter Five

'What I can't understand,' Giles grimaced as he forced down another mouthful, then put his pot down heavily on the window ledge in the corner in which they were standing, 'is how they manages to get the horse to stand still while it's pissing in the pot.'

Tom grunted in appreciation of the humour, and took another sip of his. 'At least we won't need any encouragement to make one pot last all night, so if the bugger comes in we won't be too pissed to grab him.'

They were in The White Boar in Fisher Gate, waiting to pounce on the man Susan Coleridge had described as the one who'd attacked her the previous night. Not because they were giving priority to her complaint, but because, from his description, he was one of the three they were really after, for the murder of Ed Franklin. The White Boar was a 'low' alehouse, in one of the 'low' areas of town, and its clientele was therefore far from being from the top layers of society. Most of the women in there were obviously doxies, since they were displaying sprigs of lavender on their bodices, a well established indication that the 'lady' wearing it might be acquired for a brief dalliance, if the price was right. As for the men in there, the vast majority of them were already approaching insensibility, and there was more than one pile of vomit in the rushes that one was required to navigate carefully around in order to keep one's boots clean.

'I doubt if he'll be stupid enough to show his face in here again, three nights in a row, after attacking two girls on two previous nights,' Tom observed gloomily, but Giles wasn't so pessimistic. 'He didn't attack either of them in here, did he?' he objected. 'They was both done outside, so who in here is likely to know, or even care? Certainly not that scrofulous oaf what calls himself the landlord. And both girls will be terrified to ever come back in here, so what's he got to lose? At least we know what he looks like.'

Tom shook his head. 'Does we? And how can we be sure it's the same feller? If you think about it, it were late on in the evening when he were one of them three what tried to kill us, so did he have either the time or the inclination to come over to this side of town looking for a girl to misuse? Did you talk to the girl he done over the previous night, and did she say how late on in the night it were?'

'That were Alice Winters – according to Susan Coleridge anyway –

and I haven't been able to talk to Alice yet. She maybe won't even want to talk to me, since I've run her in many's the time for parading her arse on the streets.'

'I thought you was soft on them girls?'

'Some of them, but not the likes of Alice Winters, what spreads the pox like some farmers spread cow shit.'

Two hours later there was still no sign of the man with the bald head and the scar, and Tom and Giles were not tempted to order any more of what Tom described as 'potted cows' piss', so they wandered outside and enjoyed the fresh breeze that was blowing up Fisher Gate from the Trent a half mile to the south where it was crossed by Hethbeth Bridge.

They were not the only ones abroad at that time, and as they strolled up Malin Hill, discussing in low voices how they planned, the following morning, to approach the owner of the stables on the Derby Road, they were vaguely aware of an older man walking ahead of them, slightly slow of pace. There were several side alleys between the jettied houses with shops on their lower floors, and it was from one of these that a dim shape leaped out into the main laneway and grabbed the older man around the neck, putting a knife to his throat and demanding his purse. Both Tom and Giles gave an instinctive yell and raced towards the incident, causing the would-be robber to push his intended victim to the ground and run back into the dark alleyway.

'Leave him be!' Tom instructed Giles, as they reached the man who was attempting to get back to his feet. They helped him upright, and he began to thank them profusely as he dusted down his clothes.

'I'm mightily indebted to you gentlemen,' he wheezed as he regained his breath. 'This is of course a well-known part of town for that sort of thing, but I was obliged to attend a paying customer on a boat on the river.'

'Your trade?' Tom enquired, and the man advised them that he was a bone-setter by profession, and had been called to attend on a man who'd broken his leg earlier that day when he slipped in the mud by the river bank while trying to moor his boat alongside a store house to which he'd been delivering timber from further upstream. 'Do you think we should alert the constables to what just happened?' the man enquired, and Tom and Giles both laughed as Giles replied 'We *are* the constables. Just give us your name, and we'll make a note of what happened, and leave it at the Guildhall when we report for work in the morning.'

'Gladly. My name's John Tingle, and as I said I'm a bone-setter. I live in Stoney Street, and I also have my treating room there, so if ever you should need anything from me, I'd be more than happy to assist. You must get quite a few broken limbs in your line of work.'

'Since you're offering,' Tom smiled as they continued to walk back towards the junction of High Pavement and Stoney Street, to which both constables were heading anyway on their way home, 'can you tell us if a rough type of feller, with a face full of ugly boils, come looking for you to fix an arm what my colleague here busted for him on Monday night?'

'No, not me,' Tingle replied, 'but I suggest you ask my friend and fellow practitioner Joseph Pryce. He has a treating room in Beastmarket Hill, and coincidentally we were in each other's company earlier today. We're both widowers, you see, and we enjoy playing chess against each other. We also tend to talk over business matters, and today we had occasion to commiserate with each other over those who seek out our services, then fail to pay for them. Joseph mentioned one unpleasant encounter the previous day – or it may have been the day before that – anyway, an unpleasant encounter with a ruffian who looked as if he was recovering from smallpox, but who claimed to have broken an arm when he slipped on some horse dung in the road. He was accompanied by a man who said he was his brother, and after Joseph had treated him, this other man produced a knife and threatened to slit Joseph's throat if he demanded payment. It was a most distressing incident, and I fear that it may have left poor Joseph with a reluctance, in future, to treat anyone who can't pay in advance.'

'Beastmarket Hill, you said?' Tom enquired with a broad smile. 'A bone-setter called Joseph Pryce?'

'Yes, that's correct,' Tingle smiled back. 'He's a few doors up from The Bell, on your way up the hill towards Chapel Bar.'

They escorted Tingle to the foot of Stoney Street, where Giles bid them goodnight and continued towards his lodging in Low Pavement, while Tom walked up Stoney Street alongside the elderly bone-setter until they came to the junction with Barker Gate, and it was Tom's turn to wish his companion a safe journey along the remaining few yards towards his house. Then he unlocked the door of his own darkened dwelling, got undressed, said a hasty prayer on his knees, then slipped into bed beside Lizzie.

Giles was first in the following morning, and they discussed the order in which they should follow up the two useful lines of enquiry they'd acquired the previous day. They opted for the bone-setter called Pryce, and as they passed the door of The Bell, already open for business with a few customers whose bedraggled appearance suggested that they'd never been home the previous night, Tom made the obvious observation.

'The fellers we're looking for either don't know Nottingham from a cow's arse, or they've got a limited circle of acquaintances. When one of them gets his arm busted they only travels a few yards up the hill to get it seen to, and then they goes just a bit further up, and out of the town altogether, in order to find a new stable for their horses. I wonder why they thought they needed to do that.'

'They probably noticed the bone-setter's place when they first arrived in town,' Giles mused out loud, 'which suggests to me that they were staying somewhere nearby. And if you've got a busted arm then you'd be likely to go to the first person you know of what can fix it. Here we go – this looks like the place.'

Tom hammered on the door, and from inside the premises could be heard a shuffling noise, followed by a voice calling out nervously 'Who is it?' 'Constables Lincraft and Bradbury', Tom called back in response, and the door opened a fraction to reveal the scared looking countenance of an elderly man pointing a firearm of some sort at them through the gap.

'Best put that down, before somebody gets killed,' Tom advised him, but the man seemed reluctant to do so. 'How do I know that you're constables?' he demanded. 'You doesn't,' Giles conceded, 'but we knows that you're Joseph Pryce, and that you had an unwelcome visit from a man with a face full of boils and a busted arm a couple of nights ago.'

'I never reported that!' Pryce objected, and Tom smiled reassuringly. 'No, but you told your friend John Tingle, and it were him what told us. We're not here to take your complaint, so don't worry yourself on that score. We needs to know more about the fellers what did you out of your fee, that's all.'

'But if I let you in, and the men who threatened me learn that I opened my door to a couple of constables, they'll think that I made an official complaint, and then they'll come back and finish me off, like they threatened. I can't take that risk!'

'You doesn't have to,' Tom assured him, 'because you can tell us what we needs to know while we stand here. But what makes you think that they'll be watching your door?'

'Because they're lodging only a few doors up,' Pryce whispered as he jerked his head to his left, further up Beastmarket Hill. 'I'm not sure exactly where, but they said that it was almost alongside Chapel

Bar, and that they could keep an eye on my door from there.'

'Well that's mighty helpful to learn, for a start,' Giles said encouragingly. 'All three of them, you reckons?' Pryce nodded, and was about to close the door in their faces when Giles jammed his boot in the gap and smiled. 'We'll end this conversation when we're good and ready, Mr Pryce, and the longer we stand here, the more likely them fellers is to think you're making an official complaint.'

'What else do you want to know?' Pryce demanded in a quavering voice, and Tom had a mental list already prepared. 'We know that one of them had a busted arm, because it were my colleague here what busted it. So what did you do when they come to your door, and how did they know you was a bone-setter?'

'The sign's on the door,' Pryce reminded them, 'so that anybody can see it. That's how I acquire my customers. If I was a candle-maker it would be the same.'

'So what happened the other night?' Giles persisted, and Pryce appeared to shudder at the memory. 'It was late on when there was a hammering on the door, and three men stood there, two of them half carrying the third. He was obviously in great pain, so I invited them in, gave the man a mug of wine laced with hemlock to deaden the pain he was in, and the additional pain that I was about to inflict on him, then set the bone in his forearm that had been neatly broken. The neat fractures take longer to heal, because there's no rough edges to bind together. Then I put the arm in splints, told the man that they would have to stay on for at least three months, and asked for my five shillings. That's when one of the men with him produced a knife, told me that I wasn't getting my money, and that if I told anyone what had just taken place he'd come back and slit my throat.'

'What did these men look like?' Tom enquired, and Pryce clearly retained a clear memory of the traumatic event. 'The man with the broken arm had a horrible facial complexion, full of boils that were leaking puss. To judge by the smell of him, that was because of a lack of washing. The man with the knife had a lot of greasy looking dark brown hair, again in need of a good wash. The third man was bald, but with a scar down his face. Now, is that all you need to know? If so, please leave - now!'

'One final question,' Tom persisted. 'You said something about "splints" – is them pieces of wood?'

'That's right,' Pryce confirmed. 'Two lengths of wood, one on either side of the fracture, tied together with ribbon.'

'So this feller would be hard to miss if you saw him in the street?'

'He most certainly would, and I sincerely hope that I don't,' Pryce replied as he rammed the butt of the firearm on Giles's booted foot, then slammed the door shut when Giles removed the foot with a yelp. 'We could take him up for that!' Giles yelled as he hopped up and down, but Tom merely grinned. 'We could, but the poor bugger's suffered enough, don't you think? At least if anybody's been watching from up the street, they'll think that he told us to get lost.'

'Why is it me that always has to get hurt?' Giles protested, and Tom grinned. 'Because you're too new at this game. Now, let's see if we can find them there stables up near the Castle, shall we?'

As they approached what was clearly a large set of stables on the left hand side of the road to Derby, looking down through verdant parkland towards the royal castle, Tom nodded towards its entrance. 'We done things your way in the stables of The Bell. Now it's my turn to show that I can be sneaky. Just go along with me, right?'

A man dressed in a heavy riding cloak stepped out of the entrance, and Tom called out to him 'You Master Bradwell?'

'That's me – Daniel Bradwell. What can I do for you?'

'I'm looking to buy a horse, and you were recommended.'

'I doesn't sell horses,' Bradwell objected, 'I just stables them.'

'Then I must have been misinformed,' Tom replied as he adopted a crestfallen look. 'But I was told you are a good judge of horseflesh, so can I come in and have a look at how you care for those that are left for stabling with you? If I like what I see, I might commission you to find a good horse for me. The price won't be a problem.'

Bradwell's face opened in a slow smile as he waved them inside. 'I would obviously welcome an extension to my business such as you propose. Step inside, gentlemen, and you won't find a finer groomed set of horses anywhere.'

Tom took his time working his way down the dozen or so stalls containing mounts of different sizes and breeds, making considerable show of examining their teeth before ducking down and testing their fetlocks and lifting their hooves. Giles followed patiently behind, trying to work out what Tom's objective might be, and it took the best part of an hour before Tom finally straightened up with a smile.

'Most reassuring,' he nodded towards Bradwell. 'I judge that you yourself have a well developed skill when it comes to horses, so I leave it to you to find me a fine mare. No older than two years, no younger than a year, and pure bred. It's for my daughter, and it must possess a quiet disposition. You may add two sovereigns to its price by way of your fee, and my man here will call in every few days to enquire whether or not you have met with success. And so I bid you a good day.'

'Where did you learn to speak all fancy like that?' Giles demanded, 'and what were that little performance all about anyway?' Tom grinned.

'I can talk like a fancy feller when it suits me. And back there it suited me. The third horse in on the right hand side – the chestnut stallion – has two nails missing from its front right shoe. Just like what we saw in the mud by the mill the other morning. One of them horses were there when Ed Franklin were hung out to dry, and we know from the stable lad at The Bell that the three fellers with Browne was sent to Bradwell to stable their horses. You puts all that together, and what has you got?'

It was dinner time, and they went their separate ways. For Tom it was back home, where Lizzie was clearly in one of her disapproving moods as she dumped the potage bowl down heavily on the table. 'Next time you goes out pissing it up in an alehouse, try not to come blundering home like a herd of cows and waking me up. It took me hours to get to sleep in the first place, worrying that you wasn't home, and what with that rapist still loose on the streets. Has you and Giles caught him yet?'

'I'm sorry if I made a noise coming in,' Tom replied, 'but you seemed to be asleep when I got into bed.' 'That's because I was pretending to be, in case you was drunk enough to try any of your nonsense,' Lizzie advised him, 'and answer my question.'

'No, we hasn't caught him yet, and that's because we hasn't been looking. Not for a rapist anyway. But if we're right in our suspicions, he'll be one of them what did for Ed Franklin, so we'll be solving two crimes at once. Or maybe three, since you told me there were another lassie attacked the first night – the night what Ed were in The Bell. But that lass hasn't seen fit to make a complaint, and until she does there's nowt I can do.'

'Maybe she's too scared to make a complaint,' Lizzie pointed out, and Tom nodded. 'That's Giles's first job after dinner, since he reckons that the woman called Alice Winters were one of them lying out in Leen Meadows the morning that we thinks Ed Franklin were done in.'

Giles knocked confidently on what passed for the door to the shack alongside the boneyard in Bellar Gate, and recoiled backwards as

Alice Winters flung it open from the inside, releasing a foul odour that was redolent of an unswept cow barn. She grinned through her browning gums and invited Giles inside. 'It's free to a randy spunk like yourself.'

'No thanks, Alice,' Giles replied as he held his breath. 'I'm here on official business.'

'If you was thinking of taking me in, I can make it worth your while not to,' she persisted, but again Giles shook his head. 'Just a few questions, but we'll do it out here, if that's all the same to you.'

'Yeah, sorry about that,' Alice advised him. 'I'm only just home from last night, and I hasn't had time to tidy up yet.'

'Has somebody died in there?' Giles enquired, but Alice shook her head. 'You can probably smell the privy hole out the back. It got blocked a week or so back, and the gong shoveller what normally comes to clear it reckoned that he'd need twice his normal fee to unblock it. I offered him the usual extra, and I won't tell you what his reply were, because it weren't very complimentary.'

'You has to admit, Alice, that your best years is behind you,' Giles grinned, 'and the last time I saw you, *I* has to admit that I wouldn't have been tempted.'

'I were recovering from a terrible night,' Alice nodded. 'And not just because of too much to drink, neither.'

'I heard as how some feller gave you a thumping in an alleyway down off Malin Hill,' Giles persevered, since she'd raised the matter. 'I'm here to see if you wants him taken in, and if so, who he were.'

'No fucking idea,' Alice growled, 'but when you catches him, stick something hard and blunt up his arse, because that's what he done to me.'

'He done the same thing to Susan Coleridge the night after,' Giles confided, 'so we'd like to collar him before anyone else gets the same done to them.'

'If I knew who he were, I might be interested in making a complaint,' Alice replied grudgingly, 'but I've tried doing that before, and a girl like me, what earns her money by performing a much-needed service for the menfolk of the town, tends to get nowt from you lot except a big laugh, an invitation to take my clothes off, and advice along the lines that I may be charging too much.'

'So you can't tell me owt about him at all?' Giles persevered, and Alice shrugged. 'Only that he had a bald head and a big scar down his face. I'd been watching him in The White Boar all evening, because he looked like a stranger to the town, and I thought I might get in

122

before any of the younger girls caught his eye. Then he disappeared for a long while, and I assumed that he'd found a girl. When it come to chucking-out time I were standing in the doorway when he come back up Fisher Gate from the bottom end and asked if I were interested in the business. I took him down the bottom of Malin Hill, where I normally takes fellers what likes a bit of privacy, and no sooner are we down there than he starts belting me round the head, then bending me over, lifting up my clothes, and doing me like I were a bitch in a dog yard. Then he ran off, and I never *did* get my money!'

'So how did you finish up down in Leen Meadows?'

'That's another story altogether. I were sitting by the roadside on Malin Hill, having a little cry to myself, when up comes Martha Longbottom – her from the other side of town, up by Greyfrairs – and asks me what's up. I told her, and she reckoned as how what I needed were another drink or two. So we got us a big jug of Dragon's Milk from a place what were still open, and the name of which I can't remember, and we went and sat out in the Meadows until I don't remember no more before I woke up with the sun in my face, and Martha were puking into the grass to the other side of me. I just lay there wishing I were dead, then you turned up and started asking questions.'

'About what happened in the Meadows,' Giles replied eagerly, 'you told me you saw Ed Franklin's cart going from his cottage towards the mill – that right?'

'You must have got that wrong,' Alice mumbled, 'either that or I did, because now I think about it I only *heard* the cart. I couldn't get my head upright for a long while, and when I did it made my stomach all churny, so I laid down again.'

'So anyone could have been in that cart, that right?' Giles enquired eagerly, and Alice nodded. 'Yeah, that's right.'

'And the horses you saw coming out of Turncalf Alley?'

'Not me. That were Martha. She mentioned it, in case they was coming our way and we was going to get trampled on, lying where we was lying.'

'Two horses or three?'

'Fuck, I can't remember, can I? I never got to see them, and I can't remember what Martha said.'

'But you definitely saw the miller's boy heading for the mill after that? Robert Franklin?'

'I saw a young feller, anyway, but since I doesn't know Robert Franklin from the Pope's arse I couldn't tell you if it were him or not.

Sorry – you sure you doesn't want to come inside for a free go?'

'Not even a free one, thanks all the same, Alice,' Giles replied in an attempt not to gag at the mere thought. 'There was a time you wasn't so choosy,' she chided him. 'You got a regular girl, or what?'

'Several,' Giles confirmed as he turned to go. 'And they *are* girls.'

Giles could hear the loud curses before he was halfway down the hallway that led to the office he shared with Tom, who was quite obviously back from dinner. Giles threw open the door and strode in, just in time to catch Tom hurling an inkpot at the wall, its contents splattering down the panelling and onto the bare floorboards.

'Dinner not to your liking?' Giles enquired light-heartedly, and Tom let out a string of oaths fit to curdle milk. When he had seemingly exhausted his repertoire, and apologised, he glared down at a piece of vellum on his desk, then lifted it up and handed it across. 'Read that, and see if you can outdo me for sweary words,' he commanded Giles. 'It were waiting for me when I come back from dinner, all sealed and official, like.'

Giles read it, but couldn't quite believe it. 'Tell me I'm dreaming this,' he asked, open-mouthed, and Tom let fly a few more oaths before replying. 'If you are, then make it stop, and we can *both* rest easy.'

'He can't be serious, surely?'

'Have you ever known the Sheriff of Nottinghamshire to be in a mood for jesting?' Tom snarled. 'What *we* has to decide is how long we can ignore it.'

'But we can't, surely?' Giles argued, to be met with a furious glare from Tom.

'Maybe you can't, but I certainly bloody can. There's no way on this sodding earth that I'm prepared to release Thomas Browne and hand him back his money!'

Chapter Six

They argued long and hard, well into the afternoon. Giles was all for doing as they had been commanded, and releasing Thomas Browne, while Tom was adamant that he would do no such thing.

'But,' Giles argued, 'we got no good reason for keeping him. We been reckoning all along that the three what was with him was the ones what killed Ed Franklin, and we doesn't even know that the money he were carrying were stolen. And if we doesn't release him, we'll be in the shit with the Sheriff. You've got your orders, and if we doesn't let the poor bugger out, the Chief Turnkey will.' Tom smiled unpleasantly.

'No he bloody won't – not without my say-so as Senior Constable, anyway. The way things works around here, I takes my orders from the Sheriff, and the Chief Turnkey takes his orders from me. Without me signing the paper he's got no authority to let Browne out.'

'But the Sheriff will just go over your head, and you'll be out of a job,' Giles argued.

'But at least Thomas Browne will still be alive for a few more days,' Tom argued. 'The minute we lets him out of here, them three will take him up a quiet back alley and slit the poor bugger's throat, because of what he knows. I doesn't want to have his death on my conscience, and I'm not going to release all that there money until I'm certain it weren't stolen.'

Giles absorbed that argument for a moment, then voiced his further thoughts.

'I'm still not happy in my own mind that it were them three what did Franklin in, if it comes to that. When I spoke to Alice Winters, she told me that she never saw who were in that cart what went down to the mill that morning. *And* she didn't know Robert Franklin by sight, so we doesn't know for certain that it were him what went down to the mill after Franklin were killed. And for that matter, we don't know for certain when he *were* killed. He could have been dead from the night before, and the son might have been carrying the body down there that morning, for all we knows.'

'How do you explain the hoof marks in the mud at the side of the mill, then?' Tom challenged him, and Giles shrugged. 'I'm not saying as how them three didn't go down there at some time that morning – or at least, two of them. But Alice Winters didn't see them going over the bridge, and she can't remember whether the woman she were with said that there was two, or three, of them.'

'Robert Franklin couldn't have heaved his father's body up onto that there platform on his own,' Tom countered, 'and you're forgetting that there was no muddy boot marks on the platform before we climbed up there.'

'Like I said,' Giles reminded him, 'I'm not saying that them three didn't have a hand in stringing up the body – although even if that were the case, *they'd* have left boot marks as well, wouldn't they? All I'm saying is that we may have got it wrong about when the father were killed.'

Tom sat deep in thought for a moment, then looked up. 'There's one way to find out, isn't there? The wife – Mistress Franklin – can tell us whether the old man came home alive that night, and possibly when - and if – he set out for the mill the next morning. Let's go and ask her, shall we?'

An hour later they approached the Franklin mill cottage in the meadow under the shadow of the Castle Rock, where a plump woman with grey hair was chopping wood with the aid of a small axe, and throwing the cut pieces into a pile at the side of her. Tom hailed her with a cheery 'Mistress Franklin?' The woman put down the axe, straightened up and squinted through failing eyes at her two visitors.

'That's me, right enough. Margaret Franklin, although I goes by "Maggie" to them what knows me. And who might you be?'

'Senior Constable Lincraft and Constable Bradbury. We were the ones what was called to your husband's body a couple of days past. Sorry if we're trampling all over your grieving, but there's a couple of things we'd like to ask you, if we may.'

'Haven't got no time for no grieving, what with all the jobs I've got to do around this place, Maggie advised them. 'I've got an empty wood box inside the cottage there, and for all the use that lazy good for nothing son of mine is, I might as well freeze to death of a cold night. I know it's supposed to be summer, but we gets hardly any sun, what with that bloody big rock at the back of us, and the ground down here by the river's forever damp.'

'So your son Robert don't cut wood for you?' Giles enquired, suddenly alert to a possible alternative side to Robert Franklin. Maggie gave them the benefit of a hollow cackle as she replied 'He might do if I paid him. That's all that seems to put life into his arse – money. Money what he can spend on whores and ale, and for all he helps around this place he might as well live in The Bell, up the road there.

His Dad were forever telling him that you has to work hard for money, and that it don't grow on trees. Now he's gone there'll be nobody to keep the idle little shit on the right path, and we'll likely starve.'

'So your husband and son argued over money, that right?' Tom prompted her, and she spat on the ground to the side of her. 'All the bloody time. Even on the morning Ed died.'

Tom and Giles exchanged excited glances, and Tom was the one who asked the obvious question. 'They was both up together that morning, is that what you're telling us?'

'That's right. Just before they set off for the mill, like they always did.'

'Together?' Giles enquired, open-mouthed, and Maggie nodded. 'Yeah, that's what it sounded like. I were still in my bed, but the noise of the two of them going at it – about money as usual – woke me up. Then I heard the sound of the cart being hitched to the horse, and then it went quiet again, so I reckoned that they'd left together.'

'When Robert come back with news of your husband's death,' Tom persevered, 'what did he tell you exactly?' Maggie sneered as she replied. 'The useless bugger couldn't even prevent his poor Dad hanging himself while Robert's back were turned. He were down below, opening the sluice with the iron bar, so he told me, then when he went back to the platform Ed were just hanging there. I reckon as how he were driven to do it by the disappointment of having such a lazy lummox for a son. I wager Robert didn't mention that when he called you in to deal with the body, did he?'

'Indeed he didn't,' Tom confirmed quietly, then looked back towards the mill, clearly visible less than half a mile downstream alongside the Leen. 'Is Robert at work today?' he enquired casually, 'only the wheel don't appear to be turning, from what I can see from this distance.'

'Probably in the town somewhere, with a doxie of his fancy,' Maggie sneered. 'He certainly seems to have more time for whoring than for keeping us fed. He were never much use when his Dad were alive, but since he died he don't seem to have time to turn his fat arse to owt worthwhile.'

Thanking her for her time, and declining the invitation to go inside and share a pot of small beer with her, the two constables walked back along the banks of the Leen deep in excited conversation. 'A rather different Robert Franklin from the one we met, you must admit,' Tom observed, and Giles agreed with him. 'According to what we just heard, the old man were alive when he left the family cottage, and dead by the time we found him, and the only one what were with him during the time in between were Robert. I reckon I were right all along, but what we going to charge them three from The Bell with now?'

'We got one of them for two rapes anyway,' Tom reminded him. 'And all three of them for the assault on us in the skittles alley, plus the robbery they done on John Pryce. But we shouldn't be jumping to any more conclusions just yet, and I still isn't about to release Thomas Browne and hand back all that there money. But while we're down here, let's just check for that there iron bar, shall we?'

Underneath the silent mill, they spotted a heavy iron bar lying in the bottom of the specially carved out trench through which river water was diverted in order to drive the wheel when the sluices were opened at each end. Tom scrambled down and retrieved it, then handed it to Giles. 'What does you reckon?' he enquired, and Giles nodded. 'That would have done it, no question. But I still don't see how the murderous bugger managed to get his father's body up there onto the beam by himself, and without leaving any boot marks on the platform.'

'That's something we can ask Robert Franklin, when we catches up with him,' Tom growled, 'and I don't fancy visiting every whorehouse in town looking for the bugger, so let's wait until we can stand on the bridge back there and see the wheel turning. Then we'll know where to find him.'

'Supposing he just leaves town?' Giles enquired, and Tom shrugged. 'Then we doesn't have to trouble ourselves to arrest him, does we? And in any case, I reckon we should be giving all our efforts over to finding them three what were guarding Thomas Browne and all that there money. I'm still not convinced that they wasn't mixed up somehow in Ed Franklin's death. If they wasn't, how come that Ted Hollins knew there'd been a murder?'

'Maybe because he were involved in it as well?' Giles conjectured, and Tom laughed hollowly. 'Wouldn't that be nice? But right now let's get this here iron bar back to the Guildhall. Then I think we can honestly say that we've done enough for the day.'

This proved to be an optimistic prediction. As they walked back into their section of the Guildhall, they were hailed by the Chief Turnkey, who indicated, with a disapproving jerk of the head, a bedraggled looking youth sitting on the bench reserved for those waiting to lodge complaints. 'This young scare the crows claims he's got something important to tell you. Take him into your office with you, if you'd be so obliging, so that it'll smell a whole lot better out here.'

The young boy in question had already leapt to his feet and hurried towards them, and Tom and Giles recoiled from the overpowering mixed aroma of old sweat and new horse manure as Tom tried to recall when he'd last seen him recently, and Giles answered the question for him.

'Ben Bloody Tanner! Decided to come clean about that stolen horse, have you?'

'I never stole that horse, like I said. Honest I didn't! But you was really looking for the feller what owned it, wasn't you? I reckon you was tricking me, but if I tell you where to find the crippled feller what came in with the other three when they took their horses out, then you'll have to believe me, won't you?'

Tom and Giles exchanged glances yet again, and Tom left it to his young colleague to make some sense of what the young stable groom was trying to tell them. 'You mean the feller what was with the three what had their horses in your stable last Sunday night, but took them out very early on the Monday?' Ben nodded eagerly.

'That's the feller! I were scrubbing down the courtyard outside the stable when he stuck his head round the door what leads from the skittle alley. I'm not allowed in there, on account of the smell from the horse shit, but I recognised him, and then he come right out and walked to the end of the stable yard, like he were looking for somebody. When he walked out into the lane what leads up the side of The Bell I followed him out, and I watched while he walked up Beastmarket Hill, then got himself admitted to a house on the other side of the lane, just before it goes under Chapel Bar. I can show you the house if you like.'

'Did he go into the house?' Tom enquired, but Ben shrugged. 'Dunno, because I legged it back down the alleyway in case he spotted me. But he were definitely the one what were with the three with the horses on the Monday morning. If I show you the house, will you stop saying as how I stole a horse?'

'We certainly will,' Tom assured him, and in less than half an hour they were standing a few yards up from The Bell, staring across the busy road at a well appointed jettied three storey house made from the latest style brick, and with tiles on its roof. Tom had already made a quick pass across its front facade, and come back to advise Giles that the plate on the door advertised the services of a scrivener called Ralph Gilfedder. Ben had made himself scarce after being assured that he was no longer under suspicion of being a horse thief, and Tom and Giles, in the fading light of an overcast August evening, were debating whether or not to go home for supper or continue their watch on the house when its front door opened, to allow a man to exit into the road.

The two constables flattened themselves into the doorway of the silversmith's shop in front of which they had been standing, and watched intently as the man walked quickly down the road towards the Market Place, looking furtively behind him from time to time. 'That will save us searching for him, anyway,' Tom muttered as they took up a position several hundred yards behind him, and followed his progress through the Market Place and down Bridlesmithgate. From there, if he were heading home, he'd have a choice of Turncalf Alley and a right turn into the meadow, or a right turn through Low Pavement and down into Greyfriars. His choice was made for him as Tom and Giles quickened their pace when they reached the foot of Bridlesmithgate. The man turned, saw them following him, uttered a loud oath and began running. He was overtaken and overpowered a few yards beyond the entrance to the Guildhall, and while Giles hauled him to his feet and pinioned him from behind, Tom stuck his face right into his and gloated.

'Thank you for your attendance, Mr Franklin, even though you didn't have no choice. Please join us inside, and tell us why you killed your father.'

Chapter Seven

They left Robert Franklin to sweat it out in a gaol cell while they went home for the evening, then met up in the street outside the Guildhall as the sun was rising the following morning, and sat at the foot of Weekday Cross enjoying a breakfast of fresh bread and fruit while they considered their options. They did so in order to avoid the Chief Turnkey, who had spoiled their triumph in bringing back Robert Franklin by making loud demands that Tom sign the release paper for Thomas Browne. Tom had blankly refused, assuring the man that he would take responsibility for keeping Browne in his cell for his own protection, and that unless and until the necessary paper was signed, only Tom could be blamed for disobeying the Sheriff's order.

'So how do we deal with Franklin?' Giles enquired. 'Does we accuse him of murdering his father straight out, or ask him awkward questions and see if he knuckles under?' Tom smiled. 'Which would you prefer?'

'Before I started to learn your way of doing things, I'd just have accused him of it, ignored his protestations of innocence, and kept him locked up until his trial,' Giles replied, 'but now I'm not so sure.'

'I'd say you're obviously learning,' Tom smiled again. 'We goes around it sideways, telling him what we knows already until there's no way left for him to wriggle out of what the facts point to. That way, we're sure that we're getting the full truth, and in this case I'm still not convinced that them three fellers what was guarding Browne wasn't involved somehow. Think about it – how could Franklin have got that heavy body onto the beam without leaving boot marks on the boards?'

'How could anyone else, for that matter?' Giles enquired. 'That's one of the things I hope Master Franklin can tell us,' Tom grinned, 'so if you've finished stuffing all that bread in your mouth, let's go and find out, shall we?'

The grin disappeared from Tom's face when they walked into the ground floor section that gave access, via the Chief Turnkey's station, to their own office. A man was sitting on the bench to the side, and Tom recognised him instantly. 'Master Ireton, as I recall,' he sneered at the man as he rose to his feet to intercept them. Tom turned to Giles and effected the introductions.

'Constable Giles Bradbury, meet Master Ralph Ireton, from the

County Sheriff's office. He either got out of his bed long before the first sparrow farted this morning, or he's been sitting here all night. Either way he's probably here to arrest me for dereliction of duty in not releasing Browne.'

'Much though that would give me immense pleasure,' Ireton scowled, 'I'm here to make sure that you *do* your duty. This document in my hand is from Coroner Greville, and it authorises the release of Browne whether you like it or not.'

'That right?' Tom grinned. 'And why would the Coroner have any interest in a simple stealing?'

'It's a murder,' Ireton insisted, 'and you were the one who requested a coronial inquest, so it's now a matter within the jurisdiction of one of the County Coroners.'

'And even assuming that Edward Franklin *were* murdered – which has not yet been established – why would the Coroner be seeking to release the man who's suspected of it?'

'I don't question the orders I'm given,' Ireton insisted. 'I just do what I'm told.'

'More's the pity,' Tom smiled back in a manner designed to infuriate the pompous official. 'Because if you did, you'd be wondering why Coroner Greville's taken such an interest in a case that hasn't yet been listed for a hearing, and why he wants me to release a man who's only likely to be charged with stealing a king's ransom in money from London, or wherever else he may have got it from. He says London, anyway, and until I gets a lot more information out of him, he's my prisoner, and he's going nowhere. Good morning to you, and enjoy your return trip up Bridlesmithgate, where they should be emptying the pisspots at this early hour of the day. Take my advice and keep to the middle of the roadway.'

He turned on his heel, gesturing for Giles to accompany him. As they were unlocking their office Ireton stood red-faced, staring after them and insisting that 'Sir Henry shall hear about this.' 'Good,' Tom replied with a backward glance, 'and while he's hearing that, tell him that I'll solve his murder for him before he's even had his dinner.'

'He'll be back,' Giles murmured nervously as they took to the benches behind their desks. 'You *know* he'll be back, and then he'll be carrying a warrant for your arrest. Me as well, more than likely.' Tom gave him a serious look.

'Something else I hope you'll learn from me is not to take any shit from the likes of Coroner Greville. He's a pompous bladder full of his own importance, and once you stands up to him he behaves like every other bully, and shows his cowardice. But he's well informed, it seems, and not by us. Someone's got in his ear about Browne and the money, and I'd be mighty interested to learn who. In the meantime, take a deep breath and let's go down to the cells. I wants to learn what Robert Franklin has to say for himself.'

Tom hadn't been wrong about the smell of fear that permeated Robert Franklin's cell as the turnkey opened the heavy creaking door and advised them that he'd be directly outside in the corridor if they required any assistance. Tom thanked him, then turned to look down at Franklin as he sat hunched over on the straw pallet clutching the paper thin blanket that was no doubt lice ridden.

'We went and spoke to your Mam yesterday,' Tom advised Franklin. 'From what she told us, it don't seem that you was as friendly with your Dad as you tried to make us believe when we cut his body down on Monday morning. Seems you two was always arguing about money.'

'He were tight fisted,' Franklin muttered. 'He wanted me to work all the hours God sent, and he never gave me more than few pence when I needed some money to go out of a night.'

'To spend on whores?' Giles enquired with a leer, and Franklin's gaze dropped to the floor. While he was temporarily discomforted, Tom pressed home the advantage. 'How come your Dad's body finished up dangling from that there beam without anyone climbing up there? And you couldn't have done that all by yourself, could you?'

'Why did you throw that there iron bar into the sluice channel?' Giles asked immediately afterwards, followed by Tom's suggestion that 'Them blokes from the town gave you a hand, didn't they? And you left the house at the same time as your Dad that morning, according to your Mam. That right?'

Franklin nodded without realising what he was giving away, but Tom was ready to deliver what he would have called the 'sinker'. 'He were already dead by the time them men turned up, weren't he?'

Franklin nodded again, then his shoulders began to heave with a combination of relief and remorseful grief. Tom signalled with his eyes for Giles to remain silent, waited for an appropriate break in the flow of tears, then knelt down so that his face was level with Franklin's, and enquired in a kindly tone 'Were it an accident?' Franklin looked into Tom's eyes, then nodded.

'I didn't mean it, if that's what you're getting at. It weren't an accident that I hit him, but I didn't mean to kill him, honest!'

'Best tell us the whole story, from the beginning,' Tom coaxed him, then sat back on his haunches and waited patiently while Franklin wiped his nose on his sleeve, then looked first at Giles and then at Tom before continuing in hushed tones, as if he couldn't quite believe what he was recounting as the memories came flooding back.

'Dad were playing skittles in The Bell the night before, like I told you the other day, with some feller I'd never seen before. We left after that, and on our way back home Dad told me that he reckoned the feller he'd been playing with were a bit daft in the head, because he'd been asking Dad if he was the person he were in town to deliver money to. I were just telling him that he should have said yes when these three rough looking types came down Greyfriars after us, pinned Dad up against the wall, and asked what he'd been talking about when he were playing skittles with "their friend", as they called him. Dad were daft enough to tell them the truth, and one of them asked him to keep his mouth shut about it, in return for which they'd give him some money. They promised to bring it down to the mill the next day, and we went home.'

'So that's how these men knew where to find you?' Tom enquired, and Franklin nodded. 'Must have been. Anyway, the next morning Dad seemed to have a change of mind. He seemed to think that it were something unlawful, and he didn't want to take their money. We had a big argument, then Dad said we'd talk about it while we were on the way to the mill, because he didn't want to wake Mam with the noise of our arguing. We got down there, still arguing, and I went to open the sluice to start the mill wheel. Then Dad started on at me again, calling me a useless lummox and a lazy bastard, and all the things he normally called me when he weren't best pleased with me. I shouted back that he were a fat useless shit, and as how he wouldn't have a mill business to call his own if I didn't graft for him on wages that was fit only for a slave, and how Mam must have gone to it with a better man than him to have given birth to me.'

'I bet that went down well,' Tom chuckled, and Franklin nodded. 'You're not wrong about that. Dad came at me with his fists as usual, and I finally got the guts to fight back. I still had the sluice bar in my hand, and I whacked out with it. The first one got him on the shoulder, and when he bent forward with the pain of it, I landed the second on the back of his head, and he dropped to the ground. It didn't take me long to work out as how he were dead, then the three fellers from the night before turned up, just like they'd promised. I told them what had happened, and one of them said something about I'd saved them a job.'

'Well you didn't really believe that they'd come down there to give you money, did you?' Giles enquired with a grin, then fell silent when Tom shook his head with a glare. 'Go on, friend,' Tom invited Franklin coaxingly, and when he remained silent, Tom prompted him with 'They helped you make it look like suicide, didn't they?'

'Yeah,' Franklin conceded. 'They took the rope from the wagon – the one we use for tying on loads to secure them proper – then they wrapped it round his neck real tight, dragged his body under the platform, and threw the rope over the beam. Then all three of us hauled on the rope, and Dad's body went up through the gap in the middle until it looked like he'd hung himself.'

'That explains why there was no footmarks on the platform,' Tom explained to Giles, then looked back down at Franklin.

'Whose idea was it to make it look like he'd done himself in?'

'Them fellers,' Franklin replied. 'And they said as how if I didn't keep my mouth shut, they'd tell you lot that I'd murdered my old man. Which I suppose I did, of course.'

'You was defending yourself, by another way of looking at things,' Tom assured him. 'But you could have just walked away, instead of which you come up here and told us about the body.'

'That were their idea as well,' Franklin admitted. 'And they wanted me to do something else for them as well, in return for them not reporting me for murder.'

'And what were that?' Tom enquired.

'Well, the day after you lot found the body, I got another visit from one of them three what had helped me string it up – the big feller with the bald head and the scar down his face. He told me that if they wasn't to report me for murdering Dad, I had to carry messages from the landlord of The Bell across the road to the house where they was staying. They didn't say why, but I got the feeling that them three fellers was hiding there, and that the feller what owned the house didn't want to be seen nipping backwards and forwards across the road, or talking to the landlord. He's a very obvious feller to spot, of course – him being all crippled and humpty-backed.'

'What, the scrivener, you mean?' Tom enquired, and Franklin shrugged. 'The bloke what owns that there house, anyway.'

It fell silent for a moment, then Franklin looked up at Tom. 'I suppose I'll be charged with murder now, and then they'll hang me.' Tom shrugged. 'Perhaps, but for the time being I'm going to charge you with that, then keep you locked away down here, if only for your own safety.'

'What about that other feller?'' Franklin enquired. 'You know, the one what my Dad were playing skittles with?'

'I've got other plans for him,' Tom replied, 'but that don't mean I'm going to release him.'

Just then the cell door opened, and the turnkey's face appeared from round it. 'You're wanted upstairs, Tom,' he announced. 'Urgent, like.'

'We're finished here anyway,' Tom advised him. 'This man is to be kept in his cell, but well treated and properly fed, understood?' The turnkey nodded, and Tom and Giles made their way upstairs into the front hall, where three men were standing waiting. Two of them were heavily armed – obviously soldiers of some sort – while the man they were presumably accompanying was richly dressed, although his doublet and cloak were both black, and most probably silk, by the look of them.

'Senior Constable Lincraft?' the man demanded, and Tom grunted an acknowledgment. 'If I'm being arrested for dereliction of duty, my colleague Constable Bradbury here were only acting on my orders, so leave him alone.' The man smiled.

'I'm not advised of any dereliction of duty on your part, so please don't make me aware of any. May we go somewhere more private, only my business here today is highly confidential.'

Once inside the constables' room, the man took the only available remaining stool, while his armed escort took up a position by the door. He smiled as he introduced himself.

'My name is Francis Walsingham, and I hope you've never heard of me, since my greatest value to my employer is to be both invisible and nameless. However, my employer you *may* have heard of. Sir William Cecil?'

Tom looked blank, but Giles picked up the reference. 'Don't he work for - for the *Queen*?' he enquired uncertainly, and Walsingham nodded with a smile.

'Indeed he does. Which means that I do also. And that is why I am here today, interfering with your investigations, but for the best of causes.'

'Nobody interferes with my investigations,' Tom asserted. 'And I'm not supposed to be making them anyway, so what's your business here?' Walsingham smiled confidently and extracted a vellum scroll from the pouch hanging from his belt. He unfurled it and handed it to Tom, who took his time to work his way painfully down the elaborate script, then looked back up in utter amazement.

'This here signature on the bottom. It's just a woman's name, but surely it can't be . . . ? I mean, not *her*?'

'Her indeed, Constable. My orders come from Sir William, who is of course Her Majesty's Secretary of State, but on this occasion, in view of the importance to the nation of the matter that brings me here, *his* employer has also added her signature. On the authority of Her Majesty Queen Elizabeth, I want you to release Thomas Browne and the money he was carrying.'

Chapter Eight

'Why should I release a feller what stole more money than I'm likely to earn in my whole life?' Tom demanded peevishly, while Giles held his breath as he heard his colleague challenging the order of a man who came armed with a document signed by the Queen herself. Walsingham smiled a slow smile as he replied.

'How do you know that the money's stolen?' he enquired, and Tom shrugged. 'I doesn't – exactly – but how can a draper what travels the road for a living have that much money on him? And why would he, given the risk of having it stolen? He had three fellers guarding it, but from what he said he didn't have them willingly, so something's obviously not right. And you wants him *released*?'

'You are wise to be suspicious,' Walsingham agreed, 'and your devotion to the law does you credit. More so than many a man in your position that I've had dealings with in the past. But you have my assurance that the money was not "stolen", according to the law that you uphold.'

'What, then?' Tom demanded, far from convinced, and Walsingham took time to consider the wisdom of delivering the explanation. The matter was a closely guarded State secret, but this man and his youthful looking colleague appeared honest and upright enough, and he needed their co-operation, if Elizabeth was to be properly protected.

'The money was entrusted to Browne by a man in London who had come by it at the hand of the Spanish Ambassador,' Walsingham explained. 'Where he acquired it is currently a matter of some speculation in Whitehall, but of far greater importance is where it was heading before you took possession of it.'

'So the money came from Spain?' Tom enquired, and when Walsingham nodded, Tom followed that up with 'Why?' Walsingham sighed, and leaned forward as he lowered his voice.

'What I have to tell you is so confidential that you will become only the third man in England to know of it. Third and fourth, that is,' he added with a nervous sideways glance at Giles. 'He can be trusted as well,' Tom assured him, and Walsingham continued.

'It was to be expended on the recruitment of an army to overthrow our gracious Queen and replace her on the throne with the Scots Queen, Mary Stuart.' He took advantage of the stunned silence to allow that essential point to sink in before adding further detail.

'We know that it was entrusted in London to a man in the pay of one of our highest nobles, who I cannot name, even to you. You need know only that he is a cousin to the Queen, and that it is his ambition to wed Mary Stuart. This is being encouraged by King Philip of Spain, and financed from Italy, where a wealthy noble has been prevailed upon by the Pope to supply the money with which to pay mercenaries with Catholic sympathies.'

'All these high-ranking names,' Tom muttered in total amazement. 'Why was it necessary to entrust the money to a stupid travelling draper?'

'In order to preserve the secrecy of its intended destination,' Walsingham advised him. 'Nobody would think to challenge a merchant travelling the country with money in his possession. But somewhere here in the north of the country, and possibly even here in Nottingham, is someone who is waiting to receive that money and distribute it abroad in the furtherance of the cause.'

'Who?' Tom enquired, but Walsingham shook his head. 'If we knew that, would I be sitting here? We would simply pounce, apprehend those in the plot, and convey them to certain gentlemen in the Tower who are skilled in getting answers to certain questions. By apprehending the man Browne you have effectively stopped the game from proceeding.'

'Sorry,' Tom mumbled with uncharacteristic humility, and Giles began to appreciate the seriousness of the situation they had got themselves into. Walsingham smiled reassuringly and waved his hand in the air. 'There is no need to apologise, since you were clearly only performing your duty as you understood it. But now you must do what I tell you, rather than obey the command of the County Sheriff.'

'He wants Browne released anyway,' Tom announced, 'although I think there were someone else tugging his bollocks, if you'll pardon my language.'

'Who might that be?' Walsingham enquired, and Tom was only too happy to oblige. 'One of the county Coroners – a feller called Sir Henry Greville. A lazy bastard most of the time, but he seemed to be mighty interested in getting Browne out of the cell he's currently occupying downstairs here. Since he was asking for the same thing as you, is he working on your side? If so, I'm sorry I called him a lazy bastard. Except he is.'

'Never heard of the man,' Walsingham advised Tom, 'but I'd be interested to learn of why he was so interested in securing the man's release, along with the money of course. Is he by any chance Catholic by persuasion?'

'Definitely,' Tom confirmed, 'and he don't like me, neither, because I'm not.'

'But perhaps you can see my point,' Walsingham replied patiently. 'He may be seeking Browne's release in order that the money can be distributed where it was intended. I wish to have Browne released in order that we can find out where that is.'

'If the money's not stolen, then I can see my way free to releasing him, like everyone seems to want,' Tom announced after giving the matter only the briefest thought. 'But I want them three fellers what was guarding him, because they attacked me and Giles here, and we reckons as how one of them's been attacking girls in the town late at night. And if we let Browne out of here, he reckons as how them three fellers will kill him. And I'm inclined to agree with him on that score.'

'I heard that Browne was being held on a murder charge,' Walsingham advised him, but Tom shook his head. 'he were – to begin with. That's how we got into this whole business,' he added, then went on to explain how they had been investigating Browne's suspected involvement in the death of Edward Franklin when they'd been set upon by the men guarding Browne, but had subsequently learned that Franklin had been the victim of his son's need to defend himself. Walsingham nodded as he took it all in, then had a supplementary question.

'These three men to whom you refer – are they still at large?'

'Yeah, but we knows where they are,' Giles assured him as his first contribution to the conversation. 'They're in a house across the road from The Bell, on Beastmarket Hill. We was going to summon all the other county constables and rush the place – tomorrow, as it happens.'

'I can arrange for that,' Walsingham smiled. 'Apart from these two armed members of the Yeomen Guard who are guarding the door, I have access to more royal troops at the Castle. But I suggest that we move circumspectly, so that it does not become generally known that those guarding the money have been removed from the game.'

'You keeps calling it "a game",' Tom grumbled, 'but it's deadly bloody serious, and have you given any thought to what that's going to happen if whoever it is turns up for the money and finds out that someone close to the Queen is waiting for them to make their next move?'

'Obviously that will be kept a closely guarded secret,' Walsingham explained, then his forehead creased in thought. 'All the same, it will be regarded as suspicious if Browne has no-one with him when word no doubt came up from London that he was being closely guarded.'

'But will them folks up here know who them fellers was what was guarding him?' Tom enquired, and Walsingham shrugged. 'No idea, obviously, but unlikely.'

'So if there's two blokes guarding him when the money gets collected, nobody will be any the wiser, will they?' Tom urged, and Walsingham was obliged to agree, whereupon Tom looked across at Giles with a broad grin. 'How does you fancy spending a few nights with that there Polly in The Bell?'

'Count me in for that,' Giles grinned back, but Walsingham raised a hand.

'Do I understand that you're proposing to pose as the men guarding Browne when the money's collected?'

'Bloody right and we is,' Tom gushed, 'and think about it for a minute. Whoever comes for the money will expect Browne to be guarded, and they'll suspect something if he isn't. And in the circumstances the least we owe to the poor bugger is to make sure that he really *is* protected, just in case. And,' he added with a glint in his eye, 'if I pretend as how I were ordered to keep guarding the money 'til it got where it were going, I can find out who it were that were meant to be receiving it, can't I?'

'I thought *I* were going to be spending time with Polly,' Giles protested, and Tom nodded. 'So you is, since I'll be the one in Browne's room, while you just keep an eye out for me when it happens.'

Walsingham looked far from convinced. 'Have you the remotest idea what risks you'd be running?' he demanded, and Tom smiled.

'With the greatest of respect to your good self, have you any idea how much danger we face every bloody night in this town? I wager that you've never had to break up fights between two drunken labourers what just got paid, or take on a feller with a knife what's just done his missus in. Compared with that, this will be a Sunday picnic in the Meadows.'

'Very well,' Walsingham conceded with reluctance. 'But not the part you suggested about following the money. I'll arrange for men of my own to do that; they can operate with the greatest of discretion, believe me. For my own information, this coroner you mentioned – what was his name again, and where does he reside? I'll make enquiries regarding his loyalties.'

'His name's Sir Henry Greville, and he's obviously got a town house in Nottingham,' Tom advised him, 'but he's also got a country estate called 'Swingate'', out near Strelley, on the road into the next county. I've never been there, but they say as it's pretty grand.'

With no viable alternative immediately available, Walsingham made the necessary arrangements, and in the early hours of the following morning a silent troop of royal soldiers forced the lock on the front door of the scrivener's house and arrested all four men in there, conveying them down to the Guildhall, where Tom was ready to receive them and authorise their locking up in the vilest cells that were available down below. Then he slipped back home, and did his best to persuade Lizzie that he'd been in his bed all night. When he then announced that he would be moving into The Bell for a few nights 'in the line of duty', she became even more convinced that he had a secret lover, and told Tom that he could stay there forever, for all she cared.

The release of Browne was organised for the Saturday morning – Market Day – in order to make it as public as was consistent with normal practice, and Tom and Giles accompanied him back to The Bell. When landlord Ted Hollins raised a cynical eyebrow at this arrangement, Tom told him loudly to mind his own business, since he was only making it up to Browne for the discourtesy of his unjust imprisonment, and ensuring that he was not robbed during his return to the inn of his choice. Giles lost no time in advising a very eager Polly that she'd be sharing a bed with him 'for a night or two', and Tom and Giles settled down to await an approach being made to Browne for the money that was once again hidden in his room.

Walsingham had not been idly boasting when he'd told Tom and Giles that his men were capable of operating with the greatest of discretion. They posted themselves inconspicuously around the outside of The Bell, posing as passers-by, street traders and peddlars, and keeping their weapons hidden from view. Inside The Bell Tom never let Browne out of his sight – even standing by the door to the backyard privy when he answered calls of nature – while Giles hid himself away in Polly's room immediately above Browne's, on the upper floor, enjoying all that the establishment had to offer, and more. From time to time he deigned to join Tom downstairs on guard duties over Browne, who was more than content to have been released from a gaol cell and assured that he would not be charged with anything else, provided that he did as he was told.

Saturday and Sunday passed without incident, although Ted Hollins was becoming more and more suspicious of the hidden presence of two constables on his premises, one of whom was keeping his pot girl from some of her duties. As a result, when a man sidled up to Ted's counter on the Monday morning, enquiring after Browne and slipping Ted several sovereigns, the landlord was more than happy to advise his benefactor that the man he was seeking was indeed in residence in the large back room on the first floor, but was being closely attended by two of the town constables. The man thanked him, slipped away, and advised his paymaster accordingly.

In the early hours of Tuesday morning Polly shook Giles awake. 'There's something going on downstairs,' she advised him. 'I thought I heard a fight of some sort – best go and see if your friend Tom's all right.'

Giles dressed hastily and ran down the flight of stairs, where he saw the door to Browne's room flung wide open, with the room itself empty and the money bag missing. He raced back upstairs, got fully dressed, grabbed the sword he'd brought with him on the first day, and instructed Polly to race down to the front of the inn and alert the men who were supposed to have been keeping watch that Browne had been spirited away, along with Senior Constable Lincraft, and that he – Constable Bradbury – would be heading off after them. Then the thought occurred to him that he had no clue as to where he should be heading.

In the stables to the rear he found a very sleepy Ben Tanner sitting on an empty barrel that he used for a seat in between duties. Ben blinked as he saw Giles racing towards him, then spat in the straw.

'It's like the bloody Market Place in here tonight,' he complained. 'First them three, now you. I haven't done nowt wrong since the last time you seen me, so what's going on?'

'*What* three?' Giles demanded as he gripped Ben by the collar of his grimy jacket, and Ben wriggled free before explaining. 'There was three fellers come riding in here a few minutes ago, and jumped off their horses. They told me to hold onto them, else they'd run me through with the swords they was carrying, then they kicked in the back door what goes into the skittles alley. They come out a few minutes later with that other constable feller what was with you when you come in here asking about that horse, and that bloke what was stabling his horse here until you lot locked him up. I'm fucked if I know what's going on, but I reckon it's time I found different bloody work, and that's a fact.'

'Where did they head off to?' Giles demanded, but Ben shrugged. 'They just went up the back lane, to the right there. Most likely heading for Chapel Bar, but they've been gone a little while now, if you was thinking of catching up with them.'

Giles glared along the line of stalls. 'Which is the best horse in here?' he demanded. 'The grey gelding,' Ben replied, 'and I can saddle him in no time, if you make it worth my while.'

'Do it – *now!*' Giles demanded, 'and as your reward I'll speak to the landlord on your behalf when he accuses you of stealing it. Now get on with it!'

Ten frustrating minutes later, during which Giles finally remembered that Coroner Greville had an estate in Strelley, whose precise name escaped him for the moment, he leapt onto the stallion and thundered out into the lane. Making new use of his old skill on horseback that was a legacy of his younger days working on the land, he set the horse's head westwards, breasted Zion Hill, and took the track to Wollaton and Derby at full gallop.

Chapter Nine

When Tom came round again for the third time it was to the swaying motion of the horse under whose belly his legs had been tied to keep him both upright and captive. The blow had been delivered by the hilt of a sword when the three armed men kicked in the door to Browne's room at dead of night and demanded that Browne hand over the money he had been entrusted with in London. He'd meekly reached under his bedding and produced it, but when Tom had begun to insist that he travel with it in accordance with his instructions the leader of the intruders had assured him that 'You'll be coming along with us anyway, Constable Dogshit,' and had dealt him the blow to the head.

Tom reached under his bonnet to confirm that there was indeed a massive lump where his head met his neck, and one of the group that was riding at a moderate pace through the semi darkness of an impending dawn warned him that he'd be run through if he made any effort to escape. 'I won't,' Tom grunted, 'but you arseholes will wish that I had when we get wherever we're going. Where is that?'

'Mind your own smelly business,' he was advised, and he left it at that. To either side of them appeared to be trees bordering a road, so that Tom had no way of knowing where they were, other than the fact that they had travelled out of town. Perhaps when the light improved he might have a better idea, but for the time being Tom confined his thoughts to methods of loosening the restraints that connected his boots together under the belly of his horse. He was also fearful of losing consciousness again and falling sideways, which might prove fatal. He wasn't altogether comfortable on horseback at the best of times, so for the immediate future he gripped the horse's reigns firmly and went along with playing the captive.

Some distance behind them Giles had pushed his mount to the limit as he skirted the Wollaton estate of the Willoughby family and urged the horse into the right hand fork of the road when he came to the stone in the ground that pointed towards 'Mansfield'. Although he was a County Constable, his duties thus far in his two years of service had kept him confined to the town, and as someone brought up in the fields of Tollerton, to the south, he knew nothing of the villages to be found north and west of Nottingham. But Tom had spoken of the estate of Coroner Greville being on a road leading into the adjoining county, which was Derbyshire, and Giles had chosen to risk everything on this being the intended destination for the money with which Browne had been entrusted.

The light of what they had called 'the false dawn' during his days as a farm labourer, and which had been the signal for him to rise from his bed if he was to have time for any breakfast, was now strong enough to reveal a vague cloud of dust some distance ahead, and Giles pulled on the reigns of his panting horse and stood up in the saddle for a better view. The weather had not been unduly dry, so a cloud of dust of that size must be created by several horses, and not just a solitary farmer on his early way to a local market, or a carousing squire on his way home. He reduced his gelding's pace to a gentle trot in the hope that he had caught up with the group that had captured Tom, Browne, and the all important money.

The full dawn suggested that he had, and although it was too early, and he was too far in the rear, to be certain, neither could he afford to be seen by those he was following. He also needed to slow his pace if he had any hope of being joined by the soldiers employed by Walsingham to prevent precisely what had just happened. They might be useless at mounting guard, but hopefully they knew how to put their weapons to good use. All he could do was follow discreetly behind the group ahead of him, and hope that he'd guessed correctly.

In the leading group Tom at least had some idea of where they might be heading. One didn't get to serve as a County Constable for the ten years and more that Tom had without being called out to outlying rural communities, and he had memories of being sent out to the Mansfield area in order to bring accused offenders back into Nottingham under escort in order to await trial at the next Assize while being held in a cell beneath the Shire Hall. It had been some time now, but as they came to a crossroads with a sagging sign pointing right towards Bulwell, and continued through it on the straight road ahead, Tom would have been prepared to wager a week's wages that they were headed for Strelley. If so, then he was about to satisfy his curiosity regarding the vast estate that was allegedly occupied by Sir Henry Greville.

He was proved right when the group of which he was an unwilling member turned through a large, ornate gateway to the right, and proceeded down a long drive fringed with rhododendrons on its way towards an impressive stone built mansion that appeared to have many rooms, accessed by means of a wide ornamental staircase, down which strode his old nemesis Sir Henry Greville. The retinue wheeled in a circle in front of the staircase, and Greville smiled unpleasantly at

Tom.

'You finally meddled in the wrong matter, Lincraft,' Greville sneered from the third step, 'and at long last the county will be governed in the manner of the old days. With the rightful queen on the throne, and the true religion restored, heretics like you can once again be put to the flame. But I have in mind a more fitting end for you.'

Tom glanced at the noose that was hanging from the broad oak to one side of the staircase with a horse and cart positioned under it, and Greville chuckled with glee as he followed Tom's gaze. 'That will indeed be your means of also departing this life, after I have dealt with the halfwit who was so easily persuaded to bring the money from London. Then you – and he – will be planted in the earth, in order to fertilise the new England that I and others having been awaiting for too long. You will of course recall that our last encounter was in connection with the discovery of a body under an oak tree on a country estate. Thanks to your interference the man who was intended to swing for that escaped with his life, but there will be a sweet irony in your body being similarly disposed of.'

While Tom was swallowing the bile of fear that invaded his throat, Greville demanded that the bag of money that had brought Browne from London be handed over without further delay. This done, his next order was for Browne to be pulled from his horse, for his wrists to be secured behind him with ropes, and that he be lifted onto the cart and the noose placed around his neck, while the other end was tied to the sturdy overhanging oak branch. He cackled like a rooster in a henhouse as he added

'Then remove Lincraft from that horse, and tie his hands similarly. Then lead him towards the cart, that he may have a ringside view of what will be coming to him next.'

Giles had been close enough behind to see the party ahead of him swing through the estate entrance, and even crouching low over his horse's neck he could make out the large head of his colleague Tom in the centre of the group, and realised that they had reached their destination. Unaware that Tom's true identity was known to the rest of the group, and unable to see the ropes beneath the horse that denoted his capture, Giles gave serious thought to how he might assist when the party reached the house at the end of the drive, and Tom was face to face with whoever the money bag was being delivered to. In order to assess the situation more fully Giles need to get closer to what was about to take place, but without revealing his presence.

Lying just to one side of the house, and almost encroaching onto its lawns, was a coppice of some sort that led down all the way to the lane ahead of him, so Giles trotted the horse further along it until he reached its fringe, then dismounted. Tying the horse to the first of the trees that bordered the lane, he made his way swiftly through the remaining trees, on a line parallel to the formal drive, until he was crouched down in a thicket of gorse and bracken between two sturdy elms. From there he could clearly see the noose hanging from the oak branch, with the horse and cart sitting beneath it.

He knew enough about the bad old days to recognise a lynching when he saw one, and his heart jumped to his mouth as he saw Browne being led towards the spot, struggling, screaming for mercy, but no match for the two brutes who were dragging him remorselessly to his doom. Then he also saw that Tom's hands were tied behind his back, and he recognised Coroner Greville from the inquest that he had recently attended with Tom. He had to do something, but what? There were six armed men out there, and with Tom's wrists securely tied it would be one against six.

He heard the cracking of a piece of wood to his left, and simultaneously became aware of a rustling sound to his immediate right. He was about to draw his sword and take on whoever had discovered his hiding place when there came a stern command issued in a low but authoritative voice.

'That's quite far enough, Constable.'

Chapter Ten

Tom gawped with relief and astonishment as ten armed men broke through the trees on the far side of the makeshift gallows and made such short work of the two who had been in the process of loading Browne into the wagon that the remainder of Greville's retinue fled while Browne's rescuers removed the rope from around his head. Giles ran over to Tom with a grin, cut his hands free with his knife, and invited him to join in the joyous act of arresting Sir Henry Greville on charges that they could decide on later, once they had him safely gaoled in the Shire Hall. Then they dragged Greville before Walsingham, who frowned at him before delivering the bad news.

'I don't know precisely who you are,' he advised Greville, 'but I believe you to be part of the conspiracy launched from Rome to depose Her Majesty and replace her with the Scottish whore. I wish to know whatever it is that you know regarding this plot, and all those engaged in it. You may choose to reveal it all to me now, or to my associates in the Tower of London who are anxious to try out certain new instruments of persuasion that they have lately invented.'

'All I know is that the money was to be sent north to York!' Greville bleated in terror. 'To whom?' Walsingham demanded, and Greville supplied the names of William Barker and Robert Higford. Walsingham frowned.

'I know Baker to have been the man who first handed over the money to the unfortunate Thomas Browne, who is celebrating his sudden reprieve from death by puking all over your lovingly cultivated lawn over there. Why would Baker also be in York to receive it?'

'I know not!' Greville insisted, 'other than that he did not wish to travel north with it in his possession.'

'And would these men, Baker and Higford of whom you speak, be secretaries to the Duke of Norfolk?' Walsingham enquired with his first smile of the morning, and Greville nodded. 'So it is spoken.'

'Very well,' Walsingham instructed two of the four men around him, 'take this man back into the house, let him select garments suitable for travel and a lengthy period of imprisonment, then convey him in his own coach back down to Nottingham Castle. I will send to London for his onward escort to the Tower.' Then he turned back to Tom and Giles with an even broader smile.

'Giles were just telling me how he followed us all the way from The

Bell,' Tom announced gleefully, and Walsingham nodded. 'It was as well that he did, since we were able to follow *him*. Fortunately for us, he proved indiscreet in his haste, and we were able to do so with ease. But I would hazard a conjecture that he had no idea where he was leading us.'

'I didn't,' Giles confessed, 'but I remembered Tom saying something about Strelley, and when I come up behind a group of horsemen heading north-west out of town, I took a gamble on it being the right group. But I had no idea that Tom were their prisoner.'

'You can probably thank Ted Hollins for that,' Tom growled, 'and when we get back to town, he'll be the next one down the stairs in the Guildhall, to join them three what attacked us. That were a week ago yesterday, did you know?'

'Some bloody week!' Giles grinned, then gestured towards the manor house. 'I don't know about you, but I reckon we should lay siege to Sir Henry's kitchen and wine cellar.'

'Help yourselves,' Walsingham invited them, 'but I must conclude matters here, then ride with all speed to London to advise Cecil that the plot first hatched by Roberto Ridolfi on the urgings of the Pope has been cut off at its knees. You will no doubt be hearing from me in due course, but for the time being feel free to enjoy a late breakfast.'

Two months later Tom and Giles returned to the Guildhall from their respective dinners to find that a package was awaiting each of them, delivered by a messenger wearing an unfamiliar livery. Tom opened his to discover that it contained two documents, one considerably longer than the other, and the second bearing a signature that he had seen before. While Giles simply stared at his single vellum in avid amazement, Tom read the first of his.

'To Senior Constable Lincraft, most hearty greeting.

'Due in part to the efforts of your good self, and your colleague in loyalty Constable Bradbury, the so named Ridolfi Plot has been foiled. Those responsible, identified and apprehended are now adding to the responsibilities borne by the Constable of the Tower as they await trial and almost certain execution. For their chief instigator, the Duke of Norfolk, there will hopefully be no trial, since Cecil is hopeful of having him attainted by Parliament.

'Her Majesty has been graciously disposed to approve a scheme of my conception, whereby ordinary officers of the law such as yourself and Constable Bradbury shall be enrolled in a new body under the Crown to be known as 'The Constables Royal', whose honourable duty it shall be to work throughout the realm wherever and whenever their services shall be required in order to suppress rebellion and to labour tirelessly for the enduring peace of the nation happily governed by Her Majesty in her constant endeavours directed towards the welfare of her subjects.

'It is both meet and just that the first two to be admitted to this worthy and prestigious office shall be those whose actions in seeking out those behind the Ridolfi Plot have so resolved Her Majesty to create it. Those men are Thomas Lincraft and Giles Bradbury, and I am sending each of you your letters of appointment, together with my most hearty congratulations on your award of same.

'Your ever and steadfast friend in England's cause,

'Francis Walsingham by his hand.'

Tom looked across at Giles, whose jaw had dropped as he stared, bug-eyed, at the vellum in his hand. 'This woman what's signed this here paper – her name's "Elizabeth". Surely that isn't . . . ? I mean, it can't be . . . *her*, can it?'

Tom chuckled. 'It can be, if it's the same woman what signed this one. I'll read mine out loud, and see if it's the same as yours, apart from your name of course.'

He held his vellum out in front of him and proudly read its contents.

'To my most heartily beloved Thomas Lincraft, greeting.

'I have pleasure in appointing you to the rank and status of Queen's Constable, with this charge, that you serve me loyally and faithfully in all you shall be commanded to perform in my name.

'By my hand at Whitehall this Second Day of August in the year of our Lord 1571.

'Elizabeth'.

'Bloody Hell,' Giles muttered, as Tom grinned back at him.

'Lizzie will be pleased,' he announced. 'She might even cook me lamb for supper. She's been saving it for a special occasion, and I reckon this might be it.'

Endnote

Thank you for taking the time to read this second novella in the Thomas Lincraft trilogy, and I hope it maintained your interest. It was based on historical facts tweaked around the edges, and contained real characters from the turbulent middle years of Elizabeth's reign.

There really was a Shrewsbury draper called Thomas Browne who was sent north entrusted with a bag containing a large quantity of coin intended for use in a coup against Queen Elizabeth. But unlike the Thomas Browne in this story, he panicked when he realised what he was carrying, and reported it to William Cecil, who did the rest. The real 'Ridolfi Plot' was indeed an attempt to replace Queen Elizabeth with her distant cousin Mary Stuart, financed by Roberto Ridolfi, a Florentine banker and fervent Catholic who was urged on by Pope Pius. The Pope had already excommunicated Elizabeth and urged her subjects to rebellion, and Thomas Howard, 4th Duke of Norfolk, was a closet Catholic with ambitions to marry the stunningly beautiful Catholic Mary.

It therefore required little effort on my part to re-route Browne to Nottingham and throw him into the confusion surrounding the suspicious death of a local miller. Tom Lincraft is joined in this second story of the trilogy by his younger colleague, and ladies' man, Giles Bradbury, who wishes to emulate Tom in the meaningful investigation of crimes, and not just the routine chore of locking up those accused by others. Tom and Giles have, by their joint efforts, earned themselves the status of 'Constables Royal', and in the third novella in the series, 'Queen's Constables', they will earn their keep by smoking out Catholic priests being smuggled into England.

Tom will also be able to settle a long-standing score.

The Queen's Constables

David Field

Chapter One

It was Saturday – market day – and like any other Tudor town on such a day, Nottingham's Market Place was awash with deafening noise, contrasting smells and heaving crowds. Since early light the traders had been driving their carts into town and unloading their wares, and the objects of their grunting labour and commercial ambition were now on abundant display.

Corn from the Vale of Belvoir on the Leicestershire border, the first of the season's apples and plums from Arnold in the north, and parsnips and other root crops from the villages to the west, competed for the limited purses of the local housewives with locally baked bread, pots, pans, cloth, basketry and leather goods as each stallholder loudly proclaimed their bargains into the narrow passageways between the lines of stalls. Beyond the low wall that divided the market place into two uneven halves lay the livestock pens, where one could purchase everything from a breeding cow to a goose whose neck would be obligingly wrung by the vendor for an extra penny. There were conies, capons, sheep, ducks and even ponies, each squawking, clucking or bellowing in protest against its enforced confinement.

Senior Constable Thomas Lincraft and his colleague Constable Giles Bradbury strolled slowly side by side, down one passageway between stalls, and then up another. Market Day was their busiest as they kept an experienced eye out for pickpockets, cut-purses, prostitutes and other undesirables who were always drawn to such a chaotic assembly of people about their lawful business. The two officers of the law already had three thieves and two prostitutes firmly tied to the designated post set into the ground at the eastern end of the market place, where they would remain until sunset, and the departure of the last trader. Tom and Giles would then return to their office in the Guildhall and come back with a cart in which to transport their day's crop of felons to the gaol cells.

Ahead of them through the crush of bodies they became aware of the harsh clamour of angry argument, dominated by the shrill voice of a protesting woman. They instinctively quickened their pace without a word between them, then pushed through the last of those who had been blocking their view in order to identify the source of the dispute. A young woman was competing with a dishevelled looking man for possession of a woven basket of some sort, and as Tom dived into the contest to restore order, Giles ducked behind the woman's stall and ran in pursuit of a skinny youth who had possession of a money bag. Giles brought the youth to the ground by means of a flying leap, and easily overpowered him in order to take the bag from his protesting grasp. Then he hauled the lad to his feet by the collar of his grubby shirt, and led him to where Tom had a firm grasp of the man who had been in the act of stealing the woven fruit basket, according to the young woman who was complaining bitterly to her stern faced saviour.

'This your money bag?' Giles enquired, and the woman turned, nodded and enquired 'How did you know? And how did you come by it?' Giles smiled knowingly.

'The oldest trick in the game, Mistress. They works in twos – one of them distracts you by making a big show of stealing something off your stall, while the other nips behind it and steals anything worthwhile from the back while you're too busy at the front, trying to get your goods back. You must be new around here, to have fallen for that one. And you must have been very unwise, not to have your money bag tied around your waist.'

'It's only my second market day,' she smiled up at him, 'but I were lucky that you and your friend here come by when you did.'

'We're both constables,' Tom explained, 'and we needs to haul these two away in order to tie them up until we can take them down to the gaol. Giles here will come back after that and make a note of your name.'

'I can give you that now,' the woman explained, 'It's Mary – Mary Cossall. But if this lovely young man would care to come back, I've got some elderberry wine we can share. My aunt made it.'

By dusk, the only remaining evidence that a market had been held there earlier was the occasional pile of abandoned rotting fruit that had not found a purchaser, in addition to a few portions of soiled straw from the animal stalls that were rolling around in the evening breeze. Giles walked into the square from the top end of Bridlesmithgate, and grinned as he saw that the young woman was still there. Hopefully she'd delayed her return home in order to meet up with him again. Her modest stall had already been dismantled, and now lay on top of her cart, concealing the assorted woven baskets that remained unsold, while the pony stood with its head down resignedly, awaiting the word to move on.

'I'm afraid I finished the elderberry wine,' she confessed with a welcoming smile 'since my throat got dry with all that dust. But I stayed on, in case you wanted anything more from me.'

'A kiss would be nice,' Giles flirted outrageously with one of his special boyish smiles that had won over many a maiden. 'But then we hardly knows each other, does we?'

'You at least knows my name,' Mary replied as she fluttered her eyelashes in what she hoped was coquettish encouragement to this strikingly handsome young hero with the broad shoulders and flowing auburn locks, 'but I doesn't know yours.'

'Giles. Giles Bradbury.'

'And you're one of them constables?'

'That's me. Before that I were a farmer, out by Tollerton way.'

'That's over the river somewhere, isn't it? I'm from the north side myself. At least, I were until Mam and Dad died, then I come to live at Sneinton with my aunt and uncle. He were the coachman for Earl Manvers until he upped and died, and the Master let Aunt Martha stay on in the cottage. She needed someone to keep her company around the place, and I had nowhere else to go, and now I sells the baskets what we weaves to put food in our mouths. She's teaching me how, and this were my second week at the Saturday Market. We waited ages to get the pitch.'

'So now I know all about you, except whether or not you've got any admirers,' Giles smiled back invitingly, and she couldn't help herself.

'Not at the moment, unless some young constable might be interested in applying for the position.' She winced inwardly at her own forward behaviour, and hoped that this beautiful piece of manhood wouldn't misread the signal. But his continuing warm smile was reassuring as he mentally toasted his seeming good fortune. Mary was beautiful, with long flowing light auburn locks and the most entrancing green eyes. If indeed she wasn't already spoken for, then the young men in Sneinton suffered from poor eyesight, he concluded as he pressed home his advantage.

'Does you only come into the town on market days?'

'Of course. It's not safe any other time, is it? Especially not at night.'

'It is if you're in the company of a constable,' he grinned, and she smiled back encouragingly. 'I doesn't drink ale, but I likes walking along the river on warm nights. I sometimes does that, but I never comes any further into town than the bridge.'

'Even then you'd be taking a risk, without me walking with you,' Giles said encouragingly, and she took the bait. 'It looks as if the weather's set fair for a day or two, so if I should happen to be somewhere near the bridge just as the sun starts to go down tomorrow evening, would I be likely to find a gallant young constable to ensure my safety?'

'You'd be safe from everyone except the gallant young constable,' Giles assured her with a leer, and she hid her blushes by turning back towards the cart. 'I need to get back. Could you walk part of the way with me?'

'Wasn't you planning on riding on top of the cart?' Giles enquired. She leaned forward and placed a soft hand on his jacket.

'I were until I got a better offer from a gallant young constable.'

'How come you can read and write?' Tom's wife Lizzie enquired as she removed the bowl from the table after Tom had finished his late supper, and Tom frowned.

'A long story, most of which you've heard many's the time. When Dad and my older brother Richard got burned alive on the say-so of that bastard cousin Francis, Mam and me thought it best to get out of London, and we finished up here in Nottingham. Mam and her brother Robert was brought up on an estate out Bingham way, where their dad – my granddad – had been Steward until the lord of the manor got his land confiscated because he fell out with the Earl of Lincoln what owned all the lands in them parts. You couldn't be a steward unless you could read and write, and I don't know quite where my grandad learned, because I never met him. But he'd taught my uncle, and when I were put to work as his apprentice in the carpentry business here in town, he taught me. He never had any sons, see – just a couple of daughters – and in them days it weren't thought proper for girls to be taught owt except needlework and cooking and such like.'

'It still isn't,' Lizzie snorted, 'but you've got a son, haven't you?'

'What you getting at, woman? You wants me to teach Robert to read and write? On top of my duties as a constable? You found a way of doubling the number of hours in a day, or what?'

'No, not you,' Lizzie replied with a scornful look. 'You're not home often enough to even talk to *me* beyond asking what's for dinner, and you've no patience when it comes to Robert. But he'll be eleven next birthday, and he couldn't even sign his name to save his life. No, I were thinking of that there Free Grammar School round the corner on Stoney Street.'

'It's not free,' Tom countered. 'They charges twopence a week for the dinners they gets, and the cost of keeping the fires burning, and then there'd be the cost of them books. And I'm damned if I'm going to go cap in hand to them there Guardians of the school, asking for my son to be taken on as a "poor scholar". So forget all about that idea.'

'Maybe we could afford it, now that you're being paid as a Senior Constable,' Lizzie suggested. 'There's some weeks I've got a few pennies left over, and . . . .'

'I said *forget* it!' Tom shouted as he brought his fist down heavily on the table, rattling the candle holder in the process. 'Book learning is for all them Popish lilies what swans around the place pretending they're something they're not. No good ever came of book learning, mark my words. But you're right about Robert; he needs to be set to some trade or other – maybe carpentry, like I were.'

'He certainly won't follow you into being a constable, if he can't read nor write,' Lizzie fired back in her disappointment. 'At least we'll be sparing some poor unsuspecting woman the life I've had to lead.'

'You've done well enough, for a girl what came from a family of ten whose dad were a gong farmer,' Tom sneered, and was heartily relieved when Robert and Lucy came running back indoors from wherever they'd been collecting dirt on their clothes this time, and Lizzie turned her attentions towards them, and the state they were both in.

It was their fourth Sunday evening walking out together along the river bank, and this time Giles and Mary had wandered closer to the coppice of trees that overhung the water. There were flies in abundance that they swatted away with their free hands as they chatted away happily about their lives thus far, and Giles's work as a constable whose duties required him to tangle with the most violent people in the county.

'You needs to be tough to do that,' Mary observed as she tucked her arm into his, pulled him closer towards him, then planted a kiss on his lips as he turned his head towards her. The kiss lingered longer than their previous ones, and had clearly left Mary slightly breathless as she added 'Just the sort of man a woman needs to protect her in this wicked place. Until I met you I were fearful of coming into town even on market day, but now I feels a whole lot safer, knowing that you're somewhere close at hand.'

'Not always all that far away, neither,' Giles reminded her. 'Tom's getting a bit shitty with me spending half of Saturday talking to you and guarding your aunt's baskets.'

'I've told her all about you – I hope you don't mind,' Mary advised him under lowered eyelashes. 'Depends what you've told her, don't it?' Giles grinned back, and Mary kissed him again.

'Just that you're big and handsome, and strong and brave, and beautiful, and . . . '

'And what?' Giles enquired coaxingly as they stopped in the grassy glade between two hanging willow trees whose branches drooped down towards the slow-moving water.

'Well,' Mary replied blushingly, 'just the sort of feller a woman needs to give her bubbies.'

'But not afore she's married?' Giles suggested, and she pulled him towards her, slid her arms round his broad back, kissed him hotly on the lips and ground her pelvis into his suggestively.

'That depends on the feller, don't it? And whether he intends to stay with her after the bubby's born. It don't matter whether you're married or not then, does it?'

'I don't think the minister of St Mary's would agree with you there,' Giles replied with a rapidly drying throat.

'But he isn't here to ask, is he?' Mary pointed out. 'And it's getting dark, and we're hidden from view in these here trees. A girl could easily go wrong with the wrong sort of feller.'

'What about the *right* sort?' Giles enquired as he reached out and squeezed her breast.

'It's never felt more right,' Mary breathed heavily as she pressed his hand even harder. Then they lowered themselves onto the grass in an urgent embrace without another word being spoken.

Tom cursed loudly as he broke the seal and read what Francis Walsingham had written. He'd almost forgotten the day when he and Giles had been appointed as 'Constables Royal', and considering that they'd never received a single penny by way of a stipend, it was something you could easily forget. Fancy titles like that meant nothing when you were slugging it out with Saturday night make believe prize fighters, or apprehending felons armed with knives who were accused of robbing coaches as they came into town, raping young girls in alleyways or waylaying unsuspecting merchants as they weaved their uncertain way back from an alehouse laden down with the day's takings from an advantageous deal done over a few pots of the local brew.

That was the reality of life as a County Constable – locking up those accused by others. Tom was more inclined towards making his own enquiries before condemning anyone on the urgings of others, and he had seen enough of the sort of underhanded work in which Walsingham and his paymasters engaged to want none of it. Then again, to disobey the summons would be to lose the patronage and support of someone who might prove useful if Tom overstepped the mark once too often, and he'd come close to doing that more than once.

So he sighed, folded the summons neatly into the pocket of his jacket, made arrangements for a horse to be made ready the following morning from the stables kept at the rear of the Guildhall, and went home to break the news to Lizzie.

'While you're down there, see if you can find a school for Robert what's prepared to teach the only son of a totally useless father,' was her only riposte. But at daybreak the next morning she handed him a parcel of food and a bladder of small beer, wiped a betraying tear from her eye and begged him to come home safely as she waved him off at the door.

Chapter Two

As he stepped over the insensible man lying to the side of the road and dodged yet another steaming pile of horse shit, Tom reminded himself that London was no different from Nottingham – just bigger. He'd rarely seen this part of the town before fleeing it shortly before his thirteenth birthday, although his mother would proudly remind him of when he'd been seated on his father's shoulders to witness the coronation procession of the boy King Edward outside Westminster Abbey. Tom had no memory of that, but an all too clear memory of the reign of terror that followed the untimely death of the youthful monarch and his replacement by 'Bloody Mary'. Tom spat on the ground in her memory, content with the thought that it could only make the narrow street that little bit cleaner.

He walked the final few steps into the courtyard of Whitehall, where he was to meet with Walsingham. The horse that had carried him for three days south from Nottingham was now stabled at his final inn, one that was dwarfed by the fine houses along the street they called Savoy, and he had opted to walk, rather than be refused stable space inside the pulsing heart of English government. His boots were now filthy, but at least his face was not red with the embarrassment of rejection, or his heart saddened by the curses of liveried servants as they ordered him back out into the public thoroughfare.

It was all bustle and self-importance in the entrance hall, and as he adjusted his eyes to the gloom he was all but bowled over by scurrying clerks carrying rolls of vellum and calling out to each other regarding their business. He flattened himself as far as he could against the inside of the front wall and wondered where to go next, until he was spotted lurking there by a tall man in a red and gold liveried tunic who walked over with his halberd and demanded to know his business.

Tom had retained the presence of mind to keep the written summons from Walsingham, else he might have been forced back out into the courtyard on the end of a pike. As it was, the man seemed impressed, and directed Tom up the sweeping flight of double stairs opposite the entrance, and by dint of a few more hesitant questions posed of superior faced officials, all wearing black robes and all speaking as if their noses were confined within horse feeding bags, Tom was ordered to take a seat in the outer chamber of a suite of offices on the first floor, where he heard copious references to 'the Master', 'The

Secretary' and 'Her Majesty' in the many conversations that competed for his attention.

He was contemplating a return to the outer desk at which he'd first announced his arrival what seemed like an hour ago, and advising the pompous official seated behind it that he'd return at a more convenient time for Master Walsingham, when he was approached by a scrawny little man with a dripping nose and inky fingers. 'Follow me,' the man requested, and Tom duly obliged.

Walsingham was greyer around the head than Tom remembered him as he rose from behind his desk and shook his hand. 'Welcome back to London, Constable Lincraft,' Walsingham said without any apparent movement of the lips. 'Do you find it much changed?'

'I were just a boy when I left, my lord,' Tom replied deferentially, 'and it weren't very often that we come this far west.'

'No, quite,' Walsingham nodded as he waved Tom into a chair in front of the long desk piled high with papers. 'Newgate, wasn't it?'

'You're well informed, sir,' Tom smiled politely, and Walsingham smiled back. 'In my line of work, one has to be. So how go matters in Nottingham?'

'As lawless as ever,' Tom admitted. 'Much work for constables, anyway. But I'll guess that London's much worse, from the little I remember, and from what I've seen since I got here yesterday.'

'There are places infinitely worse than London,' Walsingham advised him as his face fell. 'I myself have just returned from Paris, where the massacre that I witnessed made London seem like the gardens of Kent by comparison. Has word of it reached Nottingham?'

'Street gossip, largely,' Tom replied tactfully, 'although in the church that I goes to there were talk of a massive slaughter of Protestants whose bodies were chucked in the river what flows through Paris.'

'It was a terrible sight to behold,' Walsingham recalled with a shudder, 'and we must be ever vigilant to ensure that such never occurs here. And we may be assured that if the Catholics ever reach such a position of prominence as that dreadful Guise family in France, then we may expect similar outrages here. Hence my summons to you and your colleague. You come alone, however?'

'Yes,' Tom admitted. 'Giles has a new lady in his life, and rather than drag him away I'd thought I'd come down on my own and see what it is you're wanting of us. Is there a risk of Catholic intrigue in Nottingham?' Walsingham frowned.

'I need to remind you of the oath you swore when you became

Queen's Constables – both of you. That was not an oath that can be taken lightly, and once taken it cannot be resiled from. It requires you to work whenever – and wherever – you may be needed in the defence of the realm. You presumably understood that at the time – again, both of you?'

'Yes,' Tom conceded, 'but that were two years ago now, and we hasn't either of us heard from you in all that time. Nor has we been paid any money.'

'The first of those complaints has already been addressed, since you are here today,' Walsingham reminded him bluntly. 'As for the second, did you fondly imagine that you would be remunerated for doing nothing?'

'Suppose not, but why did you bring me all the way down from Nottingham?' Tom enquired, and Walsingham nodded, in acknowledgment that Tom was finally asking the right questions.

'Have you ever heard of "The Society of Jesus"?'

'Can't say I has,' Tom admitted, 'but it sounds like one of them Popish clubs.'

'And if it is, you would presumably be opposed to it, given your strong Protestant persuasions?'

'Of course, but so what?'

'The "so what", Tom, is that they are operating something called "The English College" across the Channel in France. A place called "Douai", although that need not concern you at present. What *must* concern you, if you are to be of service to England, is that this college is training Catholic priests, then smuggling them into England, where we believe that they are being given sanctuary in the country houses of rich nobles.'

'But they isn't preaching?' Tom enquired, at a loss to understand where this was leading.

'If they were doing so openly, we could of course have them apprehended and brought to trial, along with the nobles who are hiding them, given that the Pope peevishly excommunicated Queen Elizabeth, and called upon all Catholics to serve God by removing her from the throne. Anyone doing so would of course be guilty of treason, but the Pope anticipated that and further threatened anyone continuing to obey her orders with excommunication, and this has inspired more than one plot to replace Her Majesty with Mary of Scotland. When we last met, it was as the result of your loyal service in helping to expose one of those plots, by the Italian merchant Ridolfi. Norfolk lost his head for his part in that one, but he is by no means likely to be the last to risk his life in plots against the throne. The presence of these "Jesuit" priests in the households of the high-born can only encourage more along the same lines.'

'So where does I come in?' Tom enquired, still at a loss. Walsingham sat back in his chair as he explained.

'These priests are being smuggled into England under cover, probably at dead of night, and on board vessels that are otherwise engaged in legitimate trade. English sea captains are no doubt being handsomely rewarded for taking on this additional human cargo.'

'How does you know that?' Tom enquired, and Walsingham glared back testily.

'That is of no concern to you. I have learned that for covert schemes to be successful, those taking part in them need only know of those matters that have a bearing on the part they are to play. You need know only that these agents of Rome are being smuggled into the country on English trading ships.'

'I've never been to sea in my life,' Tom objected. 'No,' came the reply, 'but you're familiar enough with alehouses, are you not?'

'Of course, but what's that got to do with priests and sailing ships?' Tom demanded, and Walsingham sighed.

'While our intelligence sources – which are French, and are therefore well placed to confirm that these priests are being smuggled across to England – are most reliable regarding the regular departures of ordained priests from the College, they have so far not been able to identify those vessels on which they are crossing the Channel. Once the priests reach Calais or Boulogne, they disappear into a closely guarded network of houses, and for all we know they remain hidden there for many weeks before they make the crossing. We have therefore determined that our next move must be to identify the vessels in which they travel at *this* end.'

'But there's lots of ports in England, isn't there?' Tom argued. 'London's only one of them, although it's a big one.'

'The vast majority of our sea trade begins life in the storehouses at Rotherhithe,' Walsingham explained, 'and the vessels that are entrusted with those cargoes may be found moored at the wharves along Thames Street. You are not unfamiliar with that area of London, are you?'

Tom nodded. 'As usual, you're well informed. My father and older brother worked as labourers on them wharves in the days when we all lived in Newgate. That were before they was unjustly put to death on the say-so of a bastard cousin of mine, but presumably you knows all about that as well.'

'Indeed,' Walsingham smiled, 'so there are two reasons why you would be eminently suitable for what I have in mind for you and your colleague Constable Bradbury.'

'Like I said already, he's busy planning on getting himself married to a girl in Nottingham,' Tom objected, but Walsingham's returning smile was not a warm one.

'Unfortunate, certainly. Regrettable, perhaps. But hardly insurmountable when compared with the need to protect the crown.'

'I'm not sure as how Giles would agree with that,' Tom grumbled, 'and I suppose I'll be left as the one to tell him. But why us? You must have lots more of these here "Queen's Constables" up and down the country, so why a couple of fellers from Nottingham, which is just about as far from the sea as you can get in this country?'

Walsingham considered his reply carefully before delivering it. 'Do you know precisely how many Queen's Constables we have sworn in since the post was initiated?' When Tom shook his head, Walsingham added 'Five.'

Tom's eyebrows shot up in astonishment, and Walsingham hastened to add that 'You may now perhaps see why you should be so conscious of the honour bestowed upon you. Yet your only observation thus far has been to complain about the lack of payment. That will be remedied anyway, once you begin your allotted tasks.'

'I don't suppose as how we can refuse,' Tom growled, 'but you might at least tell me why the other three isn't being involved.'

'I didn't say they weren't,' Walsingham reminded him. 'I merely said that you and Bradbury *will* be, but in a different way. As I observed earlier, you need only know what you need to know.'

'So what do you want us to do?' Tom enquired with resignation, and Walsingham reached out for some papers on his desk and slid them across towards Tom.

'The lease on a very insalubrious alehouse in Thames Street. It's called the "Saracen's Head", and it's all but shaded from daylight by London Bridge, which is perhaps as well, given all the dark deeds that went on in there. We closed it down after the last death following a knife fight, but now we're obligingly allowing it to re-open in the hope that its former customers will return.'

'You going to tell me why?' Tom grumbled, 'and what's it got to do with me and Giles?'

'Second question first,' Walsingham smiled. 'You just became the landlord. As for why, its clientele consists almost exclusively of sailors and sea captains. The lowest sort, of course, and therefore the most likely to be involved in this illicit transport of priests into England.'

'So we goes in there, risks our necks every day, and keeps our ears open, assuming that they hasn't been cut off in one of them knife fights you was mentioning?'

'That sums it up very nicely,' Walsingham confirmed as his smile widened. 'Whatever profit you can make from selling whatever pigswill passes for ale in there will be yours to keep, in addition to which you'll receive a pound a week each for your special duties for me, on top of your existing stipends as Nottinghamshire Constables. I've already alerted the Sheriff that you'll be engaged on duties directly under the auspices of Secretary of State Cecil, and I'll expect you both back down here by the end of this month. That gives you almost three weeks. You may bring your womenfolk with you if you wish – in fact, that would be preferable, since it will make your assumed roles more believable.'

Tom sat there momentarily stunned by the prospect of telling Lizzie that they were leaving their relatively humdrum life in a quiet and comfortable house in a Nottingham side street in order to reside above what promised to be the roughest whorehouse in London. As for Giles's intended, Mary, the mere suggestion would probably be the end of their relationship, and Giles would be unlikely to be forgiving.

'Don't you want to know your new backgrounds?' Walsingham enquired as he cut into Tom's gloomy ruminations, and Tom nodded.

'You will be the landlord, and Bradbury your brother in law fallen on hard times. You may retain your current names, but if asked you will claim to be a farmer thrown off his land for his Catholic leanings. This gives you reason for being sympathetic towards anyone seeking to restore the old religion and bring down the Protestants who were granted lands following the closure of the monasteries. Your own farm was formerly held in fee from the local abbey, and you were dispossessed by a minor noble who declined to honour your lease, leaving you bitter and seeking revenge.'

'I can do that nicely from my own experience, without the need to invent fancy stories,' Tom replied acidly, 'but what's Giles's story?'

'He's your wife's younger brother, and a former soldier who served Elizabeth in helping to suppress a rebellion by northern earls some little while ago. The acts of brutality he was obliged to both witness and carry out when the rebellion was put down have left him sickened and disillusioned. He is seeking some new way of earning his living, and you've provided him with just such an opportunity. Hopefully, with a background like that, it will only be a matter of time before he's offered something more directly connected with guarding priests.'

'And the women?' Tom enquired, at which Walsingham spread his hands in an open gesture. 'Do I have to think everything out for you? Your own wife will obviously be keeping house in the commodious rooms above the main alehouse, and possibly supplying food for hungry sailors, while your colleague's wife – if suitably young and comely – can be the sort of pot girl that might be expected in an establishment like that, attracting in the sailors.'

'Will you be paying them as well?'

'No – you will, out of the profits you make from the liquor sales. Only you and Bradbury will be remunerated. The place is furnished, after a fashion, so you can all move in with the minimum of delay. Someone will attend your premises on a regular basis in order to collect any information you may have managed to acquire. If challenged, he will show you this ring, which has my personal seal on it. Do not, under any circumstances, allow yourself to be seen here again in Whitehall. Once you leave here today, you are on your own.

'Probably in more ways than one, once I goes home and tells Lizzie,' Tom replied gloomily as he rose to leave.

Chapter Three

'The first thing we does is give the place a damned good clean from top to bottom,' Lizzie announced with a grimace as she wiped her fingers along the grimy counter and held them up to display three months' worth of dust, along with the corpse of a long-dead insect. 'Come on, Mary – you can help. Robert, go and get some water from the conduit down the street, and Lucy can look for some old cloths, then we can get started. Nobody gets any supper until this here place is fit for decent folks to eat in.'

She'd been like this ever since the day Tom, with bated breath, had announced that they were commanded down to London. She'd been partly mollified by the prospect of additional money, and Tom's tentative agreement to at least make enquiry at the Free Grammar School regarding a place for Robert. Then she'd set about leaving their Barker Lane house as clean as scrubbing could make it, ahead of packing all their clothes into bundles and covering them with sacking that would protect them from mud and dust on the four day journey south on the wagon hired with some of the money that Walsingham had handed to Tom in a velvet bag before he left Whitehall. Tom was not entirely sure what had so galvanised Lizzie, and was fearful to ask in case she had a change of heart about spending what might be several months in London.

Giles had initially been a far harder nut to crack, when advised that his new-found relationship with Mary must be put on hold, and that the wedding that they had begun to plan in their imaginations would be even further delayed. Then, in what Giles could only regard as a miracle from God, Mary had announced that if Tom and Lizzie would ignore their sin, she wanted to accompany Giles to London. 'You're the feller I wants for the rest of my life,' she'd announced as tears rolled down her face, 'and the rest of my life starts tomorrow. Besides which, I don't want one of them London hussies to get her claws into you, so we goes together.'

Lizzie had been very accepting of the fact that Giles and Mary would be living in sin under their very noses, once she met Mary and realised that she was a cut above the sort of women that Tom and Giles normally came across in the course of their duties. She would also be a fitting companion for her, and any remaining doubts had been dispelled when the children Robert and Lucy had taken to her so naturally, and Lizzie realised that at long last here was someone who might help to keep their offspring both amused and well behaved, since Tom seemed to regard the job as beneath him.

After three days of sweeping and scrubbing Lizzie declared the accommodation on the floor above the alehouse to be clean to her satisfaction, by which time Tom and Giles had taken their first delivery from an overjoyed brewer of indifferent ale that the two men agreed they preferred to sell rather than drink. Less than twenty-four hours after they reopened the front door they were knee deep in returning customers, and although they were even rougher than Tom and Giles had dreaded, they spent freely, and within a week the establishment was as well patronised as it had ever been by the lowest dregs of the dockside community that it served.

However, all was not sweetness and light as they adapted to their new lifestyles and awaited the opportunity to overhear something that might interest Walsingham and justify their new existence. The drunken brawls, the spillages and the vomit they had anticipated, but not the surly resentment of their dubious clientele that the new landlord was not prepared to tolerate whores lounging in the doorway, or flouncing in to claim a seat on the knee of some inebriated mariner only too happy to fritter away his latest discharge money.

It was Mary who bore the brunt of this, when drunken sailors misunderstood her precise function in the place, and she swiftly learned how to fend off wandering hands and ignore disgusting invitations. Giles would hover about her like a seagull attracted to a fish market, and more than once was obliged to eject a drunk who had overstepped the mark. Tom, for his part, was obliged to block his ears to the profanities that seemed to constitute the only conversation of which his customers were capable, and, at least initially, he insisted on Lizzie remaining upstairs, safely shielded from all the foul oaths, drunken brawls and filthy personal habits that disgraced the lower floor of the premises within minutes of their opening for the day.

In any case, Lizzie had enough concerns of her own, as Robert seemed to regard their new surroundings as a playground in which he could learn bad behaviour from the ragged youths he befriended when he was allowed out into the dockside alleyways and foetid courtyards. He had soon learned to steal from vendors' carts with the best of them, and came home almost nightly with torn clothing, bruises and cuts to which Lizzie would attend while exhorting Tom to exercise some control over his son, before he was taken up by a local constable, to the severe embarrassment of the whole family. At least nine year old

Lucy could be kept indoors, although her increasingly petulant and morose behaviour, confined in the upper rooms, made her less pleasant to be around, and it was as well that she had taken to Mary like a big sister who could teach her to sew, wash and do all the other things that would be expected of her when she attained womanly status.

But the hardest thing to accept, as the weeks drifted by, was the failure of anyone to hear anything remotely related to what might be the smuggling of Catholic priests into England on ships connected with the motley crew who frequented The Saracen's Head. From time to time the same scrawny looking man dressed in the dowdy but serviceable garb of a seafarer would drift in and engage Tom in seemingly idle conversation, during which he would enquire whether anything of interest had occurred that might 'engage our friend in Whitehall'. On each such occasion Tom had been obliged to shake his head, sigh, and suggest that perhaps they were all wasting their time.

Back upstairs late at night, when Tom and Giles had finally assisted the last of the rolling drunks out into Thames Street, the four of them would sit around the table and enjoy a mug-full from the cask of 'best ale' that the brewer was prevailed upon to deliver from time to time for their private consumption. As the weeks droned on they found themselves discussing when they might decently retreat back to Nottingham, leaving a message for Walsingham that his plan, while a good one in theory, had not yielded any results. Then they were given cause to think again.

It had been the usual sort of night, with a few noisy altercations that would have developed into full-blown fights, had Giles not stepped in as usual and intimidated the disputants into conceding that they did not really disagree, before inviting them to shake hands. Then into the crowded room walked a giant of a man with lank ginger hair down to his shoulders, and animal skins of some sort wrapped around his outer clothing, suggesting that he might have been on the road for some weeks. He ordered a large flagon of ale, then leaned in a corner for a long while, eyeing all those around him with a stern stare that made everyone nervous, and ensured that he had plenty of open space all around him.

It was soon being whispered around the room that this was the infamous Phadrig Blunt, the terror of the Thames-side wharves, and the man who was currently seeking to enlist sailors into some sort of organisation that would somehow coerce the local shipowners into paying more money to their exploited deckhands. Many of those deckhands silently applauded what the man was about, but few dared associate, or even speak, with him, such was his reputation for mindless brute violence when crossed.

He had been visibly drunk when he came in, and was even worse by the time that he called out to Mary for another pot. Mary duly obliged, and as she handed him the foaming pot in exchange for his money he grabbed her arm and pulled him to her, kissing her violently on the mouth. When she began to struggle and call for Giles, Phadrig kept hold of her with his free hand, put his pot down roughly on the floor, then began clawing at Mary's bodice with his other hand. Giles came racing over and yelled for Phadrig to leave Mary alone.

The man pushed Mary roughly away from him, then gave a loud animal roar and raced towards Giles, who jinked to one side, then smashed a straight left into Phadrig's head. This seemed to daze him for a moment, then to everyone's horror, and to screams from Mary, Phadrig made another rush at Giles, and was met with a virtual windmill of fist flurries to the right and left of his head that would have killed a man half his size. As he continued to soak up the punishment Giles sank a heavy blow to his stomach that caused him to bend forward in time for a left uppercut to jerk his head backwards with a force that threatened to remove it from his head. He bounced off the back wall, and was then caught on the rebound with another hailstorm of punches to the face. He was heard to grunt in final recognition of the hammering he was enduring, then to muted applause and whispered expressions of satisfaction from the onlookers he slid slowly into the beer-stained rushes on the floor. Giles grabbed his heels and dragged him to the door, through which he rolled him into the street, then walked back inside nursing his bruised knuckles.

A grinning Tom handed Giles a pot of ale. 'It may taste like donkey piss, but it'll soak up the pain,' Giles was advised as Mary threw her arms round him and offered to kiss away any bruises he might have acquired. As she backed away, promising to come back with water and a cloth, a small middle aged man slightly better dressed than their average customer placed a hand on Giles's shoulder and enquired 'Where d'you learn to fight like that, son?'

'The Queen's army,' Giles replied, still slightly breathless from his exertions. 'You still enlisted?' was the next question, but Giles shook his head. 'No, my friend. I joined up to fight the Queen's enemies – not to butcher children and hang their mothers from trees. And who might you be, anyway, asking questions of a soldier what's seen too much of the world for his liking?'

'Timothy Barton, owner and captain of "The Kittyhawk", currently moored down the road there at Bentley's Wharf, but due to sail for Antwerp and Calais in a week's time. Ever been to sea?'

'Never,' Giles replied. 'We was supposed to be going over to the Low Countries a while back there, then we was diverted to Yorkshire. So no, never been to sea.'

'Would you like to?' Barton persevered. 'I like the way you handle yourself, and that man Blunt's long been a vexation to many a shipowner like myself. If you can do what you just did to the likes of him, I'd be glad to have you aboard even if you never lift a rope. There are plenty who can show you how, and I'll hazard that not a man on board would be unwise enough to show you any disrespect while you learn.'

'I'll think about it,' Giles promised, and Bartram took his leave after promising him a shilling a day if he took up his offer.

Later, as they sat round the table upstairs, opinion was divided. Mary sat bathing Giles's raw knuckles with vinegar and insisting that he wasn't going anywhere, certainly not for the immediate future, and perhaps not ever. 'You saw what I has to put up with down there,' she complained, 'and it were you what brought me here, so the least you can do is stay and protect me from the likes of that big oaf, and others like him. How does we know he won't come back while you're away?'

'Bullies like him is cowards as well,' Tom advised her. 'He won't dare come back in here after a thrashing like that, because it's not good for his reputation. Trust me.'

'But what about others like him?' Lizzie argued. 'This is the roughest alehouse in London, I reckon, and what was you thinking of, the pair of you, bringing us down here in the first place? It's not as if we've learned anything we can tell that feller what ordered us down here. What were his name again? Walters? Wallington?'

'Walsingham,' Tom corrected her. 'And as for whether or not Giles should go to sea – which is what we're supposed to be deciding – we might get to learn something useful. At least he'll be with other sailors, and one of them might let slip something about how them priests is being brought into the country.'

'Is anyone going to ask me what I wants to do?' Giles demanded, and Mary kissed him lovingly on the cheek as she enquired 'Does you *really* want to leave me and get yourself drowned?'

'I can swim,' Giles assured her, 'but I doesn't want to leave you, now that I've found you.'

'There were a time when Tom said lovely things like that to me,'

Lizzie chimed in dourly. 'Trust me, Mary, it stops after a while, once they've filled you with bubbies.'

'We're missing the point,' Tom reminded them with a frown. 'It don't matter what any of us thinks – what matters is what Walsingham wants us to do. I needs to ask him.'

'I only hopes that he tells us to go back to Nottingham,' Lizzie growled as she began to clear away the pots. 'And if you two fellers thinks you've maybe had enough to drink for one night, it's getting late, and some of us has to be up bright and early to fix breakfast.'

Three days later, as the atmosphere in the upstairs quarters grew more and more tense with the uncertainty of it all, Tom found himself talking once again with the man who called regularly to enquire about progress. At least this time he had something to report.

'I needs to speak urgently with our friend down the road,' he advised the man in a hoarse whisper. 'It's all very well gassing with the likes of you, but I needs some advice, and urgent like.' The man nodded.

'This was anticipated. I'll be back here sometime in the next day or two, and when I am, be prepared to take an hour away from here. It'll only be for an hour, mind.'

Two days after that, barely an hour after they'd opened for the day, the man re-appeared at the front door, and indicated with a jerk of the head that Tom should join him outside. Leaving Giles and Mary to serve the few customers who were already guzzling ale, Tom slipped out through the back door, made his way swiftly down the side alley through which the barrels were delivered, and met the messenger in Thames Street. They walked side by side under the shade of London Bridge, heading west, and Tom's curiosity got the better of him.

'We're not going to Whitehall, surely? I were told to stay away from there.'

'It's just along here,' he was told, and after another few hundred yards they slipped down the alleyway at the side of a chandler's store where the man knocked on a side door, which opened seemingly of its own accord. Tom was directed up the stairs to the upper chamber, and there stood Walsingham, warming his back against a recently lit fire. They shook hands, and Walsingham smiled at Tom's puzzled expression.

'You will have noticed the bedding in the corner?' he enquired. 'This is one of those many establishments in this part of the city where rooms can be hired by the hour for clandestine meetings. We merely take advantage of the flagrant immorality that is the curse of our current society. Would that it were otherwise, but, as you can now appreciate, even that can be used to the Queen's advantage. Now, what is so urgent?'

Tom quickly advised Walsingham of the fight in the Saracen's Head, and the offer that Giles had received from a sea captain. Walsingham nodded and smiled as he heard the details, then fixed Tom with a quizzical look.

'What made you think that your colleague should not take up this promising offer?'

'Well,' Tom replied, 'for one thing we don't know if he'll learn anything from it. And for another, I needs him in the alehouse to help out with the rough stuff. He's a lot tougher than me, and a few years younger, and . . . '

Walsingham raised a hand to silence him. 'That concern is easily overcome. I obviously have many men in my service who can handle that sort of thing, and I'll arrange for them to attend your premises, two at a time, dressed like common sailors. You won't know who they are unless they are required to restore order. As for your first objection, just think for a moment. We believe that these priests are coming in on English ships, and your colleague has just been offered an opportunity to travel on an English ship. It has to be a far more promising opportunity to acquire additional intelligence, even if it's only by way of shipboard tittle-tattle between sailors. So of course he must take up the offer. Was there anything else, or have we concluded our business?'

'Not really,' Tom conceded, 'except that the womenfolk's getting very unhappy, stuck in that dreadful shithole. The Saracen's Head is hardly the place for ladies.'

'It was your choice to bring them with you,' Walsingham reminded him, 'and you must live with that. No-one said this would be easy, but perhaps at long last we may begin to make some progress.'

Chapter Four

Giles leaned back casually against the stern bulwark and tried to look disinterested as the Kittyhawk dropped its anchor midstream in the Thames Estuary, and the small rowing boat pulled out from the mud flats in precisely the same location on the Essex north bank as on the three previous occasions. The first light of a pale dawn lit up the sky to the east, and Giles could just make out a large wooded island of some sort directly off their starboard beam, with a river estuary entering the Thames from its left.

On cue, the hatch leading to the captain's cabin opened silently, and two hooded figures emerged on deck, wrapped in dark cloaks as if to give them warmth against the morning chill. But Giles was willing to bet the shilling a day that he was being paid that they were priests, and that – as before – the two men would be assisted down the rope ladder into the boat that was gliding out to meet them, the outline of the oarsman visible in the faint light from the hooded lantern that was being held aloft by the man in its bow.

The smaller craft pulled alongside, and the two hooded figures descended into it and were rowed back to the point on the shoreline, just in front of the trees, where another lantern was being gently waved from side to side in order to guide the oarsman ashore. Giles smiled to himself as he had his initial suspicions confirmed. He now had something to report back to Tom, who in turn could alert Walsingham, and soon Giles could cease this pretence. He had no taste for seafaring, and he had been allowed simply to lounge around the deck, occasionally helping to play out an anchor rope, but in reality acting as bodyguard and general dogsbody to Timothy Barton. The other men resented him, although they also feared him, and he was not comfortable with his assumed role.

'Why aren't you below decks with the other men?' Barton demanded suspiciously as he walked back across the deck after farewelling his passengers and saw Giles lurking in the half-light.

'It smells down there,' Giles replied gruffly, 'and it's too cramped. I prefers the fresh air.'

'What did you think of what you just saw?' Barton demanded, and Giles shrugged. 'None of my business.'

'You're right, it's not,' Barton confirmed as he looked more closely into Giles's eyes for any hint of a guilty conscience. 'But it helps to pay your shilling a day, so keep your mouth shut. Don't go mentioning any of this when you go back to your brother in law and your woman in the Saracen. You must have learned how to keep quiet when you were a soldier, and all those terrible things were happening.'

'Bloody right,' Giles replied as he spat onto the deck, and Barton's eyes narrowed. 'You sure you're not one of those deserters?' he demanded, and Giles shook his head. 'We was discharged at Tilbury, further upstream there, and told that we was free to go until we was called on again. I think the Queen were feeling guilty about all them slaughters what we'd carried out.'

'Just making sure,' Barton replied, although he did not look entirely convinced. 'The thing is that I'm going to need you in Newgate on Sunday, and I didn't want you being taken up as a deserter if anyone recognised you. You're from there, aren't you?'

'I never said where I were from,' Giles corrected him. 'But if you must know, it's up north – a place called Nottingham. But what's happening on Sunday?'

'You'll find out when we get there,' Barton replied enigmatically. 'Just make sure you're up and ready by the middle of the morning. You'll be paid your usual daily shilling, which reminds me – here's what you're due for this last voyage. Just remember to keep your mouth shut, right? Now get the rest of them up on deck and let's raise the anchor.'

Back at the Saracen's Head there was the usual welcoming hug for Giles from a happy Mary, as he walked through the front door and weaved his way through the early customers towards the back room, where Tom was seated counting money.

'I hates it when you're at sea,' Mary complained as she kissed him yet again, 'and it's always so good to see you back in one piece.'

'That may be the last time,' Giles announced, and Tom looked up sharply. 'Another landing?' he enquired eagerly, and Giles nodded.

'Yeah, just like them other three. The same place, too, so you better lose no time telling Walsingham. But I think Barton's getting suspicious of me, so it's perhaps as well that I won't be going back on board, where he can have me done away with.'

Mary gave a shudder and pulled him closer to her. 'Don't say that!' she pleaded, and even Tom looked worried.

'Time you made yourself scarce, I think,' he suggested, but Giles shook his head.

'He wants me to go with him on Sunday to somewhere in Newgate, he says.' It was Tom's turn to shudder.

'That's a foul place at the best of times. Believe me, I grew up there. And if he's planning on having you done in, I can't think of a better place to do it. If you gets murdered in Newgate, like as not they'll never even find your body.'

Mary gave a shriek and clapped a hand to her mouth. 'You can't go! I couldn't bear it if you was killed, not with a bubby on the way as well!'

Both men gawped at her with gaping lower jaws, and her face reddened with embarrassment and shy pride. 'Well, why not?' she challenged them. 'After all, Giles and me's been . . . .'

'Yes, thank you, Mary,' Tom cut her off, 'I think we all know what's caused it.'

'Are you sure?' Giles demanded as he grabbed both her hands and kissed them lovingly. 'As near as I can be,' Mary beamed back at him, 'but you can see now why I doesn't want you getting yourself killed nor nothing.'

'Quite right too,' Tom added, 'so that's why he's not going to Newgate on his own.'

'He'll get suspicious if you turn up with me as well,' Giles pointed out, and Tom nodded. 'Which is a very good reason why I'll be keeping well behind the pair of you. But the first sign of any nonsense and I'll be there double quick.'

'You're supposed to be keeping an ear open in this place,' Giles reminded him, and Tom gave a derisive snort. 'So as I can learn more sweary words? And now that you've found the ship what's bringing in them there priests, our job here's done, isn't it?'

'There's probably other ships,' Giles pointed out, 'but I'm not going to sea again if I can help it, so it's for you to find out what other ships' captains is making a dishonest shilling by bringing priests into that place on the north side of the river.'

'Can you remember exactly where that spot were?' Tom enquired, and Giles nodded. 'Put me on a boat and I'll show you.'

'Not me,' Tom asserted. 'Walsingham'.

'But what about Sunday?' Giles reminded him, and Tom rose to his feet and nodded towards the public room, where the increasing noise suggested that Lizzie might be needing a hand. 'Let's go and serve some customers while we still manages this shithole, because I don't reckon as how we will for much longer. And on Sunday I'm coming with you.'

Tom was several yards behind Giles and Barton as they followed the Sunday crowds on their way down Ludgate Hill, with the spires of St. Paul's ahead of them. Although it was Sunday the streets were just as busy as on a weekday, given Queen Elizabeth's edict that everyone was required to present themselves at church on Sunday, on pain of a fine in default, in order to worship the Protestant way. This suited Tom for two reasons; the first was his distaste for anything that smacked of Catholicism, and the second, and more immediate, reason, was that he could benefit from the throng of people in order to keep his covert pursuit hidden from Barton.

Tom shuddered involuntarily as they passed the end of the Old Bailey, and his eyes were drawn down its dusty length to the grim walls of Newgate Gaol, whose dark purpose was in no way lightened by the fancy entrance gateway through which hundreds of innocent men had passed over the years. Men like his father and older brother, falsely condemned as heretics during the purges of Queen Mary, and burned alive only a few yards away from where he was following Giles and his employer. And only yards now from where he had grown up in the pious but happy house in an alleyway off Paternoster Row, in the shadow of St Paul's.

His heart sank, and his stomach bile rose, as Barton led Giles to the left, and the north end of the Row came into view. The memories began to flood back into Tom's unwilling head, and suddenly he could once again smell the rancid sweetness of burning human flesh, and hear the screams of the dying. He prayed for them to keep walking straight ahead, but as if in a sick re-enactment of his most common nightmare they turned into Paternoster Row, and Tom hung back briefly, his heart pounding and his stomach and bowels churning. He cried out in disbelief as they turned into an all too familiar courtyard, and it took all of his strength to step slowly after them, like a man in a dream. It was the dreaded courtyard, and the dreaded door, behind which the vilest of wickedness and Godless vice had been hatched in order to send his dearest family to the pyre.

The door opened briefly in order to allow Giles and Barton to slip inside. The man opening it for them had only appeared fleetingly, but it had been long enough for Tom. He gave a cry of horror, then ran back up the Row, pausing at its junction to spew up his breakfast. Then he walked like a man in a trance, against the flow of people, back towards Thames Street with unseeing eyes as his brain continued to replay the horrible events that these streets had witnessed all those years ago.

'What in God's name happened to Tom out there, and where have you been?' Lizzie demanded as Giles slipped into the back room where Lizzie was struggling to move an empty barrel. 'Looking for Tom, for the past hour or so,' Giles complained as he gently moved her aside and lodged the barrel against the side wall. 'I could see him following us when we went into that there house down in Newgate, but when we come out there were no sign of him. It were a good job nobody seemed to be in the mood to murder me, but I needs to talk to Tom, now that he's back here.'

'Good luck with that,' Lizzie complained. 'His body's out the front, as you can see, but his mind's God knows where. Ever since he come back he's been like one of them statues you sees outside fancy buildings. He's just staring into space doing nothing, even though the place's full, and poor old Mary and me's been working ourselves into the ground. And her in her condition too!'

Giles hurried back into the customer area and pushed past the silent and immobile Tom in order to work alongside Mary, who poured ale into pots from the large jugs that Giles filled from the barrel, then handed them out to yelling customers as the alehouse filled to near capacity on what should have been revered as a holy day. After what felt like the longest day of their working lives Giles and Mary assisted the last of the drunks out into Thames Street and locked and bolted the heavy front doors, embraced briefly to celebrate a job well done, then made their way upstairs, to where Tom, like a walking corpse, had been assisted by Lizzie an hour previously. A large ale pot was in front of him on the table, and to judge by the state of the barrel they kept in the corner it was by no means his first. He was roused by their entry, and looked up at Giles through watery eyes.

'Sorry,' he mumbled, then dry retched.

'Where's Lizzie?' Mary enquired, and Tom looked confused. 'I think she took herself off to her bed, after telling me what she thought of me. But it weren't my fault.' His eyes began to fill with tears, and Mary took Giles gently by the hand. 'Come on, father to be,' she smiled encouragingly, 'let's leave Tom to work it all out and get to our bed. My legs won't hold me up for much longer anyway.'

The next morning Giles found Tom in the same seat that he had left him in the previous night. The air in the upstairs room stunk like the rear yard of a brewery, and Tom was doing his best to chew on a slice of stale bread as he looked up. The two men's eyes met, and Tom dropped his gaze to the table in his embarrassment.

'You could have been done in, and I ran out on you when you most needed me. But I had my reasons, and I can only say as I'm sorry.'

'You did that last night – more than once,' Giles chuckled, and Tom grinned sheepishly. 'I don't remember nowt after coming up here to try and clear my head. When it wouldn't clear, I tried to drown it. Was I bad?'

'No idea,' Giles replied truthfully, 'since we were all too busy pouring that pissy ale into the customers. I put the money from last night into the bag under our bed, by the way,' he advised Tom, who had one issue that was still puzzling him. 'How did I finish up in this room?' he enquired, and Giles grinned. 'Ask Lizzie, because she were going on for half an hour or more about how heavy you was to help up the stairs.'

'And she hasn't finished going on about it, neither,' Lizzie announced loudly as she bustled into the room, then pierced Tom with a glare. 'You ever get into that state again and you'll be looking for your nuts in the back yard out there.'

Giles sniggered, but Lizzie shot him a venomous glare that silenced him instantly. 'If either of you's wanting some breakfast, get out of my way,' she demanded. 'But first I needs to open one of these here windows, to get the smell out of this place. Did you shit yourself or what, Tom?'

Advising her that he couldn't be certain that he hadn't, Tom gestured to Giles with his head that they should go downstairs. 'Let's go into the yard and find my nuts,' he added with a wry grin.

Out in the yard, Tom perched awkwardly on an empty barrel and apologised to Giles yet again. Giles shook his head to indicate that it wasn't necessary, but enquired what had led to Tom's disappearance in Newgate. The colour began to return to Tom's face as he looked up at Giles.

'That feller what let you and Barton into the house. What business were he about?'

'That's what I needs to tell you,' Giles replied excitedly, 'or perhaps you *and* Walsingham. So far as I could make out, he's the feller what organises the landings of the priests once they crosses the Channel. We was there for more instructions, and he told Barton as how there'd be some more for him to collect in Calais next week. He didn't say exactly when, and I'm afraid I didn't get his full name. Only that he's called "Francis".'

'Francis Fucking Covington,' Tom muttered, then stared at Giles with pain-filled eyes as he added 'The same Francis Fucking Covington what sold my dad and brother to the Catholics. They was burned at the stake not yards from where you was having your little meeting, where Newgate turns into Smithfield. You passed my old house on your way to your meeting, and Cousin Francis obviously hasn't moved house since he went to it with his sister in there, and earned his absolution by selling out two innocent souls. Now perhaps you can understand why I were missing when you come out of there.'

'At least no-one tried to do me in,' Giles advised him in an effort to raise his spirits.'Thank the good Lord for that,' Tom muttered, then looked up as he saw Lizzie in the back doorway, hands on hips in standard battle pose. 'If either of you wants any breakfast, you'd better come upstairs now, while there's some left' she shouted. 'Robert eats everything in sight these days, and Mary claims as how she's eating for two.'

'Giles tells me that we'll soon be getting away from here,' Mary announced cheerfully as she smeared mutton dripping onto her dry crust. Giles met Tom's quizzical gaze and hastened to assure him that 'It'll be your decision, obviously, but now we've got both ends of the plot I reckon that Walsingham won't have any more need for us.'

'As I understand it,' Tom replied, 'we're nowhere *near* finished yet, although you may be right that we can stop pretending to run this here alehouse. First thing we needs to do is talk to Walsingham and tell him what we knows already, then see if it's enough. We knows the name of the person what gives Barton his instructions regarding when there's priests to be collected and delivered, and you reckons that you know where some of them's being dropped off. But for all we know, there's lots more ships, lots more priests, and lots more dogs like my filthy rotten cousin doing the organising.'

'Your cousin?' Lizzie echoed, and Tom nodded. 'The same cousin what betrayed your dad and your brother?' she persevered, and Tom smashed his fist down on the table. 'Yes, the *same* bastard, so leave off talking about him!' Without another word being exchanged, they left the remains of the breakfast to a gleeful Robert, and went about their various tasks for the morning.

Chapter Five

Three days later Tom and Giles clumped up the narrow staircase to the 'convenience chamber' above the chandler's shop, where Walsingham awaited them sitting before the roaring fire in the only available chair. As they stood uncertainly, awaiting acknowledgment that he was aware of their presence, he waved them forward with a stern admonition.

'This had better be something worthy of my attention, since I have been obliged to delay an audience with Her Majesty. She does not take kindly to such slights, but hopefully Cecil can keep her amused until my tardy arrival. So – out with it.'

'We knows where them priests is being landed,' Tom announced proudly, 'and we knows who's organising things from this end. In fact we knows him very well.'

'The second point first,' Walsingham commanded as his face lightened a shade, and Tom experienced a deep sense of long delayed justice as he obliged. 'His name is Francis Covington, and I'm ashamed to say that he's my cousin. But, since you seems to know so much about my life before I went to Nottingham, then you'll know that nothing would make me happier than seeing the bastard on the end of a rope. Or maybe having his head cut off. Or being boiled alive. Or even burned at the stake, like my dad and older brother.'

'Revenge is best served cold, or so they say,' Walsingham replied as he allowed himself the hint of a smile. 'But you may have to wait a little while longer in order to see family justice prevail. I need to know precisely where he lives, in order that I may have his house watched.'

'So that he can bring other priests into the country?' Tom protested, and Walsingham's smile disappeared. 'Leave it to those who best understand these things to decide how to play the game, Constable Lincraft. He clearly cannot be acting alone, and by keeping watch on his house we may note, and follow, those who visit it. One by one we arrest them well after they have left the immediate vicinity, and it will take this Master Covington a considerable time to realise that his game is up. Then he may join the others as playthings for our torturers in the Tower. Now, what of the priest landings?'

It was Giles's turn to speak, and he did so carefully and in suitable tones of respect, since Walsingham was clearly not in the mood for levity, and the matter was too serious anyway.

'The Kittyhawk dropped anchor at the same place on four out of the seven trips we made to France,' he explained. 'On each of them trips we'd stopped in Calais, and fellers was taken on board what had their heads covered with hooded cloaks. Them same fellers was dropped off in the same place by the Thames – some sort of island with trees on it what had a river coming in from the right as you looks at it. There were a rowing boat come off the shoreline each time, and the fellers in the cloaks got into it and was rowed to shore.'

'The same place every time?' Walsingham enquired with a returning smile, and Giles nodded. 'And if you put me in a boat,' he added, 'I reckon I could take you there.'

'Excellent!' Walsingham murmured. 'When are you due to make your next trip?'

'He isn't,' Tom insisted, then explained as Walsingham raised a querulous eyebrow. 'He reckons as how the captain – a feller called Barton – suspects him of something, and I reckon the time's come to pull him out of all this. He's soon to become a father, I might add, and I reckon he's done enough already.'

Walsingham thought deeply before asking Giles 'You believe that this man Barton suspects you of being a spy for the Queen?'

'He suspects me of something, anyway,' Giles confirmed. 'He were asking if I were a deserter from that army I've been pretending to be a soldier in, so I don't think he believes the story I've been feeding him.'

'So if you were arrested for desertion, this would add some credibility to your assumed identity?' Walsingham enquired. 'Yes,' Giles conceded reluctantly, 'but I'm not sure as I want to go back on the Kittyhawk even if it does.'

'Believe me,' Walsingham advised them both, 'if Bradbury is arrested as a deserter he won't be free to rejoin his ship, or anyone else for that matter. He'll be taken to the Tower for execution.' He smiled as he watched the colour drain from both their faces.

'Clearly we would only pretend to arrest him. We would take him to the Tower, then release him after a day or two. But if we make his arrest very public – for example, inside the main room of the Saracen's Head - we could also close it down for harbouring him, which would give the rest of you the plausible excuse to leave there for good.'

'We're not running back to Nottingham and leaving Giles on his own,' Tom protested, and Walsingham nodded. 'Indeed, you are not. You can both be of further service to Her Majesty.'

'How?' Tom enquired. 'And come to that, *where*?'

'As to the "where", I can arrange for you to move into the countryside, but not far from London. Slightly to its west, to a village called Chelsea, where we have access to a house that is currently empty. You simply pretend that you're moving on in search of another commercial venture after your alehouse has been closed down, and you await further orders while enjoying the country air in the meantime. As for you, Constable Bradbury, from the Tower it's an easy journey down river, where you can show us this landing place that you mentioned. Then you may rejoin the others in Chelsea.'

'The women want to go back to Nottingham,' Tom grumbled, to be met with a grim smile from Walsingham. 'And I would much rather be on my estate in Hampshire, but we are all in the service of the Queen, and her interests – as ever - must take preference over our own. Go back to your alehouse and prepare for departure. Bradbury to the Tower, and the rest of you to the house in Chelsea that my messenger will give you directions to when the time is appropriate.'

Even though they had been prepared well in advance for what was to happen, Mary couldn't suppress a squeal of fear when, two days later, the front door of the Saracen's Head was kicked open during the busiest time of the day, and four soldiers armed with swords and pikes, dressed in the red, black and gold uniforms of the Gentlemen Yeomen of the Tower Guard strutted in and demanded 'Giles Bradbury, the filthy deserter.'

Giles made a token gesture of running through to the back room, into which he was chased and dragged back out before being hauled out into the street and thrown into a cart prior to being tied at the wrists and ankles before the wagon moved off, surrounded by the soldiers who marched solemnly alongside it. Once they had passed under London Bridge the wagon driver turned to address Giles. 'Them ropes not too tight, are they?' Assuring him that they were not, Giles lay back on the floor of the wagon and watched the clouds floating by on a stiff westerly wind until his vision was obscured by an archway, and he realised that they were entering the Tower precincts.

Back at the Saracen's Head there were several loafers demanding to know what had just happened, and an apparently shamefaced Tom admitted that his young brother in law had deserted the royal service some time previously, and had sought sanctuary in the alehouse run by his sister and her husband. 'Stupid bugger shouldn't have shown his face out the front here,' one drunk remarked uncaringly, and Lizzie made a big pretence of bursting into tears and calling him a 'rotten arsehole what doesn't deserve to be served in a decent establishment like this.'

Tom had to urgently suppress a snigger when he heard Lizzie using words like that, but so far as they could tell the ruse had been successful, and the callous conversation among the assembled drunks was all about the fate that would be likely to befall the handsome young man who'd put more than one of them in their place during the past few weeks. As for Mary, it was all too much, and even though she knew that Giles would come to no harm she was distressed by the cruelty being expressed by the uncaring and vicious louts who thought nothing of feeling her up as she served their ales, and offering their services as a replacement for Giles in her bed. She retired to the back room and allowed herself a few sobs as she wondered what was really happening to the man in her life, and the father of her unborn child.

She need not have concerned herself. Once unloaded from the wagon outside the well appointed house of the Constable of the Tower, just across the Green, Giles was met by the Constable himself, who shook him warmly by the hand, escorted him into his parlour and invited him to take a seat before the blazing log fire and partake of a mug of mulled claret.

'You come highly spoken of by Master Walsingham,' the Constable advised him, 'and I have instructions to accommodate you in the guest quarters upstairs. They've been occupied in their time by at least two Queens of England, so they should be to your liking. You'll only be here for a few nights anyway, since I expect the Master here in person by the end of the week.'

Two days later, wrapped in a heavy cloak to ward off the steady drizzle, Giles sat in the rear of a large wherry that was being rowed steadily downriver under the command of Walsingham and some grizzled individual clad in heavy leather that instinct told Giles it would not be good to get the wrong side of. After an hour with no sounds other than the muffled splashes of their oars, the raucous clamour of the swooping seagulls seeking a feed as the retreating tide exposed the occasional sandbanks, and the muted sounds of commands being called from the decks of the sailing vessels that were taking advantage of the same ebb tide to drift without sail out towards the open sea, Giles called out.

'That looks like it might be it – over on the left there.'

Walsingham ordered the solitary oarsman to pull towards the shore, and within minutes they were sinking their boots into grainy sand, and looking towards a long copse of trees that seemed to run for the whole width of the beach in front of it. Giles walked further on until he could spy the channel of fresh water that ran into the wider Thames, and he had little remaining doubt.

'Unless there's another piece of land just like this one further down that way,' he announced as he nodded downstream, 'then I reckon this is it.'

The man with Walsingham had been examining the top of the beach where it met the copse of trees, and he nodded. 'He may be right, my lord. There's lots of signs that people's been coming and going across here.'

'And it will suit your purpose?' Walsingham enquired. His companion nodded. 'If you'd care to wait just a few minutes, I'll see what's on the other side of this line of trees, but I'm pretty sure that I can hide a dozen men here every night until the next landing. Then we'll have us some fun and games.'

Not wishing to learn more about the precise nature of those 'fun and games', Giles wandered back down the beach and stood by the boat until the other men returned, and they were then all rowed back upstream. During the return trip, which was against the ebbing tide, and therefore took the heavily puffing oarsman twice as long, Giles was advised that although Walsingham and his companion would be dropped off at Whitehall Steps, the wherry would continue down to Westminster, where Giles would be met by a guide with a spare horse and taken to the house in Chelsea to which the others should already have transferred.

They were barely a day ahead of him, having taken their time to load everything worth taking from their possessions in the Saracen's Head once they had closed the doors at the end of the day's trading on the day after Giles had been taken to the Tower. Posted on the front door was a notice announcing that the premises had been closed on the order of the Lord Chancellor, and they finally left by way of the back yard, which led via a narrow alleyway into Thames Street. They'd been supplied with directions, and as the smoke began to emerge from the chimney on the late afternoon of their second day in the roomy house with the long front garden, Mary glanced out of the window, gave a yell of delight and rushed outside to throw herself at Giles as he wandered wearily up from the gap in the hedge that lined the country road used by travellers heading west out of London.

Supper was hastily prepared, and Giles recounted his adventures since being removed forcibly from their company. 'Walsingham says to wait here until he wants us again,' he advised them, 'but I don't reckon that'll be until they've caught one of them priests and tortured him for the truth about whereabouts in England they're all headed for.'

Lizzie shuddered and complained yet again that 'We'd all be best off back in Nottingham, then at least Mary and Giles could do the decent thing and get themselves married.'

'There's a church of some sort down the road here,' Mary announced as she squeezed Giles even closer. 'I saw the tower when we was coming here. If we're going to be here for a long time, can't we get married there? After all, we doesn't know how long we're going to have to wait for that there Walsington to give you more orders.'

'Walsingham,' Tom corrected her, 'and we needs to make sure that this here church isn't too Popish. We've never talked about religion, Mary, since there's been no need, but . . . . . well . . . '

'Me and Giles has talked about it,' Mary enthused, 'and I thinks the same as him, that them wicked Catholics is just blasphemers. I can't claim to be religious, and I only went to church regular in Sneinton because the law says as how I have to, and if we starts going to the church down the road, then we can soon find out if it's good enough for us to get married in, can't we? After all, the bubby's going to begin to show soon, and I can't let my bodice out any more, so what does you all think?'

There was an awkward silence before Giles slipped from his position next to Mary on the bench, knelt on the rushes, took her hand in his two and enquired 'Mary Cossall, will you marry me?' A tear formed in Mary's eye as she leaned down, kissed Giles's hand and whispered 'About bloody time, Giles Bradbury, since you was the one what put the dumpling in my oven.'

On the first Sunday of their stay they made their way to All Saints Church, just up the road, and although the service that they sat through was far too ornate and 'damnfangled' for Tom's strict and primitive tastes, he was eventually persuaded by Lizzie that they owed it to Mary and Giles to allow God to bless the union that they'd already forged, and avoid the stigma of bastardy for the child that was likely to born in the next few months. It had already quickened, and Lizzie drew on her own experience of two births in order to calculate that they'd have another mouth to feed come the New Year.

As for the mouths that they already had to feed, they'd made what for them was a small fortune from the sale of ale in the Saracen's Head, and taken together with the extra fees that the two men were earning in their clandestine work for Walsingham, they were more comfortably off than any of them could remember. Tom and Giles had never formally agreed how the money was to be divided, but Tom raised the subject tactfully as he sat with Giles two weeks before the planned wedding date, gazing up at the stars twinkling in the clear cold air of a cloudless October evening.

'Have you given any thought to where you're going to live when we gets back to Nottingham?' he enquired, and Giles looked momentarily taken aback by the question.

'I hadn't rightly given much thought to it, to be honest with you. Things has been happening so fast since Walsingham first come to see you, and I certainly didn't expect to be married this soon in my life.'

'You're not having second thoughts, is you?'

'No, course not. I wouldn't have . . . well, you know . . . if I didn't think that Mary were the one for me. But that still don't mean that I've given any thought to where we're going to live. I don't even know how much it costs to build a house – do you mind telling me how much yours cost to build? Or were it already built when you bought it?'

'I built it,' Tom replied with a proud smile. 'I weren't a carpenter for nothing, and when I worked for my uncle I helped to build lots of houses. It's all to do with how you gets the frame up and buried well enough into the ground, see? You starts with stones in the ground, then you puts the big posts in, and joins them together with plugs of other pieces of wood. The secret's in getting the right wood in the first place, then you gets lots of smaller pieces and weaves them in between the uprights. Then you gets a load of mud from the river bank, mixes it with straw, and smears it all over the weave. You'll need longer straw for the roof, so you has to wait until next harvest time for that.'

'Where will I get the land?' Giles enquired, almost totally at a loss to absorb all this detail, and Tom smiled. 'Depends who you wants for neighbours, but there's some spare land along our street, what Robert and Lucy play on when the weather's fine. It belongs to the town at the moment, but I reckon they could be persuaded to sell it to you for ten pounds or so. There'd be lots of garden ground at the back, but that won't be no problem for you, since you used to work on the land, didn't you?'

'Ten pounds is all very well,' Giles reflected, 'but where will I get the wood, how much will it cost, and how much would you charge me for the building?'

'There's plenty of green wood up Arnold way,' Tom advised him, 'and we could borrow the constables' wagon to carry it down into Barker Lane. I reckon you could get all the timber you needed for another ten pounds – maybe less. So that's twenty pounds. We can haul the mud up from Leenside ourselves, and as for the cost of the building, I'll do it for nowt if you do something for me.'

'What's that?'

'Have you seen the state of the land at the back of my house?' Tom smiled. 'Lizzie's forever complaining that we should be using it to grow parsnips and the like, but I doesn't know where to start. You make me a proper garden, and I'll build you a house.'

Giles had been doing the calculations in his head. 'I reckon I could find the first ten pounds already, what with the money I've saved, the money we gets from Walsingham, and the money I got from Barton for all that going to sea. How much do you reckon is due to me from the sales in the Saracen's Head?'

Tom smiled. 'At least another fifteen, so you see – you've already got the money. Once we gets back to Nottingham, and once winter's over, we can get started.'

Giles broke the happy news to Mary, and for the next week they sat and dreamed about what their new house would look like, what sort of furniture it would contain, whether the expected baby would have its own room, and what they'd grow in the garden. They'd almost forgotten their impending wedding until Lizzie reminded Mary that she'd need to wash her best gown, and perhaps let it out a little.

The wedding went off splendidly on a crisp November day that threatened an early snowfall, but mercifully held off. The blushing bride wiped away the tears as they stood on the steps of All Saints Church in Chelsea, and gave her own thanks to God for sending her Giles. Giles, unknown to her, was giving similar thanks to God for the gift of Mary.

Their relative wealth ensured a very comfortable Christmas with roast goose, plum pudding and generous quantities of wine, for which they'd acquired a taste while posing as publicans. The first snow fell a week later, and as Mary gazed happily through their front window into the long front garden in which Robert and Lucy were pelting each other with snowballs, she squinted through the falling flakes at the solitary figure heavily cloaked against the elements, and called out to Tom.

'Who's that coming up our front path? I hope it's not trouble.' Tom looked over her shoulder and gave a soft curse.

'Trouble for somebody, anyway. That's Walsingham. Clear the table of all them breakfast things and throw some more logs on that fire. We've got an important visitor.'

DAVID FIELD

Chapter Six

'First things first,' Walsingham smiled encouragingly as he sat across from Tom and Giles at the empty table, his back to the roaring fire, and handed each man a small velvet bag. 'Your latest payments. You may keep the bags as well, and each of them contains the ten pounds that you are due in the service of Queen Elizabeth.'

'That's twenty pounds now,' Giles whispered gloatingly as he opened his bag and counted the coins, before slipping them into his jacket. Tom was less impressed.

'You didn't just come here to give us our wages, did you?' he demanded suspiciously, and Walsingham's smile remained unbroken as he looked behind him to confirm that they were alone. The women had taken themselves into the kitchen, where they were engaged in baking bread, and Robert and Lucy were still waging a snowball war in clear view through the front window.

'As you correctly surmise,' Walsingham confirmed in response to Tom's question, 'matters have moved on since our last meeting, and we have further need of your services. Bradbury's, anyway.'

'Why not me?' Tom demanded peevishly. 'Giles has done his share, surely, and I'm not one for sitting around.' Walsingham looked into each of their faces in turn.

'Which of you has the greater skill on the land?' he enquired, and Giles was obliged to confirm that it was him. Walsingham nodded, and advised them that 'There's a certain house in Dunmow that has need of a gardener once this foul weather lifts, and the new Spring is upon us.'

Since neither of his audience had an immediate reply, Walsingham persevered.

'We were, thanks to Constable Bradbury's accurate recall of where the priests were being landed, able to capture one of them who has, for several weeks, been our guest in the Tower. His faith may have been strong, but not sufficient to surmount the experienced attentions of certain of our skilled officers in there, and eventually we obtained from him the likely location of a house in Essex to which he was to be escorted once he landed. Someone in France must have been very unguarded when giving him his landing instructions, but he was eventually persuaded to supply us with the name of his intended host, along with further advice that this gentleman has a modest manor house on the outskirts of the village of Dunmow, which is in Essex, to the east of here, and less than two hours' ride from the beach on which he was landed, prior to being intercepted. We made the necessary discreet enquiries, and the information we were given proved to be correct. The manor house is known as "Felfield", and its proprietor is one Sir Henry Felton, the only son of a former candle maker to the late Queen Mary, and a suspected Catholic of the old persuasion. It is, you would agree, highly unlikely that this captured priest, who has spent the past four years in France and was born and raised in Yorkshire, would possess that amount of information unless it were correct?'

'What was that about work on the land?' Giles enquired, and Walsingham was clearly in the mood for expanding on recent successful intelligence work.

'Our enquiries in the village that exists around the manor house revealed that the estate is currently without a head gardener. There are several youths who do the routine labouring work around the shrubberies and hedges, but no-one to direct their work, or to ensure that when the good weather returns the estate will enjoy the magnificent blooms in which Sir Henry takes such a pride.'

'So you want me to apply for the position?' Giles enquired without any obvious enthusiasm, and when Walsingham nodded, Tom objected. 'The poor bugger's only been married a few weeks, and there's a bubby on the way.'

'Even better for his assumed identity,' Walsingham smiled, 'since the Queen's spies are not in the habit of trailing pregnant women around with them.'

'You're suggesting, in all seriousness, that I expose my wife to danger, in her condition?' Giles demanded, slightly red in the face, and Walsingham merely smiled back at him, seemingly unfazed by the objection. 'I merely say that you will be less likely to be suspected of working as a spy for Her Majesty if you have a wife with a child on the way.'

'And what does you propose that I do, while all this is happening?' Tom demanded, and for the first time since his arrival Walsingham looked unsure of himself. 'You might perhaps be best to loiter in the locality, and pass on any important messages to me from Giles.'

'I'm not very good at loitering,' Tom growled. 'I'm more your man of action. And how does you propose that Giles gets information out to me – by sending Mary out with little messages?'

'Mary is your wife? The younger of the two women back there in the kitchen?' Walsingham enquired, and when Giles nodded his confirmation, Walsingham nodded back. 'That would seem to be a good arrangement. If Mary can obtain employment in Felfield House that necessitates her visiting the neighbouring village – for example, by working in the kitchens – then she can get word back to Tom.'

'And what will I be doing in the village, exactly?' Tom demanded, 'Playing the part of the local drunk?'

'A matter for you,' Walsingham replied casually. 'I can't be expected to think of everything.'

'You haven't told me what it is you wants me to find out,' Giles reminded him, and Walsingham transferred his gaze back to Tom.

'Let's see how familiar you've become with this sort of work, given your previous natural talent for solving crimes, Senior Constable. In my position, what information would *you* require from Giles, assuming that he can sell his services as Felton's gardener?' Tom thought only briefly before supplying his answer.

'First of all, I'd like to know whether or not this here manor house that you've learned about really *is* being used as the stopping off place, or whatever you call it, for priests being smuggled into the country.'

'They're known as "secure houses",' Walsingham advised him, 'and you're correct that we need to have it confirmed that this is one of them.'

'Only one?' Giles chipped in. 'Even if we manages to confirm that this here manor house *is* what you call a "secure house", you mean there's more of them?'

'Almost certainly,' Walsingham confirmed without any obvious concern, 'and if you manage to get what we want from this one, then we might send you in search of others.'

'When does we get to go back to Nottingham?' Tom demanded peevishly, and Walsingham's face set slightly as he replied 'When we've got everything useful that we can by means of your efforts. And I remind you that desertion from office is no more approved of in my service than it is in the army.'

'We're stuck like ducks' eggs up hens' arses, aren't we?' Tom conceded sadly, and Walsingham was back to smiling. 'A delightful analogy – also an accurate one, since I don't want you simply to confirm that Felfield Manor is a secure house.'

'What else?' Giles enquired, as depressed as Tom appeared to be.

'We need to know where these priests are being sent, once they've been kept in a secure location for however long it takes. We suspect that they may be travelling north, in order to render their blasphemous services to disaffected nobles who may be plotting against the Crown.'

'You doesn't ask much, does you?' Tom grumbled sarcastically, to be met by a stern stare from Walsingham. 'That's why we pay so well, and the sooner you get on with it, the better spent will be the Queen's money. When you need to get information to me, call at "The Rose" in Hendon and leave word with the landlord that you are engaged in business with "Master Francis". Someone – but not necessarily me – will contact you there.'

'Would you care to stay for dinner?' Lizzie enquired as her face appeared from round the door to the kitchen, but Walsingham shook his head. 'I have an escort waiting out on the London Road, and the less time they loiter there, the less suspicion will be attracted to this neighbourhood. And so I take my leave, gentlemen, until I receive word from Hendon.'

'Who's "Hendon"?' Lizzie enquired, but Tom shook his head sadly. 'You don't need to know, but I'd best see to them locks on the doors and windows, because you're going to be without us to protect you for a while.'

'Are you planning on running off again, and leaving me defenceless, in my condition?' Mary demanded of Giles as she appeared from behind Lizzie in the doorway, provoking a sour laugh from Giles.

'No, you're coming with me, it seems. Just don't blame me, that's all.'

'How did you find out that the Master was in need of a new gardener?' Estate Steward Matthew Prim enquired suspiciously as he looked Giles and Mary up and down where they stood humbly in the kitchen.

'We was in the village, looking for work,' Giles replied in what he hoped was a pathetic voice. 'Me and the wife here – she's due in only a couple of months, and we wasn't wanted any more where we was working in Nottinghamshire, so we've been on the road ever since.'

'You were dismissed from your last positions?' Prim enquired, and Giles nodded. He was ready for the next question, and Mary began to sniffle on cue, just as they had rehearsed.

'Why were you dismissed?'

Giles let his gaze drift shamefacedly down to the floor. 'It were on account of Mary getting in the family way. We wasn't married then, see, although we is now. We done that in Nottingham, before we come away. But that weren't good enough for the Master we worked for. He's a strict Catholic, see, like we'd like to be, except we're not allowed to be these days. Anyway, the fact that we'd – you know –

done what we did before we was married made it a wicked sin, and the Master wouldn't allow us to stay on his estate.'

'You're Catholics, you said?' Prim probed, and Giles and Mary both nodded with apparent reluctance.

'But don't hold that against us, please,' Giles begged him. 'We doesn't make a big noise about it, because we doesn't want to be prosecuted, but we may as well be honest with you, since we're hoping to get work here, and it would be a bad start to tell a lie.'

'Hmm,' Prim responded thoughtfully. 'Your information was correct, as it happens. We are in need of a new gardener, if only to get some useful work out of the idle oafs from the village that we employ as labourers. But until we know if you're any good, it will only be a temporary trial, understood? Your wife can be employed in the scullery, and you'll get all your meals supplied. There's a spare room above the stables that the previous gardener stayed in, so you can move in there straight away. In addition, you'll get three shillings a week between you for the time being. But you'll both need to prove your worth, understood?'

Mary allowed herself to burst into tears, and Giles thanked Prim profusely, assuring him that he wouldn't regret giving them both the opportunity. Then they scuttled back out of the kitchen in search of their new accommodation, embracing and giggling once they were safely inside it, and could cease the pretence.

So far it had gone very well. Tom, Giles and Mary had hired a wagon, mainly for Mary's benefit, from the bag of coins with which Walsingham had supplied them for their upkeep while travelling to Dunmow, to which he had supplied them with directions. Giles and Mary had alighted from the cart at the entrance gate to the Felton estate prior to walking up its long drive and collecting as much dirt on their shoes and clothing as would be consistent with the tale they had rehearsed regarding their sad downturn in fortunes. Tom had carried on into the nearby village on the front of the cart, and had made a big noise about being a travelling carpenter in search of work.

He had earned himself a few nights of free board in the local alehouse by repairing the sagging stable wall to its side, and was standing back, proudly congratulating himself on remembering how to make plugged joints, when he became aware of an older man standing slightly behind him.

'That your work?' the man enquired, and when Tom confirmed that it was the man stepped forward, walked under a main beam joist where it joined the new panel Tom had constructed, and enquired 'Where did you learn to make dovetail joints like that?'

'During my apprenticeship,' Tom replied drily, and the man looked back at him. 'You a carpenter, then?'

'No – a fishmonger,' Tom replied sarcastically, and the man grinned. 'You looking for work?' 'Isn't every carpenter, these days?' Tom replied sadly. 'There's not the money around for fancy houses, like there used to be. More's the pity, but hardly surprising, given that the country's in such a mess.'

'How d'you mean?' the man enquired, and Tom sensed that he had already said enough. 'Nothing, really,' he replied, 'except the big houses seems not to need the likes of me to build on new wings and suchlike. I don't think the nobility and gentry has the money they used to have, and that's why I been travelling these six months or more, looking for the sort of work I used to do back home.'

'And where were that?' was the next question, and Tom opted for a half truth, if only to give his assumed identity some credibility. 'Nottingham, where I were always kept busy on town houses for them new merchants what seems to rule the country these days.'

'So you looking for more work?'

'Didn't I just say so?'

The man looked him up and down carefully and enquired 'Do you know how to do fancy panelling, then?'

'Of course I does,' Tom replied gruffly, tiring of the conversation, 'what carpenter don't?'

'It just so happens that I've got a job coming up where I could use an extra pair of hands,' the man explained. 'In the manor house up the road there,' he added with a nod in the general direction of Felfield. 'My boy's lying in with a bad dose of the sweats, or something like it, and even at his best he can't yet do joints like those you did up there. So if you're interested I can offer you two shillings a day, assuming you to be a journeyman carpenter.'

Tom tried not to let the elation show as he nodded slowly and conceded that 'I haven't got nowt better to do, so why not?'

'I'll pick you up here tomorrow at daybreak,' the man replied. 'My name's Nicholas, by the way. Nicholas Owen.'

'Tom Lincraft,' Tom replied with a smile. 'I'll be waiting here for you tomorrow.'

Giles sighed yet again, and yelled at the two surly youths who were playing with the rose bushes instead of pruning them the way he had tried to demonstrate. 'One big snip, below the old bud growth from last year. How many more bloody times does I have to tell you?'

It was obvious to Giles that either the previous gardener had been very lazy, or he had left many months ago. It was now early March, and this basic pruning task should have been done at the end of the flowering season the previous year. This was consistent with the sadly overgrown state of the herb garden to the side of the kitchen that Giles was devoting more of his time to than the rose bushes at the front, since by this means he was able to keep regular daytime contact with Mary, sweating out her days washing utensils in the scullery. They obviously met up again every evening after work, but Giles had already seen several heavily cloaked figures coming and going from the main house, and was relying on Mary getting a closer look at them. The cloaks might be simply in defence against the cold weather, but they might also be hiding the true identities of those underneath them, and Mary was closer to the tittle-tattle of the kitchens, and might occasionally get an opportunity to venture into the main house to collect dirty dining utensils. If so, she was under strict instruction to look closely at any new visitors to the manor house.

He looked up disinterestedly at the man who stood watching him as he turned over another spadeful of last year's weeds and buried them under the topsoil, where they would serve as a crude fertiliser for the sour earth that had been long neglected. He looked down again, then back up quickly as the man spoke in a low voice.

'They found plenty of work for you, then?' Giles knew the voice like his own, and wasn't fooled by the bonnet pulled low down over the eyes.

'Tom?' he whispered, scarcely able to believe that this meeting was taking place, and fearful of what it might mean.

'The very same,' Tom grinned back from under the brim of the bonnet. 'I'm up here doing some joinery work. Where will I find Mary? Only I don't want her to give me away if she sees me.'

'Not likely,' Giles whispered back, 'unless your work takes you into the scullery. But I'll go in there on the pretence of getting a drink of water, and prepare her.'

Tom walked down into the garden proper, making his actions look like those of someone who was interested in the work Giles was doing, then it was his turn to talk in a low whisper. 'Any sign of visitors?'

'Plenty,' Giles advised him from the corner of his mouth as he continued to turn over the herb bed. 'But they goes almost as fast as they comes, and I don't get a good look at them. Mary's doing her best, but she's not allowed into the main house unless the serving girl needs another pair of hands, and by the time that the meal table's been cleared there's no-one left in the hall except the servants.'

'Looks like I'll need to keep my eyes wide open, then,' Tom replied, just as Nicholas Owen appeared round the side of the house. 'Come on, Tom!' he called. 'We can get a start, now that the master of the house has finished breakfast. No time for loitering in the garden.'

Inside the house, Tom was led by Owen to a back room in which there appeared to be no furniture. It was freezing cold, and the reason for that became apparent when Tom looked into the empty fireplace, as directed by Owen. 'There's no accounting for tastes,' he was advised, 'but Sir Henry wants this old fireplace covered over with a box of some sort. How do you best reckon we should tackle it?'

Tom cast his experienced eye over the empty hole before expressing an opinion. 'Best nail a front piece into the floor, then build the frame onto it. After that we can hammer on the boards, but it won't look very pretty.'

'Seems that Sir Henry wants to hang paintings on it,' he was further advised. 'And that isn't the daftist thing – he wants it to come out three feet from the wall, so we'll have to put sides round it.'

Tom tried in his mind to picture what the finished product would be likely to resemble, and the closest he could come to it was a garden shed standing out from the wall. But why hang paintings from the side of a garden shed, when the room could only be used in order to admire those paintings during the summer months, given that they were about to cover over the only fireplace?

He set to work measuring the width of the existing fireplace using a piece of off-cut timber from the wagon they'd travelled in at first light. He and Owen agreed that it was about the right length, and Tom then cut two additional lengths that would constitute the bases for the sides. This task took him close to the existing fireplace, and as he glanced casually towards it, something caught his eye. A ring of some sort set into the inside of the chimney flue.

On a whim he looked to the other side, where an identical ring had been set into the brickwork at the same height as the first. Then he stuck his head inside the chimney breast and looked up. He couldn't quite make out any daylight above, but there was still enough light to confirm his suspicion; there were other rings set into either side of the flue in a line going up, making a ladder of some sort for anyone prepared to open their legs a few feet. By the time that a person reached the fourth line of rings, their feet would be hidden from sight.

That was not his only exciting discovery that day. He and Owen were also commissioned to panel in the area under the foot of the main staircase, and in order to have more working room they were obliged to move several boxes that had been lying under the stairs. They were covered by damask tablecloths, but Tom waited until Owen had gone back out to their cart, then he carefully lifted the cloth covering one of the boxes. Inside were altar candles, a chalice and what looked like altar cloths. All that needed to be added were the wine and wafers, and you had all that was required for a Mass. All except the priest, and the idea had already come to Tom's mind that perhaps the priest might be accommodated up the chimney once the fireplace had been covered over.

Making the excuse that he needed to wash his hands, Tom was directed to the scullery, where he could see Mary bent over a sink, her back to him as she scrubbed hard at a bowl that had no doubt been used for dinner. Whispering that she shouldn't turn round, but simply nod if she could hear him, Tom poured water from the pitcher into a hand basin, which he placed on the flat surface to the side of the sink and whispered again.

'They're definitely receiving priests in this place, and planning to hide them up the chimney if anyone comes calling. Tell Giles to make ready to follow one of them. The sooner the better. You'll find me at the village inn if you needs me.'

Mary nodded, and whispered back 'God help us if we gets caught.'

Chapter Seven

If Tom had expected an excited reaction when he arrived at The Rose in Hendon's only street and announced that he was there on business to meet 'Master Francis', then he would have to swallow the disappointment. A seemingly disinterested proprietor replied somewhat listlessly that he would make Tom's arrival known, and continued serving the handful of customers who were lounging around his taproom. Tom wasn't sure if he imagined the sudden departure of the other man who had appeared to be serving from behind the counter, but once he reached his allocated room and opened the door his doubts were resolved. The same man was standing in front of the mullioned window that looked out over the stable yard, and he smiled at Tom's expression of surprise.

'What did you expect – tabors and horns lined up outside to welcome your arrival? Give me your message, then take time to rest. I'll be back by daybreak tomorrow, so make sure you come down for breakfast, if dinner in this shithole hasn't killed you already. For myself, I'll be glad to get a decent meal for once in Whitehall.'

'Tell our friend to move immediately on the house in Dunmow,' Tom advised him, hoping that he was not being deceived. 'The men he's seeking are being hidden in there.'

With that the man nodded and took his departure. Tom spent an afternoon lying on the threadbare pallet, resting his aching thighs and reminding himself to keep horse-riding to a minimum while wondering how Giles was faring, and whether, by the time that Walsingham's men invaded the Dunmow house, he would be trailing the latest priest to leave. After the implied warning regarding the likely quality of any meal served in his resting place he opted to lose some of his expanding waistline and to catch up on some sleep, but the next morning, as a distant cockerel somewhere not far away advertised to his hens that he was open for business, Tom walked downstairs, well prepared to assuage his hunger on whatever swill might be served up.

The bread and cheese that was placed down in front of him was served by the same man who had been in his room the previous day, and who advised him in muted tones that were probably not necessary, given that there were no others taking such an early breakfast, that 'Our friend has the information, and will be riding north in a few days, when his other business permits. He wishes you to be at the house when he arrives with a company of men.'

Tom nodded his understanding, and gave orders for his horse to be made ready, as he grimaced at the thought of another day that would end with aching thighs.

Giles looked up from the channel that he was attempting to create in unyielding earth that still retained the stubborn frost of the retreating winter, to see a tall young man, spare of frame and with little obvious hair, watching his efforts. He smiled encouragingly, and the man smiled back.

'What do you plan on planting?' the man enquired, and Giles was ready with an answer. 'Beans, probably, which is why I'm opening the ground for the seed planting once the warmer weather arrives. It's still cold and hard from winter, and I needs a fine tilth before I can plant any seed.'

'I find that a deep early mulch helps,' the man replied, betraying both his education and his knowledge of soil management. 'Perhaps some of that rotted weed that you placed in that pile to the side there?'

'You're a gardener yourself?' Giles enquired, and the man nodded. 'My name's Ralph.'

'I'm Giles. Why are you here, or is the Master not happy with what I been doing?'

'Just interested,' Ralph replied guardedly. 'It used to be my main activity.' He paused, as if in acknowledgement that he'd said too much already, and changed the subject. 'Those rose bushes out at the front certainly got a heavy pruning, didn't they?'

'The only way,' Giles replied. 'They say as how you should get your worst enemy to prune your roses, and them lazy lads from the village was going at it like they was cutting their Dad's hair until I told them to go deeper down the stems.'

'I must be going now,' Ralph replied after a further moment of hesitation. 'It was nice to have this little talk.'

'You can come and talk to me about gardens whenever you likes,' Giles replied invitingly, but Ralph shook his head. 'I have to be leaving soon. I was only staying here for a brief while.'

'Where are you from?' Giles enquired, suddenly intrigued, but Ralph shook his head. 'Nowhere in particular, these days. Good luck with the beans.'

He wandered off towards the house, and Giles became more alert when he noticed how the man tucked his hands crosswise in the sleeves of his cloak as he walked. It could simply be a means of keeping them warm, but the only men that Giles had ever seen adopting that habit had been monks and friars, although that was some years in the past now.

Young Ralph must be one of those priests brought in from France, Giles reasoned as his conscience stabbed at him. Tom had left word with Mary that Giles was to lose no time in following a priest to his intended destination, and so far he'd done nothing to that end. Life was too comfortable living with Mary in the room above the stable, and the weather had hardly been welcoming. But soon he'd have to stop being a gardener and go back to being a Queen's Constable. After all, that was what he was being paid for.

His opportunity arose within hours. He was washing his hands in the water butt at the side of the stables when he overheard the Steward giving orders to the young stable groom who he always enjoyed bullying.

'Off your backside and give all the horses the good rub down that you should have given them before you had the cheek to come up to the kitchen for your dinner,' the Steward instructed him in his usual harsh tone. 'And if they're not gleaming by nightfall, you'll get one of these horsewhips across your back - understood?'

Giles was unable to catch what the fearful young lad had to say by way of reply, but his ear caught the next angry response from the Steward. 'None of your pathetic excuses, you useless wretch! If those horses aren't fit to travel to Cambridge by nightfall, you'll be back to begging in the streets. See to it!'

This was his long awaited opportunity, Giles concluded with a shiver of anticipation as he bent his head over the butt in a pretence of washing his face while the Steward strode past him with the complaint that 'Those rose bushes look as if they'd been on a battlefield.' Giles bit back the angry retort that came to his mind, and hastened upstairs, where Mary was resting flat on her back, the prominent swelling in her belly pointing at the ceiling as he began to explain that he would have to leave her once it got dark.

'Where to?' she enquired as her face betrayed impending tears, 'and for how long?'

'No idea how long,' Giles replied as he reached down for her hand and kissed it, 'but only as far as Cambridge. That's just up the road from here, isn't it?'

'No idea,' Mary admitted, 'but make sure that you keeps out of danger, that you eats plenty before you sets off, and that you gets back here before the bubby's due.'

'You haven't felt it coming, have you?' Giles demanded in alarm, and Mary shrugged. 'Who knows? I keeps getting these funny feelings inside, and I hope as how it's only the bubby moving around. But since this is my first I doesn't know, does I?'

'Make sure that *you* eat proper while I'm away,' Giles instructed her. 'When I'm gone, just tell whoever wants to know that I've gone into the village to look for a midwife to come and look at you. If Tom managed to get that message to Walsingham, his men should be here in a day or two anyway, and they can set off behind me.'

'How can you follow fellers on horses, anyway?' Mary enquired. 'Are you going to try and run behind them, or what?'

'Don't be silly,' Giles smiled as he leaned forward and kissed her playfully on the nose. 'I'll take one of the spare horses from the stable down below.'

'Won't they miss it?'

'I doubt it. But even if they do, it'll be too late to warn the ones who've already left, won't it?'

Mary shuddered. 'I've got a bad feeling about this,' she complained, but Giles ignored her as he looked out his spare clothes, and shook out his cloak, ready for travel. They both went to the kitchen for their supper, but while Giles followed Mary's advice and took two hearty helpings of bread and potage, Mary merely picked away absent-mindedly at a single slice of manchet loaf.

After they'd retired for the night Giles kept his ears wide open as he heard the gentle heavy breathing from Mary at his side. His patience was rewarded when he heard the unmistakable sound of horses being saddled and led out into the courtyard, and he slipped from the pallet and looked down carefully through the narrow window. Seven horses were snorting and pawing with impatience, but all their riders were heavily cloaked as they swung into the saddles, wheeled the horses' heads and set off towards the drive that led to the road. After counting to sixty, Giles turned back, hurriedly donned his cloak and leaned down to give Mary a goodbye kiss. She murmured softly in her slumber, and Giles tiptoed down the perilous wooden steps that led him outside, then ducked into the stables, saddled one of the remaining horses and set off at a fast trot after the departing party. As he did so, the stable boy raised himself from the straw that constituted his bedding, scratched his head to see the gardener departing in the dead of night, then fell back into the slumber that had already been disturbed twice.

Mary awoke to find Giles missing, and instinctively looked to where he normally draped his cloak over the only available chair. It was gone, and she realised with sadness and some concern that Giles had embarked upon what to her seemed like his foolish plan to follow priests out of Dunmow to some unknown destination in Cambridge. She eased herself off the bed, made use of the pisspot in the corner, then wandered off downstairs to wash the first dishes of the day once they came in from the breakfast table. She barely raised her head at the commotion in the kitchen, since it was fairly normal, given the cook's short temper. However, this time one of the voices was the familiar one of the Steward, and she felt the first frisson of fear as he stormed into her scullery and brought his face within inches of hers as he demanded to know 'Why has your man stolen a horse?'

'Beg pardon?' she replied as she began to tremble, but the Steward was in no mood for guessing games.

'Your man – where is he?'

'No idea,' Mary replied truthfully, 'although he did say as how he was going to ask in the village about a midwife. I been feeling the baby move, you see . . . '

'A pox on your baby!' the Steward bellowed in her face. 'The stable groom reports that your man stole a horse during the night. There's no midwife in the village anyway, but why would he be seeking one during the hours of darkness – you're not about to give birth, are you?'

'No,' Mary conceded in a small voice constricted by her sudden apprehension. 'But that's what he said, anyway.'

'Come with me!' the Steward ordered her, and all but dragged her by the arm into the Morning Room, in which Sir Henry Felton was talking with another man. 'Stand there and don't move!' the Steward commanded as he turned to address Sir Henry.

'Sorry to interrupt, Master, but that new gardener stole a horse during the night, and his woman here can't give a satisfactory explanation for his actions. I can only apologise if I made a serious error of judgment when taking on the pair of them, but I was unwise enough to believe their lies when they assured me that they were in search of work after being sent away from their former positions somewhere in Nottingham.'

'Nottingham?' the man with Sir Henry echoed. 'That's probably more than a coincidence, I think. The man Tom who was working with me on your new panels said *he* came from Nottingham. He's been missing for several days now, and it looks as if all three of them may have been in it together. It may not only be a horse that was stolen, Sir Henry. Perhaps you should look to your silverware as well.'

'Do that,' Sir Henry instructed the Steward, 'and while you're about it, send two of the footmen in to guard this wretched woman while we decide what's to be done with her, pending the arrival of the Constable. Master Owen, this man to whom you refer, who was helping you with the new panelling in the house here – where was he residing?'

'The village alehouse, sir,' Nicholas Owen advised him. 'I had no reason to doubt that he had once been a carpenter, since his work was very skilled, and . . . . '

'Yes, yes,' Felton replied testily, 'no-one's blaming you, so set your mind at ease for the moment. I want you to go back to the village and see if there's still any sign of this so-called carpenter. If you find him, bring him back here on some pretext, and I'll deal with him along with this whore who's obviously one of his accomplices.'

'I'm no whore!' Mary protested without thinking, then howled with outrage as Felton slapped her across the face. 'I'll be the judge of your character,' he sneered, adding 'I begin to suspect that the three of you were involved in something deeper than the mere theft of a horse.' He then called for two footmen to take her away 'and store her for later where our former guests would have been hidden from view had we needed to do so.'

Mary was bundled out of the room, squirming and protesting that this was no way to mishandle a woman who was in the final few weeks before her lying in. Once out of the room she was blindfolded and led forward to a colder spot where she heard a strange collection of sounds. She was ordered to remain silent and not to move, then after a few moments she was further manhandled into what felt like a confined space. She was told that she might sit down, and as she was lowered into a sitting position she heard more strange sounds, followed by the unmistakable echoing of footsteps on a bare wooden floor as they retreated into the distance. She called out for someone to remove the blindfold, but all around her was silence. Silence, coldness and the uneasy feeling that wherever she was, she was about to be left to die alone.

At least they had not tied her hands, and she removed the blindfold, only to find that there was almost no light, that her prison appeared to be constructed of wood, and that there was a dark aperture of some sort above her head, from which came an unnerving fluttering sound that chilled her even further.

Back in the drawing room, Owen was receiving his final instructions from Felton, and the two footmen who had locked Mary safely away in another room were being detailed to accompany him to the neighbouring village. 'It's a pity that the armed men have gone as an escort to Cambridge,' Felton advised him, 'but the three of you should be enough to overpower a mere carpenter. Assuming that he's still there of course, and hasn't fled the coop with his companion in crime, leaving the little baggage to face the consequences all on her own, and her in that condition. Don't bother involving the local Constable at this stage.'

After his return to Dunmow Village following his brief trip to Hendon, Tom was debating within himself whether or not to seek out Nicholas Owen and request more work in order to have an excuse to visit Felfield Manor again, unaware that Giles had taken off in pursuit of the group destined for Cambridge, and that Mary had been imprisoned within the house itself. Then he looked up with a smile from where he sat at the table in front of the alehouse as the question in his mind seemed to answer itself and he saw Owen walking towards him, accompanied by two other men who didn't appear to be dressed for outside labouring.

'Sorry I've been missing for a couple of days,' Tom smiled at Owen, 'but there were some business down south what needed my attention. Does you want me back up at the house?'

'We most certainly do,' Owen replied as he gestured with his head to the two men slightly behind him armed with cudgels, who walked round to stand behind Tom at the side of the table. 'And these two have accompanied me to make sure that you don't decline the invitation. Your dishonest scheme has come undone, and you're to be taken in charge.'

'Don't know what you're talking about,' Tom insisted, 'but if you reckon I done something wrong, then you'd best call in the local Constable.'

'That won't be necessary,' he was assured by Owen, 'since we intend to deal with this ourselves, up at the house. Start walking.'

Tom quickly thought through his options as they walked up the long drive, Tom in the lead with the two house servants behind him brandishing their cudgels threateningly every time he turned round. He might be able to overpower the two armed men, and perhaps Owen at the same time, but then what? He'd still have to approach the house in order to find out if Giles had gone after suspected priests, and he needed to reassure himself that they hadn't hurt Mary or the baby she was expecting. Best to wait until Walsingham turned up with reinforcements, and for the time being at least it suited Tom's requirements to go along with being a prisoner. He might even succeed in bluffing his way through it all by clinging to his pretence of being a carpenter fallen on hard times.

As they approached the main building, Tom looked in vain for any sign of Mary. What he could see was the face of Sir Henry Felton, red with anger, as he glared at him from the entrance doorway. Sir Henry didn't bother to wait until they'd reached the door, but bellowed down the driveway.

'Never mind any more pretence – who are you, and who sent you?'

'Don't know what you're talking about,' Tom insisted. 'I'm just a carpenter – didn't you like the work what I done on your new panels?'

'You come from the same place as the man who stole my horse, and his woman who was working in my scullery. The three of you were clearly in league with each other, and I want to know what for!'

'I don't know who told you all that shit,' Tom replied defiantly, 'but it's a lie.'

'Really?' Felton demanded, then looked over his shoulder at the two men with cudgels.

'Take him into the back room and confront him with that woman we confined in there. If she shows any sign of recognising him, kill the pair of them!'

Tom was obliged to think quickly again. From what he had just been advised, it seemed that Giles had somehow escaped, and was perhaps chasing after priests on their way to their allocated positions in English Catholic houses. Why else would he have stolen a horse? And Felton obviously had Mary held captive in some place – probably inside the false cabinet that Tom had helped to build in front of the old fireplace – and if she, in her innocence, betrayed the fact that she knew him when they were brought face to face, then they were both likely to be killed because of what they knew.

Somehow or other he had to avoid that confrontation, and buy time before Walsingham got here with his soldiers, hopefully tomorrow or the day after. So when he was led into the back room he began to struggle with the two men who were holding him, one arm each. As he had hoped, he sensed the movement of an arm behind him, and heard the swish of the cudgel as it was brought down onto the back of his head. Then it all went black.

When he came round, it was to the sensation of almost total darkness and a pounding in his skull. But at least he was still alive, and he was not the only one, to judge by the rustling noises close by as he felt a soft hand on his forehead in response to his groans.

'Tom? Is that really you, and are you still alive? Thank God!'

'Sh!' he urged her, then continued in a hoarse whisper. 'They may be listening outside, trying to find out whether or not we knows each other.'

'Outside where?' Mary whispered back. 'Where in Hell are we?'

'A false cupboard in front of the old fireplace,' Tom whispered back. 'If it can open to let in a priest what needs to be hidden, then I reckon as how it can be opened from inside here as well, somehow or other. But it's too dark in here for me to find out how, so we got to keep quiet until we knows that there's nobody in the room out there.'

'I keep hearing these horrible scrabbling noises from somewhere above our heads,' Mary complained hoarsely, and Tom was quick to reassure her. 'It's only birds, nesting in the chimney breast.' Then he remembered something else, and smiled in the darkness as an idea came to him.

Chapter Eight

Giles sat by the side of the stream, allowing the horse to drink its fill, and thanking God for the fact that the one he'd stolen at random, and in the dark, had proved to be a good one. No doubt the best had been taken by those he'd been following, but Sir Henry obviously kept a good stable, and this chestnut gelding certainly had certainly demonstrated its stamina for two days or more, although Giles was fearful that it might be tiring with Cambridge still ten miles ahead of him, to judge by the milestone he'd passed shortly before ducking down below road level to the side of the water.

The party he was following was somewhere behind him, and he dared not venture any further in case he had already passed the house to which they were heading. He'd overtaken them at the end of the first day spent following their dust cloud a safe half mile to the rear, when they'd stopped off at a local inn at a place called Linton. Giles's first instinct had been to pull on the reins and take cover under some overhanging trees, but then inspiration had kicked in.

If they were heading for Cambridge, and given that there appeared to be only one road, then he would be less likely to alert suspicion if he rode ahead of them and waited for them to pass him again. His only immediate concern had been whether or not the horse was up to another day of riding, but once past the inn in which those he was following would no doubt stop for at least an hour or two, if only to eat, he'd taken the road ahead at a slower pace, allowing his mount to take water, and graze on the grass at the side of the road, whenever the opportunity arose. His earlier life on the land had given him a basic understanding of horses and how to handle them, and hopefully he hadn't been asking too much of this one, which in his mind he'd christened 'Chester'.

The thought of food had set his stomach rumbling again, and he was glad that he had taken Mary's sound advice and eaten a good supper two evenings ago. Even so, he would have welcomed the opportunity to stop and buy a meal at one of the several inns along his route, had he possessed any money. Hopefully he could think of some suitable role to adopt when the party from Dunmow reached their destination, and in that role he could prevail upon some kitchen wench to sneak him a loaf of bread or a bowl of potage.

He smiled as he remembered the days when he could acquire almost anything his heart desired from a comely wench, simply by turning on the charm with which Dame Fortune had equipped him. Inevitably his thoughts drifted to the one he had most recently charmed, then fallen in love with; the one who was carrying his child, and for whom he offered a silent prayer as he tried to imagine the reaction to his departure from Dunmow in suspicious circumstances.

Subconsciously he became aware of the soft rumble of an approaching body of horsemen, and he flattened himself into the grass and looked up towards the road above him. There were seven of them, just like the party he had set off in pursuit of, and so far as he could tell they were the same ones, although he'd only seen them from half a mile to the rear, and for much of the time in poor light. But he'd need to take a gamble, and Chester appeared to have eaten and drunk enough, so after a decent interval he led him back onto the road and looked north, where the party that had passed him was still just visible. He quickened the pace slightly in order to gain a little ground on them, then sat back at the same slightly slower trot until he saw them swing into a gateway to the left up ahead. They had just passed a crossroads with a signpost of sorts that announced the existence of a village named 'Cherry Hinton' half a mile to the north. Time to dismount again, and decide how to handle this next stage in his mission, which involved gaining entry to this new house by some form of subterfuge.

He sat by the side of the road deep in thought. He was tired of pretending to be a gardener, and wished he were a Constable again. Then he chuckled as he remembered how, in his former life, he'd arrested men for doing precisely what he'd done back in Dunmow when he stole a horse. The chuckle died in his throat as the answer came to him – he could pretend to be a Constable in pursuit of a horse thief!

Head held high he cantered the weary horse up the main drive and dismounted, throwing the reins to a stable groom who scurried out to meet him. 'Where will I find your master?' he demanded, and the youth nodded towards the house. 'In the Main Hall, sir, where he just received a party of guests – are you one of them, arriving late?'

'Not exactly,' Giles replied as he headed for the front door, and instructed the menial standing just inside it that he required an audience with the Steward without delay. The man in question met him in the hallway and demanded to know his business.

'I'm Constable Giles Bradbury, and I'm in pursuit of a man who stole a horse further south of here. Has anyone of that description been seen in this vicinity?' Giles asked in what he hoped was 'proper'

English. 'I've no idea,' the Steward replied with a puzzled expression, 'but a party arrived from down south less than an hour ago. They're in the Main Hall with the Master – do you wish me to announce your arrival?'

'If you'd be so good,' Giles smiled, and less than a minute later he was introducing himself, announcing his business, and enquiring as to the identity of his host. A florid faced man in expensive looking attire answered his question with a haughty sneer.

'I'm Sir Humphrey Audley, and this is my estate of Cherry Hinton. These gentlemen are my guests, and I can assure you that none of them is a horse thief.'

'And I can assure your lordship that this man is no Constable,' one of the group announced as he stepped forward. A thin young man with little hair, but a familiar face. 'The last time I saw this so-called Constable he was posing as a gardener in Dunmow. He must have followed us up here, and I suspect that he's a spy sent by Queen Elizabeth.'

'Seize him!' Audley commanded, and two of the men who had presumably just arrived stepped forward and grabbed Giles's two arms in a firm grip. With a sinking feeling in the pit of his stomach, Giles recognised the man who'd just denounced him as the one he'd chatted idly with in the garden at Dunmow, and attempted to bluff it out.

'You must be the man I'm after,' Giles announced with all the air of authority he could summon up. Audley stepped forward with a curse and struck Giles hard across the face with a hand hardened by many years gripping a sword and a bridle.

'That man is no horse thief, you scum! He's an ordained priest of the Church of Rome!' He seemed to realise what he had just divulged, and nodded to the two men holding Giles firmly by the arms.

'Take him out and hang him!'

Tom stretched both hands upwards into the darkness and located the second pair of metal rungs set into the chimney breast. Then he carefully located each of his boots firmly on the lowest pair of rungs and pulled himself up. Satisfied that he could maintain his balance in this way, and that the rungs would support his weight, he reached up for the next set of rungs and pulled himself up onto the next level. There was a flurried twittering sound from somewhere above him, as nesting birds took off and showered his head with soot. The chimney had obviously not been used for some time, but had once known blazing logs, to judge by the amount of choking black powder that now covered his head and his clothes. He coughed as some of it landed on his nose and mouth, and there was an anxious call from Mary a few feet below him.

'You all right?' 'Yes!' he whispered hoarsely, 'but keep silent, for both our sakes!'

He continued the climb, inch by hesitant inch, and on the fifth rung he risked another face full of soot by looking upwards. There was light of a sort up there, but not very much, bearing in mind how bright the day had been when he had been escorted back to the house. If the chimney top was decorated with all those fancy turret chimneys, he might not be able to break through, but he would never know if he didn't keep climbing. Then when he reached up for the seventh rung, his hand met nothing. Frantically he waved his hand in a wide circle, but to no avail – he had come to the end of the rungs. This made sense, since the rungs had only ever been intended to allow a priest to hide in the chimney, not to scale it to the roof, but it meant the end of Tom's escape bid unless he could find a substitute for the rungs.

He suddenly felt insecure with only his feet planted on rungs, and his arms hanging by his side, so he reached out carefully and discovered to his relief that the sides of the chimney breast were now narrow enough for him to maintain his balance simply by pressing outwards against them. Another inspired idea came to him, and he reached upwards with his left hand to discover that the inner core of the chimney had been so roughly laid by the masons who had constructed it, no doubt working for a miserly fee and with poor materials, that there was an outcrop of rough stone some two feet up to his left. When he discovered an equivalent one off to his right he decided to take the risk of plummeting ten feet down into the fireplace if he was wrong, and placed, first his left boot, and then the right one, on the outcrops and pushed upwards with a heartfelt prayer. Mercifully, both his hands encountered further outcrops.

Wreathed in the sort of sweat that only fear can generate, he inched his way another ten feet or so up the inside of the chimney by the same means, until his broad shoulders were almost touching both sides as the channel narrowed. Then his head brushed up against something soft and prickly, and instinctively he let go of the latest outcrop to his left and punched upwards. There was a series of outraged squawks and a cascade of something light and sticky, then suddenly he was bathed in bright daylight as the remains of the destroyed birds' nest, complete with its now broken eggs, tumbled down over his shoulders and fell towards the fireplace.

Elated, he pulled himself free of the top of the chimney by reaching upwards and pressing down on its narrow circular top. Mentally noting that he was fortunate not to be a larger man, he squinted hard against the bright daylight that had previously been obscured by the birds' nest, and enjoyed the sudden onset of a fresh breeze and warm light on his face. Then he looked around carefully in all directions until his gaze fell finally on the front drive, and he couldn't resist a gruff cheer that turned into a cough as he expelled the last of the soot from his besieged lungs.

A large group of horsemen was pounding up the drive towards the house, and the one in the lead was carrying a royal banner.

Giles lay on the rear lawn of the country estate that he had foolishly entered without any thought that one of those he had followed would be able to recognise him. He rolled over and retched as another kick rattled his ribcage, and waited resignedly for the next one to land. Instead he heard a commanding shout from somewhere behind him.

'Don't kick him to death, you oafs! I said he was to hang – but before you do that, bring him indoors and let's see what he can tell us about who sent him.'

Giles groaned inwardly at the prospect of finally learning how well he could withstand torture. He'd heard enough about it from the horrible tales brought into Nottingham by those tradesmen with their origins in London, some of whom had in turn heard tales of what went on in the Tower of that town, in which Giles had briefly been a mere guest during the pretence of his arrest for desertion what now seemed like a lifetime ago. He'd heard about the 'rack', the 'thumbscrews', the hot irons, and the knotted string in the eyeballs, all of which were allegedly employed to extract information from the more reluctant of the Tower's inmates, and he'd often wondered, in idle moments, how long he could resist telling the torturer what he wanted to know, whether it was the truth or not. Now, it seemed, he was destined to find out.

His two days as a guest of the Constable of the Tower had been before he married Mary, he recalled, and tried to decide in his own mind whether it was better for him to die a brave man who refused to betray his colleagues, leaving behind an unborn child who would grow up with no memory of the hero of whom many tales were recounted by its heartbroken mother, or to tell them what they wanted to know and live to hold the next generation of Bradburys in his arms.

Then, as he was being carried back indoors, the thought occurred to him that there might be a third alternative. His captors didn't know what he knew, which was why they were no doubt seeking to learn of it by dint of fear and physical agony. So whatever he told them, if he put on a sufficiently convincing show of being mortally terrified, they would perhaps believe. All he had to do was invent a suitable story that sounded believable, but did not involve Walsingham, Tom, or the fact that Queen Elizabeth was on the hunt for Catholic priests.

His inventive brain was working at high speed as they dumped him on the bare floor in the back room, where an indifferent fire was being pumped into renewed life by means of a bellows. He was rolled over so that he could witness the actions of the grinning henchman as he thrust a long thin brand of wood into the flames, held it there for a minute, then withdrew it to display the glowing redness at its tip.

'Hot enough for our purpose,' the man leered at his companions. 'Now lower his hose.'

Walsingham looked up towards the roof when he heard the familiar voice shouting down at him, then issued his instructions to the ten or so men who had ridden in with him.

'Enter the house, secure everyone inside it and herd them into the same room. I'll join you in just a few moments.'

The armed men ran inside, and Walsingham dismounted and grinned up at Tom. 'They have strange birds on this estate, it would seem,' he shouted, to a cursing rejoinder by Tom. The two men stared at each other for a moment before Walsingham broke the silence.

'Well, don't just stay up there playing games on the roof, man. Get down here and join me.'

'I would, if I knew how!' Tom yelled back as he looked fearfully down at the roof tiles that sloped away alarmingly to the edge of a twenty foot drop onto the roughcast driveway. 'I got up through the chimney, but I'll be buggered if I intends to go back down the same way.'

Walsingham looked towards the stables, outside which was a cart containing fresh straw bales intended for bedding. A few minutes later he'd ordered the terrified stable groom, at sword point, to manhandle the cart under the eaves of the house, then he yelled up at Tom.

'If you can make it down that slope of roof tiles without breaking your neck, here's a soft landing. Now get on with it, since I have more important business inside!'

Advising himself with curses that he was finished with chimneys and roofs for the rest of his life – if he lived – Tom lowered himself onto the tile ridge, then attempted to slide in a measured fashion down the tiled slope. It proved slippier than he had calculated, and it was undoubtedly a miracle that when he reached the bottom edge and flew into open space with a terrified shriek, it was immediately above the straw cart, into which he bounced with nothing worse than a jarred spine and a punctured dignity. Satisfied that he was still alive, Walsingham ordered Tom to follow him into the house.

There were a dozen or so estate servants gathered in the Main Hall, under the pretended authority of a very frightened Steward. Footmen mingled with maids, and the cook was surrounded by menials from the kitchen, all under the stern supervision of half a dozen armed men, as Walsingham strode into the room with Tom limping slightly behind him.

'Where are Giles and his woman?' Walsingham demanded, 'and are there any priests left here?'

'A long story,' Tom advised him. 'Giles must have headed off somewhere after priests who had been hidden here, as I instructed him to do, but I don't know where to. As for the rest of your question, come with me.'

Tom led the way into the back room from which he had only recently escaped via the chimney, and pointed to the wooden frame around the former fireplace. 'That's where they hides the priests if anyone comes calling, and there's another hiding place under the stairs. As for Mary Bradbury, you'll find her inside there,' he added as he nodded towards the covered fireplace.

'If that's Tom Lincraft, I'm in here right enough, so shift your arse and get me out!' came a woman's voice, to which Tom replied 'Watch your language – I've got Walsingham with me. You're lucky he didn't bring the Queen as well!'

'How do we get in there?' Walsingham enquired as he stared at what, to all intents and purposes, was a panelled outcrop of the main wall. Tom grinned as he replied 'I been wondering about that myself, but I reckon as how there must be some sort of catch at the side of one of the panels. There wasn't when I left off putting it up, but they must have added that while I were down in Hendon'

'Well hurry up and find out,' Walsingham instructed him, and Tom limped to the covered fireplace and began exploring with his fingers between the panels and the frames that supported it. There was a click, and a shout of triumph from Tom as he slid back the panel to reveal Mary on her knees, deathly white in the face and looking down at a pool of liquid that was soaking the hem of her gown.

'About bloody time, Tom Lincraft,' she snorted. 'And if it's all the same to you, you can assure me that you knows all about delivering babies, because unless I'm very much mistaken there's one on its way.'

Chapter Nine

Walsingham strode into the main room in which the household of Sir Henry Felton had been gathered, and demanded their complete attention.

'You are all under arrest on suspicion of treason against Her Majesty!' he announced, before allowing the collective gasps and wails to subside. Then he continued. 'However, there may be an opportunity for at least one of you women to work towards your freedom. Does any one of you have any experience of childbirth?'

In the silence that followed it was the cook who seized her chance. 'I reckon I could say that,' she shouted back, 'since I've had four of my own. And I helped to deliver two of my sister's.'

'Very well,' Walsingham announced after a nod of agreement from Tom, 'take two of your best women into that room at the back with the covered over fireplace, and assist the lady you'll find in there upstairs to the Master's former bedchamber. He won't be needing it, since his new abode will be in the Tower. Once you have her up there, see to it that she has the best assistance of which you're capable. If she and her baby survive, you may well have earned your freedom. Now set about it without delay!'

Calling on one girl to begin boiling some water, and another to tear up some bed linen into strips, the cook bustled out into the back room and assisted Mary to her feet, sniffing at the drying moisture on the floor. 'That's your waters, right enough,' she tutted. 'Can you walk, my dear?'

Mary assured her that she could, trying not to giggle at the kind concern for her welfare that she was receiving from the old witch who had previously only ever yelled orders at her. As she wobbled rather unsteadily out of the room, she was met by Tom and Walsingham, who first enquired after her health before Walsingham asked 'Do you happen to know where Giles went?' Mary nodded.

'He went after some priests what had been staying here. To a place called "Cambridge", I think. Would that be right?'

Walsingham nodded. 'I believe it may be, and thank you. God be with you during your lying in.'

'You're welcome,' Mary replied with a grim smile as she was led away, and Tom looked enquiringly at Walsingham. 'Cambridge is a big place, isn't it?'

'Yes, but it has only a few staunch Catholics well established enough to risk involvement in the smuggling in of priests. And one in particular. I'll have to hazard everything on my belief that he may be the one to whose estate Giles has ridden, but if I'm wrong then there are others we can visit.'

'We?' Tom echoed. 'Can't I stay here and look after Mary?' Walsingham shook his head vigorously. 'What do *you* know about childbirth, compared with what you appear to know about where priests may be hidden? You'll be riding with us, but first I need to send ahead, in case Giles has already got himself in above his head in matters he doesn't fully understand. Wait here a moment.'

Walsingham strode into the room where the rest of the household had been given permission to sit on the floor, guarded by those who had ridden in with him. He pulled one of them aside – the biggest and roughest looking of them – and gave him a new set of instructions.

'Robert, time to earn your keep. Ride hard north, to the estate of Sir Humphrey Audley on the south side of Cambridge, and do what you can to preserve the life of Queen's Constable Giles Bradbury.'

'No! Please! Not that! Mercy!' Giles pleaded, not necessarily in pretence, as he felt the heat from the burning brand that was being held close to his opened buttocks while a heavy ruffian sat on each of his wide-apart legs, pressing them firmly to the floor. 'Tell me what you want to know, and I'll tell you! But God's mercy, not *that*!'

A grinning face appeared before his where he lay face down on the floor, and he was conscious of the man's rank breath as he asked his first question.

'Who sent you here?'

'Francis Covington!' Giles yelled in a moment of inspiration. 'Hold there!' Audley yelled to his torturer from his seat in the corner of the room. 'Leave off with that brand and sit the man upright.'

Heaving a massive sigh of relief, Giles allowed the blood to flow back through his body and hastily concocted the rest of his story as he was turned to face Audley. 'What about Covington?' Audley demanded, 'and why did he send you both here and to Dunmow?'

'I was supposed to be making sure that you were conducting the transfers in accordance with the instructions from our mutual friends,' Giles gargled. 'I was ordered not to reveal my identity, but to ensure that there was no risk of anyone being exposed.'

'And of what interest is that to Covington?' was the next question, but Giles could tell that he had Audley worried, and opted to maintain the uncertainty. 'You have no need to ask me that, if you are true to the cause. But when I last met with him in Newgate, those were my orders.'

'And what have been your findings so far?' Audley demanded, and Giles managed a smile. 'You caught me out, didn't you? I can report back that there is no risk of our being discovered.'

'Tie him up and take him down to the wine cellar,' Audley ordered, and Giles was lifted by rough hands and forced out of the room, into the main entrance, along a rear corridor and down a flight of stairs. There was a brief delay while the Steward was located with his keys, then Giles was bustled between lines of bottles to the end of a long dank room where he was bound hand and foot, then tied in a standing position to a bracket set into the wall that was presumably intended to be the start of yet another wine shelf. The door closed behind the men who had brought him there, and he was left in total darkness, thanking God for sparing him from the hot brand but wondering why his make-believe story had not led to his immediate release.

The reason for this was Audley's discontent that the overall management of the English end of the plot to flood the nation with Jesuit priests who would minister to the chosen had been left to a cringing nobody in the lowest area of London whose only claim to such an honour was his alleged loyalty to the true faith that had been demonstrated when he had betrayed members of his own family. The man Covington, or so Audley had heard, had no breeding, no pedigree and no connections among the nobility, so who was he to be granted such a privileged role in the glorious scheme to place the rightful Queen Mary on the throne of England, following the overthrow of the Anti-Christ Elizabeth?

This was surely a matter that should be entrusted to the highest born nobles in the realm, and he, Sir Humphrey Audley, could claim kinship with the Howard family that for generations had proudly produced Dukes of Norfolk. He was not content to receive orders from some low-born whelp from the stews, and he might best demonstrate his scorn and contempt for the man by hanging his spy. How *dare* the upstart Covington presume to question how matters were conducted at Cherry Hinton? Even if the rogue currently locked in his cellars had demonstrated that there were problems with the management of the secure house at Dunmow, was this not a matter best left concealed from Covington, in case it threw the entire network of willing nobles under suspicion? His prisoner must hang, but for the moment Audley had more important matters to attend to.

His first priority had to be the accommodation of the two new arrivals, Ralph Ireton and Edward Blount. They were both ordained priests from the Jesuit College in France, and they would ensure the preservation of the souls of all those in Cherry Hinton who still clung to the true faith, for which they risked persecution and death. Sir Humphrey had taken the necessary steps to minimise the risk of either, but both young men required to be shown their designated hiding places, made available by the excellent work carried out by Nicholas Owen before he travelled south to Dunmow. Audley called the men in from the garden where they had been taking God's good air after their somewhat uncomfortable journey north, and showed each of them where they were to be hidden should the need arise. Then he invited both of them to conduct a welcome Mass in the Main Hall, to which the most trusted members of the household were invited, with armed men guarding the door and keeping a careful look out down the drive.

It was by one of these men that Sir Humphrey was advised that he had a visitor who claimed to have travelled north in search of a horse thief. He had the man shown into the kitchen and given bread and small beer, while he urgently ordered that all trace of the recent Mass be hidden from view before he had the man admitted to his Morning Room. He was tall and grizzled, and dressed as if for the Hunt. He lost no time in announcing his business.

'Thank you for receiving me, Sir Humphrey,' he smiled. 'My name is Robert Higham, and I'm a Constable from down south. We've had trouble with a man who's been gaining access to wealthy estates on the pretence of being a gardener, and then stealing horses. Ordinarily we wouldn't make such an effort to track down a mere horse thief such as he, but during his most recent deception, at a place called Dunmow, a girl from the neighbouring village was violated and left for dead. Fortunately she seems to be recovering, but the description she gave of her attacker fits the horse thief, and I'm most anxious to secure him and bring him to justice.'

'What sort of justice can he expect?' Audley enquired, and his visitor grinned. 'The sort to be found hanging from a local gallows.'

'After trial?' was the next question, and Higham's grin became less pleasant as he replied 'Not if I can get my hands on him first.'

Audley smiled. 'I think we can be of mutual service, Constable. Earlier today my men had occasion to apprehend a man lurking around our stables. He gave the name "Giles Bradbury", and he claimed to have been riding from Dunmow in pursuit of a horse thief. He's aged about twenty-five or thereabouts, a large-built man with long flowing brown hair much in need of a barber. Could he be your man?'

'He fits the description perfectly,' Higham grinned again. 'Do you have him securely held?'

'In my cellar,' Audley smiled back, 'and since nothing would give me more pleasure than to see him hanged, would you care to undertake the process?'

'Gladly, should you agree to say nothing about my avoidance of the prescribed due process,' Higham agreed, at which point he was invited to stay for dinner while suitable arrangements were being made.

Giles look up and blinked as light flooded into his place of confinement with the opening of the door. He was untied from the wall, and his legs freed from their binds so that he could stumble back through the house, his hands still tied in front of him, on the insistent physical urgings of his two captors. He was pushed through the scullery door and out onto the rear lawn, where there was a large oak tree, and underneath it a farm cart with a horse harnessed to it. His suspicions were confirmed, and his bowels lurched, as he saw the rope hanging from one of the lower branches of the oak. Inside the wagon stood a man who looked vaguely familiar, although in his immediate terror Giles could not place him.

He was thrown roughly into the wagon by the men who had brought him up from the cellar, who were then verbally castigated by the man installed inside it. 'It's easy to see that you blushing violets have no idea how to conduct a hanging,' the man advised them, then he turned his attention to Giles, untied his hands and ordered him to stand up and turn round.

'Is everybody here who wishes to see what we do to horse thieves and rapists?' he yelled, and received his answer from a red-faced Audley, who was standing with four of his bullies in the centre of the lawn. 'Get on with it, man!' he yelled.

'First of all,' Higham yelled back, 'you should know that a man who's about to be hanged should have his hands tied *behind* him, not in front! I need to attend to that oversight on your part, then the entertainment can commence.' He took the rope and moved behind Giles, hidden from view by those on the lawn.

Giles felt something being pressed into his hand, and from memory it felt like the hilt of a knife. But there was so far no attempt to tie his hands, and he was puzzled.

'Don't I know you from somewhere?' he enquired of his executioner, but was ordered to shut up and pay attention. 'This is a knife, as you may have realised,' the man mumbled as he tried to hide from others the fact that he was talking to a man he was supposed to be hanging. 'In just a moment I'll put the noose round your neck. Try not to shit yourself when I pull the wagon forward and leave you hanging; that's when you grab the rope with your free hand and pull upwards to loosen the noose from round your throat. Then reach further up with your other hand and cut the rope. When you hit the ground, head for those trees to the side and keep running. Good luck.'

It all went as predicted, and Giles needed no further encouragement to pull hard on the rope and slash through it with the knife as he felt the rough hempen cord tighten round his throat. He hit the ground awkwardly and went over on one ankle, but as the spectators gave roars of anger and began to converge on him he found the strength to fight through the pain as he made it as far as the copse of trees on the boundary of the lawn and crashed through the foliage like a mad bull escaping from a market stall.

He kept running without looking back, and made it into some sort of cornfield in which the first shoots of the season were barely a foot out of the ground. Beyond it was another line of trees, and his damaged ankle finally gave out as he reached what proved to be the bank of a stream, which he gratefully rolled down and landed with a splash in water so cold that it seemed to kick his flagging heart into further action. Then with a stab of terror he felt a hand on his shoulder as he was dragged under the decaying trunk of a large tree that had fallen over the stream, and by which he was hidden from view from above.

He rolled over, expecting to come face to face with one of his pursuers, but instead he was lying next to his pretended hangman, who handed him a broken tree branch. 'If they come this far, be prepared to use it. Constables always come equipped with staffs of office, do they not?'

'How did you know I were a Constable?' Giles enquired through labouring breaths brought on by his race for freedom, and the man smiled. 'Did you imagine that you were the only Queen's Constable in England? Robert Higham, pleased to renew our acquaintance.' Suddenly Giles remembered.

'You're the feller what come with us down to that place on the Thames, aren't you? The one what captured the next priest what landed there?'

'That's me,' Robert smiled. 'I've been a Constable along the lower reaches of the Thames for most of my life. Now keep quiet, so that we can hear anyone who comes after us.'

There had been no immediate pursuit, since Audley had unwisely elected to order all his horses to be saddled and led from the stable for his men to mount prior to making a thorough and painstaking search of the entire estate, which was so vast that it would be impossible for the two escapees to leave its confines before dark. He rode to the head of his men, and was about to command them to split up into groups of two and begin at the estate boundaries when his attention was drawn to another group of horsemen. They were riding in from the road to the south, and they appeared to be in a great hurry.

An hour later, he was the one bound hand and foot, staring disbelievingly into the stern countenance of another upstart, Cecil's grubby spymaster Walsingham, who was explaining with obvious satisfaction that Audley had a choice between confessing his part in a treasonous plot against Her Majesty here and now, or delaying that moment until he had made the acquaintance of the torturers in the Tower. Audley denied any involvement in any plot, and made outraged protests when he was accused of harbouring Catholic priests. Walsingham turned to the stern-faced individual by his side and smiled smugly.

'Tom, please make use of your recent experiences as a carpenter and prove this oily rat to be both a liar and a traitor.'

'I'd be honoured,' Tom replied drily as he led Walsingham and two of his men on a tour of the lower floor of the grand house. In the so-called Library he stared hard at a section of the panelling on the inside wall and nodded to himself before walking forward, and fiddling for a brief moment with something to the side of it. There was a sharp clicking sound, and the panel slid back to reveal the pale face of a young man in a long brown robe who had been in the act of fingering a rosary. The man was seized and dragged away muttering something in Latin, but Tom was not yet finished.

Having tested all the remaining walls in the Library he led the way into the Great Hall, where he stared for a moment at the panelling behind the top table, then smiled at Walsingham. 'That middle panel looks newer than the rest. Put your fingers between the new panel and the one on its left until you feel a small catch of some sort. Then pull it down.'

Walsingham did as advised, and another priest was found on his knees, praying under his breath. A further lengthy search of the house having yielded no more hidden priests, they moved back into the entrance hall, where Tom performed his carpenter's magic on the fresh panel under the central staircase and pointed to a box full of what proved to be implements of Catholic worship. He was in the process of being congratulated by Walsingham on his trained eye when there was a commotion behind them, and Tom turned. Then he burst into peals of laughter when he saw the state that Giles was in.

'I hopes you won't be asking either Lizzie or Mary to wash them clothes,' he joked as the two friends rushed towards each other and embraced, while Walsingham enquired of Robert Higham whether or not there were any of Audley's men still on the loose. Assured that they had all been flushed from their hiding places and rounded up, Higham was instructed to lock them all in the stables, with guards all around the building, then join Walsingham, Tom and Giles as they made free with their noble prisoner's larder and wine cellar.

Two days later they were riding back south with their prisoners trussed together in a wagon when a rider approached them from the south. He jumped from his horse and ran towards the southbound party, coming to a halt beside Walsingham's mount.

'You may wish to delay your journey overnight at Dunmow, sir,' the man advised him with a smile. 'It's only a few leagues further on, and there are matters that require the attention of you all.'

'Such as?' Walsingham enquired, and the man's smile broadened.

'Sir Henry is prepared to make a full confession, and to implicate the man in London who was behind it all, who you previously advised me is Constable Lincraft's cousin. And Constable Bradbury has a two day old daughter.'

Giles gave a hoot of glee and kicked his horse into action without seeking anyone's leave. As they watched his dust cloud disappear south, Walsingham turned to Tom.

'Time for that cold revenge, my friend.'

The sun was beginning to sink behind the tenements of Aldersgate three afternoons later, as Tom and Walsingham walked at a measured pace down to the junction of Newgate Street and Paternoster Row. Further down the Row a contingent of eight Yeomen of the Tower in full uniform could be seen walking up towards them with halberds in their hands and swords at their belts. They met up at the entrance to the courtyard, the centre of excited attention for the ragged urchins who had been playing in the street. On a command from Walsingham the soldiers formed up in a semi-circle in front of the peeling front door and stood at full attention. Then Tom wiped a tear from his eye as he thanked Walsingham for this long dreamed of moment and knocked on the door.

It was opened furtively by a rat-faced man whose jaw dropped as he saw the armed guard. Then his eyes opened in fear as he recognised Tom.

'Good day, cousin Francis,' Tom smiled grimly. 'I come with a message from my father and brother.'

Endnote

Dear Reader,

Thank you for investing your valuable time into reading this third novella in the series, which was based on well documented historical fact.

When Pope Pius excommunicated Elizabeth 1st, he also declared that her subjects were forbidden, on pain of excommunication, to follow her commands. He also impliedly invited them to remove her from the throne, and this gave encouragement to the many Catholic families, some of them noble, to plot her downfall. To assist, and to give them spiritual succour in what could prove fatal if discovered, a seminary was established in France to train priests who could be smuggled into England and hidden away in country houses. When intelligence of this reached Secretary of State William Cecil and his spymaster Francis Walsingham, the cat and mouse game began.

Priest hunters known as 'pursuivants' were sent in search of these covert priests, and their protectors took to redesigning their country houses in order to hide them when the Queen's men came calling. The most popular locations were in false wall cavities, under staircases, down in cellars or inside fireplaces, and as the pursuivants became more skilled in finding them, so the hiding places became more ingenious. Many an English country house still boasts these 'priest holes', and many a Gothic horror story has been written about the ghostly wraiths of former priests who died of suffocation, starvation or thirst while hidden away from their pursuers, only to return as resentful ghosts.

The most active of those who constructed these hiding places was the Nicholas Owen of this novel, a lay Jesuit Brother and a skilled carpenter. He was not captured until after the failure of the Gunpowder Plot in 1605, and regrettably he died under torture in the Tower of London the following year.

Historical fact as dramatic as this makes the work of a historical novelist both easy and rewarding, and I hope that you enjoyed the fruits of my research. I should be grateful for any review you would care to leave on *Amazon,* and/or I look forward to chatting with you more directly on my Facebook website davidfieldauthor.com. I can also be contacted on Twitter.

David

*

Printed in Great Britain
by Amazon